ALL MY TOMORROWS

ALL MY TOMORROWS

As enemy planes bomb the East End, Ruby Clark is fighting for her life against her brutal husband and is forced to flee London. Ruby's billet in Cliffehaven is comfortable and the job in the tool factory is well-paid. But when her landlord makes unwelcome advances, Ruby faces life on the streets. Until an unexpected turn of events brings her to Peggy Reilly's boarding house. Ruby dares to hope for a brighter future now she has the love and support of those at Beach View. But swiftly-moving events in London mean that it is all about to change...

ALL MY TOMORROWS

by

Ellie Dean

Magna Large Print Books
Long Preston, North Yorkshire,
BD23 4ND, England.

British Library Cataloguing in Publication Data.

Dean, Ellie
All my tomorrows.

A catalogue record of this book is
available from the British Library

ISBN   978-0-7505-3994-4

First published in Great Britain by Arrow Books 2014

Published in Large Print 2014 by arrangement with
Random House Group Ltd.

Magna Large Print is an imprint of Library Magna Books Ltd.

Printed and bound in Great Britain by
T.J. (International) Ltd., Cornwall, PL28 8RW

Acknowledgements

Once again I give thanks to my wonderful editor, Georgina Hawtrey-Woore, and my equally wonderful agent, Teresa Chris. They have encouraged and supported me throughout this new adventure, and I know my work is all the better for it. Thanks, too, to the lovely readers who so enthusiastically review my Beach View Boarding House series, and who send me very encouraging and informative emails.

Author's Note

I am aware that the Royal Regiment of Canada was sent on the 20th May 1942 to the Isle of Wight which was sealed off during the rigorous training needed before the raid on Dieppe. I have taken artistic licence in this story so that the young Canadian officer is present in Cliffehaven towards the end of the book. I hope this does not spoil your enjoyment of *All My Tomorrows*.

Chapter One

East End of London, 1942

The small tenement room that Ruby Clark shared with her husband Raymond was musty with the odours of unwashed bedclothes, long-forgotten meals and grimy heat. An iron-framed bed took up most of the space, and apart from a table, two rickety wooden chairs and a dilapidated chest of drawers, there was precious little else, just a few pegs on the back of the door to hang their clothes.

This was where Raymond Clark's suits hung from hangers, along with his carefully ironed shirts, and a line of his highly polished shoes sat on a sheet of newspaper by the meter for the gas fire. The superior pedigree of all this finery simply made the little room look shoddier than ever, but Raymond had a reputation to keep up and he thought nothing of spending his ill-gotten money on bespoke suits and handmade shoes, even though Ruby had to wear hand-me-downs she found in the Salvation Army clothes store.

As Ruby finished washing in the bowl of tepid water she could hear the shrieks and shouts of her neighbours penetrating the thin walls and echoing along the landings and down the concrete stairs. It was never quiet in the block and although she was inured to it from childhood, it seemed louder than usual today, making her long for just a few moments of precious silence in which to mourn.

A fly buzzed with annoying regularity against the single dirty window which overlooked yet another tenement block, and the ticking clock on the narrow mantel above the gas fire reminded her that she was in danger of being late. She glanced wordlessly at her mother, whose expression was as dark as the cup of tea she'd been drinking, and sank onto the thin mattress. The bedclothes were sweat-stained and in a tangle, but regardless of the trouble it might cause later, she simply didn't have the energy or the time to replace the linen and tidy up.

Ruby dragged on her underwear, pulled the worn cotton frock over her head, tugged it down and, with trembling fingers, began to do up the buttons that ran from waist to neckline. It was an old dress, the once cheerful colours muted by too many washes, the material as thin and fragile as her spirit. Yet the softness of it comforted her, wrapping itself around her bruised body like a gentle caress.

She ignored the baleful glare from her mother and slipped her bare feet into the high-heeled shoes Ray liked her to wear when she worked behind the bar at the Tanner's Arms. 'I have to go to work, Mum,' she muttered. 'We need the money.'

'It's only been a week and you ain't well enough, gel,' retorted Ethel Sharp, her skinny arms folded tightly about her waist. 'If it were up to me, you'd be back in that bed for at least another few days.'

'But it ain't up to you, is it, Mum?' she said

softly. 'Ray said I have to go, so I'm going.' She picked up the almost toothless comb and scraped it through her thick brown hair, her defiant words belying the awful dragging ache in the pit of her stomach, and the desperate yearning to climb back into bed and curl beneath the blanket.

Ethel's metal curlers bobbed beneath her head-scarf and the wrap-round pinafore quivered over her slight bosom as her pent-up anger could no longer be held at bay. 'He's a wrong 'un, Ruby. No decent man would do what he done and then expect you to go–'

'Stop it, Mum,' she interrupted wearily. 'I know you mean well, but he's my husband, and there ain't nothing you can do about it, so give it a rest.'

Ethel took hold of Ruby's shoulders and gently turned her to face the scrap of fly-spotted mirror that was propped on the old chest of drawers. 'Look at yerself,' she said, her voice breaking with emotion. 'You're eighteen, Ruby, and yet you look as old and worn-out as me.' Her tone softened, and there were tears in her eyes as they regarded each other's reflection. 'You gotta learn to dodge them fists, Ruby, and keep yer gob shut, or he'll kill you one day – just like he killed that poor, innocent little baby you was carrying.'

Ruby flinched at the words that struck so deeply, but determinedly masked her emotions. To give in to the pain and the sorrow would be her undoing – and nothing could turn back the clock and save her precious baby. 'He said he was sorry,' she replied as she turned away from the mirror, 'and he promised he wouldn't thump me again.' She sniffed back the tears. 'I gotta believe him, Mum,'

15

she whispered.

'His promise don't mean nothing, and you know it,' her mother retorted.

Ruby looked into her mother's careworn face and silently acknowledged this truth before she embraced her. 'You know what it's like, Mum,' she murmured. 'There's no point in going on about it.'

Ethel remained silent as they held one another, perhaps remembering her own black eyes and bruises that had been meted out by Ruby's step-father, Ted Wiggins. 'At least Ted's gorn for a soldier,' she said eventually as she drew back from the embrace and shot her daughter a wry smile. 'It's just a pity your Raymond don't do the same, then we'd both get a bit of peace.'

'Well, that ain't gunna happen, is it?' she replied with a sigh. 'Ray's got flat feet and poor eyesight. The army wouldn't have him.'

'For all his bluff and bluster he ain't worth a light to no one but them cronies of his what run the black market.' Ethel sniffed with derision and folded her arms more tightly beneath her scrawny chest.

Ruby silently agreed with her, but would never dare voice it. Ray's fragile pride had been severely dented by the rejection, making him a very angry man – and even in her silence, she was terrified he would imagine he could see the same scorn in her eyes that his uncles had shown when he'd been assigned to the Home Guard. It was like walking a knife-edge every day, and she wondered if she would ever learn how to endure it.

Ethel seemed to realise there was no point in

carrying on this conversation and reached into her apron pocket. 'I brought the last of me face powder,' she said as she handed Ruby the tarnished compact. 'You need to cover them bruises.'

Ruby gingerly dusted the powder over the yellow and purple bruises and eyed her reflection without much joy. She'd been quite pretty once, with lively green eyes, a cheery smile and shining hair the colour of cobnuts. Now she looked dowdy and drained of any spark of life, and living in this shabby room with a man who could lose his temper in a heartbeat was slowly defeating her.

Ethel seemed to read her thoughts, and her expression softened into weary acceptance. 'You made yer bed, gel, and now you got to lie in it – just like we all do.' She sighed and gently cupped Ruby's cheek with her work-roughened hand. 'It ain't easy being a woman, love, but you always got me to turn to when things get too bad.'

Ruby momentarily nestled her cheek into the warm hand and then turned away. Her mother could do very little but patch her up and offer tea and sympathy – and if Ray caught her here, there'd be ructions again. 'We gotta go, Mum.' She returned the compact, slipped on a knitted cardigan and picked up her cheap handbag.

'I'll stay and clean the place up a bit,' said Ethel as she eyed the grubby bed and polished one of the brass knobs with the hem of her pinafore. 'Don't want him coming home to this and losing his temper again.'

Ruby gave a deep sigh. 'Better not, Mum. You know he don't like you coming in here.'

17

'It comes to something when a mother ain't allowed to visit her only daughter,' sniffed Ethel. 'If your dad were alive he'd have his guts for garters and no mistake.'

Ruby didn't reply as she held the door open and waited for her mother to step outside. Her dad had been a tough, no-nonsense docker who had never raised a hand to Ethel or Ruby, and considered men that did to be beneath contempt. He would certainly have defended Ruby and seen to it that Raymond got a taste of his own medicine – but he'd been dead for over ten years and there was little point in wishing things were different. She and Ethel had both made mistakes, and now they had no choice but to live with them.

Ruby locked the door and dipped her chin so her hair fell forward and shadowed her battered face. The knowing looks and sympathetic smiles from the other women they passed on the landing spoke silently of sisterhood and understanding, but Ruby had never wanted membership to such a club – had vowed she'd never be like them. And yet, from the moment she'd met Raymond Clark, it seemed it was inevitable.

They weaved past prams and bikes as they headed along the narrow fifth-floor landing and down the concrete steps. Neither of them looked at their surroundings, for they did little to raise the spirits, and they were inured to the sounds and the odours to the point they hardly noticed any more.

Tenement building 41 was an exact copy of the others which lined the mean little streets of Bow. It formed a square around a grubby concrete

18

yard where washing lines had been strung across it from every landing. Having miraculously escaped from too much damage during the Blitz, it still teemed with life – although not all of it was human.

Fleas, lice and cockroaches were a part of everyday life. Rats skittered through the rubbish and the overflowing communal lavatories on the ground floor; dogs fought over scraps and cats prowled in search of mice while grubby, half-naked urchins played on the broken concrete beneath the lines of defeated-looking washing as their mothers gossiped by the taps which provided the only clean water. As ugly as sin, scarred by enemy bullets, blackened by fire and soot and mouldering from lack of care and grinding poverty, the tenement was home to hundreds.

Ethel lived on the third floor with a couple of young lodgers, and Ruby said goodbye to her and continued down the steps until she reached the yard. She felt light-headed and had to pause for a moment before she hurried towards the narrow alley which led to the main road. She was already late and knew there would be trouble if Ray turned up at the pub before her, but it took every ounce of her determination to put one foot in front of the other.

The East End had taken a pounding over the past two years and a great many of the buildings had been reduced to burnt-out shells. The spring day had been unusually warm and now a pall of dust clung to that lingering warmth as the evening closed in, and she could smell the acrid stench of smoke which still rose from the blackened skeleton of a nearby warehouse.

She carefully avoided the worst of the debris as others scavenged for firewood or anything else that might come in use. A group of boys were hunting for bits of shrapnel which could be used for barter, or for scrap metal and waste paper which they could sell. A lot of the kids had been evacuated at the beginning of the war, but a good many of them had returned, for another pair of hands meant another wage in these tough times.

Ruby continued down the street and then turned into a much narrower lane, avoiding the alley which was a favourite haunt of the local prostitutes, and the pub customers who used it as a lavatory. Stinking to high heaven, it was littered with rubbish and overflowing dustbins, and she hurried past it, heading for the front door of the Tanner's Arms. Taking a deep breath to bolster her courage, she pushed the scarred door open and stepped inside to the usual wall of noise.

The Tanner's Arms had served this community for over a hundred years. Scant light managed to penetrate the small, filthy windows, the gloom deepened by the dark wood panelling, the heavy beams and nicotine-stained ceiling. The old-fashioned gaslights were so dim they hardly cast shadows and the enormous bar which took up an entire wall was a looming presence of heavy oak and fly-spotted mirrors. A few tables and chairs were the only other furniture, but the majority of the regulars preferred to stand at the bar.

Ruby felt her eyes stinging from the cigarette smoke which hung like a thick fog from the ceiling, and the noise of so many raised voices rang in her ears as she slipped behind the bar and stowed her bag and cardigan under a back shelf. Thankfully there was no sign of Ray or his cronies, so she could afford to relax a little.

Fred Bowman's eyes widened as he caught sight of her. 'Blimey, gel. Weren't expecting you in today – but I'm glad to see yer. Me and Glad have been run off our feet.' The middle-aged landlord's penetrating gaze rested momentarily on her bruises before he looked her in the eye. 'You sure you're up to this, Rube?'

Ruby felt the colour flood her face as she nodded, for she knew his life would be so much easier if she just handed in her notice and found work in one of the factories instead – but of course that wasn't possible now she was married to Ray, who had his own reasons for keeping her there.

Despite having the build of a heavy-weight boxer, and the ability to handle most trouble that came his way, Fred was a good man, and he and his little wife Gladys had taken her under their wing since she'd started working for them. They'd done their best to dissuade her from marrying Ray, but of course she'd been young and dazzled and had refused to listen. Poor Fred didn't like having Ray and his thugs as regular customers but couldn't do much about it. The safety of his wife, family and business was paramount, but precedents had been set as a warning to those who might try to resist this growing menace. They all knew the score, and neither he nor Gladys would say anything to Ruby about how she'd come by the bruises, or why she'd had a week off work.

'If you can't cope, then just tell me,' he murmured. 'I'll still pay yer wages for the session.'

She flashed him a grateful smile and did her best to appear ready for a busy night, for Ray would come in sooner or later and she needed to keep him sweet – and the only way to achieve that was to keep her head down, get on with her work and bring in the money.

Ray sauntered in just before closing time, and like every other woman's in the pub, Ruby's gaze was immediately drawn to him. There was no doubt about it, Ruby thought, he was the hand-somest man in the room, and despite everything, she felt a flutter of something akin to pride.

Tall and broad-shouldered, Raymond Clark wore his tailored suit like a man used to the finer things in life. His white shirt, smart tie and hand-made shoes merely added to the illusion, and as he slipped the velvet-collared overcoat from his shoulders and handed it to one of his minions, he acknowledged respectful greetings with the merest inclination of his head. At twenty-three, he exuded a sense of power in the way he carried himself and was fully aware that his presence underlined the fact that he was a name around these parts – a man to be reckoned with. With his strong family ties, to some of the most powerful and feared villains in the East End, it paid to keep him onside and informed of everything that was going on in his manor.

His dark eyes were shadowed by the brim of his fedora, and although he was very short-sighted, vanity meant he refused to wear glasses – and yet his gaze found Ruby in an instant and held her as firmly as a moth stuck with a pin. When he looked away Ruby found she'd been holding her breath and hurried to pour him his usual tot of whisky, which she carried to the other end of the bar where he always sat.

Ray eased himself onto the bar stool, surrounded by his heavies and the usual hangers-on who wanted to be seen with him and thereby inflate their own reputations amongst the hard men of the East End. Ruby plastered on a smile as she fluffed her hair over her bruised cheek and brow and set the whisky in front of him.

His myopic brown eyes trawled from her face down her body to her high-heeled shoes. 'Looking well, gel,' he drawled. 'See, I told yer it would do yer good to get out.' His gaze held her again as he swallowed a mouthful of whisky.

Ruby felt much as a mouse must do when cornered by a cat. She could see command in his gaze – an unspoken pleasure in bending her to his will. 'D'you want another?' she managed as he put the empty glass down on the bar.

'Yeah, why not? I had a good run of the cards tonight, and Stan here owes me.' He rested a heavy hand on the shoulder of the nervous-looking man who stood next to him. 'Get yer wallet out, Stan. It's your round.'

Ruby shot them both a stiff little smile and hurried to refill the glasses. She knew he didn't like her chattering at him when he was with his mates – but there again, he didn't like what he called her dumb insolence when she said nothing. She was all too aware of his steady scrutiny and her hand trembled as she battled to think of something to

23

say, but all reasoned thought was scrambled and she ended up spilling some of the whisky on the bar. With a muttered apology she wiped it away and was saved from further confrontation by Gladys shouting from the other end of the bar that she needed a hand.

When Fred clanged the bell for last orders Ruby was almost dead on her feet. The ache inside was a dragging weight, her back was stiff with tension and her head was splitting from all the noise and the cigarette smoke. But there were still customers clamouring to be served before they were chucked out, and even after they'd gone there would be the cleaning up and restocking before she could go home and crawl into bed.

She shot a glance at Ray, who was still sitting at the end of the bar, and although he seemed to be listening to the wild stories from his coterie of admirers, his gaze followed her every move. She bit her lip and went to help Gladys clear the glasses and empty the ashtrays as Fred determinedly manhandled his more reluctant customers out of the door. She could only pray that Ray's run of luck with the cards had mellowed him, and that the amount of whisky he'd had would send him to sleep quickly rather than stoke his temper.

As she wiped down the bar and the tables and swept the fag ends off the floor, she kept a wary eye on him. There was a fresh whisky bottle doing the rounds of his little group despite the fact it was now way past closing time. She could hear him telling Fred not to worry about his dwindling supply of spirits, and that he could expect a delivery the next day – subject to the usual fee and a heavy skim off the profits. Fred couldn't refuse, but Ruby knew how much it cost him to have to agree to this black-market trade. Although Fred didn't bat an eye at the odd fiddle here and there, this sort of carry-on could see him heavily fined or imprisoned, his reputation in tatters, and his pub shut down. Ruby's face burned with shame at the thought of a decent man being dragged to such depths by someone she'd once thought she loved.

She carried on sweeping the floor, her thoughts skittering over the past year and a bit. She'd been just seventeen when she'd first met Ray, and with his film star looks and rather dangerous connections, she'd been flattered and excited when he'd made it clear he wanted her to be his girl. During the next six months she'd been swept along in the glamour of the basement nightclubs and private drinking bars where they drank champagne and watched exotic floor shows. He gave her jewellery and expensive clothes because he said he liked her to look good when she was on his arm, and enjoyed showing her off.

Her hands gripped the broom as she recalled how eagerly she'd agreed to marry him, and how quickly she'd been faced with the cold, hard truth. It was all a sham. There was no posh flat; the jewellery and furs were on loan and behind that winning smile and handsome façade was a man of quick temper and even swifter fists. With her new clarity of vision she'd seen that the gambling clubs, strip joints and private bars that she'd once thought so glamorous were merely seedy hangouts where tough men negotiated deals, and rivalries between the different factions that ruled the East End were dealt with swiftly and violently.

Ray, she soon realised, knew he was simply a minor cog in the great wheel that his family turned, and because his mother had committed the heinous sin of running away, he would never attain the same status as his much older half-brothers. But he'd clung on, milking his connections, ducking and diving and doing shady deals wherever he could to prove to his family that he deserved a larger share in their enterprises. The family name was his only asset and this earned a certain amount of respect, but he was all too aware that could change in an instant if he displeased his father and uncles – and that knowledge made him very dangerous indeed if he thought his fragile authority was being questioned.

In her naïvety, she'd hoped they could be happy – had prayed that the coming baby would sweeten him. But leopards didn't change their spots, and his beating had left her empty of the child she'd been carrying and bereft of all hope.

'Wot you doin', gel?' Ray shouted from the bar. 'Get yer arse in gear. It's time we was leaving.'

She snapped out of her reverie and hurried to put away the broom and fetch her cardigan and handbag. As she turned back she saw him demand her wages from Fred and fold them into his pocket. She stifled the protest and, with a nod of goodnight to a shamefaced Fred, followed Ray outside.

It was as black as pitch, with scudding clouds racing across a pale moon as the wind picked up. There had been no raids and all was still but for the shriek of a drunken woman coming from the side alley. Ray flung his arm round her shoulder and rather unsteadily propelled her down the road. 'Mind how you go in them heels,' he muttered. 'Don't want you falling over and hurting yerself, do we?'

She heard the sly snigger and shivered as she pulled the cardigan more firmly across her chest. His words chilled her far more than the cold April night, and she could only hope that he wouldn't keep up his taunting when they got home.

He didn't seem to notice her discomfort as he weaved his way along the deserted road. 'We'll pop into Flannigan's for a quick one first,' he said casually. 'Micky owes me for that last delivery.'

Ruby's spirits plummeted further. She was feeling wrung out and on the point of collapse. The last thing she wanted to do was sit in yet another smoky bar and witness Ray's intimidation of someone who couldn't fight back. 'Shall I make me way home on me own then?' she asked tentatively. 'You won't want me hanging about if you're gunna talk business.'

His arm seemed to grow heavier across her shoulders, the grip on her upper arm tightening. 'Best you come with me,' he said. 'Don't want you wandering about in the blackout on yer own.'

'I know me way,' she replied softly, 'and it ain't far now.'

He came to an abrupt halt and glared down at her. 'I said we was going for a last drink at Flannigan's,' he said flatly. 'You wanna give me an argument about that, Ruby?'

She shook her head. 'No, of course not,' she

said quickly.

He tucked her hand into the crook of his arm. 'I'll make it a quick one,' he said with a wink, 'and then we can get home to bed.'

Ruby saw the gleam in his eyes and her stomach clenched. It was far too soon after the miscarriage for intimate relations, but Ray had clearly decided he'd waited long enough, and for the life of her she couldn't think of any way to change his mind. She blinked up at him, dumb with a fear she dared not show.

His gaze was steady as he moved closer and kissed her.

Ruby had to steel herself from flinching as his hand traced the bruises on her brow and cheek-bone. He was toying with her, making it clear who was in charge, and when he purposefully steered her across the street to Flannigan's Bar she had no choice but to go with him.

Chapter Two

Cliffehaven

The April sunshine glittered on the sea as the waves rolled lazily against the shingle and swirled around the concrete shipping traps which formed a forbidding chain beyond the low-tide mark of Cliffehaven bay. Gulls hovered in the light breeze that still held the chill of the dying winter, their mournful cries echoing across the water to the white cliffs that stood sentinel to the east of the town.

Peggy Reilly pulled up her coat collar as she sat on the stone bench, the pram beside her. Despite the beauty of the day and the promise that summer would soon be here, the reminders of war were everywhere. They lay in the coils of barbed wire along the promenade; in the warning signs that the beach was mined; in the gun emplacements that were dotted along the shore and strung along the clifftops; and in the clumps of oil that stained the shingle – a terrible epitaph for the hundreds of lost mariners and airmen whose crafts now lay in that glassy blue tomb.

Peggy shivered as her gaze drifted along the seafront she'd known since childhood. Cliffehaven had become a popular holiday resort once the railway had been established back in Victorian times, with gracious hotels lining the seafront, colourful deckchairs and parasols fluttering in the breeze, and the sound of music and laughter coming from the amusement arcades and the ballroom at the end of the pier. There had been the sweet scents of candyfloss and toffee apples, and the alluring smell of vinegar and frying fish and chips to tempt the hungry holidaymaker.

Now the only scents were the oil on the shingle, the faint whiff of smoke from a recent bomb site and the tang of the sea. Bomb craters marked the demise of many of the elegant hotels, and in the place of parasols and deckchairs were barrage balloons and gun emplacements. The pier had been separated from the beach at the beginning of the war to deter enemy landing craft that might have made it through the traps, and now, with the remains of a German bomber still jutting from its burnt-out skeleton, it would have been a kindness to blow it up and let it sink.

Peggy turned her gaze from this gloomy scene and concentrated on Daisy. At four months old her youngest daughter was a little beauty. Plump and forever smiling, she had Peggy's dark brown eyes and the black hair of the Reilly clan and, even at this tender age, possessed the same innate charm as her father and grandfather in getting her own way. There was a danger she would become spoiled by all the attention she got from the inhabitants of Beach View Boarding House, and Peggy had had to be quite firm about a strict routine.

Peggy smiled as Daisy watched the birds in wide-eyed fascination as they swooped and hovered overhead. She was the image of her father, and at times like these Peggy ached for Jim to be with her. He was missing so much of his daughter's growing-up, and right this moment, she herself needed his solid presence and his comforting arm about her. But he'd been called up and was miles away somewhere in the north of England, and it was doubtful she would see him again for many months.

Peggy experienced a wave of debilitating loneliness and self-pity and swiftly controlled it as she manoeuvred the sturdy old pram so the wind didn't blow in Daisy's face. Her emotions were all over the place, and she knew that if she didn't keep a tight rein on them, she would be lost. And yet her hands still trembled as she cupped them round a match and lit a cigarette. She wasn't ready yet to return home to the usual chaos of Beach View, for she needed these few moments to come to terms with what she had learned that morning.

She felt the chill wind on her face and blamed it for the tears which she quickly blinked away. Crying wouldn't change anything, and she had to keep strong and focussed. After all, she reasoned, her condition wasn't life-threatening – merely highly inconvenient, and rather worrying.

She watched the smoke from her cigarette spiral away on the breeze, and then followed the wheeling path of the black-headed gulls whose only concern was the need for food. If only life could be that simple, she thought with a deep sigh. But it wasn't, and now she was faced with the prospect of having another baby before Daisy had even celebrated her first birthday.

The doctor had confirmed her suspicions half an hour ago, and he hadn't been at all pleased, for he'd warned her after Daisy's difficult delivery that another pregnancy at her age would simply exacerbate her anaemia and high blood pressure. He'd tutted and clucked as he'd weighed her and taken blood and urine samples, and she'd had to promise to slow down, to take his horrid iron pills, drink a pint of milk stout every day and try to put on weight.

Peggy puffed on the last of her cigarette and mashed the butt under her shoe as she folded her arms tightly about her waist. 'I know he means well, Daisy,' she muttered crossly, 'but how on earth can I put on weight when rationing's so tight?' Her sour mood was born of frustration and worry. 'As for slowing down – well, he should spend a day in my shoes and see just how impossible that is.'

Daisy batted the rattling plastic ducks that were strung across her pram and gurgled up at her mother.

Peggy's flash of sourness disappeared and she smiled back at her tiny daughter. This pregnancy was all her own fault, for she'd thought she couldn't get caught while she was breastfeeding Daisy. 'It just goes to show,' she said, 'how much rubbish all those old wives' tales are and how stupid I was to believe them.'

She turned her gaze back to the waves that were hissing against the shingle. She'd worked out that she'd fallen for this baby in the days leading up to Jim's leaving for his army posting, and of course the last thing on her mind had been the possibility that their lovemaking would lead to another pregnancy. She felt a tiny flutter of apprehension in the pit of her stomach and decided there and then that however inconvenient it might be, this new life was a precious gift, and it would be loved and nurtured as all her others had been.

Daisy crowed and giggled as she waved her arms about and tried to kick off her blankets.

Peggy grinned and tucked her back in. 'You might laugh about it now, young lady,' she said softly, 'but you wait until you have a rival for everyone's attention. You won't be the Queen Bee of Beach View then, you know.'

Daisy's bright brown eyes regarded her solemnly for a moment, and then she plugged her thumb into her mouth and settled down to sleep.

Peggy knew in that moment that her momentary lapse into self-pity would not be repeated. There was a house to run, people to tend to and Daisy to care for. Air raids, rationing and the day-to-day struggle for survival were enough to be getting on with, and she was being selfish by sitting here feeling sorry for herself when there was so much to do back at home.

She stood up, ready to continue her walk, but a wave of light-headedness made her grip the pram handle, and she had to wait until it passed. This pregnancy was still in the very early stages but was proving to be unlike any of the others, with various niggles and aches and a sense of being tired and out of sorts all the time. But then that was probably due to her age and the galloping anaemia the doctor had been going on about. No doubt the iron pills and a drop of stout each evening would soon sort that out.

'I must remember to ask Ron to bring some home from the Anchor,' she said as she set off down the promenade, 'though Lord only knows how I'll swallow it down – I hate the stuff.'

She was still feeling a little light-headed as she slowly walked along the promenade, and when she turned from the sea and looked up the long, steep climb she had to tackle to get home to Beach View, she wondered if her legs would carry her that far. Accepting there was no alternative, she gritted her teeth and determinedly traipsed towards home.

Beach View Terrace was a cul-de-sac about halfway up the steep incline which led eventually to the top of the surrounding hills and the Cliffe estate, which had recently been taken over by the Women's Timber Corps. Cliffe airfield lay some miles beyond the estate in a broad valley, and the sight and sound of Spitfires, Wellingtons, Stirlings and Halifaxes overhead had become so commonplace no one really noticed them any more.

Beach View Boarding House was a Victorian terraced house which had been in Peggy's family for two generations. Almost indistinguishable from all the others which lined the hill on this eastern side of Cliffehaven, it had managed to escape serious damage during the air raids. Tall and narrow, its only view of the beach was from the corner of one of the upstairs front windows, but its depth provided seven bedrooms, a dining room and kitchen on three floors, and another two bedrooms and a scullery in the basement.

Peggy had a stitch in her side and was out of breath by the time she reached the alley which ran between the backs of the houses and continued on as a muddy track into the hills. She paused for a moment to catch her breath before opening the rickety gate.

The flint wall had been damaged early on in the war and Jim and his father, Ron, had done some makeshift repairs which unfortunately had not withstood time and the elements. There were some loose tiles on the roof and several of the windows had been boarded up – glass was expensive and difficult to find, and it made sense not to keep replacing it when Gerry was constantly dropping bombs all over the place. The neighbouring houses also had boarded windows, but some had lost their chimneys, and the two houses at the end of the cul-de-sac had been ripped apart by a gas explosion. All in all, she thought, they'd been lucky to escape so lightly.

As Peggy wheeled the pram along the garden path she eyed the ugly Anderson shelter which was going rusty beneath its turf-covered roof and then turned her gaze to the shed, the outside lav, the chicken coop and Ron's flourishing vegetable garden. The eggs and fresh vegetables certainly helped them to eke out their miserly rations, as did Ron's forays into the hills with his dog, Harvey. The pair of them were disreputable and unruly to the point where Peggy often despaired at the mess they made and the scrapes they got into – but their hunting trips were always successful and they'd come home with rabbits, wild berries and herbs – and the odd game-bird which had wandered by accident from the safety of the Cliffe estate into the deep pockets of Ron's ankle-length poacher's coat.

Peggy smiled as she passed the woodpile and coal bunker, and wrestled the pram over the back step into the basement. Her father-in-law might be in his sixties now, but he was sturdy and strong, still with a twinkle in his eye and the soft brogue of Ireland in his speech. He had enough blarney to sink a battleship, the dress sense of a tramp, and the heart of a lion. Peggy adored him, and couldn't imagine life without him – even though he persisted in keeping ferrets in his bedroom and let Harvey sleep on his bed.

She wrinkled her nose at the smell of damp dog as she parked the pram beside the stone sink and copper boiler. The basement had been divided into a scullery and two bedrooms. Her two youngest sons, Bob and Charlie, had once slept down here in the front room while their grandfather slept in the other. Now the boys were in Somerset, Ron had the place to himself, and he used the empty room to store all his junk. The place smelled of dog, pipe tobacco and old socks, but at least the two new ferrets didn't pong as well and their bedding was always fresh.

Peggy eyed the mound of washing that awaited her in the basket and decided it could wait. Daisy was stirring and would need feeding and changing, and she was in desperate need of a cup of tea and a bit of a sit-down after that long haul up the hill.

She carried Daisy up the concrete steps and into the kitchen, surprised to see it was deserted for once. Having changed Daisy's nappy and fed her with a little mashed vegetable, she settled down in the armchair by the Kitchener range and gave her a bottle of formula milk. The kitchen was her favourite room in the house, for although it was shabby and the furniture bore the scars of years of rough treatment, it was homely and welcoming, and held precious memories, not only of her childhood, but of her own family gathering here before war had torn them apart.

The glow from the range warmed her as she relaxed into the chair and gazed up at the photograph of Jim which she'd framed and placed with pride on the mantelpiece. He looked so handsome in his Royal Engineers' dress uniform, the beret tilted low over one eye, his sensuous mouth curved in a smile that told her he'd been thinking of her when the photographer took the picture.

Her gaze drifted to the other photographs she'd placed on the dresser next to the wireless. Her two young sons grinned mischievously at her, arms entwined about each other's shoulders as they stood in the back garden in their short trousers and wellingtons. Charlie was eleven now, and Bob had just turned fifteen, but they were growing up without her, far away on a farm in Somerset. It had broken her heart to have to send them back there after their all-too-short visit – but at least they'd had a chance to see their father and say goodbye as he'd left on the train with his brother Frank for the army barracks so many miles away.

Peggy blinked back the ready tears and regarded her eldest daughter, Anne, who'd just celebrated her twenty-sixth birthday when the photograph was taken. Standing beside her husband Martin, who looked so dashing in his RAF uniform, she held their little daughter, Rose Margaret, in her arms and smiled bravely for the camera. Dark-haired, slender and beautiful, only Peggy knew the torment that lay behind that smile, for Martin had returned to flying again, and with each sortie, his odds of surviving this war were shortened.

And then there was Cissy. Peggy smiled. Cissy was twenty now and her fair hair had been styled in fetching waves which fell to her shoulders and almost covered one eye. Cissy had always been rather theatrical, and liked to emulate the Hollywood beauties Hedy Lamarr and Lana Turner. Thankfully her yearnings to go on stage had been nipped in the bud by an unfortunate run-in with

37

a sleazy theatre director, and she was now enjoying life to the full in the WAAF and driving some RAF bigwig about in a staff car.

Peggy realised Daisy had fallen asleep, and she gently laid her in the playpen in the corner and covered her with a blanket. As she looked down at her sleeping child she couldn't help but wonder how she would cope when she had two babies to look after.

'Hello, dear. You're looking thoughtful. Anything I can help with?'

Peggy turned and smiled at the elderly woman who was watching her from the doorway with such concern. 'Just wool-gathering,' she said lightly. 'The tea's fresh in the pot. Sit down and I'll pour us both a cup.'

Cordelia Finch fiddled with her hearing aid. 'Do speak up, dear. You know I can't understand a word you're saying when you mutter.'

Peggy poured the tea, added a bit of precious sugar and hunted out the biscuit tin as Cordelia discarded her walking stick and gingerly settled in the other chair by the range. Cordelia Finch was aptly named, for she was delicately boned and small in stature, with a tendency to twitter and blush every time Ron or Jim teased her. She was in her seventies and had been living at Beach View for many years. The family, as well as the evacuees and lodgers, had come to regard her as a surrogate grandmother, and it was clear she enjoyed this position of love and trust and felt very much at home here. Peggy loved her dearly, although it was a bit of a trial at times to hold a sensible conversation when her hearing aid was

38

on the blink.

The house was very quiet, and as Peggy had left straight after breakfast for her clandestine appointment at the doctor's she had little idea of her lodgers' timetable for the day. 'I suppose we ought to enjoy this lull while we can,' she said as she munched on a rather soggy digestive biscuit. 'They'll be home soon enough, starving hungry and in a rush to go out again.'

'I don't think anyone's gone to Hull, dear,' said Cordelia. 'Fran and Suzy are on duty at the hospital and Rita's out with that motorbike of hers – no doubt racing about like a madcap as usual.' She clucked and rolled her eyes in disapproval, though everyone had long realised she rather envied the freedom the young women had these days. 'My Sarah will be at work on the Cliffe estate and dear little Jane is going straight from the dairy to her office job at the uniform factory.'

Peggy gestured to her to adjust her hearing aid. 'You must be very proud at how well your nieces have settled in,' she said clearly.

Cordelia nodded. 'I think that once they got those letters from their mother, and could write back, it helped enormously. Though of course none of us know what has happened to their father – or to Sarah's fiancé after Singapore fell.' She paused, her expression sombre before she rallied again. 'But still, they seem to be coping very well, all things considered.'

Peggy knew how deeply Cordelia had fretted over her late brother's family when the Japanese had invaded Malaya, and it had been a joy to learn that they had come through safely, and that

39

their mother had managed to get on one of the last ships to Australia. Cordelia had perked up no end, and thoroughly enjoyed playing the great-aunt now she had family of her own to fuss over. Poor Cordelia, her sons were far away in Canada, and there had been little communication between them, so it was a blessing that she now had Sarah and Jane to watch over.

'By the way,' said Cordelia. 'Ron said to tell you he'll have his lunch at the Anchor and then take Harvey into the hills before he has to open up for the evening session.'

'At least all this running about is keeping him out of mischief,' said Peggy dryly.

Cordelia grimaced. 'That's as maybe, but he's working far too hard for a man of his age,' she murmured. 'What with running the pub for Rosie Braithwaite, and fulfilling his commitments to the ARP and Home Guard, I'm amazed he can find the time or the energy to tend to his garden as well as go poaching with Harvey.'

'He's only in his mid-sixties and as fit as a butcher's dog,' protested Peggy mildly. 'He might moan about his moving shrapnel, and try to pull a fast one now and again to get out of doing things around the house, but I don't think you need worry about him at all.'

Cordelia giggled. 'He got another letter from Rosie this morning, and I suspect all this new-found energy of his comes from knowing she's still thinking of him.'

Peggy's smile was soft as she thought about Ron's deep and abiding passion for the glamorous Rosie Braithwaite. He'd fallen in love with her from the moment she'd taken over the Anchor, and had patiently and determinedly courted her until she finally surrendered to his undoubted charm. A few short months ago she'd suddenly left Cliffehaven and, thinking she no longer loved him, Ron had been devastated. And then he'd found the letter she'd left in her treacherous brother's safe-keeping and all had been explained. From that day on Ron had been revived, and he'd taken over the Anchor to ensure Rosie had a thriving business to return to – and to prove that although he might be a scruffy old Irishman with few refinements, he was the right man for her should she ever be free to take him on.

'I know it's wicked to think such things,' murmured Peggy, 'but it would have been a blessing for all concerned if Rosie's poor sick husband had been killed when the insane asylum was bombed.'

'I agree,' said Cordelia. 'Death would certainly be a blessed release from a life spent in torment.' She eyed Peggy over the lip of her teacup. 'You look peaky,' she said flatly, 'and there's no good denying it, Peggy. What's wrong?'

Peggy might have known those sharp old eyes would miss nothing, but it was still early days in her pregnancy, and she had yet to tell Jim and the rest of the family. 'I'm just a bit run down and tired,' she replied, 'but it's really nothing for you to fret about.'

Cordelia's gaze was steady as she regarded Peggy. 'I always said you do too much, but then you rarely sit still long enough to listen to any of my advice.' She reached across and took Peggy's hand. 'I'll help all I can, but you have to stop

41

worrying about everyone else and start looking after yourself, Peggy'

Her loving words brought Peggy close to tears again as she patted her hand. 'I'll take care, Cordelia,' she promised. Then she glanced at the clock and reached for her wrap-round apron. 'Goodness, look at the time. Half the day's gone and I haven't even started on the washing.'

Chapter Three

Cliffehaven

Cordelia's arthritis was playing up something shocking, for the tentative warmth of the past two weeks had been replaced by bitter winds and heavy rain that lashed the windows and battered the delicate green shoots in Ron's vegetable garden. It was four in the afternoon of a late April day which had never really recovered from a gloomy beginning, and she was sitting close to the range with a blanket over her aching knees and mittens on her misshapen hands, feeling decidedly sorry for herself.

The house was quiet, for everyone was out, and she missed the noise and kerfuffle and having someone to talk to. She would have liked a cup of tea as well, but her hands were so bad today, she didn't dare try and lift the heavy kettle from the hob for fear she'd scald herself. She gave a deep sigh as she listened to the wind buffeting the house, and thanked her lucky stars that she didn't have to be out there.

Cordelia perked up when she heard the garden door slam and Ron stumped up the cellar steps into the kitchen with a crate of milk stout, quickly followed by a soaking wet Harvey who proceeded to shake himself vigorously and splatter everything with muddy water. Before she could stop him, the brindled lurcher made a beeline for Cordelia, his great paws landing heavily in her lap as he dripped all over her and tried to lick her face.

'Oh,' she cried out in distress. 'Harvey, get down, you're hurting me.'

'Get out of it, ye heathen beast,' growled Ron as he hastily dropped the crate on the draining board, grabbed the dog's collar and hauled him away. 'Sit there and stay,' he ordered firmly.

Harvey slumped on the floor, ears drooping, eyes liquid with sorrow as if he was facing a death sentence.

Ron ignored this fine piece of acting and turned back to Cordelia. 'Are ye bad hurt, Cordelia?' he asked in softer tones, his Irish brogue still strong despite the years he'd lived in Cliffehaven.

Cordelia shook her head, although the weight of the dog had sent deep pains shooting through her legs and hands and her lovely blanket was now wet and muddy in patches. 'I'll be fine,' she muttered as she plucked at the blanket. She looked up at him, saw the concern in his blue eyes and hurried to reassure him. 'Harvey's just a bit too big to be throwing himself all over me,' she said lightly, 'and he took me by surprise.'

Ron dug his hands into the pockets of his

43

disreputable old corduroy trousers and regarded her steadily from beneath bushy eyebrows. 'To be sure, Cordelia, 'tis sorry I am.' His gaze dropped to her hands which she'd cradled in her lap. 'Ach, your poor wee hands look terrible cold. Would you like me to fix you a hot water bottle and a cup of tea?'

She felt the blush spread over her face as she nodded. 'That would be lovely,' she murmured, unable to meet his eyes. Ron was still a handsome man despite the shaggy brows and wayward hair, and the ragged clothes which looked about fit only for the dustbin, and Cordelia always felt a pleasurable little flutter in her heart when he smiled at her. She knew it was silly, for Ron was at least ten years her junior, but he had such a lovely way with him, she couldn't help it.

Ron shook out the worst of the muddy water from the blanket and placed it tenderly back over her knees. Then he stomped about the kitchen in his muddy wellingtons, his long poacher's coat dripping onto the lino as Harvey lay with his nose on his paws, eyebrows and ears twitching as he watched every move.

Ron unearthed the stone hot water bottle from behind the gingham curtain under the sink, and when he'd filled it from the whistling kettle and secured the bung, he wrapped it in a tea towel and gently placed it within the fold of the blanket.

She nodded her thanks and closed her eyes as the lovely heat slowly melted away the pain. She'd been living here for years, but the warmth and affection Ron and his family showed her still brought tears to her eyes, and she counted herself very blessed.

Ron poured them both a cup of tea, slopped some in a saucer for Harvey by way of forgiveness, and then sat at the table, still in his wellingtons and dripping coat, the old tweed cap flung on a nearby chair.

As Harvey noisily lapped up his treat, Ron filled his pipe. When the dog had finished chasing the saucer round the room to garner the last smear, he sternly sent him back to his corner. 'Where's Peg?' he asked once he'd got his pipe going satisfactorily.

'She took Daisy down to the station to help man the WVS tea waggon and make sandwiches. Another troop train's due to stop here on the way to the naval base.' Cordelia had fretted over Peggy all afternoon, for the weather was terrible and she really shouldn't have been out in it while she was still so tired and run-down.

'To be sure, that wee girl does too much,' muttered Ron around the stem of his pipe, 'and standing about in this weather is not good for man nor beast.' He finished his cup of tea and pushed back his chair. 'I'll set to and peel some spuds to go with that stew I can smell simmering in the oven – then I'll fetch in more logs and clean up the mess I've made on her floor.'

'She'll appreciate that, but don't do too many spuds,' Cordelia said quickly. 'There'll only be the three of us eating at home tonight.'

Ron raised a greying brow. 'Oh, aye?'

Cordelia was feeling much brighter now the pain in her hands and legs had been eased. 'The Americans have invited the girls to another party up at the Cliffe estate, and if it's anything like the last time, there'll be a huge spread laid out.' Cordelia grinned. 'The Yanks don't seem to have a problem with rationing, and Fran said the tables were fairly groaning with roast beef, chicken and ham.'

Ron carried the crate of milk stout across the room and stowed it away on the marble shelf in the larder. ''Tis a pity they can't sneak a few bits home with them,' he muttered. 'I can't remember the last time I had a decent bit of ham.' He returned to the sink and began to peel the potatoes. 'Are Sarah and Jane going this time?'

Cordelia smiled at the mention of her great-nieces. 'They certainly are,' she replied. 'The last party was too soon after they got those letters from their mother, so of course they were in no mood for socialising then. But they've since had time to digest the news and realise that their father's fate, and that of Sarah's fiancé, is out of their hands – and that life must go on regardless of what the future might hold.' She stared into the fire. 'At least their mother and baby brother are safe in Australia with their grandparents, and while there is life, there is hope.'

'I suppose there'll be all sorts of shenanigans in this house from the minute they get back from work,' grumbled Ron. ''Tis a mystery to me how much fuss and noise it takes to get ready for a bit of a dance with a few Yanks.'

Cordelia giggled. 'I seem to remember someone making a terrible fuss every night when he was going to see Rosie Braithwaite. Those young girls are not the only ones with stars in their eyes, Ron.'

'Aye, well,' he replied with a shrug, 'but at least I'm not the one for changing me clothes a dozen times and spending hours doing me hair.'

'You've only got one set of decent clothes,' she retorted, 'and a month of brushing wouldn't bring that mop of yours under control.'

He turned from the sink and winked at her. 'At least I'm not as bald as a coot like most of my contemporaries. To be sure, Cordelia, I've a fine head of hair.'

'Not short of a bit of vanity either,' she said with a sniff.

'Ach, Cordelia, you're a hard, woman to please, so y'are.' His eyes twinkled as he looked at her, and then he turned back to the sink.

As Ron chopped the potatoes and dropped them into the saucepan of cold water, Cordelia noticed that Harvey was on his belly, slowly edging his way towards the range as he kept a wary eye on Ron. She didn't encourage him, knowing he would leap up at her again, but she didn't stop him either, for he loved to stretch out and warm himself in the glow – and he'd been punished long enough.

She smiled fondly at him as he tentatively squirmed onto the rug and softly rested his nose on her shoes, his big amber eyes liquid with a plea for forgiveness. He was a lovely, highly intelligent dog who had proved his bravery time and again by helping to sniff out and rescue those trapped in the rubble of an air raid. Blessed with a whole catalogue of expressions, he knew exactly how to get around her – as did his sidekick and fellow conspirator, Ron.

Peggy was almost dead on her feet, for she'd been standing for most of the afternoon, making endless sandwiches. But at least she hadn't had to go and stand in the rain by the tea waggon to greet the young men on the incoming train and dispense cups of tea and cigarettes while they ate the sandwiches, for she'd been asked to stay in the Town Hall and oversee things there.

She'd had about enough of bread, marge, Spam, corned beef and fish paste, which was all they'd had to offer the boys, and as the last box of sandwiches was carried out of the Town Hall by one of the volunteers, she dropped her knife and sank into a nearby wooden chair. It wasn't the most comfortable of seats, but at least it took the weight off her feet and eased the ache in her back. She shot a glance towards the pram on the far side of the room before lighting a well-earned cigarette. Daisy would be waking soon and then it would be time to walk home and start all over again.

Peggy sighed, the cigarette smoke streaming towards the ceiling as she tipped back her head and closed her eyes. She felt completely drained, and the thought, of having to walk home in the wind and rain simply defeated her. If only she could use the car, she thought, life would have been so much easier. But it was propped up on bricks and locked away in a friend's garage for the duration, and even if she had the money, petrol was so tightly rationed she wouldn't have been able to use it anyway.

'Margaret! Do pull yourself together and stop lounging about like that.'

Peggy almost jumped out of her skin. She

opened her eyes and regarded her elder sister, Doris, with little affection. Doris was bossy and overbearing, a terrible snob and the laziest person she knew. The fact that she'd clearly just come from the hairdresser's was simply another irritation. 'I've earned a few minutes' peace,' Peggy replied flatly.

'I hardly think that making a few sandwiches can be classed as heavy labour,' Doris snapped, her cold gaze sweeping over the mess on the table.

Peggy refused to rise to the bait as she ground out her cigarette in the tin ashtray and slowly began to clear things away. She regarded Doris from head to foot, noting the fresh hairdo under the silk scarf, the immaculate make-up and suspiciously new-looking gabardine raincoat. 'Did you want something, Doris? Only I have to finish here and get home.'

'I just called in to ensure that everyone was pulling their weight this afternoon,' she replied. 'As the local WVS supervisor, our patron, my friend Lady Charlemondley, expects me to keep a finger on the pulse of things here.' She pronounced it Chumley, her voice raised just loud enough for everyone to hear and appreciate her intimacy with the upper classes.

'Your fingers would have been put to better use by lending a hand with all those blasted sandwiches,' muttered Peggy as she gathered up the empty meat tins and threw them in a cardboard box.

Doris raised a severely plucked eyebrow, her expression flat with disapproval. 'My role in the WVS does not include such things, Margaret, as you very well know.'

Peggy took a deep breath and carried on clearing up. Doris didn't do anything very much, she thought wearily, and yet she couldn't resist her little digs. She had a girl to do the housework and most of the cooking, a husband who gave her a generous clothing allowance, and a son who saw to the garden and any of the repairs that needed doing around her posh house in Havelock Road. She had a regular weekly appointment at the hairdresser's, could shop in the expensive department store in the High Street and afford to have tea in the swanky restaurant upstairs. All in all, she and her sister lived in different worlds.

'It seems to me, Doris,' she said as she cleaned the breadboard and stowed it away with the knives and the last tiny portion of margarine, 'that you are a very fortunate woman. Now, if you'll excuse me, I have to finish up here, and you're getting in my way.'

Doris stepped back hastily as Peggy wiped a cloth over the table and sent crumbs flying. 'Anthony has managed to borrow a car from the MOD and will be arriving at your house on the dot of seven to pick up that girl. Be sure she doesn't keep him waiting.'

Peggy looked up from her task and frowned. Doris's lovely, shy, clever son Anthony had been courting her lodger, Suzy, for a few weeks now, and Doris had made it clear she didn't approve. 'I don't see why she should,' she replied. 'Why, what's the occasion?'

'As Anthony seems determined to go against my wishes by seeing the wretched girl, I have decided to invite her to dinner.'

Peggy felt a stab of alarm. 'When did you arrange this?'

'This morning. Anthony is off duty for the day from his important work for the MOD, and I sent him to the hospital to issue the invitation.'

Peggy folded her arms and regarded her sister steadily. 'I hope this invitation was sent with the best of intentions, Doris. Suzy's a lovely girl, and I will not have you making mischief.'

Doris's expression hardened as she lifted her chin. 'I don't know what you mean by that remark, Margaret. Susan has been invited to an intimate family dinner so that we can all get to know one another better. I cannot see why you should think there is any mischief involved.'

Peggy almost shuddered at the thought of an 'intimate family dinner' with Doris playing the grande dame, and waiting to pounce on the slightest sign that Suzy felt uncomfortable or daunted. She needed to get home quickly and have a quiet word with the girl, who was no doubt already quaking with nerves, for she knew how awful Doris could be when on her high horse.

Doris looked at the thin gold watch on her wrist. 'Edward will be closing the shop soon, and I need to get home to lay out his suit and so on. Phyllis is cooking dinner, and if I don't keep an eye on her, she'll burn the chicken.'

'Chicken, eh? My word, you are pushing the boat out, Doris,' she said wryly.

'One has standards, Margaret – even in these troubled times.'

Peggy didn't doubt it as she dragged on her

worn raincoat and tied her headscarf under her chin. Doris liked to show off and had the means to do it.

She quickly handed over the box of tins to another volunteer and followed her sister out of the canteen and into the vast room that had been turned into something resembling a jumble sale. Trestle tables groaned beneath piles of donated clothing, bedding and kitchen appliances, while prams, toys and stacks of books had been set out by the Almoner's office. The mattresses which would be used at night by the homeless had been stacked against the far wall, the pillows and blankets safely locked away in the recruiting office's store cupboard. The Town Hall had become a refuge, an advisory centre and a recruiting base, and it was always busy.

Daisy was crying and had kicked off her blankets, and one glance outside confirmed that the rain was coming down in horizontal stair-rods as the wind howled up from the seafront. She held the squalling baby in her arms and eyed the Bentley that was parked at the bottom of the Town Hall steps. 'I thought you'd locked that away for the duration,' she remarked.

'I did,' replied Doris as she unfurled a smart black umbrella. 'But the weather is so ghastly, and I have enough petrol stored away to use it occasionally.' Before Peggy had the chance to ask for a lift home, she'd hurried down the steps, climbed into the car and within minutes was driving down the High Street.

Peggy gaped at her thoughtlessness and glared as the brake lights flashed at the bottom of the hill and the indicator arm flicked out. 'Thanks for nothing, Doris,' she muttered beneath the baby's yells. 'You really are the absolute limit, and I hope Phyllis burns your rotten chicken to a ruddy cinder.'

She felt marginally better for venting her rage, but the memory of her selfish sister's car sailing off blithely through the wind and rain still rankled as she changed Daisy's nappy and stuck a dummy in her wailing mouth.

By the time she reached the back door of Beach View Boarding House she felt – and probably looked – like a drowned rat.

'Get yourself inside,' said Ron as he threw open the door and ordered the overexcited Harvey to get back into the kitchen. 'There's tea in the pot, dinner in the oven, and the fire's burning a treat.' He pulled the pram in after her and plucked the yelling Daisy from her blankets. 'See to yourself, Peggy, girl. I'll be dealing with this wee wain.'

Peggy smiled at him with profound gratitude as she pulled off the sodden headscarf and raincoat and left them both to drip dry over the stone sink that stood beneath the copper boiler and mangle.

Slipping out of her wet shoes, she carried them upstairs to the kitchen where Harvey was waiting for her, his tail thumping on the floor in wel- come. Peggy patted his head, kissed Cordelia's soft cheek and dropped her shoes on the mat in front of the range fire. 'I can't remember the last time I felt so tired,' she admitted as she poured a cup of welcoming tea. 'It's been an endless day.'

'Ron brought some more milk stout,' said Cordelia. 'Perhaps you should have a glass of that instead of weak tea?'

Peggy grimaced. 'I'd rather have tea, however weak.'

Daisy was still hiccuping with fury at not being fed, but had become fascinated by Ron's sweeping eyebrows. She made a grab for one and held on, broke into a beaming smile as he winced, and gave it a hefty tug.

'To be sure, the pain is worth it to have no more crying,' Ron groaned as the tiny fist took a tighter hold.

'You should have let Fran give them a trim when she offered,' said Cordelia with a glint of humour in her eyes. 'It's your own fault they stick out like that.'

'Did I hear my name being taken in vain?' Fran came into the kitchen, her auburn curls dancing about her shoulders in disarray as she plumped into a chair at the table and reached for the teapot. 'That's a fair hold she has on you there, Uncle Ron,' she said and laughed. 'Are you sure you'll not be letting me trim them brows?'

Ron tried glowering at her, but didn't quite manage it, for he was trying not to laugh as he fended off the tiny pugilist who seemed determined to batter him.

Peggy sank into her chair by the fire and lit a cigarette as the little Irish nurse and her father-in-law teased one another. Just being at home in her kitchen and sitting down was enough to restore her. 'Is Suzy back yet?' she asked.

'Aye, that she is, and in a terrible lather upstairs, worrying the life out of herself about what to wear to this awful dinner at Doris's.'

Peggy told them about seeing Doris earlier. 'It's just so typical of my sister to give out such an invitation with no notice and expect everyone to jump. I'd better go up and have a word with Suzy. Warn her what to expect.'

'I t'ink she already has a fair idea, Peggy, and she's girding her loins to prepare for battle, so she is.' Fran giggled. 'What I wouldn't give to be a fly on the wall in that house tonight.'

'It's not funny, Fran,' said Rita as she came stomping into the room in her heavy waterproof trousers, thick boots and moth-eaten WWI flying jacket. She dumped her rain-soaked goggles and leather helmet on the table and poured a cup of tea. 'Doris can make things very sticky for Suzy, and she'll have to be on her guard all night. Just be thankful it's not you.'

'To be sure, Anthony's a lovely wee man, but he's not my type. One look at Doris, and any girl worth her salt would be running for their lives, so they would. Suzy deserves a medal.'

Peggy watched as Rita discarded the sodden jacket and the two girls drank the stewed tea. Fran was from Ireland and, like Suzy, was a nurse at the hospital. Rita was a local girl who'd come to live at Beach View after she'd been bombed out, and now drove fire engines for a living when she wasn't organising motorcycle races out at the old track. Fran's blue eyes and wild autumnal hair were in direct contrast to Rita's sleeker black curls and dark eyes – and although their personalities were very different, they seemed to rub along without too much falling out.

Peggy gave a sigh of contentment as she settled

55

into the fireside chair and enjoyed not having to do anything for a few minutes. The stew was in the oven, the potatoes cooking on the hob while Ron fed Daisy her mashed veg and warmed her bottle in a jug of hot water. Left to her own devices, Peggy could have nodded off then and there.

'Right,' said Ron as he handed Daisy and the bottle of formula milk over to Fran. 'I'm off to open up the pub. I'll be back for me tea, and then I've got a Home Guard meeting at the church hall.'

As he left the house with Harvey trotting at his heels, the kitchen was invaded by Sarah, her younger sister Jane, and the rather pale-looking Suzy. 'I think I've settled on the right thing to wear,' she said distractedly, 'but it's awfully hard to know what an intimate family dinner really means in your sister's house.'

Peggy eyed the sleeveless black dress with the sweetheart neckline and the lovely cut that skimmed the material over the girl's narrow hips to fall just to her knees. Her long, slender legs were bare, but shown off to their best advantage in black high-heeled court shoes. She carried a small black satin bag and her only jewellery was pearl studs and a string of more pearls around her elegant neck. 'You look wonderful,' said Peggy truthfully.

'She looks like a model in one of those fashion magazines,' breathed Jane as she perched on the arm of Cordelia's chair. 'Do you like the way Sarah's done Suzy's hair up into a chignon? Mummy always had hers like that, and I think it's very sophisticated.'

'You don't think it's all too much?' asked Suzy with a worried frown. 'Black's a bit formal, but I didn't think a blouse and skirt was smart enough, and–'

'Believe me,' interrupted Peggy, 'you look just perfect.'

But as Cordelia sighed in delight and Suzy did a twirl for the other girls and basked in their admiration, Peggy was sharply reminded of the day when her daughter Anne had been invited to lunch with Martin's snobbish parents. It had been ghastly for her, poor lamb, and she'd come home in tears having been looked down upon and sneered at all the way through that awful meal. But she and Martin had married despite his horrid parents, and although the war meant they were rarely together, she knew it was a strong and enduring marriage. She just hoped Suzy showed the same fortitude, for she wouldn't put it past Doris to do her best – in a subtle, but cutting way – to make the evening hell for her.

'Right, come on Rita,' said Fran as she handed a sleepy Daisy over to Peggy. 'The staff car will be here in less than two hours, and you can't go to a party looking like that.'

'I haven't got anything else,' retorted Rita. 'And if they don't like me the way I am, then I'm not interested in going.'

'Will you be listening to yourself?' replied Fran crossly. 'Anyone would think you were one of those odd women who never marry and live with their "friend" Sybilla or Enid – and who breed dogs and stride about in trousers, smoking a pipe with their hair cut like a man's.'

'I'm not like that at all,' retorted Rita hotly. 'I got dressed up for the cocktail party the other week, didn't I?'

Fran rolled her eyes. 'I do *not* call an old jumper and skirt dressing up – and you sat in the corner and glowered at everyone so no one dared talk to you, and then you just left without a word to anyone after half an hour and came home.'

'I think Rita just needs to feel a bit more confident about herself,' interrupted Sarah quietly. 'If she's not used to parties, then it can be terribly daunting to find yourself in a crowded room full of strangers.' She turned to Rita. 'Would you mind terribly if I helped you to get ready, Rita? Only I really do think the right clothes for the occasion make such a difference to how one feels, and the dress we've picked out for you is very pretty.'

Peggy silently blessed sweet little Sarah for her kindness, but she could see the inner battle going on in Rita, and silently willed her to agree. Rita liked to think she was tough, but under that fierce, prickly exterior Peggy suspected there beat the heart of a little girl who longed to be pretty and popular, but who'd not really had much chance to learn how.

Rita glanced at Peggy and then back at Sarah. 'All right,' she muttered, 'but I'm not having ten inches of make-up all over my face, and my hair stays loose.'

Sarah nodded and took her hand. 'Come on then, we'd better get started. I'll get dressed while you use the bathroom, then Jane and Fran can take turns in there, and before you know it, we'll all be ready for a lovely evening out.'

Suzy decided she'd rather supervise and help than sit about getting more nervous by the minute as she waited for Anthony, and the five girls hurried out of the room and pounded up the stairs, their happy voices ringing through the house.

Peggy and Cordelia exchanged glances and grinned. This was more entertaining than any show at the theatre, and they were both on tenterhooks to see what sort of transformation Sarah made of Rita.

Daisy was asleep in her cot in Peggy's room on the ground floor, the door ajar so they could hear if she woke up crying. Ron, Peggy and Cordelia had tucked into the hot, tasty, vegetable stew that was so welcoming on such a dirty night, and Suzy had spent the last few tense minutes nervously flicking through the stack of old magazines that sat next to the wireless.

Ron had left for his Home Guard meeting when the knock on the front door heralded Anthony's arrival and Suzy rushed to meet him.

'I think she's glad the waiting's over,' said Cordelia, 'but utterly dreading what's to come.' She took off her half-moon glasses and pinched the bridge of her little nose. 'Oh dear. I do hope it doesn't all end in tears. They make such a lovely couple.'

'If there's one tear shed after tonight then I'll make sure my sister pays for it,' said Peggy flatly. Her mood lightened immediately when her nephew Anthony came into the room, for she'd always been extremely fond of him, and couldn't for the life of her understand how someone as awful as her sister Doris could have given birth to such a sweet-natured son.

Tall and rather too thin, he had a well-defined mouth and his horn-rimmed glasses framed expressive eyes. The shoulders of his thick overcoat sparkled with raindrops, and as he undid the buttons, she could see he was wearing a suit instead of his usual corduroy trousers, sweater and tweed jacket.

Anthony greeted them both with a soft kiss on their cheeks. 'Don't worry, Auntie Peg,' he said warmly, 'I'll look after Suzy and make sure she has a pleasant evening.'

'I know you will,' she replied, 'and I'm relieved that you realise this could be quite an ordeal for her.'

He smiled his lovely shy smile and patted her shoulder. 'Mother can be a little bit difficult at times,' he said with admirable British understatement, 'but don't fret, Auntie Peg, I won't let her spoil Suzy's evening.'

As Suzy came back into the room Peggy saw the love that shone from his eyes and knew his promise would hold good. She kissed them both goodbye and waved them off as they quickly ran out into the rain and down the steps to the little black Austin parked by the kerb. She closed the door, heard the giggling and chatter coming from upstairs and, with a smile of contentment, returned to the kitchen.

'Whatever is keeping those girls?' grumbled Cordelia some time later. 'It's past seven o'clock and we haven't seen hide nor hair of them for nearly two whole hours.'

As if on cue they heard footsteps on the stairs and the click-clack of heels on the hall's tiled floor and both turned towards the doorway. They could hear muffled giggles and hoarse whispers and wondered what on earth they were up to out there.

'We thought we'd give you a fashion show,' said Fran from the other side of the doorway. 'Are you ready?'

Peggy and Cordelia smiled in pleasurable anticipation and replied that they were.

Sarah came in first, her fair hair elegantly coiled at the nape of her nape, the string of pearls gleaming at her throat, the plain cream sheath of her linen dress skimming over her slight figure. She looked sophisticated and completely self-assured as she gave a twirl, acknowledged their happy applause and then went to stand by the table.

Jane's long fair hair had been swept back into victory rolls which emphasised her fine cheekbones and blue eyes. She looked rather bashful as she teetered a bit in her borrowed high-heeled sandals and showed off the deep blue dress Suzy had lent her for the occasion.

Fran had no such inhibitions and sashayed in wearing a dress of emerald green, her beautiful hair rippling down her back and over her shoulders as if she'd stepped out of a Pre-Raphaelite painting. Scarlet glass beads were at her throat, and she'd finished off her outfit with rather saucy red shoes.

Cordelia and Peggy applauded enthusiastically and then waited with bated breath for Rita.

She emerged shyly from the doorway, her eyes

downcast. Her dark curls fell about her face, held back only with a pretty butterfly-shaped slide above one ear. Her dainty figure, hidden so long beneath thick trousers and her old flying jacket, was quite remarkable. The tight bodice of the flowery pink and white dress was nipped in at the waist with a narrow white belt, from which the full skirt swirled almost to her knees. She wore low-heeled court shoes, had a sparkling bangle round her wrist and looked so sweet it brought tears to Peggy's eyes.

'Goodness me,' said Cordelia, reaching for her handkerchief. 'What a transformation. You look absolutely lovely, my dear.'

Rita's dark eyes regarded them all from beneath the curls, her cheeks burning with embarrassment at being the focus of everyone's attention. 'I do feel very different,' she admitted, 'but it's cold without trousers and my jacket.'

Fran waved a pink cardigan at her. 'Put that on,' she ordered, 'and stop moaning.' She grinned and gave the younger girl a hug. 'You look gorgeous, so you do, and I lay odds that you'll not be off the dance floor all night.'

'That's all very well,' retorted Rita, who seemed to have found her prickliness again, 'but I don't know how to dance.'

'You will when it comes to the smoochy ones,' said Fran. 'It's easy, you just hang on and let them steer you about the floor.'

The rap of the door knocker brought this exchange to an end and had them all rushing about hunting for bags and coats and doing last-minute things to their hair. Peggy clucked and smiled and went to open the door.

Two very tall, handsome young American officers stood on her doorstep in their smartest dress uniform. They whipped off their peaked hats and saluted, their pristine white gloves glimmering in the light from the hallway. 'Good evening, ma'am,' said their spokesman. 'Lieutenant Jonathon Cable at your service. This is Lieutenant Randolph Yates. Are the young ladies ready?'

He pronounced it 'lootenant' and as this was the first time Peggy had managed to get a close-up view of any Americans, she could instantly see why the girls had been all of a flutter. 'I'm Peggy Reilly,' she said. 'Please, come in out of the rain. The girls won't be a moment.'

She closed the door and beckoned for them to follow her into the kitchen so she could introduce them to Cordelia.

Cordelia went pink and giggled as they saluted her. 'My goodness,' she twittered. 'You both look like film stars. Are you from Hollywood?'

'No, ma'am,' said Jonathon Cable, 'I'm from Texas, and Randolph here is from Chicago.'

'Goodness,' breathed Cordelia. 'Is that anywhere near Kalamazoo? I do love that song, don't you?'

'Sure do, ma'am,' he replied and smiled, showing wonderfully white and even teeth. 'But Kalamazoo is in Michigan, ma'am.'

Peggy realised this could go on for ages and decided it was time for them all to leave. She chivvied the girls into their coats and herded them into the hall while the American boys said goodbye to Cordelia and swiftly followed.

Ignoring the rain that was still hammering onto

the pavement, she watched from the doorway as the girls climbed into the large grey saloon car that was parked at the kerb. It was at least four times larger than Anthony's little Austin, with white-wall tyres, acres of gleaming chrome, and American pennants fluttering on the wings.

Waving goodbye as the car roared off down the terrace to the main road, she closed the door and slowly returned to the kitchen. It was lovely to see Rita looking so feminine and pretty in her borrowed party dress. Lovely, too, that all her girls were living life to the full and having fun, for the world was a dark place, the future uncertain.

She gazed up at Jim's photograph, remembering her own youth and the excitement of dressing up to go out dancing. Jim was a good dancer, and she had felt as light as a feather as he'd twirled her around the ballroom at the end of the pier. She gave a soft sigh. It all seemed a very long time ago – but the memories lingered and warmed her as she settled into her chair and prepared for a cosy night in with Cordelia.

Chapter Four

Bow

Ruby had been back at work for two weeks now and although the bruises had gone, she felt empty inside, and in the few quiet moments she had, she still mourned the loss of the tiny baby that had not been allowed to live.

She had finished the lunchtime session at the pub and wasn't due to go back until the next day, so she'd queued for what felt like hours at the butcher's stall in the market only to return home with a mutton bone and a few scraps of dubious-looking offal. Placing this meagre offering in her only heavy cooking pot, she lit the gas ring which stood on the scarred table by the hearth and boiled it up with some pearl barley.

Once the few strips of meat had fallen off the bone, and the offal had made a thick stock, she peeled and chopped the last of the whiskery potatoes and shrivelled carrots, then shredded the cabbage leaves she'd managed to forage from beneath the grocer's stall, and added them to the pot.

It didn't smell too bad at all and her mouth watered at the thought of mopping up the rich gravy with some of the wheatmeal bread the Ministry of Food was calling the 'national loaf'. It didn't taste of much, but it was filling, and that was the important thing.

She ignored the pangs of hunger and looked round the room to make sure everything was neat and tidy as she took off her apron. The floor was swept, the bed was made with clean linen, the brass knobs polished to a gleam. Ray's shirts and freshly pressed suit trousers hung waiting for him on the back of the door. His shoes had been polished and were lined up on newspaper by the dilapidated dresser where his brushes, soap and razor had been placed neatly on a clean towel next to the bowl and jug of water he would need when he got in. She'd even managed to clean the window and nail the blackout curtain back onto the frame where it had come loose. Ruby gave a sour grimace of satisfaction. He would find no fault today.

Waiting for him to come home always made her nervous, for she never knew what sort of mood he would be in, and with everything ready and nothing to occupy her, she became restless and began to pace the small room. She checked her appearance in the mirror, glad she'd had the time to wash her hair and put on some powder and lipstick. The bruises might have gone, but she couldn't hide the apprehension in her eyes, or ignore the growing resentment and hatred for the man who'd so cruelly robbed her baby of life and treated her like dirt.

Tamping down on these dangerous emotions, Ruby turned from the mirror and looked out of the window to see what the weather was doing – it was still light, so she didn't untie the blackout curtain but left it knotted to one side – and then gave the soup another stir.

Her gaze flitted to the meter. It was running low and she'd spent the last of her meagre house-keeping on tonight's meal. If the gas ran out then the soup would get cold, and she wouldn't be able to heat his shaving water. The thought of what Ray might do if that happened made her stomach churn. She should have remembered – should have made sure she had a spare tanner for just such an occasion. But she'd been tired and in a rush to get everything done in time and had forgotten.

She looked at the cheap clock that ticked on the mantel and decided to risk going down to her mother's room. Ethel always had a few tanners put by, and she only needed to borrow one. Turning off the gas beneath the saucepan, she quickly opened the door and raced down the stairs to the third floor.

Ethel was in the middle of ladling her own soup into bowls for her two young lodgers who worked alongside her on the assembly line in the canning factory and slept on a mattress in the corner of her tiny room. They all looked startled by Ruby's sudden appearance.

'Whatever's the matter?' Ethel asked.

'I need to borrow a tanner for the meter,' she replied breathlessly. 'I'll pay you back tomorrow when I get me wages.'

Ethel raised an eyebrow but said nothing as she delved into her purse and handed over the small silver coin.

'Thanks, Mum, you're a diamond.' Ruby kissed her mother's cheek, charged back out onto the landing and raced up the stairs.

Ray was waiting for her, framed in the open doorway, arms folded, expression thunderous.

Ruby's heart was hammering and her mouth was so dry she could barely speak. 'I just popped out to get–'

'Shut the door,' he snapped.

Warily, she stepped into the room and, with her heart banging against her ribs, closed the door behind her. 'I was only gone for a few seconds,' she said softly.

'I told you never to leave this room unlocked.'

His voice was deadly calm, his face almost expressionless as his eyes bored into her.

She could smell the whisky on his breath as he came nearer. 'But I was only at Mum's to fetch a tanner for the meter.' Her back was pressed against the door, the sixpenny piece biting into the palm of her hand as she clenched her fist around it. 'I didn't want your soup to get cold.'

'But you didn't lock the door.' His gaze was arctic.

Ruby was so nervous she had the sudden terrible urge to giggle – but that would have been fatal, and she fought to control it. 'It ain't as if we've got anything to steal,' she managed in a hoarse whisper.

'That's what you think,' he snapped. 'I don't make idle rules, Ruby – they all have a reason. But it seems you can't get that through yer thick head for more than a minute at a time. When I say the door is to be locked, then that's what should happen.'

She saw how his fists curled at his sides. Noted how his lips formed a thin line, and his eyes narrowed to a steely glare. 'I won't do it again, I promise,' she gabbled. 'Please don't hit me, Ray. I don't mean to upset you. Really, I don't.'

The lightning strike to her belly took her breath away, and before she could react, his fist slammed into her jaw and sent her stumbling across the room.

She fell against the unyielding iron frame of the gas fire but hardly felt the blow to her head, for the agony in her belly and jaw was all-encompassing. She tried to heave air into her lungs as she scrabbled along the floor in a desperate attempt to escape him. If she didn't get to her feet quickly, he'd put the boot in and break her ribs again.

Her terror gave her strength and she twisted away just in time to avoid the heavy boot and somehow got to her feet. The table was between them now, the hot soup still simmering in the cast-iron pot. She saw his gaze flicker to the long-handled pot – knew what he was about to do – and braced herself to stand firm and then dive away at the last minute.

She was fast, but not quite fast enough, and some of the scalding soup sprayed over her shoulder and neck and down her arm before the pot crashed to the floor and splattered its contents everywhere.

His face darkened as he eyed the mess that had spewed from the flying pot and now dripped like vomit down his expensive clothes and into his shoes. When his gaze fell back on Ruby, there was murder in his eyes.

Ruby felt no pain now – just sheer, blind terror as he threw the table aside and advanced on her. She snatched the heavy pot from the floor and swung it hard, feeling it judder right through her as it hit his arm.

With a mighty roar of rage and pain he faltered and then made a grab for her.

She dodged out of his way, slipping in the soup that had puddled on the floor as she brandished her only weapon. A great surge of defiance and fury rushed through her. 'Stay away from me, Ray,' she yelled at him. 'I'm not a punchbag and if you hit me again I'll kill you!'

He made a noise deep in his throat and made a grab for the pot. 'You're already dead, *bitch*,' he growled.

Ruby dodged away and managed to keep hold of the heavy pot, but the room was too small – Ray was too big and too angry to listen to reason – and despite the rush of rage-filled energy that had given her the strength to fight back, she knew she couldn't hold out much longer. A pot, no matter how heavy, was not a real deterrent to a man like him. Her gaze flickered to the wickedly sharp carving knife that had slid from the table to the floor. She had to find some way of getting out of the door before he saw it too.

Ray's eyes gleamed with fury and malevolence as he followed Ruby's fleeting glance and snatched up the knife. 'No one defies me, Ruby,' he snarled as he flashed the blade between them. 'Least of all a little tart like you, and I'll get you in the end – you know it.'

She stayed out of his reach, her mind working furiously as she kept an eye on the knife and moved warily across to where the soup still puddled the floor. She was in danger of getting trapped in a corner, and instead of swinging the heavy pot at him like he probably expected, she risked the slash of the knife and darted forward, jabbing him as hard as she could in his midriff.

Ray lost his footing in the mess on the floor, and as he dropped the knife and tried to regain his balance, Ruby gathered up the last of her dwindling strength and courage, swung with all her might and hit him squarely between the legs. As he howled in agony, clutched his balls and slid in the mess of soup, Ruby dropped the pot and raced for the door.

She flung it open and was poised for flight when she heard a sickening thud followed by the sound of a deep grunt and something heavy hitting the floor. She dared to look over her shoulder.

There was blood on the brass bed-knob – and more slowly pooling beneath Ray's head as he lay in a motionless heap amid the spilled soup.

Ruby froze in the doorway. Ray was dead. She'd killed him – and would be hanged for murder.

She didn't know how long she stood there, her gaze fixed to the still figure on the floor as the pool of blood widened and began to soak into the floorboards. And it was only the insistent wails of the air-raid sirens that broke the trance and galvanised her into action. With a sob of terror, she grabbed the key and locked the door behind her. She had to get to her mother's before she left for the tube station. Ethel would know what to do.

The sirens were going off all through the East End and, as she pushed and jostled her way through the mass of humanity that blocked all the landings and stairs, she could see the search-lights stutter into life. Ignoring the curses and questions thrown at her from the other women, she finally made it to Ethel's door. But one glance into the room told her that Ethel and her lodgers had already left.

Ruby's despair was a sob in her throat as she spun on her heel and raced down the rest of the steps, shoving her way through the great tide of humanity that was heading for Bow Street Underground. She didn't care that she must look like a mad woman, with soup in her hair, blood trickling down her face from the gash to her head, and a jaw that felt as if it had swollen to twice its size. She had to find her mother.

The ARP wardens were shouting orders, babies and small children were screaming as the residents of Bow pushed and shoved their way through the station entrance and the sirens shrieked with maniacal insistence. Above the noise, Ruby could hear the approaching enemy bombers, but her whole being was centred upon finding her mother in the crush of people that filled the two Underground platforms.

Ethel was in her usual place, close to one of the exits, comfortable in the old deckchair she'd found months ago on a bomb site, and sipping tea quite happily as if she was at a garden party. But then Ethel was an old hand at living down the tube stations during the raids, and enjoyed the camaraderie and the singsongs.

Ruby suddenly realised she couldn't just rush over and tell her mother what had happened – there were too many people about, she must look a fright, and questions would be fired at her from all directions. She hovered impatiently close by where the shadows might just hide the state she was in, and tried to catch her mother's eye.

Ethel finally saw her frantic arm-waving and beckoned her to join the group, but as Ruby shook her head and made it clear she needed her to come over, Ethel frowned and finally hauled herself out of the deckchair. She took one look at the blood on Ruby's face and the swollen, bruised jaw, and clucked with sympathy. 'I can see what's happened,' she said wearily. 'Blimey, gel, don't you never learn?'

Ruby grabbed her mother's arm. 'I think I've killed him,' she rasped. 'Oh, Gawd, Mum, what am I gunna do?'

'You're gunna keep your voice down for a bleedin' start,' muttered Ethel grimly as she glanced about and then roughly steered Ruby into the deeper, less populated shadows. 'Right, gel. Tell me what happened.'

The evening's events were beginning to take their toll, and Ruby's voice wavered as she described the terrifying scene and battled the almost overwhelming need to collapse at her mother's feet.

Ethel's expression was unreadable as she listened without comment, arms folded tightly about her waist, her gaze never leaving Ruby's battered face. She waited until Ruby had come to a stuttering halt. 'Are yer sure he's dead?'

'He wasn't moving and there was blood – lots of blood. He looked dead to me,' stammered Ruby.

'Half the blokes round here look dead when they've passed out drunk,' muttered Ethel, 'it don't necessarily mean they actually are – more's the pity,' she added with a sniff.

'He didn't pass out, Mum,' she persisted. 'I heard his head hit the bed.' She took a shuddering breath. 'It were an awful sound.'

Ethel nodded. 'Then we'd better go and take a look at 'im before the raid finishes and all them nosey parkers are back on the landings.'

'But we're not allowed out during a raid, and I

73

forgot me gas mask. The warden–'

'Bugger the warden,' snapped Ethel. She lit a fag, stuck it in the corner of her mouth and adjusted her headscarf over her rollers. 'It's only old Eric, and he's probably sleeping off the drink somewhere. C'mon.'

They ran up the steps where people had settled with their few belongings because there was no more room on the platforms. Ethel's glare rebuffed all comments and Ruby forced her trembling legs to carry her towards the main door.

It creaked open, but the sound was lost in the roar of enemy planes and the thunderous booms of exploding bombs. Searchlights wavered across the smoke-shrouded sky as ambulance and fire-engine bells clamoured and flames devoured the shattered remains of a nearby row of buildings. There was no sign of Eric.

Ethel grabbed Ruby's hand. 'Ready for this?' At Ruby's nod they ducked their heads and scrambled over the debris which spilled across the pavement and into the road.

The red glow of fire lit their way as the enemy bombers droned overhead amid the zip and zing of tracer bullets, the rattle of the ack-ack guns, and the bright pom-pom bursts of shellfire coming from the batteries of guns that defended London. The ground shuddered beneath their feet as explosions rocked the very foundations of the buildings that were still standing. They cringed as masonry toppled with a crash in front of them – and then flattened themselves into a doorway as a low-flying enemy plane spat bullets which thudded into the walls inches from their heads.

'Bloody hell,' breathed Ethel. 'That were too bleedin' close.'

Ruby grabbed her hand. 'C'mon, Mum, we gotta get outta here.'

'Oy! What you doin' there?'

The loud shout made them flinch, and as the grim-faced ARP warden emerged from a cloud of smoke and ash, Ruby yanked her mother away from the meagre shelter and hauled her into the surrounding darkness.

They kept to the deepest shadows, running, stumbling and sliding over the shattered concrete and splintered remains of an old warehouse until they reached the pitch black of the tenement building yard. Both were out of breath and sweating as they leaned against the grimy wall and watched the dogfights that were going on overhead as the Spitfires and Lightnings harried the enemy bombers and engaged in a deadly dance with the Gerry fighter escort planes.

'Looks like they'll be a while,' muttered Ethel as she relit her fag. 'C'mon, let's see what's what.'

Ruby followed her mother into the courtyard square, guided only by her familiarity with the tenement building and the red glow of Ethel's fag end. They climbed the stairs to the third floor as the dogfights continued overhead, bombs exploded nearby and fire and ambulance bells urgently clanged.

Ethel hurried into her room, pulled the old dresser from the wall and reached into the hidden recess. Pulling out a hessian bag, she scrabbled about for a moment and then produced a claw hammer and a heavy wrench. 'I were going to sell

Ted's tools, but it's a good thing I didn't,' she said grimly.

She handed the wrench to Ruby. 'We might need these if that Ray ain't dead, 'cos you can bet yer life he'll be madder than a bull with an 'eadache, and I ain't going in there without some kind of back-up.'

Ruby eyed the heavy wrench, sickened by the thought that she might have to use it. The violence of the night had drained every ounce of strength she possessed, and as they slowly climbed the concrete stairs to the fifth floor, she stumbled repeatedly and had to cling to her mother's supporting arm.

They both cringed as a bomb exploded nearby and they clung to one another as the old tenement building shuddered and bits of masonry came loose and crashed to the yard below. Sick with fear, they waited a moment for things to settle, and then warily carried on up the stairs.

Ethel took her hand as they approached the door, but Ruby hung back. She didn't want to go in – didn't want to be faced with what she'd done – or, even worse, have to defend herself all over again.

'I know you're frightened, love,' murmured Ethel as she gave Ruby's fingers a squeeze, 'but we gotta make sure what's what.' She released Ruby's hand and pressed her ear to the thin plywood door. 'Can't hear nothing, but that don't mean he ain't sitting there waiting fer us.' She checked that Ruby had a firm hold on the wrench. 'Unlock the door, gel, then, on my say-so, we'll go in together.'

Ruby's hand was slick with sweat as she fumbled the key into the lock and gingerly turned it. With a nod of encouragement from her mother, she grasped the wrench in both hands and Ethel kicked the door open.

It had still been light when Ray had come home and so she hadn't pulled the blackout curtain across the window. Now the room was eerily lit by the fleeting sweeps of searchlights and pom-pom bursts, but Ruby could see enough. Ray was still lying on the floor exactly where she'd left him.

'Bloody hell,' breathed Ethel as she slammed the door behind them and took in the scene.

'What am I gunna do, Mum?' Ruby's voice was barely above a ragged whisper as she looked fearfully at Ray's inert form.

Ethel took a firmer grip on the claw hammer. 'Better see if he's dead first – or just playing possum.' She slowly inched her way towards him, stretched out her foot and prodded him with the toe of her shoe. Getting no response, she prodded him again and then stepped closer, the claw hammer raised to strike should he suddenly make a grab for her.

'He's dead, ain't he?' sobbed Ruby. 'Oh, Gawd, Mum, I killed him, didn't I?'

Ethel looked grimly at the man on the floor before she squatted behind him and pressed her finger into the side of his neck. 'He ain't dead,' she shouted over the roar and whine of the fighter planes overhead. 'I can feel a pulse.'

'Thank Gawd fer that,' Ruby breathed as the spectre of the hangman's noose faded. Then she realised what Ray would do to her when he came round, and the prospect was even more terrifying. 'He'll kill me for this,' she moaned.

'He ain't going nowhere for a while,' said Ethel as she stepped away from him and eyed the bloodstained brass knob on the end of the bed. 'That done a lot of damage to his head and could still be the death of him if he ain't treated quick.'

'I'll go to the phone box and ring for the doctor.'

'You'll do no such thing,' snapped Ethel.

'But if I leave him here he could die and...'

Ethel's expression was grim as she folded her arms and regarded Ruby steadily. 'Dead or alive, you're in trouble, gel. If he comes out of this yer life won't be worth nothing. If 'e dies, then the rozzers and his family will come looking for yer. We gotta get you outta here and long gone before someone finds him.'

'But I can't just leave 'im 'ere to die,' Ruby protested.

Ethel eased the wrench from Ruby's tight grip and placed both tools on the bed before embracing her. 'You ain't thinking straight, love,' she said softly, 'and I don't blame you after what you been through. But you gotta pull yerself together if yer gunna stand any chance of having a proper life.'

Ruby swiped away her tears with the back of her hand and tried to get her thoughts straight. 'But it was obviously an accident, Mum. Anyone can see that. We should get him seen to.'

Ethel gave a sigh of exasperation. 'You ain't been listening, gel. Accident or not, Ray's linked to some of the hardest nuts in the East End. They'll

78

come looking for you, Ruby. You gotta leave London.'

'But where can I go, Mum? I got no money and I ain't ever been outside London before.'

Ethel gripped her arms and gave her a none-too-gentle shake. 'This ain't the time to be feeling sorry for yerself, Ruby – you gotta think straight and remember how you was before you got mixed up with Ray.' Her grip loosened and she smiled. 'You was a tough, no-nonsense little fighter – a right chip off the old block who stood her corner and let nothing get 'er down. You gotta find that old Ruby again if yer gunna come through this.'

Ruby took a deep, shuddering breath and tried very hard to remember that other Ruby – but the last eighteen months had wiped away her self-confidence and changed her into someone she didn't recognise any more. And yet, she realised, she'd finally fought back tonight, so there must still be a spark of the old Ruby somewhere.

Ethel nodded as if she could read her thoughts and then quickly felt Ray's pulse again. 'It's getting weaker,' she muttered. 'We gotta be quick.'

She regarded Ruby solemnly as they stood in the flickering shadows cast by the searchlights flashing intermittently against the shabby walls. 'Ray lost his temper 'cos you didn't lock the door. But why was that so important? No one locks doors in this place – unless they got something worth nicking.'

Ruby's thoughts were clarifying as calm returned and she remembered the short, angry exchange. 'That's what I said to him, but he said, "That's what you think. I don't make rules for nothing."'

Ethel nodded and glanced again at the unconscious man on the floor. 'Flash suits and shoes, gold cufflinks – there's money coming in from all the illegal booze and fags he's flogging round the place. He's got a stash somewhere – I just know it.'

Ruby knew every dingy corner, had been through the dresser drawers only this afternoon to tidy the few bits of clothes. The walls were bare, there was no hatch into the roof and the door was too thin to hide a secret panel.

As the dogfights continued overhead and the evening sky glowed red from the nearby fires, Ruby helped Ethel to move the chest of drawers, and once it was clear nothing had been hidden behind or under it, they tested all the floorboards and then stripped the bed and began to prod and poke at the lumpy mattress.

Ray groaned and they froze.

Ruby and her mother waited breathlessly to see if he was about to come round, the sense of panic rising with each second that passed. But when it became clear he was still out for the count, they frantically resumed their search.

'I think I've found something,' said Ruby triumphantly from beneath the bed as she began to prod at the one section of skirting board that wasn't begrimed and rotting. She was aware of her mother scrambling alongside her, but continued to work her fingers over the neatly cut, loose section until it finally fell away to reveal a long, hollowed-out space.

'I told ya,' breathed Ethel. 'What's 'e got in there?'

Ruby's scrabbling fingers found a small book, a square tin that rattled, and something that felt solid and heavy, rolled in a piece of material. Handing each item to her mother, she searched for anything she might have missed and, finding nothing, crawled from under the bed to see what she'd unearthed.

Ethel flicked through the little leather-bound book and tossed it aside. 'You don't wanna get involved in that,' she said. 'It's his record of his dodgy deals.' She picked up the square tin and shook it. 'This sounds more promising,' she muttered and set about trying to break the lock with one of her hairpins.

As the sounds of the air raid continued all around them, Ruby picked up the material roll and felt the weight and shape of it. The cloth was an old remnant of cotton which was stained with what smelled like oil and she gingerly unwrapped the folds, already suspecting what lay beneath them. As the pistol fell into her lap she shuddered and was about to toss it across the room when her mother's sharp command stopped her.

'Don't touch it,' snapped Ethel. 'Wrap it up again and stuff it back into the wall.'

Ruby's hands were trembling as she did as her mother ordered and tossed the notebook in after it. She wanted nothing to do with either of them, and shivered at the thought of all the nights she'd slept in that bed with that deadly thing hidden less than a foot beneath her head.

'Don't worry about that,' said Ethel as she emptied the metal box onto the bed. 'There's enough here to get you out of London and set yourself up somewhere safer.'

Ruby stared in amazement at the rolls of notes, the glittering coins and the countless food and clothing stamps that lay on the mattress. 'What a bastard,' she breathed as the anger returned full-force. 'He kept me short of everything from the moment we was married, and all the time...'

She leaped from the bed, resisted giving the recumbent Ray a hefty kick as she stepped over him, and then began to stuff her few bits and pieces into the pannier basket she used to carry her shopping. 'Put the money and some of them stamps in me handbag, Mum, and keep some for yerself while yer at it.'

Ethel took a few ten-bob notes and some stamps, then stuffed the rest into Ruby's handbag alongside her ration book and identity card. 'Gawd knows we've earned all of this tonight.'

Ruby finished her meagre packing, discarded the soup-stained dress for a clean one and pulled on her warmest cardigan. Her neck and arm had been slightly scalded by the soup, but the sting of it was manageable. A glance in the mirror showed there was one hell of a bruise blossoming on her jaw and blood had streaked her face from the nasty gash on her head where she'd hit it on the-gas fire. The water in the jug had been spilled during the fight, so she couldn't wash, but luckily there was a raid on and if anyone saw her they'd think she'd come a cropper and was simply one of the many walking wounded.

She reached for the gas-mask box and turned to her mother. 'I don't know where to go,' she said, suddenly afraid to leave her and the only place she'd ever known.

'Head straight into the city. Find a main line station and get on the first train outta there. It don't matter where you go, you got money now – just get as far from here as you can.'

Ruby's fragile confidence fractured. 'Can't you come with me, Mum?'

Ethel's expression was sorrowful as she shook her head. 'I'm too old and fixed in me ways to do a moonlight,' she admitted softly. 'But you got the rest of yer life ahead of you, and the chance to make something of yerself. Get out of this place, Ruby, run for all you're worth and don't look back.'

Ruby heard the passion in her words, saw the desperate pleading in her eyes and knew her mother was right. And yet there was danger for Ethel if she stayed here. 'It ain't safe, Mum. You gotta come with me.'

Ethel shook her head again. 'I can handle meself, never you mind, gel.'

Ruby could see she wouldn't be persuaded and shot a glance at Ray. 'What about him?'

'Leave that to me, love.'

'But Mum...'

Ethel enfolded her in a hard embrace. 'Trust me to do what's best, love. Now, you take care of yerself, you hear? And don't write to me, neither. Just send a short note to Fred Bowman at the Tanner's Arms when yer settled – you can trust him to keep his gob shut.'

'I'm frightened, Mum,' Ruby whispered.

'I know, darlin', but you gotta do this.' Ethel cupped her battered face gently in the palms of her work-worn hands and softly kissed Ruby's lips. 'I love yer, darlin'. Don't you never forget that.'

Her mother's parting words still rang in her head as Ruby darted in and out of the shadows. The enemy bombers had gone now and the rescue services were at full stretch, trying to dowse fires, rescue people trapped beneath shattered buildings, turn off gas mains and defuse unexploded bombs.

Ruby's tears dried as she stumbled through the smoky darkness that was diffused with the red and orange glow of the many fires. The all-clear had yet to sound and there were still dogfights going on beyond the great clouds of smoke and dust that rose above London's East End. The once familiar landscape was now confusing. Entire streets were reduced to blackened skeletons, landmarks had disappeared, and roads and alleyways were blocked by vast craters or mountains of smouldering rubble.

Ruby felt a glimmer of her old self returning as she headed towards the city of London. She had to remember she'd been born to the sound of the bells of St Mary-le-Bow and was a Cockney to the very bone: strong, determined and streetwise. She would overcome the events of this awful day and her inner compass would lead her unerringly into the heart of the city – and perhaps to a brighter, more hopeful tomorrow.

Chapter Five

London

Ruby heard the all-clear sound as she stumbled her way around mounds of rubble. As people who'd spent the raid in tube stations and public shelters came pouring into the streets to stand and stare in horrified fascination and dread at the devastation, she pulled on a headscarf and kept her chin tucked down in case she was recognised.

She'd been walking for some time when she found her way blocked by wardens and a team of soldiers working frantically in the bright lights they'd set up. An unexploded bomb had been found and she had to make a long detour which confused her for a while as she became lost in an unfamiliar maze of backstreets and alleyways.

Despite the confusion and chaos, her inner compass didn't fail her, and she suddenly realised she was actually walking along the Embankment. The air was full of dust and smoke which stung her eyes and caught in her throat, each cough jarring the bruised muscles in her midriff where Ray had punched her, and sending a shaft of pain through her swollen jaw. But Charing Cross Station wasn't far away now, so she bore the pain, dredged up the last of her strength and plodded on.

She was not alone, for others were making their

slow way through the wreckage, burdened with precious belongings, their faces grey with weariness and set with a stoic determination to make the best of things no matter what they might find at their journey's end. There were no buses, trams or trolleys running, and the Thames slid past like a grey steel ribbon between the heavy iron and barbed-wire barricades that lined both embankments and surrounded the gun emplacements. London's skyline was still tinged with red, the billowing, acrid clouds of smoke and ash whipped up by the sudden squall of wind that came down the river.

Ruby stumbled past the Home Guard sentries who stood by the towering stacks of sandbags that shielded the entrance to the huge station building, and entered the concourse. The few dim lights barely cast a shadow and every sound was magnified beneath the vast ceiling which had been boarded over for the duration. A sea of milling people raised their voices to be heard above the shouts of the porters and guards as unintelligible announcements blared from the many loudspeakers and the last few weary stragglers emerged from their shelter in the tube station.

Ruby stood for a moment, wondering what to do and where to go. Charing Cross serviced Kent and the south coast, she knew that much, because some of her neighbours had gone from here to Margate for the day on a factory outing before the war. But the noticeboard was blank, the ticket barriers and platforms were deserted, and the announcer seemed to be telling everyone that there would be no trains running for at least

86

another hour while the tracks were inspected before they could be declared safe.

It seemed to Ruby that despite the noise and the ever-moving sea of people, they were all trapped here, and the thought made her anxious. She needed to get away – needed to find a safe haven where she could rest and try to ease the terrible, pain, for her jaw was throbbing so badly it felt as if all her teeth were loose.

'You look a bit lost, love. Are you all right?'

She looked at the young woman in the guard's uniform and gave a wan smile. 'I was just wondering when the trains would get going again,' she replied.

The girl eyed the dried blood on Ruby's face and the swelling on her jaw. 'Depends on how quickly they check the lines and clear any damage,' she said. 'It could be hours yet – there again, it could be in the next twenty minutes.' Her gaze flickered once more over Ruby's injuries. 'The Red Cross people are over by platform two if you want to get that cut seen to.'

'I'll live,' she returned with a shrug. 'What I really need is a cuppa and a sit-down.'

'Join the club,' said the other girl with a grimace. 'I've been on my feet for hours and my shift doesn't finish until midnight.' She pointed to the other side of the concourse where the WVS had set up a canteen. 'You'll get your cuppa over there,' she said and then hurried off before Ruby could thank her.

The sight of the women in the familiar dark green uniform was comforting, and Ruby headed for the tea waggon. Within minutes she had a big mug of hot, sweet tea grasped in her cold hands, while a nice motherly lady cleaned up her head wound and stuck a plaster over it.

'Got caught in the raid, did you?' the woman asked as she finished gently dabbing some foul-smelling oil on Ruby's swollen jaw.

'Something like that,' said Ruby, handing her the empty mug. 'Thanks ever so much for the tea.' She shot her a cheeky grin. 'I don't suppose you could spare another?'

The woman must have felt sorry for her, for she clucked in sympathy and refilled the mug before bustling off to help someone else. Ruby didn't mind; she had a belly full of hot, sweet tea, and she'd just spotted a spare place on a nearby bench.

Ruby quickly claimed it and sat down with a sigh of gratitude. Having drunk her tea to the last drop, she placed the mug on top of the basket between her feet and tried her best to ignore the ache in her jaw. She carefully tested her teeth with her tongue and was relieved to discover that none of them seemed to have been knocked loose – and then, without warning, the full horror of what she'd been through suddenly hit her.

Overwhelmed and unable to fight the great wave of emotion that swept through her, she wrapped her arms about her waist and curled over until her head was almost touching her knees. Her thoughts raced, teeming with anxious questions. Had her mum got help for Ray? Was he still alive? Why hadn't she insisted upon Ethel coming with her? It couldn't possibly be safe for her in the tenements now. Would the rozzers be asking their endless questions – and had Ray's family already spread the word to numberless, anonymous people who were out there this very minute looking for her? She had no answers, just the almost crippling certainty that she had put her mother in terrible danger by leaving her behind. And that was the hardest thing to bear.

As she sat on the end of the bench, curled against the noise and bustle of the vast concourse, she felt hot tears roll down her face. She had never felt so lost or alone before, had never experienced such anguish or indecision, and she didn't know how to deal with any of it.

She felt the woman sitting next to her shift about and then, moments later, her soft, nudging elbow against her arm. 'Here you are, ducks,' she said softly, 'the hanky's clean, and you look as if you need it more'n me.'

The stranger's kind words brought things back into focus again, and as she used the scrap of cotton, she regained firmer control of her emotions. Tears weren't the answer, but she had to admit she felt better for them. She gave the elderly woman a watery smile as she returned the rather soggy hanky. 'I don't usually bawl me eyes out like that,' she said shamefacedly.

The curlers bobbed beneath the headscarf and the faded eyes were sympathetic as the woman stuffed the handkerchief into the pocket of her shabby coat and tucked her two brown paper parcels more firmly between her feet. 'I expect you're just tired and fed up like the rest of us,' she said. 'I been bombed out three times now, and I've 'ad enough too.'

Ruby looked into the wan, lined face and the

kindly eyes and felt like crying again. The woman was a much older version of Ethel, with her head-scarf and curlers, her work-worn hands clasped around her gas-mask box, and cheap handbag. 'It's been a long day,' Ruby muttered, 'and by the looks of that empty noticeboard, it ain't over yet.'

'Every day's flamin' long since that 'itler got above 'imself,' the woman replied, her arms folded tightly beneath her bosom. 'I'm off back to me billet in Clapham Junction if the bleedin' train ever arrives,' she said without rancour. 'What about you?'

Ruby knew she had to be careful what she said. There was a complicated network of families and acquaintances amongst the working people of London, and although she didn't know this woman, it didn't necessarily mean she wasn't related to someone in Bow or the surrounding districts. 'I'm off to Margate,' she said.

'Blimey, best of luck,' the woman said with a grimace. 'They say the bombin's just as bad there as it is here.' The faded eyes regarded her and the wicker basket with more than a hint of curiosity. 'You gotta job there then?'

Ruby nodded.

'So you got a ticket?'

Ruby nodded again, unwilling to admit she had no such thing.

'That's good, 'cos there's always a queue,' she said comfortably, 'and you'd 'ave ter move sharpish if you left it to the last minute.'

Ruby shot a glance over at the ticket office. There was already a queue although there were no trains arriving or leaving, and the large noticeboard nearby still had nothing showing. She thought about asking the woman if she had a timetable and then decided it was too risky and probably wouldn't help much. If the schedules were all messed up by the raids, there was no telling what the next train might be.

She settled back onto the hard wooden bench and tried to appear relaxed.

The woman regarded her thoughtfully for a long moment and then obviously decided that Ruby's travelling arrangements were none of her business, for she scrabbled about in her large handbag and lit a fag.

Ruby wished she had a paper she could hide behind, for conversation was dangerous, and the woman was clearly still curious about her. They sat in silence and watched the ebb and flow of the people through the concourse. There were servicemen and women, harried housewives and office clerks – all in a hurry to be somewhere and frustrated by the delay. Men in bowler hats leaned on tightly furled black umbrellas and re-peatedly looked at their watches while an im-patient gathering formed by the noticeboard, more in hope than expectation.

And then the noticeboard clicked and buzzed and an announcement blared out from the loud-speakers. The reaction was instant and there was a general rush to the far side of the station. The train for Clapham Junction, East Croydon and a dozen other places south of London had arrived at platform fourteen.

'That's me,' said the older woman as she gath-ered up her parcels, handbag and gas-mask box.

'Stay lucky, love, and mind 'ow yer go.'

Ruby watched her plod across the long concourse towards the other end of the station, her broken-down shoes slapping on the concrete. The announcements were coming thick and fast now and she listened hard as she watched the board. The next train was due to arrive in ten minutes and would be going to Margate. But having dismissed Margate after the conversation with the old woman, Ruby looked for another train.

There were several going to the London suburbs, but they wouldn't do at all. Then she noticed there was a train due in twenty minutes and it was going quite a long way by the look of it, for there were lots of stops before it reached some place called Cliffehaven. She had no idea where that was, but it sounded as if it might be by the sea and she couldn't sit here all night being picky. She gathered up her things, took the empty mug back to the WVS lady and hurried over to join the long queue at the ticket office.

She heard the train's arrival being announced and anxiously looked up at the clock as the queue slowly shuffled forward. She'd miss the bleedin' thing if this queue didn't move any quicker, she thought impatiently. How on earth could it take so long just to buy a flamin' ticket?

She shifted from one foot to the other as the woman in front of her prolonged the wait by asking questions and taking forever to get her money out of her purse. As she finally collected her change and continued to dither by the counter, Ruby gave a great sigh to let her know what a

92

ruddy nuisance she was being, and eased round her.

'Cliffehaven one way,' she said firmly to the middle-aged woman behind the glass.

'Is your journey really necessary?' The reply was accompanied by a hard stare.

'Yeah. I gotta factory job to go to,' Ruby replied blithely.

The ticket was shoved under the window and Ruby slammed the right coins down, grabbed the ticket and raced towards the platform at the far end of the station. Her train was due to leave in three minutes, and she simply couldn't afford to miss it.

She darted through dawdling groups, swerved to dodge porters' waggons and piles of kitbags and suitcases, ignored clucks of annoyance, and wolf whistles from a group of sailors, and was out of breath and sweating as she skidded to a halt at the end of yet another long queue.

She could see around the bobbing heads that the train was a long one which ran right to the very end of the platform, and the announcement had said something about one half going to one place, the other somewhere else. But which half did she need? Would someone tell her when she got to the ticket barrier?

Ruby shuffled along impatiently with everyone else, certain that the train would leave without her, for she could already see the porters loading baggage into the carriages and the guard striding up and down with his whistle in his hand.

'Rear eight coaches for Cliffehaven,' said the man at the barrier as he clipped her ticket and handed it back. 'That's the lot nearest the barrier,' he added helpfully as she hesitated.

Gripping her basket, the gas-mask box and handbag dangling from her wrist, she hurried along the platform and climbed into the second carriage. It was an open one with row upon row of uncomfortable seats on either side of a narrow aisle. Thick blackout blinds covered all the windows, and the only light came from a couple of low-watt bulbs that had been fixed into the roof.

Ruby found a space on the end of a row and sat down, the basket on her knees. 'This is the right bit for Cliffehaven, ain't it?' she asked the man in the bowler hat who was sitting next to her.

He looked down his nose at her before returning his attention to his open newspaper. 'Indeed it is,' he replied from its depths.

Ruby kept a tight hold of her basket, not wanting to risk it in the overhead rack where it might fall off and spill her clothes all over him. She had to bite her lip to stop herself from giggling at the thought of her camiknickers draped over his bowler hat and snooty nose, or her brassiere landing in his pinstriped lap.

She looked away and began to take an interest in the other people in the carriage, which was filling up fast. There were housewives and young women in uniform, soldiers, sailors and airmen, all with bags and parcels which they stowed away in every available space. The carriage was now so full that some of the servicemen had resorted to perching on their kitbags in the aisle while they chatted up the younger women and lit their cigarettes.

Ruby tried to relax, but she was still jittery, her watchful gaze flitting from one face to the next, in dread of spotting someone she knew – or someone who seemed to be taking an unnecessary interest in her. She had no idea how long it would take to get to Cliffehaven, but did wish the train would get going after all her rushing to catch it. What were they waiting for?

Just as the man next to her tutted in annoyance at her fidgeting, she finally heard the slam of many doors echoing along the platform and the piercing shrill of the guard's whistle. She tensed, waiting for that initial jolt – and then gave a deep sigh of relief as the train's whistle blew and it began to slowly pull out of the station.

Ruby felt the gentle sway as the great iron wheels got into their rhythm and the train chugged and chuffed along the rails. The waiting was over, she was on her way.

And yet her anxiety would not be shaken off and it lay heavy in her heart as the train carried her away from everything she'd ever known. She was leaving London and her mother for the first time in her life, heading for an unknown destination and uncertain future. Would she ever see her mother's face again, or the landmarks of the city where she'd been born?

Ruby closed her eyes on the tears that threatened and silently prayed that she would return – that fate would be kind and Cliffehaven would prove to be the sanctuary she needed.

The train clattered and chuffed away from London, and at each stop there was a bustle of movement as bags and parcels were gathered up, and the servicemen who were perched on their kitbags in the aisle had to shift about for people to get through. The snooty man beside her had gone, and now there was a young Canadian officer in his seat. She glanced at him and coolly returned his 'hello', but then kept her gaze fixed away from him, for the concern in his eyes as he saw her battered face was not something she wanted to discuss. He seemed to take the hint and began a conversation with one of his fellow officers.

Ruby sat and fretted over the situation she'd left behind and the uncertainty of what lay ahead. She had absolutely no idea of where she was, for although the guard had come through on each occasion to tell everyone the name of the station or halt they were approaching, they meant nothing to her now they'd left London behind. She wished the blackout blinds weren't down, for she would have liked to see out of the window – but then it was pitch-dark out there, the stations all observing blackout, and she wouldn't have been any the wiser.

As the train came to yet another stop there was a general exodus by the majority of the service people and Ruby could only guess it must be some large station from which they would be ferried to their various bases. The carriage was almost empty but for a few elderly civilians and the smartly dressed Canadian soldiers in their bright red tunics, so she eased over to sit by the window, the basket on the seat between her and the young officer.

'Excuse me, ma'am,' he said, his voice pleasantly deep. 'I think you've dropped your paper.'

The bowler-hatted man must have left his paper behind. She was about to explain that it wasn't hers, but then realised it would be something to occupy her and serve as an excuse not to talk to him. 'Thanks,' she murmured as she reached for it.

He didn't relinquish his hold of the paper. 'Are you all right, ma'am? Can I offer you a sip of brandy or a cigarette?'

She was forced to look at him and was taken aback at the brightness of his blue eyes. 'I'm fine,' she stuttered as she took a firmer grip of the newspaper.

His handsome face lit up with a beaming smile as he relinquished the paper. 'I guess you're not the sort of girl who talks to strangers on trains,' he said. 'The name's Michael Taylor, but my buddies call me Mike.'

She couldn't ignore the large hand he held out to her and she found her fingers swamped in a sturdy warmth. 'Ruby,' she replied, unable to continue her frostiness in the light of his smile.

'Well, Ruby, now we're acquainted, I guess we can pass this long, tedious journey more pleasantly. Are you sure I can't offer you a smoke, or a nip of brandy?' He drew a slim silver flask from his scarlet jacket pocket.

'I don't smoke,' she replied warily, 'and brandy don't agree with me.'

He frowned as he eyed the plaster on her forehead and the swell on her jaw. 'That looks painful. Did you get caught in the raid?'

97

'Yeah,' she replied, dipping her chin.

'I'm sorry, Ruby, I'm just naturally curious, that's all. If you don't want to talk about it, I understand.'

She looked down at the newspaper and tried to iron out the creases with her fingers. 'It ain't nothing fer you to worry about,' she muttered. She realised she was being churlish and as this was so out of character, tried to make amends. 'So what you doing on this train, Mike?'

'We've all been posted to Wayfaring Down.' He seemed to realise the name meant nothing to her and hurried to explain. 'It's an army camp that's been set up a few miles back from the coast. We've been on garrison duty both in Iceland and Scotland since I enlisted, so it'll make a nice change.' He cocked his head, his eyes bright with curiosity. 'What about you, Ruby?'

She looked round warily to see if anyone was listening to this exchange, but most of the civilians were at the far end of the carriage and the Canadian boys were deeply involved in games of cards. 'I'm going to Cliffehaven,' she said quietly.

His bright blue eyes widened. 'Hey, that's just a few miles from Wayfaring Down. Perhaps we could meet up sometime when I'm off duty?'

She felt a frisson of panic. 'I don't think that would be a good idea,' she said quickly. 'I'm a married woman.'

'Aw, gee, that's a shame,' he replied with genuine regret. Then he grinned. 'I have only good intentions, Ruby. Perhaps we could have a cup of tea or something, and you could bring a friend along as a chaperone.'

She smiled despite herself. 'Maybe,' she murmured.

The train began to slow and then ground to a jarring halt as the ticket inspector shouted out the name of the station. 'Aw, gee, that's us,' said Mike, grabbing his kitbag and large suitcase. 'How will I find you, Ruby?' he asked urgently as he stood up and towered over her while the others began to shuffle towards the door. 'Where are you staying?'

'I don't know yet,' she replied.

His smile was slow and warm. 'Then I guess we'll just have to leave it to fate to bring us together again,' he said quietly. 'It's been a pleasure meeting you, Ruby.'

She returned his smile and then he was gone, lost in the chaos of men and kitbags swarming down the aisle and out of the door. Leaning back into her seat, Ruby closed her eyes and took a deep breath. He'd seemed genuinely nice, and she'd liked the way he'd smiled and had found the soft, deep tones of his accent very attractive – but for all his charm, he was a man, and that was the last thing she needed. From now on, she vowed silently, she would keep well away from men, however handsome, for they brought nothing but trouble.

She opened her eyes as the train chugged away from the station and realised there were only three other people left in the carriage, and they had fallen asleep. She did her best to forget about the Canadian and conquer the pangs of hunger and the throbbing pains in her face and stomach by picking up the discarded newspaper and slowly reading the headlines. Her reading wasn't up to much, but at least it gave her something else to concentrate on.

The Germans were continuing their bombing raids on Exeter, Bath, Norwich and York, which the newspapers were calling the Baedeker Blitz. The targets had no strategic significance but had been listed in the German tourist guide as places of historical interest and great beauty, and given three stars.

Ruby had no idea what that meant, and only had a vague conception of where the cities were in relation to London, but the grainy pictures in the paper showed the devastation the Luftwaffe had left behind in retaliation for the RAF's attack on some place in Germany called Lübeck.

As the train slowly rattled southwards, Ruby turned the page and read an article about the Spitfires that had been delivered to a beleaguered Malta, whose people had been recently awarded the George Cross for their unceasing bravery in the face of the German onslaught. The mission to get the Spitfires to Malta by using an American aircraft carrier to carry them into the Mediterranean had not been a rousing success, for over twenty had been shot down before they had even landed, and several others were in such a bad state it would take days before they could be operational again.

Ruby sighed and set the paper aside as the train slowed and then stopped.

'Stonebridge Halt,' shouted the inspector. 'Tickets, please.'

No one got out at the halt and Ruby scrabbled

in her cardigan pocket for her ticket as the train continued to sit in the station. 'How long before we get to Cliffehaven?' she asked as he clipped the ticket with a flourish and handed it back.

'I couldn't really say,' he said dolefully. 'They're still repairing part of the line, and as there's no buses available, we've got to wait here until it's done.'

Ruby digested this disappointing information, realising she didn't really have any choice in the matter and was a hostage to the railway repair teams. 'How many stations are there before we get to Cliffehaven? Is it at the end of the line?' she asked quickly before he moved on.

'This service terminates there usually, but what with everything being so behind, we'll probably turn round and come straight back to the Smoke again.' He eyed her suspiciously. 'You ask a lot of questions,' he said sourly.

'Well I ain't been on this line before,' she fired back, 'and I don't wanna nod off and find meself halfway back home again.'

He nodded sagely, his gaze drifting from the plaster on her forehead and the swell of her jaw to her skimpy dress and cardigan. 'Better make sure you don't fall asleep then,' he said unhelpfully before he continued on his way.

Ruby was tempted to stick her tongue out at him, but realised it was childish and snatched up the paper again. Without a watch she had no idea what the time was or how long she'd already been travelling, and she just hoped his sense of duty didn't match his lack of manners and that he would continue to come through the carriages calling out the names of the stations.

As time dragged on and the train sat and waited, Ruby realised the print was blurring before her eyes, and that she hadn't in fact read the last bit about the new Archbishop of Canterbury at all. She gave up on the newspaper, hugged her handbag to her chest, and rested her head back against the antimacassar. A little sleep now while the train waited at the station would do no harm, she decided as her eyelids grew heavy.

She knew she was dreaming, but that didn't make it any less real. She was running through London, with flames all round her and enemy planes strafing the street within inches of her feet. She could hear her mother calling her from the deep shadows up ahead, and the sound of train wheels rattling along a track behind her.

She dared to look over her shoulder and her heart began to pound. Ray was driving the train and he had the pistol in his hand – but the pistol was changing shape and now it was as big as one of the battery guns that lined the docks. She tried to run faster, but it was as if her feet were stuck in mud and the harder she tried the slower she became.

'Cliffehaven. Cliffehaven. All change here.'

Ruby was startled awake, the terrifying threads of her nightmare still enmeshed in her mind as she stared up in bewilderment at the inspector.

'You gotta get off here,' he said gruffly. 'Hurry up. We're running very late as it is, and this is a quick turnaround.'

Ruby blinked away the fog of sleep, grabbed

her things and rose stiffly to her feet. Her feet were numb with cold and she had cramp in her toes, but she hurried as best she could down the long aisle between the seats and then clambered down the steps to the deserted platform.

She was engulfed by the great clouds of smoke coming from the train's funnel, but as she tentatively walked along the platform and the smoke cleared, she could see the welcome glow of a small lantern up ahead.

'It's all right, love,' said a kindly male voice as the bearer of the lantern emerged from the darkness to lead the way. 'I'll see you safe.'

Ruby saw the peaked cap and black uniform and realised it was the stationmaster. 'Thanks ever so,' she murmured as she let him lead her to the end of the platform and through the remains of what had clearly once been an elegant booking hall. 'This is Cliffehaven, isn't it?'

'It certainly is,' he replied as he raised the lantern so they could see one another.

He was probably well past retirement age, with white hair and a bristling moustache, but his face was kindly and Ruby realised she must look a right fright, for she saw how his eyes widened as he took in her bruised face and the sticking plaster on her forehead. 'We had a bombing raid in London and then the train got delayed all the way,' she said by way of explanation. 'It was ever so kind of you to wait for so long.'

'It's what I'm paid to do,' he replied. 'But now you're here, I can get home to me bed.'

Ruby glanced up at the huge clock that hung outside what was left of the station building. It was

103

three in the morning, still dark, with a bitter wind that penetrated her thin clothes and chilled her to the bone. 'Goodnight, then,' she murmured as she gripped the basket and looked uncertainly down the dark and empty street.

'Hold on a minute, love.' He touched her arm so she turned to look into his concerned face. 'You got a billet fixed, or people waiting for you?'

She shook her head. 'I thought I'd find somewhere to kip down until the billeting office opens in the morning.'

'You can't be traipsing about on your own in the middle of such a cold night,' he said purposefully. 'Come on, you can sit in the booking office and keep warm until the Town Hall opens.'

His broad smile revealed a full set of very white dentures as he pointed to what looked like a Nissen hut. 'I've even got a little spirit stove in there and a kettle, and you look as if you could do with a cuppa.'

His kindness was so unexpected, and his offer so tempting that she didn't quite know what to say. 'Are you sure? Only I don't want you getting into no trouble.'

He slotted the key into the door and stepped inside. 'There's only me, and I make up my own set of rules.' He hung the lantern from a hook in the roof, lit the spirit stove and placed the tin kettle on the top.

Ruby shivered with cold as she hovered in the doorway. She was still uncertain, but the thought of a warming cuppa was alluring.

'Come in and shut the door. The wind's coming off the sea and it cuts right through you if you're not dressed warmly enough.' He fiddled with the kerosene heater until heat radiated through the hut.

Ruby tentatively stepped into the warm fug and closed the door behind her. She was still unsure of whether he was being kind, or if he had something else on his mind. He was an old bloke and looked quite harmless, but you never knew – men were men, after all, and in Ruby's experience, most of them couldn't be trusted an inch.

He glanced at her, plucked a tartan travelling rug from a nearby pile and handed it over. 'This might be the seaside, love,' he said with a shake of his head, 'but it's not summer yet by a long chalk. Put that round your shoulders and sit down.'

Ruby snuggled into the lovely warm blanket, still tense and wary as he pushed a canvas stool towards her. She could see that the hut was kitted out as a ticket office and somewhere to leave luggage. It would have been quite big if not for the wide shelves at the back and the deep desk beneath the shuttered window, but it seemed he'd made it a cosy place to sit and while away the time when he wasn't busy.

'You're quite safe with me, you know,' he said as he rinsed out two tin mugs and poured boiling water into the teapot. 'You're young enough to be my granddaughter, and I don't like to see anyone with no place to go in the middle of the night – least of all a young girl who's clearly a stranger to my town.'

Ruby eased onto the canvas stool and kept the blanket tightly around her shoulders as he handed her a steaming mug of tea. 'Thanks,' she murmured.

'The name's Stan, by the way,' he said as he turned off the spirit stove, prised open a tin and offered her a sandwich the thickness of a doorstep.

'Ruby,' she replied, her gaze fixed on the sandwich.

'Go on, love,' he said softly. 'I can see you're hungry.'

Ruby was embarrassed by his pity, but her stomach had less inhibition and growled loudly, making any protest rather pointless. Her mouth watered as she eased the enormous sandwich out of the tin. She'd last eaten the previous morning, and that had only been a hunk of stale bread smeared with dripping. As she took the first bite of thick, greasy Spam smothered in lashings of brown sauce and margarine, she thought it had to be the most delicious thing she'd ever eaten, and although her jaw ached with every mouthful, she was so ravenously hungry, she munched until every last crumb was gone.

Licking the residue of margarine and brown sauce from her fingers, she smiled up at him. 'Ta ever so,' she said. 'That were lovely.'

'Have the other one,' he said gruffly. 'It's too late for me to eat now, and it would be a shame to let it go to waste.'

'Are you sure?' At his nod, Ruby took the sandwich and devoured it before slurping the hot tea. Her belly was full and she was warm for the first time in hours. 'You're ever so kind,' she said softly as she handed him the empty mug. 'Thank you.'

He shrugged off her thanks, his eyes suspiciously bright as he stowed his sandwich tin back in his canvas satchel, picked up his gas-mask box and unhooked the lantern. 'I'll leave the heater on so you stay warm and have a bit of light, and here's the key to the ladies' washroom which is just by the entrance to the station. Now you try and get some sleep, and I'll be back in time for the eight o'clock from Hastings.'

Ruby watched as he trudged away into the darkness, and then swiftly closed the door on the cold, salty wind and examined her accommodation for the night. He probably wasn't allowed to let people sleep in here and she hoped he wouldn't get into any trouble, for he'd been so kind.

In the flickering light of the heater, she noticed there were several more blankets piled in a corner, and if she moved some of the suitcases to one side, there would be plenty of room to lie down on the bottom shelf. Having sorted out her bed, she quickly ran through the darkness and found the lav. It was pitch-black and every sound echoed, but the water was hot in the tap and the towel on the roller was clean and dry.

Shivering with cold, but feeling much better after her wash, she raced back to the Nissen hut and shut the door. Not bothering to undress, she lay on the folded blanket, rested her head on another, pulled a third up to her chin and snuggled down. The warmth from the kerosene heater soothed her and she felt snug and cosy and safe for the first time in many months.

She watched the flickering flames dancing behind the wire mesh in the heater until her eyelids began to droop with weariness and all the terrors and tensions of the past few hours drifted away to be lost in deep, comforting sleep.

Chapter Six

Cliffehaven

Peggy had tried to stay awake until all the girls came home, but she'd been so tired that after the nine o'clock news she'd helped Cordelia upstairs to her room, given Daisy her last feed and then gone to bed. She'd been vaguely aware of footsteps crossing the hall and muffled whispers, but was still too deeply asleep to be roused.

She was woken before dawn by the sound of Jane tiptoeing down the stairs and into the kitchen to make her flask of tea to take with her to the dairy. Snuggling back beneath the blankets, she heard the girl leave by the back door and then dozed on and off until Daisy began to grizzle.

She climbed out of bed, pulled on slippers and Jim's nice thick dressing gown and plucked the fretful Daisy from her cot. Her little cheeks were bright red and she was gnawing at her knuckles. 'Poor little love,' she soothed as she carried her into the kitchen, stripped off the sodden nappy and wrapped her in a warm blanket. 'Those nasty old teeth are coming through, aren't they?'

Daisy wasn't to be consoled, even when Harvey came bounding up the steps into the kitchen to see what all the noise was about. He danced on his toes and whined as Peggy bathed Daisy in the sink and then dressed her warmly in the lovely layette the girls had knitted for her. Harvey loved babies, but he also loved porridge, so he sat at Peggy's feet, nose on her knee, watching every mouthful as she fed some to Daisy.

Peggy smiled and patted his head: 'You'll get your breakfast when she's finished her bottle,' she soothed.

Ron came stumping up the steps a few minutes later, armed with a small basket of eggs. 'There's breakfast in your bowl downstairs, Harvey,' he said gruffly. 'Go and eat it and stop pestering Peggy.'

Harvey shot down the steps to the cellar and within seconds they could hear the metal tag on his collar pinging against the tin bowl as he scoffed his food and made horrible slurping noises as he drank some water. Before Ron could make a pot of tea he was back up the steps, his whiskers and beard soaking wet, his tail windmilling with joy.

'I'll be taking him out for just a short run this morning,' said Ron as he warmed the pot and spooned a few tea leaves into it. 'I managed to get a pot of paint from a mate of mine, so I'll be spending the morning freshening up Rosie's sitting room.'

'I don't know about Rosie's sitting room – this place could do with a bit of freshening up,' Peggy replied without rancour as she eyed the faded paint, the worn woodwork and the rotting window frame. 'In fact, the whole house could do with a lick of paint and some new wallpaper – it's looking decidedly shoddy.'

'Ach, Peggy. That will take a month of Sundays, so it will – and there's no point in doing anything while Gerry is bombarding us. Better to wait until this war's over, and then me and Jim will go through the place like a dose of salts.'

Peggy gave a wry smile. It seemed that Ron's priorities lay beyond the shabby walls of Beach View – as usual. She sighed. One of these days she'd pin him and her husband down and get the jobs done around here, but she knew better than to hold her breath while she waited. They could voice their good intentions most eloquently, but were always far too easily distracted by other, more interesting projects.

'Before you go, I could do with a few more logs for the fire and some spuds from the garden,' she said as Daisy finished her bottle. 'And if Fred's in his shop, could you get us some fish for tonight?'

'Aye, I'll do that. Anything else?'

'We need more bread, margarine, sugar, flour and salt. I'll write you a list if you like. It would save me having to queue for half the morning.'

'Aye. I'll get the shopping, but only if you promise to sit down and do your knitting instead of rushing about.'

'I've got more important things to do than sit about all day knitting,' she protested.

'No knitting, no shopping.' He eyed her sternly from beneath his brows, his tone brooking no argument.

Peggy thought of all the things she had to do today and was about to protest again when she saw how determined he was to make his point. 'I'll sit and knit,' she said with a sigh of resignation.

'Aye, see that you do. And while you're about it, you can make some headway with that milk stout.'

'It tastes horrid,' she said with a grimace.

'If the doctor said you should have it, then there's a reason, Peggy,' he said, glowering at her. He took the sleepy Daisy from her arms and carried her across the room to the playpen which was jammed in a corner. Having covered her with a soft blanket, he stumped back to the stove, filled a bowl with porridge and added some top of the milk and a large helping of sugar.

'You're to eat all of that, Peggy Reilly,' he said firmly as he set it on the table, 'and then you're to have the egg and toast I'll be making for you.'

'That's far too much, Ron,' she protested as she saw the size of the helping.

'Eat,' he said firmly, 'and you're not leaving this table until it's all gone.'

Peggy blinked away her tears as she picked up the spoon. Ron was a rogue, and a ruddy nuisance at times, but God love him, he had a heart of gold beating beneath that ratty old jumper and it was lovely to be so well cared for.

The telephone rang just as she'd finished her egg and toast, and because it was not yet eight o'clock, Peggy raced to answer it, certain some disaster had befallen a member of her family.

'Hello, Peggy. Stan here – from the station.'

She frowned. 'Hello, Stan. Is there something wrong?'

111

'I was wondering if you've got room to take in another lodger,' he said hesitantly. 'Only this little waif turned up on her own in the middle of the night on the last train from London, and hasn't got anywhere to go.'

'A child on her own? Well of course I'll take her in, but the authorities will have to be informed, Stan.'

'She's not a child exactly,' said Stan. He cleared his throat. 'It's difficult to tell how old she is, but I reckon her to be about seventeen or so – married, too, 'cos she's wearing a ring. She's only a wee thing, no bigger than a bug and half starved. Been through the wars by the look of her face – and probably not got two pennies to rub together if her clothes are anything to go by.'

'Poor little thing. You send her to me, Stan. I've got a spare room she can have.'

'Bless you, Peggy. I knew I could count on you.'

Peggy replaced the receiver and listened to the sounds from upstairs. Everyone was stirring and they would all want their breakfast. She returned to the kitchen, her thoughts on her conversation with Stan.

He'd been the stationmaster at Cliffehaven for years and should have retired long ago to potter in his allotment and tend his beloved roses, but his sense of duty was such that he'd stayed on and was one of the mainstays of the town. He knew everyone and was happy to chat and pass on gossip, for he'd been widowed for some years and enjoyed the company of others. It was typical of him to want to help this latest waif and stray, and Peggy suspected he'd made her comfortable for the night somewhere warm and probably fed her too.

She explained to Ron what the telephone call had been about and he nodded. 'Salt of the earth is Stan,' he agreed. He finished his cup of tea and reached for his cap. 'Get the girls to help you today, Peggy, and put your feet up,' he ordered. 'I'll see you at teatime.'

Peggy shooed him and the dog out of her kitchen and rescued the porridge, which was in danger of sticking to the bottom of the pan. It was all very well for Ron to be issuing orders, but the girls had long shifts and were out of the house for most of the day. As long as they tidied their own rooms and helped with the cooking and cleaning when they could, she was happy and perfectly capable of doing everything else.

'I fell asleep after Jane left and now I'm running late,' said Sarah breathlessly as she rushed into the kitchen in the jodhpurs, green sweater and heavy shoes that were the uniform for the WTC.

'Drink a cup of tea and I'll make you a quick sandwich to take with you,' said Peggy as she reached for the bread knife. 'You can't possibly walk all that way over the hills to the estate without something to line your stomach.' She sliced the rather stodgy wheatmeal loaf, made a thick sandwich with the last of the cheese and a smear of her home-made tomato relish, and wrapped it in a piece of newspaper. 'How did it all go last night? Did you have fun?'

Sarah had pulled on her warm WTC coat and was standing as she finished her cup of tea. 'We had a wonderful time. The Americans are terrific

113

hosts. But Rita will tell you all about it.'

'Did she enjoy herself and join in this time?'

Sarah nodded as she rammed her beret on her head, stuffed the sandwich in her coat pocket and turned to open the back door. 'She had the best time of all,' she said and grinned. 'I'm sure she'll tell you all about it. TTFN.'

'Ta-ta for now,' murmured Peggy in reply, but Sarah was already running down the garden path towards the twitten which would lead her up into the hills to the Cliffe estate and the WTC office where she worked.

Fran and Suzy came down together, their starched aprons crackling over their striped dresses as they greeted Peggy rather sleepily and helped themselves to porridge. 'To be sure, Peggy I have a yearning for me bed still. 'Tis terrible early to have to be facing Matron,' said Fran.

'Perhaps you shouldn't have come in so late,' said Suzy mildly.

'It's not my fault we had to hang about waiting for Rita,' Fran protested. 'If she hadn't gone off with that Yank, we'd have been at home in bed long before midnight.'

Peggy was on full alert. 'What do you mean, she went off with a Yank? What was she doing alone with him? Why weren't you keeping an eye out for her?'

'Because I'm not five years old and don't need a chaperone,' said Rita as she came into the room in her usual boyish attire. She put porridge in a bowl, poured a cup of tea and sat down. 'Honestly, Fran, trust you to make a mountain out of a molehill. We were only talking motorbikes and you couldn't

114

have been waiting more than five minutes.'

'Five minutes is a long time in the back of a Lincoln with someone who seemed to have grown another three pairs of hands,' muttered Fran. 'Honest to God, Peggy – I never thought I'd get out of there alive.'

Peggy glared at both of them. 'I think it's time I put a stop to you going up there,' she said darkly. 'It's clearly not as safe as I thought.'

There was a loud protest from all three girls and in the end Peggy put up her hands for silence. 'You will stick together in future, and there's no more getting into back seats of Lincolns unless it's just you girls. Understand me?'

Fran looked mulish and Rita blushed – but they both nodded.

Peggy looked more closely at Rita and realised, with something of a shock, that although she was in her fireman's uniform she was wearing make-up. The American, and the night out, had clearly left a lasting impression. 'So,' she murmured. 'Who is this American who likes to talk about motorbikes?'

Rita's blush deepened and she dipped her chin. 'His name's Paul Schaffer and he comes from New York where his family own a motorbike dealership.' She glanced up at Peggy through her curls. 'We were only talking,' she said softly.

'I believe you, Rita,' said Peggy with a sigh. 'But please be careful. Those American boys are very attractive, and you don't have much experience of these things.'

'You sound just like my mother,' grumbled Fran.

'That's because while you're living under my

roof I *am* your mother. Just remember that, Fran.'

'Well, I had a very strange evening,' said Suzy as an awkward silence fell. 'Doris laid on a super dinner, ran poor Phyllis ragged and ignored her sweet husband, who looked as if he'd rather be on the front line facing the enemy guns than at home.' She giggled. 'All the best silver was out with the crystal, each place setting a minefield of knives and forks that I think was supposed to flummox me completely.'

'I hope she didn't upset you, Suzy,' said Peggy.

'Not at all,' she replied with another giggle. 'In fact, I think you could say it was an even match in the end, and I rather enjoyed the skirmish.'

'Good for you,' said Peggy with a sigh of relief. 'She always makes me feel clumsy when she brings out the bone china and the silver teapot.'

Suzy shrugged. 'Luckily I'm used to all that, so I let her get on with her airs and graces and enjoyed the dinner. Then, just as we were preparing to leave, I mentioned in passing that Winston Churchill was a family friend.' She grinned at Fran's gasp and Peggy's wide-eyed disbelief. 'That seemed to take the wind out of her sails, and before she could recover, Anthony brought me home.'

'Good grief,' gasped Peggy. And then she burst out laughing. 'I would have loved to have seen her face,' she spluttered, 'but is it true?'

'Of course. He and my grandfather were at prep school together,' Suzy replied as she took her dirty dishes to the sink. 'We have to get going, Fran, or we'll be late.'

Peggy waved them off and sat at the table smoking a cigarette as she tried to imagine the shock Doris must have had at that little revelation. 'Serves her right for not giving me a lift yesterday,' she muttered.

Her moment of reflection was interrupted by the ring of the telephone, and with a cluck of annoyance she went into the hall to answer it. 'Beach View Boarding House,' she said automatically as she put the receiver to her ear.

'It's me, Stan, again. Sorry, Peg, but the little bird has flown and I can't leave the station to go in search of her. Will you be going into the Town Hall today? Only I think that's where she'll head first if she's looking for a billet.'

Peggy thought of her promise to Ron to rest, and knew that for once she should actually heed his advice, for she really didn't feel the full ticket this morning. 'I wasn't really planning to, Stan,' she said. 'But I'll ring the billeting office and let them know I can take her in. What's her name, by the way?'

'Ruby,' he replied, 'but I don't know her other name. Sorry to be a bother, but she's such a lost little thing, and I don't like the thought of her wandering about all alone.'

'You're just an old softy, Stan,' she teased. 'Get back to your trains and I'll ring round and see if I can't track her down.'

Ruby had tidied away the blankets, turned off the fire and left the key to the lav on Stan's desk after she'd washed and prepared for her first day in Cliffehaven. It was just after seven when she left the Nissen hut and walked down the hill, fascinated by the streak of blue at the bottom: she had never seen the sea before. Curious as she was, she resisted the urge to take a closer look and stopped at the billeting office, where there were already several people waiting, their few bits and pieces tied together with string and brown paper.

It was almost an hour later before she could register her name with the woman at the front desk and she was now sitting in the noisy waiting room. It seemed there were a lot of people in Cliffehaven looking for somewhere to stay, and she wondered how big the town was – and if indeed she would actually get a bed somewhere.

To while away the time until she was called, she'd taken a sheaf of pamphlets from a nearby table and was reading through them in search of a job. She didn't fancy joining any of the armed services, the WTC or the Land Army, and certainly didn't reckon much to the NAAFI, where she'd be on her feet all day working as a waitress. Plumbing, plastering and electrics were beyond her, but there were plenty of factory jobs going, and as they all offered a short course of training, she had little doubt she could get herself fixed up quite quickly.

She gathered the pamphlets together in a neat stack, pushed her hair back from her face and glanced around the room. There were still four people ahead of her, and many more coming through the doors to take the last few empty seats behind her. With so many in need of accommodation, Ruby suspected she would be very low down on the list of priority. Being a single girl with no dependants, she would probably end up in some hostel – not that the idea bothered her at all, for she was used to sharing, and at least that way she might make a few friends.

She clutched her handbag to her chest, aware of all the money she had hidden in there. She knew she should feel guilty at having stolen it from Ray, but as he'd no doubt come by it dishonestly in the first place, she had no qualms on his account. Once she had a job and a billet organised, she would go shopping for some warmer clothes and find a small gift for Stan, who'd been so kind to her last night. If he hadn't rescued her, she'd have had to sleep on a doorstep or in an alleyway, and probably wouldn't have survived the bitter cold.

'Mrs Ruby Clark! Counter eight.'

Ruby grabbed her basket and hurried to the other side of the room where counters had been set up between tall hessian screens. The woman behind the desk was middle-aged and very neat in a lovely blue suit and silky blouse, her dark hair pinned into a thick bun at the back of her head.

Ruby sat down on the wooden chair as the other woman smiled distractedly and rummaged through the paperwork on her desk. 'Mrs Clark?' At Ruby's nod, she picked up a pen. 'Are you a resident of Cliffehaven?'

'No. I come down from London yesterday.'

'Do you have a job here?'

'Not yet. I wanted to get somewhere to live first, but I'll be looking for work the minute I leave here,' she added hastily.

'It's all a bit irregular,' said the woman as she

119

glanced up from the paperwork. 'Most people only come here because they already have work, and our priorities have to lie with the residents of Cliffehaven. Why did you come down from London? Do you have relatives here?'

'I don't know no one,' she confessed, 'but I had to get out of London 'cos me house was bombed and I didn't have nowhere else to go.' Ruby crossed her fingers in her lap and just hoped her lie sounded convincing enough.

The other woman regarded her steadily. 'Cliffehaven is not the first place I would have chosen if I was living in London,' she said. 'There are other towns much nearer to the city that would have suited.'

'I come 'ere for an 'oliday once when I were a kid,' lied Ruby, who was beginning to get desperate. 'Look, I can see you got a lot of local people wanting places to stay, but I really don't want to go back to the Smoke. I don't mind staying in a hostel or sharing a room with another girl. I just wanna settle in, find some work and do me bit like everyone else.'

The woman's gaze was appraising. 'How old are you, Mrs Clark?'

'Eighteen.' She saw the look of surprise in the woman's eyes and handed over her identity card. 'I might look like a kid,' she said with a wry smile, 'but believe me, eighteen's quite old where I come from.'

The woman asked endless questions as she filled in a long form and Ruby wondered if they'd check up on her, find she was on the run for murdering Ray, and hand her over to the police. She would just have to take her chances, she decided, but the tension and the worry were starting to get to her, and if she didn't watch it, she'd let something slip and then she'd be for it good and proper.

The other woman didn't seem to notice Ruby's discomfort as she looked through a large card index and finally pulled one out. 'You're in luck,' she said. 'Mr and Mrs Fraser have a single room free, and they've specifically asked for a young woman.'

She wrote down the address, clipped it to a rough map of the town and added the form Ruby would have to give to Mrs Fraser when she arrived at the house. 'It's a nice respectable house,' she said, 'and they're a well-thought-of couple who've lived in Cliffehaven for years, so I have no worries about sending you there.'

The relief was like a huge weight being lifted from her shoulders, and Ruby's smile was broad as she took the map and tucked it away in her handbag alongside her identity card and form of introduction. 'Thanks ever so,' she said as she pushed away from the desk.

'I very much doubt you'll have any problems, but if you do, come and see me,' the woman replied with a warm smile.

'Just one thing,' said Ruby, 'could you point me in the direction of the Labour Exchange?'

'Go down the hill a bit further, and you'll find it on the other side of the road opposite Plummer Roddis, the department store.' The woman smiled. 'Be prepared for a long wait, they're always busy.'

Ruby left the office and took a deep breath of

121

the clean, crisp air which was very different from the London smog she was used to. The rain of the previous night had passed on and the sky was quite blue this morning, the temperature much milder. Ruby looked down the hill to the glittering line of blue at the bottom and made a silent promise to go and look at the sea once she'd got herself a job.

The Labour Exchange was musty with the smell of too many people in a confined space, and Ruby had to queue to register her name and show her identity card. As every seat was taken, Ruby perched on a low windowsill at the back and prepared for a very long wait.

It was almost three hours later when she emerged from the Exchange, but she now had a job to go to first thing the next morning at the tool factory. The wages were much higher than she'd expected, so she decided to celebrate her successful day by buying a, bag of chips, a Spam fritter and a bottle of pop from the chippy.

She perched on a stone bench and gazed at the sea as she ate from the cone of newspaper, marvelling at how big it was. It rolled and splashed on the shingle as the big white gulls hovered and screamed overhead, and she could smell the salt in the light wind that ruffled her hair.

Cliffehaven must have been lovely before they put all the ugly barriers and gun emplacements along the front, she thought. The cliffs at the far end were a gleaming white, and it looked as if there'd been a pier and a bandstand, and lots of very posh hotels. She munched on the fried food and drank the fizzy pop straight out of the bottle as she tried to imagine the holidaymakers coming in the summer. She'd seen postcards of seaside places, so she knew there would have been striped deckchairs and bright parasols, music playing on the bandstand, and flags fluttering all along the pier.

She gave a sigh of contentment, refusing to dwell on the black worries over her mother and what had happened to Ray. It was lovely sitting here in the sun by the seaside, so clean and clear and sparkling despite the bomb sites and the obvious damage to a lot of the buildings. Cliffehaven was a new start, an opportunity to make something of herself, and so far, it had proved to be everything she could have hoped for.

Licking the salt and vinegary grease from her fingers, she finished her lunch and threw the bottle and the newspaper into a nearby rubbish bin. After a careful study of the map, she hoisted up her things and began the long trek back up the hill towards the station. There was no sign of Stan, but she would thank him properly another day.

Nelson Street lay to the west of the huge factory estate that sprawled on the northern border of the town, and was lined with small terraced houses with front steps leading straight onto the pavement. It was similar to many of the East End terraces, but in much better condition, and Ruby felt quite at home as she wandered down it looking for 'Mon Repos'.

It was almost at the end of the street. Ruby took a firmer hold of her basket as she knocked on the shiny black door. The windows were gleaming

123

and the nets were as white as snow behind the heavily taped glass – something her mother would definitely have approved of and envied.

The door opened and a large, motherly-looking woman stood on the threshold in a flowery wrap-round pinafore, her greying hair covered by a matching scarf. 'Yes, dear?'

'The billeting office sent me, Mrs Fraser,' Ruby replied, handing over the form she'd been given. 'I 'ope you still got the room.'

Mrs Fraser glanced at the form before giving Ruby and her scant luggage the once-over. She eyed the swollen jaw and the sticking plaster on her forehead. 'My goodness, you have been in the wars, haven't you?'

'There was a bombing raid in London just before I left.' Ruby smiled. 'It looks worse than it feels,' she said lightly.

'Well, you'd better come in,' said Mrs Fraser, her smile warm and welcoming. 'You look as if you need somewhere nice and comfy after such a horrid experience.'

Ruby followed the broad back and hips along the short, narrow corridor. Mrs Fraser showed her the spotless sitting room, with its carpet and pristine antimacassars on the backs of the comfortable chairs, and then the dining room, which had a large, highly polished table and four chairs taking up most of the room.

The kitchen was square, the lino polished to a gleam, the stone sink so clean it looked new. She looked through the snowy net curtains to the back garden, which was more of a walled yard. The paving was clean and swept and there were plants growing in pots by a small shed, and a large metal tank which had a tap on the side.

'That's the outside lav and the water butt,' said Mrs Fraser. 'Baths are once a week and cost thruppence, but you have to have your own soap and choose a night when my husband is out. The tub is hanging on the back of the lav door and must be used in here where any spills can go on the lino. When you've had your bath, you must pour the water away into the butt so it can be used to water the plants. If you want washing done, then that'll be another thruppence.'

'I can do me own washing,' said Ruby hastily.

'That's as maybe,' said Mrs Fraser, 'but I still have to heat the water, and it all costs money, as I'm sure you are aware.'

She led the way back out of the kitchen, and Ruby followed her up the steep staircase with its runner of carpet and shining stair-rods, wondering what other extra charges the woman would add to the list.

'This is your bedroom,' said Mrs Fraser as she opened the door to reveal a single bed, a narrow wardrobe, a chair, small chest of drawers and a corner washbasin. A square of carpet lay on the polished floorboards and the pretty curtains matched the counterpane. Everything was spotslessly clean and smelled of lavender. It was a million miles from Ruby's squalid tenement room.

'It's ever so nice, Mrs Fraser,' said Ruby with a gasp of pleasure.

'You will be responsible for keeping it clean and tidy. Bedding is to be changed on Monday mornings, food is not to be eaten up here, and of course I have a strict rule about male visitors. This is a respectable house, and I expect you to behave accordingly.'

Ruby flashed her wedding ring at her. 'You'll have no trouble from me, Mrs Fraser.'

The woman seemed to relax a little as she noted Ruby's ring and earnest expression. 'Hubby away at war, is he?'

Ruby nodded. 'I come down to work at Simpson's tool factory,' she said blithely.

'The shifts can be a bit erratic there, but I can always leave you a plate warming for when you get in, and they've got a good canteen, so you won't need a packed lunch. If you're doing nights, then you'll have to fend for yourself. My hubby and I usually have breakfast at nine.'

'Is Mr Fraser working at the factory too?'

'Goodness me, no,' she replied with a sniff of disdain. 'My Harry's on the local council and is in line to be Mayor at the end of the year.'

Ruby looked suitably impressed, and Mrs Fraser patted her arm. 'I'll leave you to settle in, dear,' she said. 'If the sirens go, the public shelter is three streets down in the recreation ground. Tea is at six sharp, and remember to give me your food stamps. I'll need those if you want me to feed you properly.'

Ruby sank onto the bed as Mrs Fraser closed the door behind her. Fate had smiled on her for a second time in as many days. It was a lovely room, the bed was soft and clean and comfy, and Mrs Fraser seemed ever so nice, even if she did scrape for every last penny. She'd fallen on her feet and no mistake.

Chapter Seven

Ruby had folded her few bits of clothing into the chest of drawers and placed her best shoes on the floor of the narrow wardrobe where the empty hangers reminded her of how little she possessed. With her basket tucked away on top of the wardrobe, she washed her hands and face in the tiny corner basin and dried herself on the fluffy hand-towel Mrs Fraser had provided, and then ran her worn comb through her hair and fastened it back with a slide.

She looked a fright and no mistake, she thought as she regarded the dark bruising on her jaw, the grubby plaster on her forehead, and the angry red scald marks on her neck. But she'd suffered worse and knew that by the end of the week she'd look better. The sun shone through the window and winked on her wedding ring, and she was tempted to take it off, for this was a new beginning and she wanted to erase all reminders of her marriage to Ray and the torment he'd caused her. And yet Mrs Fraser would no doubt notice and ask questions, and a wedding ring was a sort of protection against unwelcome advances.

Ruby shook off these thoughts and checked on the rolls of money and clothing coupons that were crammed into her bag. She had at least two hundred quid, which was a fortune in anyone's money, and over five hundred clothing coupons –

though she'd have to be careful with those; they were rationed to sixty-six a year and questions would be asked if she tried to use too many in one shop. She extracted thirty quid and a year's clothing stamps from the bundle and stuffed the rest out of sight in her gas-mask box. It was late afternoon and she needed to get to the shops before they closed.

With a thrill of anticipation for this extraordinary treat, she shot a quick glance round to make sure everything was tidy, and then went downstairs.

'Off out, are you, dear?' Mrs Fraser was peeling spuds in the sink.

'I thought I'd 'ave a look about,' Ruby replied. She put the food stamps for the week on the top of the nearby dresser. 'Could I have a front door key, please?'

Mrs Fraser snapped off her rubber gloves and reached into a drawer. 'If you lose it you'll have to pay to get another one cut,' she warned. 'That's my only spare.'

Ruby nodded and then carefully stowed the key in her handbag. 'I'll be back in time for me tea,' she murmured as she backed out of the kitchen. Closing the front door behind her, she breathed in the wonderful clean air before hurrying along the street.

It was late afternoon but Cliffehaven town was still busy, with trams and trolleybuses rattling along and delivery boys swerving their bicycles in and out of the slow-moving traffic. Heavy army lorries lumbered down the High Street and off-duty servicemen strolled along with their girls or stood in groups talking and smoking. There were the usual stacks of sandbags protecting the doorways to the more imposing buildings, and several prams were parked outside the Home and Colonial general store, their small passengers asleep, or happily gurgling at the passers-by.

It was all very posh, Ruby realised, for there were no half-naked urchins playing in the street, no rough men loitering on street corners, or women screeching from their doorways in rollers and pinnies with fags stuck in the corners of their mouths. The women here were well dressed and quietly spoken as they did their shopping or gossiped on the pavements, and the few non-servicemen that were about wore nice suits and doffed their hats at the ladies.

She found a stationer's and bought a notepad, a pencil and some envelopes, then went into the post office and bought stamps so she could write to Fred Bowman at the Tanner's Arms and let him and Ethel know she was safe. Discovering the chemist, she went in and used some of her ration to buy face powder, mascara, lipstick, a bar of cheap soap, some shampoo, a brush and comb, and a packet of plasters. She dithered over the pretty pink nail varnish and decided it wasn't worth it. Her nails were ragged and almost bitten to the quick, and nothing would make them look nice.

Ruby came at last to Plummer Roddis and looked through the criss-cross of tape on the only surviving window of the large department store, expecting to see lovely clothes to tempt her. But the display consisted of what she considered to be a rather dowdy navy costume, an equally dull hat and a pair of sturdy lace-up shoes. It was all very grown-up and she wondered if she was too young to even consider shopping here.

She felt her nerve desert her as she eyed the door. She'd always got her clothes from the Sally Army or the market, and had never been into a shop like this before. But she did need to get some new clothes, and this looked as if it was the only place that sold them. She was trying to stoke up the courage to go in when a very elegant woman emerged with several packages, adjusted the luxurious fur around her neck and set off down the street, her expensive perfume lingering behind her.

Ruby watched her for a long moment, then gathered her courage, gripped her handbag and pushed through the door. Her money and clothing coupons were as good as anyone else's – and she'd been looking forward to this all day.

The hushed interior of the department store was rather daunting, but Ruby ignored the blatantly snooty stares of the elderly saleswomen and took her time to look at every counter. She didn't want to miss anything, for it was like a treasure trove, with gorgeous bottles of scent, glittering paste jewellery, real leather handbags and shoes – and dozens of glamorous hats with feathers and ribbons of every colour. There were boxes of coloured soaps, bottles of lotions and creams, and numerous powder compacts and silver cigarette cases. It seemed that war didn't touch those who had money to spend on such luxuries.

Like a child in a sweet shop, Ruby continued

her exploration of this wondrous place, resisting the urge to touch and caress the things she saw, for she was aware that her every move was being watched as she passed through the different departments. They no doubt thought she was in here to nick something, and she couldn't blame them, for she certainly looked out of place amongst the smart ladies in their tweed suits and fur wraps.

She finally came to the clothing department and gazed in awe at the rows of ballgowns and cocktail dresses which wouldn't have looked out of place in a Hollywood film. The women of Cliffehaven must be very rich indeed, and Ruby suddenly wondered if she wasn't pushing her luck by even coming in here.

'Can I help you, modom?'

Ruby looked up into the snooty face and suspicious eyes of a woman who was probably in her late, well-preserved forties. In a black dress and high heels, she was as thin as a rake and wore far too much make-up. 'Yeah, you can,' said Ruby, bolstered by the knowledge she had money to spend. 'I'm looking for a warm coat and some other bits and pieces.'

The cool gaze went the length of the narrow nose and the bony shoulders stiffened. 'Modom might find something more suitable in Hathaway's,' she replied flatly.

Ruby had never heard of the place, but could imagine the racks of cheap clothes that wouldn't last more than a couple of washes. She smiled back, ready to do battle. 'Really? And why's that?'

There was the hint of a disdainful sniff. 'Modom

will find that Hathaway's prices are suited to the more modest budget. Plummer Roddis prides itself on selling only the finest of merchandise.'

Ruby grinned. 'That's why I come in 'ere,' she replied, and set off towards one of the racks of coats before the other woman could stop her. She reached out and touched the lovely softness of a caramel-coloured three-quarter-length coat that had a silky brown lining and two real leather buttons. Her eyes widened in shock as she glanced at the tag. The price would have fed a family of four for a month, and take twenty of her clothing coupons – but Ruby was in no mood to let that stop her. 'Have you got this in my size?'

The woman reluctantly plucked one of the coats from the rail and took an inordinate amount of time undoing the buttons and the belt before she held it out for Ruby to slip on.

Ruby felt the downy weight of the coat settle on her narrow shoulders as the lining slithered with a whisper over her tatty cardigan and thin dress. When she turned to look at herself in the cheval mirror she couldn't help but grin with pleasure. The caramel went lovely with her nut-brown hair, even if the coat did look a bit silly with a cotton dress, socks and sandals. 'I'll take it,' she said as she tied the belt round her waist and turned this way and that to get the full-effect.

The woman was clearly taken aback, and after a quick glance to make sure they weren't being overheard, she leaned towards Ruby, her voice low. 'Are you sure about this, dear? The price...'

'Yeah, it's steep all right, but I got the cash and enough coupons,' replied Ruby, glad that the woman had lost her stiffness and was actually being nice. 'Now, I need to look at the skirts and jumpers, and 'ave you got trousers? Only I'm gunna need a pair for work.'

'If they're for work, then I suggest you go to Hathaway's,' she said quietly. 'They do a good line in utility clothing, the cost is very reasonable, and of course you'd need fewer coupons.'

Ruby conceded that this was a good idea, and happily followed her across the vast department to where the skirts and sweaters were displayed. Now the other woman had shown her more human side, Ruby felt far more relaxed as she tried on several of the lovely skirts they had in her size. She chose one in a lovely lavender tweed, and then picked out a blue sweater that was as light and soft as a feather.

'If you're going on a real shopping spree, then you'll need some shoes,' said the woman, who'd unbent enough to tell Ruby her name was Lois Chapman and who seemed to be enjoying herself despite her initial frostiness.

'I think we'd better add this lot up first,' said Ruby. 'Don't wanna get too carried away.' She rested her cheap handbag on the top of a glass cabinet displaying trays of leather gloves and silk scarves while her purchases were totted up. She was feeling a bit nervous now, for this place could get through money and clothing coupons in a heartbeat, and by her reckoning she was at the limit of her clothing allowance.

'That all comes to twenty guineas and fifty-six coupons.' Lois Chapman looked at her anxiously. 'That's almost a whole year's clothing coupons.

Are you sure you've got enough?'

Ruby sighed with relief as she snapped open the clasp on her handbag and pulled out the thirty quid she'd set aside for her shopping spree. She counted out twenty-one pounds and added the right number of coupons. There was plenty left over – certainly enough for a pair of shoes.

She looked up in triumph at Lois, saw the shock in her eyes as she regarded the roll of money, and hurried to reassure her. 'I been saving up me coupons, and me 'usband's ever so generous,' she said with a grin.

'It's a good thing you came in today,' said Lois. 'The clothing ration is being cut to forty-eight a year from tomorrow.'

Ruby popped the receipt and the change in her bag and snapped it shut. 'Then we'd better go and find them shoes, eh Lois?'

The shopping expedition turned into a happy occasion as Lois got into the swing of things and brought shoes for Ruby to try on and helped her decide what would be best to go with the new outfit. Ruby finally chose a lovely pair of navy and white ones with a low heel, which were so comfortable she felt she could walk in them for hours.

The department store was about to close by the time Ruby walked confidently through the door in her new overcoat, lavender skirt, sweater and low-heeled two-tone shoes. She felt warm and knew she looked ever so smart despite the bruise and the sticking plaster – and that she smelled nice too, for once she'd said a grateful goodbye to Lois in the dress department, she'd treated herself to a little bottle of rose scent from the perfume counter, There was a lovely red woollen scarf for Stan the stationmaster tucked away in her bag with her old dress and cardigan, and now all she had to do was find Hathaway's and get a couple of pairs of cheap trousers, some underwear, socks and sturdy lace-up shoes.

She walked happily down the High Street as the sun began to sink behind the rooftops and the breeze turned chilly. After Hathaway's she would go back to her billet, have tea and climb into that lovely comfy bed for a long, well-deserved kip so she'd be fresh for her new job in the morning. Life away from London and Ray was definitely looking much brighter, and she refused to let the darker worries trouble her on such an extraordinary day.

Peggy had fulfilled her promise to Stan, and had telephoned him later that morning with the news that Ruby Clark had found a very good billet with Councillor Fraser and his wife, and work at the tool factory, and was obviously not quite as helpless as she'd looked. He'd sounded relieved, dear man, and had thanked her profusely.

She had helped Cordelia wash and dry the breakfast dishes, and then, as it was such a pleasant day, she'd unearthed the old deckchairs from the shed and they'd sat in the sunshine with their knitting, Daisy gurgling happily in her pram beside them. Lunch was leisurely, for all the girls were at work and Ron was at the pub, so Peggy had made them both a hot cup of Bovril and boiled egg sandwiches which they ate in the back garden after she'd fed Daisy.

It was now mid-afternoon and Peggy had even managed to drink most of a bottle of the hated milk stout. 'It's good to see you taking it easy for a change,' said Cordelia as she peered over her half-moon glasses and rested her knitting in her lap.

'I do feel better for it,' admitted Peggy, 'but there are a dozen and one things I should be doing instead of sitting out here like a lady of leisure.'

'The dust and the cobwebs will only be back again tomorrow even if you do sweep and polish,' she replied comfortably. 'I'd give in gracefully if I were you, Peggy, and let things slide for a bit.'

They both looked up as a squadron of RAF planes roared overhead on their way across the Channel. 'There's no sliding for some,' murmured Peggy as she thought of her son-in-law, Martin, who was no doubt up there on yet another sortie.

'We need to show Hitler we won't be bullied,' said Cordelia. 'If he will insist upon bombing our loveliest cities then we must retaliate.'

Peggy finished the horrid milk stout and was about to go upstairs and make a pot of tea to take the taste away when Ron came stumping through the back gate with Harvey held back on a lead so he didn't rush at them or the pram in his over-enthusiasm.

'Nice to see you're doing as you're told for once,' he said with a twinkle in his eye as he saw the empty stout bottle. He let Harvey loose with an admonition to sit and behave, and the dog flopped down beside the pram and eyed them all piteously.

Peggy noted the spots of paint clinging to

Harvey's fur and Ron's hair and eyebrows. There were also splatters of white down Ron's trousers and sweater and on his boots. 'I see you painted more than Rosie's wall,' she said dryly.

He grinned back at her. 'Aye, I did that,' he said, deliberately misunderstanding her. 'The walls and the ceilings of all the upstairs rooms are snowy white now, so they are, and I'll be making a start on the bar tomorrow.'

'I wish you were that enthusiastic when it comes to our poor old place,' Peggy muttered as she continued to knit another sock for Jim.

Ron ignored this small protest and went indoors, crashed about for a few minutes and came back out again with another bottle of stout and his two ferrets. 'Drink that,' he ordered. 'I'll be taking Flora and Dora up top for a wee while. Brenda and Pearl are opening up for me tonight, and these wee wains need the exercise.'

Harvey sprang to his feet, tongue lolling, ears pricked and eyes gleaming. Ferrets meant a walk on the hills and perhaps a good hunt for rabbits and squirrels.

Ron popped the ferrets into one of the deep pockets of his poacher's coat. 'I'll be back for me tea,' he added cheerfully before he marched back down the path and through the gate, Harvey racing ahead of him.

'I don't know where he gets the energy,' sighed Peggy, who was feeling unusually languid and lazy as she sat in the sunshine, the knitting forgotten in her lap.

She closed her eyes and relaxed into the chair, lulled by the warmth of the sun, the gentle clucking of the chickens in the pen and the soft coo of the doves in a nearby tree. In the peaceful silence she could almost believe they were not at war – that Jim and the rest of her family weren't miles away, and that Cissy would be home for her tea instead of driving some Air Vice Marshall about.

She woke with a start to discover that almost two hours had passed, and there was no sign of Cordelia. Daisy was beginning to grizzle and the sun had sunk over the roofs of the nearby houses, leaving the garden in deep, chill shadow. Dragging herself out of the deckchair, she lifted Daisy from her pram and carried her up to the kitchen.

Cordelia was busy at the sink, preparing vegetables to go with the lovely bit of fish Ron had brought home earlier, and which she'd made into fishcakes with lots of potato and a sprinkling of parsley and chives from the pots of herbs by the back door. 'You're getting as bad as me,' she said cheerfully as she chopped cabbage. 'We both fell asleep out there, you know.'

'I must be getting old,' said Peggy as she changed Daisy's nappy. 'I didn't mean to nod off, and now I'm all behind.'

'Well, if you've got a cold behind, you should put something warmer on. You know the old saying, Peggy. "Ne'er cast a clout 'til May is out" – and May doesn't start until tomorrow.'

Peggy smiled. Cordelia's hearing aid was on the blink again.

Despite having fallen asleep for a good part of the afternoon, they managed to get the tea ready by six. Ron appeared with Harvey and the ferrets right on cue, and dropped four rabbits on the drainer to be skinned for the pot later.

'Get those ferrets out of my kitchen,' said Peggy with a sigh, 'and take off those boots and wash your hands before you sit down at the table.'

'Ach, Peggy, you're a hard woman, so y'are. A peck of dirt never killed anyone.'

Peggy eyed the filthy hands and grubby face. 'There's more than a peck of dirt on you, Ronan Reilly,' she said, trying not to giggle. 'To be sure, you're a walking germ factory, so you are,' she teased in her best Irish accent.

He wagged a dirty finger at her and chuckled. 'I can see that a day of rest has done you the world of good, Peggy Reilly, but that doesn't mean you can be cheeky.'

He clumped off down the concrete steps, and reappeared some time later looking much cleaner, having changed into different trousers and one of his new shirts. He held his hands out to Peggy for inspection like a naughty small boy. 'Are you sure you'll not be wanting to look behind me ears as well?' he teased.

'Get away with you, Ron,' she said, playfully swiping him with a tea towel.

He sat down at the table, listened for a moment to the girls' chatter and decided he'd find something more interesting on the wireless. He fiddled with the knobs until he had a clear reception and then turned the volume up so he could hear 'Listen with Mother'.

Peggy rolled her eyes. As if there wasn't enough noise in the room with all the girls talking at once. And yet Ron's choice of programme was rather sobering, for it reminded her that Bob and Charlie were probably listening to the same thing down in Somerset. Not wishing to dwell on how far they were from home, she got on with dishing up the meal.

Everyone tucked into the fishcakes, fried potato and cabbage as the girls discussed their plans for the evening. Sarah, Jane and Suzy had theatre tickets for *The Merchant of Venice*, and Fran was meeting three of the other nurses and going to play bingo at the church hall to help raise money for the local Spitfire fund.

'What about you, Rita?' asked Peggy as they sat round the table after the meal, drinking tea.

'I'm going out too,' she said, carefully avoiding everyone's eyes.

There was a chorus of teasing from the others and Rita went bright red. 'I'm just going for a drink with Paul at the Anchor,' she said defensively.

'That's how it starts,' said Fran and giggled. 'To be sure, Rita, you'll soon be billing and cooing like Suzy.'

'I will not,' she snapped as she pushed away from the table. 'He isn't the first American I've been out with, you know, and I'm fully aware of all the pitfalls, thank you very much.' She turned on her heel and stomped out of the room as a stunned silence fell in the kitchen behind her.

'Well, well,' said Fran. 'Our little Rita isn't so innocent after all. Now there's a surprise.'

'That's quite enough of that, Fran,' said Peggy firmly. 'Rita's a good girl, and I won't have you casting aspersions.'

'I wasn't,' Fran protested as she shook back her fiery curls. 'Surely to goodness, I was only teasing.'

'I'm sure you were, but Rita's only just beginning to find her way, and remarks like that aren't helpful.' Peggy stared her down until she looked away.

'To be sure, I'm sorry, Peggy,' Fran muttered.

Satisfied that everyone knew how strongly she would defend every one of her girls, Peggy's flash of anger died. 'If you're all going out tonight, shouldn't you be getting ready?' she suggested. 'I think Ron wants to listen to the early news before he goes to the Anchor.'

They all trooped out and Ron gave Peggy a wink. 'I'm glad I'm not the only one round here who gets it in the neck,' he teased. 'But not to worry about Rita. I'll keep an eye on her tonight.'

Ruby was quite shocked to realise that she had spent almost all of her thirty pounds and used up nearly three years' worth of clothing coupons on her shopping spree. She carefully hung her beautiful new coat in the wardrobe and put away the rest of her more utilitarian purchases, then stroked the buttery soft leather of the shoes and nestled her cheek against the downy sweater. She'd never possessed anything as beautiful – had never imagined even touching such luxury – and just seeing it all and knowing it belonged to her, made her feel warm inside.

She washed her hands, combed her hair, and decided not to use her new make-up as she would be going to bed after tea and it would be wasteful after all the money she'd spent today.

With a happy smile, she went downstairs and found Mrs Fraser in the kitchen.

'There you are,' said Mrs Fraser who'd removed the headscarf and apron to reveal tightly permed greying hair and a grey button-through dress which strained at every seam over her generous curves. 'My goodness,' she said as she eyed the sweater and skirt and new shoes, 'you do look smart.'

Ruby grinned with pleasure. 'I went on a shopping spree.'

'I didn't realise Hathaway's did that sort of thing,' said Mrs Fraser. 'I must pop in there tomorrow.'

Ruby could see she was a bit put out that her lodger was able to afford such lovely clothes, so she didn't say anything about the department store. She glanced round the kitchen for some sign that the meal was ready, but there just seemed to be some empty saucepans in the sink. 'Do you want some 'elp with the tea?' she asked.

'It's already on the table,' Mrs Fraser replied. 'I did warn you to be down at six.'

'I sort of thought you might call up to let me know when it were ready,' said Ruby.

Mrs Fraser didn't bother to reply to this but picked up the water jug and led the way into the dining room. Sitting at the head of the table was a balding, tubby little man in a pinstriped three-piece suit. There was a gold watch-chain across his rotund belly and his many chins rippled over the tight white collar of his shirt. 'Harold, this is the new evacuee I was telling you about.'

Harold looked up from his half-eaten meal, his

142

eyes beady behind round, horn-rimmed spectacles as they trawled over her from head to foot. 'Good evening, Ruby. I'm afraid your food won't be very warm. We eat promptly in this house.'

Ruby didn't like the way his eyes crawled over her, but she shot him a nervous smile and sat down. 'Nice to meet yer, I'm sure,' she muttered. 'Sorry I were late, but I ain't got a watch.'

Mrs Fraser filled Ruby's glass with water before she picked up her knife and fork and resumed her meal. 'Perhaps it would have been wiser to spend your money on a timepiece instead of fancy clothes,' she said in a soft tone that belied the steeliness in her expression.

Ruby didn't flinch beneath that hard look, even though she was disconcerted by it. 'I'll get one tomorrow when I finish me shift,' she replied.

She looked down at the plate of food and her spirits sank even further. A tiny lamb chop was congealing in watery gravy that shone with grease, and beside it sat a boiled potato and a few strands of sliced cabbage. She glanced across at the other plates and saw the remains of carrots, swede and buttery mash, and the bones of at least half a dozen chops. She got the message immediately. Being a lodger meant half rations in this house. Without commenting, she picked up her knife and fork and began to eat.

There was barely any meat on the chop, the boiled potato was as watery as the disgusting gravy and the only edible thing on the plate was the cabbage. The whole meal was lukewarm, there were no more vegetables going by the look of the empty pots in the kitchen, and no bread on the

143

table to bulk the meal out and take the edge off her hunger.

'That was a lovely dinner as always, my dear,' said Councillor Fraser, as he dabbed his mouth on a linen napkin and took a sip of water from his crystal glass.

Ruby swallowed down the last of her unappetising food, then noticed how Mrs Fraser put her knife and fork together on the plate and did the same. She looked up and saw their expectant faces. 'That were very nice,' she lied politely. 'Thank you.'

Mrs Fraser dipped her chin in acknowledgement, gathered up the plates and took them into the kitchen.

Councillor Fraser shifted in his chair. 'I understand you come from London,' he said. 'That's quite a long journey for such a young woman on her own.'

Ruby shrugged. 'It weren't so bad. Once I were on the train I didn't have to do nothing 'til it got here.' She moved her legs to one side, for the Councillor's knee had accidentally nudged her thigh.

'I suppose your husband is away fighting,' he continued, his gaze steady through the spectacles. 'It must get very lonely without a man about the place.'

'I got me mum, and I had work at the pub, so I didn't get much time to meself.'

'So you were a barmaid, eh?'

The knee was back again, and Ruby now knew for certain it had been no accident. She regarded him steadily. 'Yeah, and I learned pretty quick how to deal with blokes what try to take liberties.'

He gave her a sly smile as he moved his knee away. 'I'm sure you did,' he murmured as his wife came back into the room.

'It sounds as if you two are getting along nicely,' she said as she placed the tray on the table and began to pour weak tea into the cups.

'We're getting to know each other very well, thank you,' said Ruby, her tone flat as she kept her gaze fixed meaningfully on the Councillor's face.

'That's nice, dear. Now drink that up, and then we can sit in comfort and listen to the wireless before bedtime.'

Ruby drank the tea, her earlier high spirits deadened by the realisation that Councillor and Mrs Fraser were not at all what they had first appeared to be. She was as mean as her meals, and he was an old lech who would have to be avoided at all costs. The thought of spending any more time with either of them didn't appeal at all. 'I think I'll go for a bit of a walk and then turn in,' she said. 'My shift starts at eight tomorrow morning.'

'Harold always brings me up a cup of tea around seven,' said Mrs Fraser comfortably. 'He'll knock on your door to make sure you're awake.'

Ruby felt a prickle of unease 'That's really kind,' she said hastily, 'but I'm sure I'll be up in time.' She put her cup and saucer on the tray and pushed back from the table. 'Thanks fer tea. I'll see ya later.'

It was still twilight as she stepped through the front door, but the wind was cold and she was glad of her lovely new coat. Walking down the street, she heard her stomach rumbling, and won-

145

dered if the chippy was still open. If Mrs Fraser was planning meals like that every night, then she'd have to have a word with her.

The chippy was still open, and she wandered into the park down by the seafront to eat her second portion of chips that day. Havelock Gardens were nice, with rose bushes and little paths and a pond with a weeping willow drooping over it. Through the trees she could see the big houses that lined the seafront, and tried to imagine what it must be like to live in such a lovely spot.

Despite the warm coat and the hot food in her belly, she was soon feeling chilled, so she slowly walked back to Mon Repos, taking note of the recreation ground and how to get to the public shelter along the way.

As she stuck her head round the sitting-room door to say goodnight, she saw that Councillor and Mrs Fraser were settled in the armchairs by the wireless, a large plate of cheese and biscuits set out with jars of pickles and a slab of butter on a low table between them. Neither of them offered any to Ruby, and after a brief acknowledgement of her presence, they continued to ignore her as they tucked into their supper and listened to the wireless.

Ruby felt a surge of anger as she went through the kitchen to use the outside lav. Their house might be as shiny and clean as a new pin, but they had marred a lovely day.

It was dark now, and she had to fumble her way back to the house. Harold would need watching, that was for sure, and from now on she'd make sure she was in the kitchen when his wife dished

146

up the food. She was blowed if she'd buy chips every night, and the Frasers were being well paid by the government for her keep, so she had a right to a decent meal at least once a day.

Back in her room, she pulled the blackout curtains and switched on the light. But as she closed the door, she saw there was no key in the lock. The thought of Harold creeping about early in the morning made her go cold, so she grabbed the small wooden chair and jammed it tightly beneath the doorknob.

Satisfied she could sleep in peace, she washed in the handbasin, sorted out her clothes for work in the morning and pulled on clean knickers and vest before climbing into bed. It was as soft and comfortable as it had promised, but something was niggling at Ruby and wouldn't let her sleep.

She lay there staring into the darkness, trying to think what it was that she hadn't done. And then it struck her. The Frasers might have a good reputation in this town, but they weren't to be trusted, and she wouldn't put it past Mrs Fraser to come in here and start poking about the minute her back was turned. Ruby still had a lot of money and coupons in her possession, and with such riches came responsibility. She wouldn't be able to take her bag with her to work tomorrow, for even if there were lockers, they could easily be opened by a determined thief – and she certainly couldn't leave it here where Mrs Fraser might help herself.

Throwing back the blanket, she felt her way across the room and switched on the light. There had to be somewhere in here that she could hide

147

everything until she got the chance to open a post office account. She slowly took stock of the room. The floorboards were tightly jammed together and firmly nailed down. The wardrobe and chest of drawers were too obvious, and there was no hole behind the basin's waste pipe. Her gaze drifted to the window and the pretty curtains that hung over the blackouts, and an idea slowly began to form.

She dug about in her gas-mask box and pulled out the three remaining rolls of money and the sheets of food stamps and clothing coupons. She kept back enough stamps to buy an alarm clock, two ten-bob notes and the small change. Then she flattened the rest out and carefully rolled them up tightly, fixing them with two of the rubber bands. Easing the third band through the others, she secured it with a knot, leaving a generous loop at one end. She wasn't at all sure if this would work, but she had to give it a go.

She could still hear the wireless downstairs, so she eased the chair away from under the doorknob and carried it over to the window to inspect the floral curtains. They had brass hooks inserted into a special tape that had been sewn along the top edge, and these hooks slotted into the small rings that hung from the metal runner above the window. With a sigh of disappointment she realised that as the hooks were upside down and the rings were too small to take the rubber band and the hook, she would have to think again.

She took the right-hand-side curtain down and sat on the bed to work out the conundrum. There had to be some way, if only she could see it. Then, as she examined the tape, she realised there were special slits for the hooks and not all of them had been used. Using one of the hooks, she carefully wriggled the looped end of the rubber band into the slot next to the last hook and tied it firmly in place. Then she climbed back on the chair and hung the curtain over the blackouts.

She tested the curtain by pulling it back and forth, and then stepped away from the window and examined it for any sagging or bulges. But being right on the end, and closest to the wall, it didn't show at all, even when the curtains were fully closed, and she breathed a deep sigh of relief. Her money would be safe there until she could get it to the post office.

As she replaced the chair beneath the doorknob she heard voices and the tread of feet on the stairs. Swiftly turning out the light, she made sure the chair was solidly jammed and then tiptoed back to the window and opened the blackouts. She could sleep now, secure in the knowledge that she and her money were safe and that the early light would wake her long before Harold came tapping at her door.

Chapter Eight

Peggy was having a very strange dream. She was running down an endless corridor with doors on both sides, urgently seeking something, or someone. But every door she opened led to more doors and she could feel the panic rising as the urgency increased and the pain deepened. She needed help, but the shadowy figures that shifted around her watched and waited in silence and didn't respond to her frantic calls.

She could hear the sirens begin to wail. Saw Jim and Ron and Cordelia in the wavering beams of the searchlights – but they were too far away and couldn't hear her, couldn't show her the way out of this bewildering maze, or lead her to the place or the person she so desperately sought. Turning this way and that, she moaned in frustration and fear as the deep pain took a tighter hold and she felt the trickle of something warm seep from her.

She woke with a gasp of anguish to discover that her dream was firmly rooted in reality. The sirens were screaming, Daisy was crying and she'd wet the bed.

Throwing back the covers, she sat up and was immediately bent double by a hot spear of agony. It took her breath away, freezing her ability to gasp or even cry out as it burned through her. She tried to contain it, to control her panic and her dread, but it was persistent, and the damp patch beneath her seemed to be spreading. Somewhere deep within that haze of pain she understood what was happening, and although she knew it would take a miracle now to save the baby inside her, she silently pleaded with God not to take it.

The sirens were screaming, drowning out the wails of her small daughter as Peggy curled into the pain and fought to overcome it. She couldn't stay here – had to see to Daisy and go and wake

Cordelia while they still had time to get to the Anderson shelter. But she couldn't move – couldn't escape the all-encompassing agony that had her within its grip.

At long last the pain ebbed to a dull, deep ache and Peggy fumbled for the bedside light. One glance told her that all her fears were confirmed. The sheet and the nightdress were soaked in blood. She took a trembling breath and pulled off the sodden nightdress and then hunted frantically in the nearby drawer for the packet of sanitary pads and belt. She was shaking so badly her fingers were clumsy, but once she had the thick sanitary pad in place, she stuffed the nightdress between her legs for extra padding, and dragged on the large knickers she'd worn while expecting Daisy. She had to hurry now, for soon the sirens would fall silent and the enemy bombers would come, and she had to make sure Daisy and Cordelia were safe before she sought help.

Ignoring the deep, dull ache in her abdomen, she grabbed a pair of Jim's pyjamas and struggled into them before yanking on his dressing gown and stuffing her feet into her slippers. The pain had ebbed enough for her to breathe through it, but she knew she was still bleeding. The thick wadding between her legs made it difficult to walk and she had to shuffle over to Daisy's cot, but as she reached down and lifted her, she felt another stab of pain so strong, she almost dropped her back onto the small mattress.

Daisy waved her arms and legs, her little fists curled in anger as her piercing cries went through Peggy's head. 'I can't lift you, darling,' she panted through her tears. 'I'm sorry, but I'm going to have to leave you here for a bit.'

Daisy's cries tore at Peggy's heart as she turned her back on the baby and shuffled to the door. She managed to stumble into the dark hall and then collapsed on the chair by the telephone, her breath coming in ragged gasps as she reached for the receiver.

There was only the dead silence of a disconnected line at the other end.

Peggy left the receiver dangling from its cord, dredged up every ounce of strength and determination she possessed and stumbled to the stairs. They seemed endless but, spurred on by Daisy's cries and the wailing of the sirens, she took the first step and then the next, slowly making the long climb towards the first landing and Cordelia's room.

She was almost at the top with only four more steps to go, but her legs were trembling with the effort, and she swayed so alarmingly that she had to cling to the bannisters as she blinked away the salty sweat that stung her eyes. She sank to her knees and gripped the faded carpet as she crawled towards the landing. She lay there for a moment, breathing in the dust of the old carpet, feeling its rough texture against her cheek as Daisy's wavering cries threaded through the sirens' warning of the enemy's approach. She had to move, had to find the strength somehow to get to Cordelia.

Peggy usually woke her softly so as not to frighten her, but tonight was different, for there simply wasn't time for niceties. She flung the door open, managed to stagger to the bed, switch on the bedside light and roughly shake the old lady out of her sleep.

'What? What's going on?' Cordelia sat bolt upright, fear etched into her face until she saw Peggy kneeling beside the bed, and then she was all concern. 'What is it, Peggy? Are you hurt? You look awful.'

Peggy didn't have the strength to waste words, so she urgently pointed to the hearing aid on the bedside table as she tried to breathe through the pain.

Cordelia quickly fumbled it into her ear and adjusted the volume until she could hear the sirens and the wailing baby – but her whole focus was on Peggy as she saw the blood soaking through the pyjama trousers. 'Oh, my dear, whatever is the matter?' she gasped.

'I need you to go to the Anderson shelter with Daisy,' Peggy shouted above the noise of the sirens and the squadrons of Spitfires which were roaring overhead.

'But I can't leave you here, Peggy. You're bleeding and need help.'

'The phone's not working,' she yelled back. 'See to Daisy. I'll manage.'

Cordelia was close to tears, but she was made of stern stuff and knew this was not the time to argue or fall apart. She pulled on her dressing gown, tugged on her slippers and grabbed her walking stick and small torch. 'I'll be back as soon as I can,' she shouted.

'No!' Peggy yelled back urgently. 'Stay with Daisy in the shelter. I'll join you there.'

Cordelia gave a curt nod, her expression unreadable as she squeezed Peggy's shoulder and then hobbled out of the room.

Peggy was on her knees by the bed and she closed her eyes as Cordelia made her slow way down the stairs. It was terrifying to think of her going down the cellar steps with Daisy in her arms, for she was unsteady on her feet at the best of times and Daisy was likely to wriggle and squirm now she was so upset. But she couldn't let herself think like that – couldn't allow anything to weaken her resolve. She had to get downstairs again before the sirens stopped.

As she slowly dragged herself to her feet and leaned on the bed to gather her strength, she heard more squadrons of RAF fighter planes leaving Cliffe airfield to engage the approaching enemy. By the sound of it, they were prepared for a large raid.

Peggy stumbled and swayed her way across the room and out onto the landing. The floor seemed to be rocking beneath her and the long flight of stairs went in and out of focus. But the thought of Cordelia and those cellar steps kept her going, and she realised it would be quicker if she sat on the top step and slid her way down to the hall.

The sirens stopped, the echoes of their wails dying away to be replaced by the distant, ominous drone of heavy-bellied enemy bombers – and Daisy's persistent, angry cries. But Daisy should have been in the Anderson shelter by now, so why could she still hear her?

Peggy was drawn to the sound, the urgency giving her renewed strength as she tottered across the hall and into the kitchen. She stumbled and grabbed the back of a chair to steady herself, for if she fell now she wouldn't be able to get back up again, and her baby needed her – Cordelia needed her.

She staggered round the table, reached the door that led to the basement and froze.

Cordelia was sitting on the cellar's concrete floor, the sobbing Daisy lying across her sprawled legs.

'Oh, dear God,' she breathed. In her horror and fear Peggy found a surge of energy and almost fell down the concrete steps as she rushed to get to them.

'Daisy's all right,' shouted Cordelia over the drone of the enemy bombers. 'I didn't drop her – she's not hurt.'

Peggy sank to the floor beside her and grabbed Daisy, holding her to her heart as she kissed the tear-stained little face and reassured herself that her baby hadn't been injured. But Cordelia was ashen, and Peggy could feel her trembling as she put her arm gently around the narrow shoulders and drew her close. 'What happened, Cordelia? Are you hurt?'

'I think I might have done something to my wrist,' she replied. 'I can't seem to move it.' She eyed Peggy tearfully. 'I'm so sorry, Peggy, but I slipped on the last step, and to protect Daisy I sort of rolled over so she didn't hit the floor and banged my arm on the blasted mangle. But I'm more concerned about you. Are you still bleeding?'

Peggy shifted so her back was also against the wall, Daisy's weight resting in her lap, her arm still around Cordelia's shoulders. 'I'm having a miscarriage,' she replied, the tears streaming down her face as the shock and fear began to take their toll.

'Oh, my dear,' murmured Cordelia. 'Can I do anything to help?'

'I think it's too late to do anything now.' Peggy battled the debilitating weariness that had suddenly overtaken her.

'It might not be,' said Cordelia as she nursed her painful wrist. 'I seem to remember from a first-aid class I once had that in circumstances like this you should lie down and put your feet higher than your head.'

Peggy placed Daisy back on Cordelia's lap and slowly eased down the wall until she was lying on the cellar floor with her feet halfway up the concrete steps. Then she reached for the still-squalling Daisy and held her to her chest. 'I don't suppose there's a bottle to give her?' she asked hopefully.

Cordelia reached into her dressing-gown pocket and smiled in triumph. 'I remembered to pick it up as I went through the kitchen, but it won't be warm.'

'You're a star, Cordelia,' sighed Peggy as she took the bottle and coaxed Daisy to drink.

'I'm nothing but a liability,' replied Cordelia crossly. 'I can't even get down those blessed steps without going head over heels, and now look at us.'

Peggy held tightly to the now silent Daisy and reached out her free hand to Cordelia. 'We'll be fine,' she said as the enemy planes thundered overhead and the house shook with their vibration. 'And you have never been, or ever will be, a liability, Cordelia – for without you, I would never have managed to get Daisy even this far.'

They held hands as Daisy finished the bottle and went to sleep on Peggy's chest. The bombers were flying very low now, and through the cracks in the ill-fitting back door they could see the wavering searchlights and the bright bursts of the anti-aircraft guns that had opened up all along the hills. They both knew there would be no help until the raid was over, but they had each other, and that was a great comfort.

As time went on and the cold of the concrete floor began to seep into their bones, Cordelia managed to get to her feet and grab the blankets off Ron's bed. They smelled a bit of Harvey and ferret, but they were warm, and both women huddled into them, the sleeping baby still on Peggy's chest.

They could now distinguish the distant booms and thuds of bombs exploding at the airfield and along the coast where there was a naval dockyard. They heard the Spitfires and Hurricanes engaged in dogfights with the German fighter planes that always escorted the bombers, and the terrible screams of planes in their death throes as they spiralled out of control and exploded on impact.

And then they heard the erratic throb of the bombers coming back, and the thunder of the Bofors guns along the hills interspersed with the rat-a-tat-tat of the smaller guns which shot tracer bullets like red darts into the black swarm of the marauders. The enemy bombers had completed their onslaught and were on their way back across the Channel with their escort of fighter planes which were still being harried by the RAF boys.

Peggy was feeling very sleepy despite the hard concrete beneath her and the ache in her arm as she held onto Daisy with one hand and gripped Cordelia's fingers with the other. The house was vibrating with the rumble of the enemy planes overhead, and echoed with every boom of the big guns and rattle of the ack-ack. But the need to sleep was overwhelming, and she eased Daisy from her chest onto the floor and the loose folds of the two blankets and then curled round her. The waiting was almost over, and soon, soon they would hear the all-clear and be able to get help.

The explosion came with no warning. It shook the ground beneath them, shuddered in the walls, blasted the glass in the windows and blew the back door in. There was no time to react, no chance to escape as the wreckage of bricks, mortar, wood and glass flew in and buried them.

Ron had been busy all evening, but he'd kept a close eye on Rita and the young American. Ron had known her father, Jack Smith, for years, and he knew Jack would want him to look out for his motherless young daughter while he was away at war. It was not a responsibility he begrudged, for he'd always liked little Rita, and had come to think of her as one of his own now she was living with the family.

When the sirens had gone off he and the two middle-aged barmaids had swiftly got everyone down into the cellar. Ron had cleared it after he'd taken over the pub from Rosie's crook of a brother, and had kitted it out with benches and tables and a makeshift bar so the customers didn't have to run all the way to the public shelter on the other side of town, and could continue their drinking while the raids were going on overhead.

Harvey hated the sound of the sirens and set up his usual howling until they'd quietened. Now he was lying peacefully at Ron's feet while Brenda and Pearl dispensed bottles of beer, cigarettes, matches and even cups of tea. The little primus stove had been a good idea, he thought, as he watched Pearl make yet another large pot of tea, for not everyone wanted to drink alcohol during a raid and some preferred the comfort of a good cuppa.

Rita and her American had joined in with the others as they sang along to the records playing on the wind-up gramophone that Brenda had suggested they bring down here to help pass the time and lighten the mood. It was certainly a good idea, for singers got thirsty, and the takings had shot up over the past few weeks.

The enormous boom of a nearby explosion rocked the pub on its ancient foundations and brought a fine mist of dust, cobwebs and plaster raining down. The music was forgotten, the song unfinished as everyone froze and listened.

'That was very close, Uncle Ron,' said Rita as she edged to his side. 'I wonder what took the hit?'

'Difficult to tell down here,' he replied with a consoling hand on her shoulder.

She nodded. 'Wherever it was, I'm going to have to go on duty the minute the all-clear sounds. That was a big explosion and there are bound to be fires.'

Ron fiddled with his pipe so she couldn't see his anxiety. It had sounded as if the explosion was no further than a few streets away, and he could only pray that Peggy, Cordelia and the baby were safe in the Anderson shelter – and that the other girls were sheltering beneath the theatre or in the dugout behind the church hall. But he could do nothing until the all-clear sounded.

As the minutes ticked away there was a general restlessness amongst the people in the cellar, and when the all-clear finally sounded there was a rush towards the steps. Ron herded them all out of the side door of the pub – it was way past closing time and he didn't want them straying back into the bar.

He caught hold of Rita as she passed with the American close behind her. 'You come straight home after you've finished at the fire station,' he ordered gruffly. 'I don't want to be coming looking for you in the wee small hours.'

Rita grinned at him. 'I'll be back as soon as I can,' she promised. 'Paul has to go back to the estate anyway.'

Ron nodded and was about to go back down to the cellar to thank Brenda and Pearl for all their hard work when he saw Harvey freeze by the side door. His legs were stiff, ears pricked, head cocked to one side. 'What can you hear?'

Harvey gave a sharp bark, then shot out of the door and along the narrow alleyway into Camden Road.

Ron raced after him, his heart thudding like a drum as the dog reached the end of Camden

Road, tore up the hill, and down the twitten that ran behind Beach View. He could now see the fires devouring the row of terraced houses in the street behind the boarding house, the flames' orange glow bringing a false dawn as the first of the fire engines roared past him, the bell clanging with urgency.

Ron kept running up the hill and into the twitten. The swirling smoke and ash stung his eyes and filled his dry throat as the dread of what he might find squeezed his heart.

'Help! Please help! We're in here.'

Harvey followed Cordelia's cry, leaped over the remains of the flint wall and bounded across the debris of a shattered shed and outside lav to the place where there had once been a door and a scullery wall. He barked again and began to scrabble furiously at the wreckage which blocked the doorway.

Ron's fear was copper in his mouth as he grabbed Harvey's collar and stopped him from digging. This part of the back wall formed an essential load-bearing section of the house. With the door gone and the beam over the entranceway collapsed, there was a very real danger that if they moved too much of the debris the whole back of the house would come tumbling down. 'Where are you?' he shouted.

'Here. Over here,' called Cordelia from the depths of the rubble.

Ron tightened his hold on Harvey, who was whining and dancing on his toes in his desperation to get to those he loved. 'Are Peggy and Daisy with you?'

'Yes. But Peggy's in a bad way and needs a doctor. You have to hurry, Ron. She's unconscious and feels very cold.'

'Dear Lord, save us,' he exclaimed. He kept a tight hold on the anxious Harvey, pulled out his ARP whistle and gave six sharp blasts on it to alert anyone nearby that he needed urgent help. 'Stay absolutely still, Cordelia,' he ordered as he knelt down to peer into the darkness beyond the rubble. One false move on his part could kill them all.

'I can't move anyway,' she said, her voice much fainter now. 'I seem to have something heavy pinning me to the wall.'

Ron knelt and took Harvey's large head in his hands and looked directly into those trusting amber eyes. 'Find help, Harvey. Go fetch help.'

The dog whined and skittered, clearly torn between his need to obey Ron, and the urgent yearning to find his loved ones beneath the rubble.

Ron held him firm, his voice commanding. 'Fetch, Harvey. Go for help.'

Harvey yanked his head from Ron's hands and sped back across the ruined garden, over the wall and was gone.

'I'm going to need help to get you out,' Ron called into the cellar. 'Can you hear me, Cordelia?' He had to strain to hear her reply, for her voice was very weak. 'How are Peggy and Daisy?'

'Daisy's too quiet and I'm worried about Peggy. I can't seem to wake her. Hurry, Ron. Please hurry.'

'I'm doing the best I can,' he called back as he began to tentatively pluck some of the rubble out of the way. The stone sink lay on top, broken into two, the mangle still firmly bolted to one half. 'Keep talking to me, Cordelia. Don't fall asleep.'

Cordelia muttered something, but his attention had been drawn to the sound of running water and the dribble of it seeping beneath the rubble. The pipes had been broken when the sink had been ripped away, so he dug about in the remains of the shed, found the large metal tool he needed, slotted it into the mains stopcock and twisted it off.

Cordelia had fallen silent again. 'I can't hear you, Cordelia,' he shouted. 'Turn your blasted hearing aid on, woman.'

'There's no call for rudeness, Ronan Reilly,' she retorted faintly.

'That's better,' he said, his anxious gaze searching for some sign that help was coming. 'Shout at me all you like. I need you to stay awake, Cordelia.'

The welcome sight of Harvey bounding over the wall, closely followed by a fire crew and several soldiers, made him grin. He patted the dog and ruffled his ears as he explained the situation to John Hicks, the fire chief.

John listened carefully and started giving orders to his men and women. 'You were wise to follow your instincts and not start to clear the debris,' he said as his crew helped the army boys shore up the hole with the steel scaffolding poles they always carried in their trucks now. 'Without that supported, the whole house could have come down on top of all of you.'

Ron waited with an equally anxious and impatient Harvey as the wall was made secure. 'Cordelia, are you still awake?' he shouted.

There was no reply and he looked fearfully at John. 'We've got to hurry,' he said. 'Both women need medical help and God alone knows what's happened to the baby, because I haven't heard her crying since I got here.'

John nodded and tersely ordered the men to get on with the job so they could start clearing the wreckage. Within minutes the wall was made secure and everyone was frantically grabbing at the rubble, tossing it aside in the desperate need to get to the women and baby trapped beneath it. Harvey scrabbled and dug, the soft whine in his throat revealing his own sense of urgency.

Ron was sweating as he heaved bits of concrete and brick out of the way. 'Cordelia,' he called. 'We're coming. Hang on, old girl. We're nearly there.'

'Less of the old, you rude heathen rogue,' she said weakly.

'Aye, that I am. And you're as deaf as a post and as daft as a sack of frogs.'

He kept digging, Harvey working furiously by his side. And then he tossed aside a large section of the back door and saw Peggy lying curled around a silent and ominously still Daisy. Cordelia was beside them, her frail body pinned against the cellar wall by a pile of rubble. 'I need the medics over here!' he shouted as Harvey whined and sniffed at Daisy and Peggy.

The fire crews and soldiers pulled away the last of the debris and the ambulance medics clambered in to check on all three of them and hand

164

Harvey over to John Hicks so he was kept out of their way.

'Well, it's about time,' Cordelia said with a ghost of a smile on her begrimed and bloody face. 'Not that the sight of your ugly mug is anything to celebrate.'

'You're not exactly a picture of loveliness, either. But 'tis thankful I am that you're alive.' Ron held her hand and watched anxiously as the medics searched for vital signs in Peggy and Daisy. He could see the copious amount of blood on Peggy's clothing and prayed that they'd found her in time.

Daisy miraculously seemed to have been asleep, for when the ambulance girl picked her up she opened her eyes and gave her a broad, almost toothless smile.

'We need to get Mrs Reilly to hospital as quickly as possible,' the other medic said. 'She's lost a lot of blood by the look of it, and her pulse is very weak.'

As the stretcher was brought and they laid Peggy on it and covered her with a blanket, the medic checked on Cordelia. 'Superficial cuts and bruises, and a possible fractured wrist.' She smiled at Cordelia as she gently placed her arm in a sling. 'You've been a very lucky lady.'

'I know,' she said weakly. 'Just concentrate on Peggy. She's had a miscarriage.'

Ron's eyes widened at this piece of news but he kept his own counsel. 'I'll bring Cordelia,' he said to the young girl as she packed her medical bag.

He squatted down, eased his arm behind Cordelia's back, tucked his other beneath her knees and gently carried her over the rubble and out into the smoke-laden garden where the haze of fire still lightened the sky. He felt the frail little body relax in his arms, and the meagre weight of her head against his shoulder, and knew in that moment just how very much she meant to him.

The first ambulance had already raced off for the hospital with Peggy and Daisy, the bell clanging stridently. Ron thanked John Hicks and his crew, took Harvey from him and sat in the second ambulance, Cordelia cradled on his knee, Harvey lying on the floor at his feet.

'You can't bring the dog in here,' said the sour-faced driver.

'You'll drive your ambulance to the hospital with my dog in it, or I'll be giving you a bloody nose,' he growled. Harvey's hackles rose and he curled his top lip and snarled too. The man gave no further argument, and within seconds they were roaring down Camden Road.

The hospital was an enormous building which sprawled the width of an entire block and serviced a vast area of isolated villages, hamlets and small towns. It was a busy night, with four ambulances already unloading patients at the accident and emergency wing, and lots of walking wounded being brought in by friends and family.

Ron carried Cordelia straight into the emergency department, took one look at the mayhem, spotted an empty bed and put her down.

'She'll have to wait out there like everyone else,' said the harassed nurse. 'You can't leave her here.'

'She's an old lady who's earned the right to be treated immediately after what she's just been through,' he said quietly. 'She has a broken wrist,

166

cuts and abrasions – but I want a doctor to give her a thorough examination to make sure we haven't missed anything.'

The girl seemed to realise he wouldn't be shifted and gave a sigh. 'All right, but you'll have to take the dog out of here. Matron will have a fit if she sees it.'

'Harvey stays with me,' he said firmly. 'And I'm staying with Cordelia until I'm satisfied she's been examined and treated properly.'

The girl smiled with sudden recognition. 'You're Ronan Reilly, aren't you?' At his nod her smile widened. 'I thought so. Fran and Suzy are always talking about you.' She patted his arm. 'I'll fetch the doctor.'

Ron pulled the curtains round and sat on the end of the bed while Harvey crawled beneath it, nose on paws, as patient as ever.

Cordelia opened her eyes and winced as she tried to move her damaged wrist. 'I'll be fine, Ron. Go and find out what's happened to Peggy. I won't rest easy until I know she and Daisy are all right.'

'I'll be going the moment I know you're in safe hands,' he replied softly.

'I've been in safe hands since the moment you carried me out of the cellar,' she murmured, her eyes bright with unshed tears. 'Thank you, dearest Ron.'

Ron blinked rapidly and folded his arms. 'To be sure, Cordelia, you talk a lot of nonsense sometimes,' he said gruffly.

The middle-aged doctor arrived, looking as frazzled as the young nurse who accompanied him. He barely glanced at Harvey or Ron as he sent them out of the cubicle while he examined Cordelia. A few minutes later the nurse fetched a wheelchair, and shortly after that she wheeled Cordelia off to the X-ray department with the promise of a cup of strong, sweet tea to counter the shock of her ordeal.

'We'll plaster her wrist and find her a bed for the night so we can keep an eye on her,' the doctor said as he smothered a vast yawn. 'She may have suffered concussion during the bomb blast, and she'll be safer here.'

'My daughter-in-law, Peggy Reilly, came in with her baby Daisy as well. Where can I find them?'

The other man dug his hands into the pockets of his white coat. 'I was with the team when she came in,' he said, his expression too solemn for Ron's liking. 'She's had to go straight into theatre. But Daisy is absolutely fine, and she'll be kept in the nursery overnight.'

'Cordelia said Peggy had had a miscarriage.'

The doctor nodded. 'I'm afraid so, but there were added complications which I can't go into without breaking patient confidentiality. Can her husband be contacted?'

A shaft of fear speared Ron. 'She's not going to die, is she?' he breathed.

'All operations carry some risk, but one must remain positive in situations like this.'

'My son's somewhere up north with the Royal Engineers,' Ron said fretfully. 'I don't even have a phone number for his unit's barracks.' His voice quavered and he found his hand was shaking as he felt Harvey's wet, consoling nose nudge the

168

palm. 'Can I wait until the operation's over?'

'Go down that corridor and keep going until you come to a set of double doors. You'll find a row of chairs there where you can wait. But it could be a long while, Mr Reilly, and you really cannot take your dog with you.'

'Aye, I understand that. Thank you, doctor.'

Ron led Harvey outside and ordered him to sit and wait by the steps where he wouldn't get in the way. He gave the soft head and ears a loving stroke and then hurried back up the steps and navigated his way along the endless corridor to the theatre wing.

The chairs were hard and uncomfortable, and he could have done with a large mug of tea – but Peggy was as beloved as a daughter, and he would sit here for as long as necessary, and pray that she would survive this terrible night.

Chapter Nine

As the long night progressed the girls arrived one by one to sit quietly beside him. Ron didn't have to tell them very much, for they had learned what had happened from Peggy's neighbours, and seen the damage to Beach View and the houses behind it. He explained about Cordelia and Daisy and the scant news he had about Peggy, and thought himself blessed that these girls cared so deeply for his little family.

Suzy had brought a flask of tea and two doorstep-sized sandwiches, whilst Jane had a packet of digestive biscuits. Fran had a small bottle of brandy in her coat pocket, which Brenda had given her as she'd passed the Anchor on her way to the hospital, and Sarah was carrying Ron's poacher's coat in case he was feeling the cold after his ordeal.

Ron sat and waited, cursing the clock on the wall as it slowly ticked away the endless minutes. And yet the girls were a great comfort to him, always making sure he was never alone as they took turns to check on Cordelia and Daisy, and to try and get a progress report on Peggy's operation.

Sarah and Jane returned with the news that their beloved great-aunt was comfortable now her arm was in plaster, and fast asleep on the women's ward. Suzy then went to the nursery to check on Daisy, who was also asleep and blissfully unaware of the dramatic events of the night – and once she'd returned, Fran went to see if anyone could tell her what was happening in the operating theatre.

She came back and plumped down next to Ron. 'No one will tell me anything,' she muttered as she took his hand. 'But Mr Simmons is the best surgeon we have here, and I'm sure everything will be fine.'

Rita turned up an hour later with another flask of tea, her little face streaked with soot, her hair and heavy-duty clothes still damp from the hoses. She asked immediately for news and was disappointed to find there wasn't any. 'I would have been here earlier, but what with the number of fires and everything...' She gave Ron's arm a comforting squeeze. 'Everyone at the fire station sends their best love, and I managed to get someone to give Harvey a bowl of water – poor old thing, he looked so sad sitting there on the steps. Is there anything else I can do to help?'

'Aye,' he muttered, 'you could find him some food. The poor wee beast must be starving by now.'

'Of course I will.' Rita hurried off, her heavy boots squeaking on the highly polished linoleum.

Ron ate the sandwiches, even though he really had little appetite, and drank the tea, which he'd laced heavily with the brandy. The clock on the wall told him it was past one in the morning. He'd been sitting here for almost two hours, and every minute had felt like an eternity.

Rita returned some time later, still in her uniform. 'I took Harvey to the fire station and we gave him a saucer of beer along with his water, and some scraps with biscuits. He's currently lording it by stretching out in John's office in front of the heater.' She sat down with the other girls. 'Any news yet?' As they all shook their heads, Rita gave a long sigh of despair, slumped in the chair, and fell silent.

Nurses bustled past, orderlies clanged buckets as they mopped the floor, porters pushed squeaking trolleys and doctors could be seen at the far end of the corridor rushing past, their white coats flapping – but no one came near, and they all began to wonder if they'd become invisible, or had simply been forgotten.

'I don't understand what's taking so long,' said

171

Ron peevishly. 'For the love of God, you'd think someone would come out and let us know what's happening in there.'

Purposeful footsteps came down the corridor and they all turned expectantly. But it wasn't Matron or a doctor with news – it was Doris.

'I do think one of you could have had the decency to let me know that my sister is in hospital,' she said before she'd even reached the line of chairs.

'The phone lines were down and as I don't possess a carrier pigeon, I assumed you'd hear the gossip sooner rather than later,' said Ron sourly. He couldn't stand Doris – knew the feeling was mutual, and didn't care a fig.

Doris sniffed and eyed them all disdainfully. 'Will one of you at least tell me how Peggy is?'

'We know as little as you do,' said Suzy. 'They're operating on her now.'

'I see.' Doris folded her fur coat around her and sat down in the line of chairs opposite, her glossy leather handbag clasped on her lap. Her hair was neat, the make-up flawless as usual, the sheer stockings and expensive shoes positively shouting wealth and privilege.

'I see you rushed out the moment you heard,' said Ron, eyeing her in disgust.

She glared at Ron. 'There are certain standards to be maintained even in moments of crisis, Reilly. Discipline and order, those are my watchwords – and it is a shame that you do not live by the same ethos.'

Ron hated it when she talked to him that way – using his surname as if he was some forelock-tugging peasant. He took a long swig of tea and brandy and closed his eyes. The night was already endless and distressing. Did he really have to put up with this sour-faced old witch as well? He peeped through his lashes. It seemed he did, for Doris was settling down to read the paperback she'd taken from her handbag.

The clatter of the double doors swinging open startled them from their morose stupor, and they looked up as the grey-haired surgeon strode towards them.

'Mr Reilly?' He shook Ron's hand. 'I'm sorry you've had such a long wait, but there were complications which had to be addressed immediately. Your daughter-in-law has come through with flying colours, and I expect her to make a full recovery.'

'I am Mrs Williams – Mrs Reilly's sister – her next of kin,' said Doris with a glare at Ron. 'What was the matter with her and what exactly do you mean by complications?'

The surgeon looked from Ron to Doris with a frown, then clearly realised Doris was not someone he could ignore. 'Mrs Reilly was in the early stages of pregnancy, but it appears that the foetus was forming in the fallopian tube instead of the womb. We call this an ectopic pregnancy,' he explained carefully. 'The pain and the bleeding she suffered were due to the rupture of the tube, and this led to an internal haemorrhage. Such cases are often fatal if not caught in time and it was only the swift actions of Mr Reilly and the ambulance medics that saved her.'

Doris was ashen as she sat down. 'But she will be all right, won't she?' she murmured.

'I expect her to make a full recovery, Mrs Williams, but there will be no more babies.'

'That's not a bad thing,' sniffed Doris. 'She's far too long in the tooth for such nonsense anyway.'

Ron heard the girls gasp at her rudeness and lack of care, felt the stress and worry of the night build to breaking point, and exploded. 'If you can't keep a civil tongue in your head, woman, then you should go home,' he barked.

Doris went pale as she gripped her handbag.

Feeling slightly better, he turned back to the doctor before Doris could think of some nasty retort. 'Can we see her?'

He shook his head. 'She's in the recovery ward and will stay there until she comes round fully from the anaesthetic. The operation was a long, fairly complicated ordeal for her and she needs time to recover.' He smiled at Ron and the girls. 'But I can see she has loving support and a close-knit family to look after her, so no doubt she will soon be on the mend.'

Doris snorted as she collected her things and, with a glare of contempt at all of them, strode away down the corridor.

Ron caught the astonishment in the surgeon's face and shot him a weary smile. 'Doris can be tricky,' he explained with breathtaking understatement. 'Just ignore her.' He shook the surgeon's hand. 'Thank you for taking such good care of our girl, Mr Simmons. You have no idea how grateful we are, to be sure.'

174

'I suggest you all go home and get some sleep. You may visit her tomorrow in Women's Surgical.' He gave a vast yawn and went back through the double doors, which clattered behind him.

'Come on, girls,' said Ron. 'Let's fetch Harvey and go home and see what the damage is.' They collected up bags, gas-mask boxes, flasks and sandwich wrappings, and then Rita and Fran tucked their hands into the crook of his arms and they all set off down the corridor, united in weariness and the profound relief that their darling Peggy was safe.

Chapter Ten

Ruby hadn't slept well after returning from the public shelter with her basket filled with her precious new clothes. She'd been keyed up over the need to be out of bed before Harold started his morning prowl, and subsequently kept waking up throughout what was left of the night.

As the light began to stream through the open curtains she groggily climbed out of bed, washed in the basin and quickly pulled on her new trousers and old sweater, and tied the laces on the sturdy boots she'd bought the day before. Dressed and ready for the day, she made the bed, checked on the hidden money and went downstairs.

There was no sign of Harold Fraser, but that was hardly surprising, for the kitchen clock showed it was barely five-thirty. She unlocked the

175

back door and stepped into the yard, which was still in heavy shadow and glittering with dew. Now she could actually see it properly, the outside lav was a gleaming example of Mrs Fraser's housewifely skills for, unlike the ones at the tenement, it didn't stink to high heaven, the concrete floor was scrubbed clean beneath the hessian mat, and there was a proper wooden seat.

It flushed efficiently, too, and there was even newspaper cut into neat squares to wipe her bum afterwards. All in all, Ruby thought, the billet was top-notch – and if it hadn't been for the Frasers, it would have been perfect.

She returned to the kitchen and, having worked out how to use the gleaming white cooker, turned on one of the gas rings, quietly filled the kettle and placed it on top. Opening the nearby cupboard, she found a brown teapot and a large china mug, and in the narrow larder she discovered a packet of tea, a bottle of milk and some sugar. She liked her tea strong and sweet and didn't even hesitate before putting three scoops of tea into the pot. After the measly meal the previous night she was entitled to something decent.

Once the tea had stewed to just the way she liked it, she poured it into the mug and added two scoops of sugar. Leaning against the stone sink to drink it, she let her thoughts wander as she regarded the pots of bean and tomato plants that grew in the yard.

Everything was very different to what she was used to, and she'd been quite shocked the night before when they'd gone down to the public shelter, to discover how well regarded the Frasers were in this posh little town. There had been respectful greetings, offers of seats, cigarettes and cups of tea, and Harold had become somewhat pompous as his wife preened in the reflected glory. The townspeople obviously didn't know what the Frasers were really like, and the thought galled her.

And yet she didn't know why she was so surprised, for they were fundamentally little different from a lot of people she knew in the East End – their public faces so very unlike the ones they showed behind closed doors. She grimaced as she sipped her tea. Ray was a prime example, and she'd been fool enough not to look beyond the handsome, smiling face before she married him.

She turned her thoughts from Ray and the Frasers and felt a tingle of apprehension as the time approached for her to leave for work. It wouldn't be at all like her shifts in the pub, where she was left to her own devices to deal with the mostly male customers. She knew from her mother that standing for hours beside a production line was far from easy, and that some of the women could get clannish and bullying if they saw the slightest sign of weakness in a newcomer. Ethel, of course, was an old hand at factory work and took it all in her stride. Although Ruby had few fears about her ability to learn the job quickly and handle any awkward situation that might crop up, she just hoped that her first day would go smoothly, that the line manager wasn't a cow, and that she'd meet some nice girls to pally up with.

But thinking of her mother made her fretful, and she wondered again if she was all right; if Ray was dead, in hospital, or out looking for her. And whether the rozzers were already asking their questions and trampling their size twelves all over the tenements. Not that it would do them much good, she thought. No one had witnessed anything – and even if they had, the entire tenement population was adept at turning suddenly blind and deaf to everything when the police came calling.

'My goodness. You're up early.' Harold was rotund and resplendent in a tartan dressing gown, velvet slippers and striped pyjamas, his thinning hair smeared over the balding dome of his head.

'I'm due at work soon,' she replied as she poured another mug of tea and added sugar.

'Go easy with that,' he said hastily. 'It is rationed, you know.'

'Yeah, and you've got me food stamps, so I reckon I'm entitled to a bit of sugar in me morning cuppa.'

He raised an eyebrow as he peered at the dark colour of the stewed tea, but seeing the defiance in Ruby's eyes he made no comment and put the kettle on.

Ruby watched him set out a tray with a cloth, cups and saucers, sugar bowl, milk jug and four sweet biscuits. 'What can I have for me breakfast?'

'There's bread in the larder and a pot of dripping,' he replied as he refreshed the pot of tea with boiling water and placed it on the tray.

She wasn't about to be fobbed off with bread and flaming dripping. 'I saw eggs in there, and a bit of 'am,' she replied.

'The eggs are for Marjory,' he said firmly. 'My

wife has a delicate constitution, and it's important she has her boiled egg every morning.'

Ruby pursed her lips at the thought of the fat and far from delicate Marjory. 'Reckon I'll just have the 'am and a bit of toast then.' Without waiting for him to respond, she got the bread and the knuckle of boiled ham out of the larder and began to scrape off the few bits of meat onto a plate while the bread toasted under the grill.

'I do believe that Marjory was planning to use that for soup,' he murmured.

'There ain't enough here to poke in yer eye, let alone make soup,' she retorted. 'Best not to waste it.'

She heard him cluck his tongue before he picked up the tray and took it upstairs, but she ignored him. If she didn't eat something proper before she went to work she was likely to keel over, and that wouldn't do at all.

She couldn't find the butter she'd seen the previous night – Marjory had probably hidden it away with the cheese and crackers – so she spread a thin layer of dripping on the two bits of toast, slathered them with the tomato sauce she'd found in the cupboard and sandwiched the scrapings of ham between them. It was a small victory and by the time she'd munched her way through it and finished her second mug of tea, she was ready for anything.

The Frasers were still upstairs as she left the house, the front door key safely tucked into her trouser pocket. Swinging her gas-mask box in her hand, she felt the warmth of the early sun on her face and the clean, salty air ruffling her hair as she strode away from Mon Repos and headed for the factory estate.

She reached Jenkins' dairy just as the gates opened, and she stood and watched as the four enormous shire horses emerged with their youthful drivers, the drays loaded with crates of rattling bottles. They were a lovely sight, reminding Ruby of the days before the war when the draymen would come to the pubs to deliver the barrels of beer, and the rag and bone man would slowly plod the streets with his patient old nag, the dray loaded with all sorts of unwanted junk.

She grinned back at the fair-haired girl who waved a cheerful good morning and looked as if she was having the time of her life up there on that high wooden seat. But she didn't envy her, for as much as she admired the lovely big horses, they frightened the life out of her. She waited until the horses had gone their separate ways and the gates were shut behind them before she set off again and wandered past the sprawling allotments.

The residents of Cliffehaven had obviously answered the call to dig for victory with some enthusiasm. There were already a couple of hardy souls working in the rich, dark soil, and someone was sitting in the doorway of one of the little sheds smoking a pipe and looking out at the row upon row of sprouting greenery. Frameworks of poles supported beans and peas, and wire mesh protected delicate seedlings. She had no idea what most of the vegetables were, for she'd only seen them on a market stall before today, and wouldn't have known the green shoots of a carrot from a spud.

She finally came to the factory complex which sprawled over several acres behind a high wire fence. As she had a bit of time before she was due to clock on, she showed her ID and work docket to the guard on the gate and then wandered round to get her bearings.

Silvery barrage balloons drifted above the many buildings, glinting in the sun and swaying in the light breeze, and as she strolled beneath them she found an enormous underground shelter, a huge canteen, washrooms, and sheltered rest areas for when it rained.

The factories seemed to make everything from tools, parachutes and ammunition, to barrage balloons, plane parts, engines and leather boots. She could see trucks parked by enormous storage sheds, could hear wirelesses blaring from every building above the rumble and crump of heavy machinery, and felt the energy of this busy, productive place.

'You look about as lost as me. Is this your first day?'

Ruby turned and smiled at the small, plump girl with the pretty round face and bright blue eyes who grinned back at her. 'It certainly is. You too?'

'Yes.' She hitched her gas-mask box over her shoulder and shuffled her feet in their sturdy boots as she glanced at the bruising on Ruby's face. 'I hope you don't mind me saying, but that looks awfully painful,' she said.

Ruby had forgotten about the bruises now the swelling in her jaw had gone down. 'It's a coupl'a days since I done it, so they don't hurt no more.'

181

The girl accepted this explanation and eyed Ruby's trousers, boots and sweater. 'You look very workmanlike,' she said, 'but I must confess I feel a bit silly in this get-up. My mother had a complete fit when she saw I was wearing overalls – said it wasn't the done thing at all for respectable girls of seventeen.'

Ruby giggled. 'I think you look just fine – and of course they're practical. You'd look proper daft in a skirt and high heels.'

The other girl chuckled and brushed her long fair hair from her eyes. 'I'm Lucy Kingston, by the way,' she said as she stuck out her hand.

'Ruby Clark.' The small hand was soft, the nails like little pale pink shells. There was only a year between them, but Ruby could tell that she'd had a lifetime of experience compared to Lucy and that, with her soft hands, plump sweetness and posh accent, she'd be an instant target of the bullies. She felt suddenly protective of her, even though they had only just met. 'You from round here, then, Lucy?'

She shrugged as if in apology. 'I've lived here all my life, and if it wasn't for Mother, I'd be off and doing something exciting like delivering Spitfires.'

'Blimey,' breathed Ruby, 'you got more guts than me, gel. But I suppose yer mum don't want you doing dangerous stuff like that.'

Lucy gave a sigh. 'I don't think she'd mind, actually,' she said thoughtfully. 'But she isn't very well and I have to look after her now Daddy's gone back to sea.' She glanced at the wedding ring on Ruby's finger. 'I suppose your husband's

182

away fighting as well?'

'He certainly is,' she replied lightly, 'that's why I'm down here.'

'But you're from London, aren't you? Is it as bad as they say?'

'Round where I come from it is, but that's because of the docks and suchlike. The city's in a pretty bad way too, but we all just get on with it – there ain't much else we can do, really.'

'I know. Ghastly, isn't it? But at least we girls have got the chance to take on jobs we would never have had before the war. I'm looking forward to earning my own money and being independent. It's getting a bit tedious having to traipse round the shops with Mother, who of course chooses everything I wear because she's the one paying.'

'I'm surprised you went for a factory job,' Ruby murmured. 'A girl like you could find all sorts of better things to do than stand in a production line.'

Lucy shrugged delicately. 'I was so desperate to get out of the house and do something useful I took the first thing they offered me,' she admitted.

They both heard the hooter which signalled the end of the midnight-to-eight shift, and stood watching as a stream of women came clattering out of the factories like great flocks of squawking geese.

'Looks like it's our turn, Lucy,' said Ruby as she pulled a headscarf from her pocket. 'You got a scarf? Only you can't have yer 'air floating about with machinery going.'

Lucy bit her lip, the sunny smile fading into a frown. 'I didn't think to bring one. Oh dear, will it matter terribly, do you think?'

Ruby handed hers over. 'My hair's shorter, and I expect I can get a lend of one,' she said lightly. She helped Lucy bundle her baby-fine hair under the scarf and tied it securely at the front.

Lucy's little face was still concerned as she suddenly noticed they were surrounded by a large group of women who were waiting to start the same shift. 'Have you done factory work before, Ruby?' she asked fretfully. 'Only this is my first ever job and I haven't a clue. I'm terrified of making a fool of myself.'

Ruby smiled at her encouragingly. 'We can learn together, 'cos I ain't done this sort of thing before neither.'

Lucy gave a long sigh of relief. 'I'm so glad we met, Ruby,' she said as she tucked her hand into the crook of Ruby's arm. 'It's always nice to make a friend on your first day, isn't it?'

'It certainly is,' said Ruby warmly as they joined the other women and headed for the vast corrugated iron shed. They came from different worlds, but circumstances had brought them together, and this was a new day, a new beginning, and perhaps the start of a close friendship that would see them both through these confusing times.

They were greeted by a wall of noise, for the shifts overlapped and the machinery never stopped. As they shuffled along with the other women towards the clocking-on station, they took the chance to look around.

Ruby saw banks of bright lights hanging from

184

the steel rafters, line upon line of heavy machinery, with women pulling levers, turning knobs, and chucking bits of heavy metal into nearby boxes. There were coils of waste metal on the floor beneath every machine, and these were being swept up and tossed into large storage bins where no doubt they were melted down to be used again. Everything looked grey and gloomy, and the pungent smell of oil, hot metal and sweat combined with the noise made her regret eating such a big breakfast.

Ruby noticed that Lucy looked a bit green around the gills as they approached the small office window by the clocking-on board, but her shoulders were squared and her chin was tilted determinedly as she handed over the docket she'd been given at the Labour Exchange.

Ruby stood beside her as their dockets were examined and they were given their time sheets. She had to lean almost through the window to hear what the woman was saying, and then nodded her understanding and nudged Lucy towards the board where she showed her how to clock on.

'Where do we go now?' shouted Lucy.

'Over there with the other new lot,' Ruby yelled back. At this rate, she thought sourly, she'd have a sore throat by the end of the day as well as a headache – and she almost wished she was back in the pub dealing with drunks and lechers.

The six women nodded at each other, realising there was little point in trying to hold a conversation. Ruby saw that three were middle-aged, but the fourth was about eighteen or twenty, and looked so out of place it was hard not to stare.

Her hair was the sort of colour that could only come out of a peroxide bottle, her lips were as scarlet as her long fingernails, and her eyelashes were heavy with mascara. There was a sneer to the tilt of her lips and her scathing glance over the rest of the women was more telling than any words.

'She's frightfully glamorous, isn't she?' shouted Lucy in Ruby's ear.

'She's trouble, Lucy. Steer well clear, gel.'

Lucy frowned. 'But how can you tell? You don't even know her.'

'I seen enough like her to know, all right.'

The foreman was a man in his sixties with bushy grey eyebrows, trim moustache and the bulbous nose and ruddy cheeks of a man who liked a drink or four. He carried a clipboard and his clothes were protected by a long brown duster coat.

'My name is Mr Hawkins,' he said above the surrounding noise. 'You will all be taught how to use the machines and your work will be assessed at the end of your shift. There will be a ten-minute break at eleven, half an hour for lunch, which will be provided in the canteen, and another ten minutes at four.' He took a breath. 'There is absolutely no smoking on the factory floor, and if alcohol is found on your person, or it is deemed you are drunk on duty, then you will be dismissed instantly without a reference.'

Ruby wondered if he was ever guilty of taking a quiet nip of something in his office and suspected he did. She caught the peroxide blonde giving her the snooty once-over and held her gaze defiantly until she got the message she wasn't about to be cowed by any of her nonsense.

The foreman was still droning on. 'As you are aware, this is a tool factory, but we also make nails, screws, nuts, bolts and washers. You will all be assigned to the washers for now until you get a proper hang of things.' He turned as a woman in dungarees and the ubiquitous headscarf app-roached. 'This is Mabel and she will be your line manager until it's deemed safe enough to consign you to the other parts of the factory.'

Mabel was probably well past thirty, with a sturdy figure and a face devoid of make-up be-neath the knotted headscarf. She looked extremely capable, and Ruby suspected she wouldn't stand for any nonsense. They all trooped after her to the other side of the vast, echoing factory where six machines sat on a steel bench waiting for them.

Ruby edged between Lucy and the blonde and listened hard as Mabel began to explain how to start the machines and keep them well oiled, and how to feed each thin metal disc onto the stamp-ing block so the hole could be punched through it. If there was a problem with their machine, they were warned, they were to put their hand up and wait for someone to come and fix it. It was dangerous, dirty work, the machines were very valuable, and to avoid accidents there was to be no talking.

Ruby smiled at that, for chance would have been a fine thing with all this racket going on – but the work wasn't exactly complicated, and within minutes she had done her first washer, shown it to Mabel and had it passed as correct.

She threw it in the box beside her, aware that

the blonde on her left was having trouble with her long fingernails and getting it in the neck from Mabel. But a glance told Ruby that Lucy was getting the hang of things very well and already had three washers in her box. They shared a grin and set to work with a will, relishing the thought that they could get to know one another better during the break.

Chapter Eleven

Ron and Harvey had slept in the Anderson shelter for what remained of the night, but as dawn broke on the horizon and they stepped outside into the garden; the full effect of the bombing raid was made startlingly clear.

The flint wall at the bottom of the garden had another gaping hole in it, and the neighbouring fence had come loose from its moorings and was leaning drunkenly over the coal bunker and wood pile. The shed and outside lav had been blown to bits, and the poor chickens were pecking about in what was left of their nesting box as the rooster perched on top of it and began to crow. The trampling feet of the firemen and medics had put paid to at least three rows of onions, and in amongst the wreckage, he could see that some of the tiles had been blown off the roof and were embedded in the earth.

A path had been cleared through the rubble to get to the women, but there was still a mountain of it to be shifted before he could start work on cleaning up. But they had fared better than the poor people in the road further up, for he'd heard from Rita that two houses had been completely flattened and two others would have to be demolished because they were deemed unsafe. The house directly behind Beach View hadn't escaped either, he realised as he looked beyond the shattered garden walls and saw that the roof was almost gone and not an inch of glass had been left in the windows.

He took a moment to light his pipe, thankful that his neighbours had all been in the public shelters at the time, and no one had been hurt. He eyed the damage to Beach View and knew that with a lot of hard work, it could be fixed, but that wasn't really the thing that bothered him at the moment. It was the fate of his young ferrets, Flora and Dora, for he hadn't been able to get to them last night, and he was very much afraid that they hadn't survived.

Harvey was quartering the garden with his nose to the ground, sniffing out all the strange smells. He came to the chicken pen and looked back at Ron as if to ask if he should round them up like he did the quail on Cliffe estate.

'You leave them alone, ye heathen old scoundrel,' Ron muttered as he hitched up his sagging trousers and rolled back his ragged shirtsleeves. 'Come on. Let's find Flora and Dora.'

The rubble had blown in right to the very end of the narrow corridor, and a pall of dust hung in the air still. Ron used a spade to shovel it all into his wheelbarrow and made endless journeys to the bottom of the garden, where he tipped it out. There were the remains of the stone sink, shelving, bits of piping, chunks of brick and mortar, the remnants of the frosted window, and even three of his wellingtons amongst it all. He set these aside with the mangle and Peggy's washing basket.

The pile was high and wide by the time he mansaged to clear a path to his bedroom door, which, by some miracle, had been blown shut. Pushing it open he heard the rustle and scrabble of the ferrets, and with a deep sigh of relief, he pulled their cage from under the bed and knelt down to check on them.

The dust lay in a thick grey coating on everything, including the ferrets' fur, but their eyes were bright and they didn't seem to be injured. He gently drew them from the cage and stroked them as Harvey buffeted them with his nose. They were all right, he realised; just a bit bewildered, dusty and probably very hungry.

He carried them up the cellar steps and into the kitchen in search of some bread and milk, his boots crunching on the shattered glass of the window pane which had been blown in. As he fed his babies and gave Harvey a drink of water and some biscuits, he eyed the dust and the debris on every surface of Peggy's kitchen, and was glad she couldn't see it like this, for it would have broken her heart.

Once the ferrets had been fed and brushed clean, he returned them to their cage and carried it outside, well away from the dust. He would have a cup of tea, he decided, and then make a start on cleaning the kitchen before the girls came down.

He didn't want to think of the dust that was probably all over the house – that sort of challenge could only be faced after a hearty breakfast.

Peggy's eyelids fluttered momentarily and as the strange, muffled sounds of people talking and moving about began to penetrate the thick fog which seemed to fill her head, she opened her eyes. The curtains weren't familiar, there was a strange sort of antiseptic smell, and someone's shoes were squeaking as they walked past. Where on earth was she? What had happened?

She fought off almost overwhelming drowsiness as she tried to focus her thoughts and keep her eyes open. The only thing she could remember was being in the cellar with Cordelia and Daisy when the world seemed to explode.

'Daisy! Where's Daisy?' She bolted up from the pillows, but immediately collapsed with a strangled cry as a searing pain shot through her.

'It's all right, Peggy, she's safe upstairs in the nursery, and there's not a scratch on her.' Suzy gently took her hand. 'Don't try to sit up,' she said softly. 'You've had an operation, and you'll pull the stitches if you move about too much.'

Peggy looked blearily at Suzy, who was in her nursing uniform, and tried very hard to clear the fog in her head and understand what she was saying. 'Daisy's all right? Are you sure?'

'She's absolutely fine, I promise. And so is Cordelia. They'll both be going home later today.'

Peggy ran her tongue over her dry lips as she digested all that Suzy had told her. The relief was tremendous, but there was still the nagging pain in her belly and Suzy had said something about an operation. It was then that she remembered the blood. 'I've lost the baby,' she stated on a sigh.

Suzy perched on the bed and took her hand. 'I'm so sorry, Peggy, but there was nothing the surgeon could do to save it.'

Peggy listened groggily as Suzy kept a tight hold of her hand and explained about the emergency operation that had saved her life. 'But there was a great deal of damage, Peggy,' she continued softly. 'Mr Simmons had no option but to perform a hysterectomy.'

The words hit her like a hammer blow. 'But that means...'

Suzy's grip tightened on her fingers. 'It means you have survived a very dangerous situation, Peggy,' she said firmly. 'You have Daisy and Bob and Charlie, Anne and Cissy – as well as your little granddaughter, me and Fran and the other girls. And then there's Ron and Cordelia, and of course Jim. We all love you, Peggy, and the thought that we could have lost you was unbearable.'

Peggy was still trying to come to terms with the fact that part of her was missing, that she had lost the precious little baby she'd been carrying and there would be no more. 'Was it something I did that caused this?' she asked tearfully.

'Absolutely not,' said Suzy firmly. 'It was just an accident of nature which occurs sometimes through no fault of the mother.'

'I see,' she murmured, the weight of her loss lying heavy round her heart. 'Has Jim been told?'

'Jane sent a telegram to his barracks first thing. We didn't want to alarm him, so we just said you'd had an operation, but that you were on the mend and expected to make a full recovery. No doubt he'll telephone sometime today, and then we can—'

Peggy gripped her hand. 'You're not to tell him about losing the baby – or how serious the whole thing has been. I don't want him worrying himself sick up there and going AWOL – and he will, I know my Jim.'

'He'll have to know at some point,' said Suzy mildly. 'Otherwise, how are you going to explain the scar?'

'I'll do it when he comes home on leave. I'll be up and about again then, and he'll see that I'm all right.' This little speech exhausted her and she closed her eyes, trying desperately to gather the strength to say all the things she needed to.

'Peggy, you need to rest,' said Suzy as she took her pulse.

'Promise me you won't tell Anne,' she rasped. 'I don't want her taking that long journey from Somerset with Rose Margaret – and try to keep it from Cissy, too. She'll only get over-dramatic and cause a fuss.'

'I'm afraid Cissy already knows,' said Suzy as she helped Peggy to drink some water. 'She'd heard about it from someone who'd been drinking at the Anchor, and is asking her CO for permission to visit you this evening.'

The few drops of water were nectar, and slightly restored her senses. 'If Cissy knows then so does Martin,' she murmured. 'Which means he'll tell Anne.' She grasped Suzy's hand. 'Please don't let them worry,' she begged. 'I couldn't bear it.'

193

'I'll make sure everyone knows you're on the mend and there's no need for worry or fuss,' said Suzy calmly as she adjusted the flow of drugs through the drip.

Peggy's eyelids fluttered and she lost the ability to fight the swirling darkness that seemed so determined to overwhelm her. Within moments she was in a deep, dreamless sleep.

Ron was overwhelmed by everyone's kindness, for the mammoth task that had faced him at dawn had been lifted from his shoulders in a great tide of goodwill.

Sarah, Jane and Suzy had risen after only a couple of hours' sleep to give their rooms a thorough clean before they had to go to work. Brenda and Pearl had come to clean Peggy's room and the kitchen before they were due to open the Anchor for the lunchtime session. They had assured him they could cope quite well without him, and told him to take all the time he needed to get things straight.

Two of Rita's colleagues at the fire station were retired builders and bricklayers, and they'd turned up with their tools and immediately started to replace the broken load-bearing beam with a sturdy railway sleeper and then repaired the scullery wall. Two other off-duty firemen brought ladders and fixed the tiles back in place and checked that the chimney was safe. A neighbour donated a door which had been sitting in his cellar for years, and Stan from the railway station brought a stone sink he'd been using in his allotment as a seed propagator.

An elderly man appeared from down the road and, without being asked, began to repair the garden's flint wall, and another neighbour arrived with sheets of hardboard which he nailed over the shattered windows. Peggy had been a stalwart help to both of them when they were widowed, and this was their way of paying her back.

Fred the Fish and Alf the butcher had closed their shops during the lunch hour and got stuck into helping Ron repair the chicken coop, fix the fence and put the shed back together again. They all agreed that the outside lav was beyond repair, and so they added its remains to the bonfire Ron had lit in the far corner of the garden, where there was now also a pile of hard core.

When the fishmonger and the butcher had to leave to reopen their shops, their delivery vans were laden with the broken sink, lavatory and bits of metal, wire and piping that couldn't be used or burned. It would all be taken to the town dump after their shops closed.

While the men were busy hammering, brick-laying and plumbing, Rita and Fran were organising the army of pinafore- and headscarf-clad women who'd arrived with buckets and mops, brooms and dusters. Peggy had always lent a hand when needed, had been a good friend and neighbour and a great source of comfort in darker times, and they were only too willing to show her how much she meant to them.

Ron and the other men had been barred from going into the newly cleaned kitchen in their dirty boots, but they were kept refreshed by copious amounts of tea that were brought into

195

the garden on trays. The beds and windows had been stripped, the linen and curtains washed in the kitchen sink, the blankets and rugs beaten clean of dust out in the garden. Once Ron's bonfire had gone out, the washing was pegged out on the newly repaired lines.

Harvey was petted and spoiled with biscuits and sweet tea, and he rushed about enthusiastically, getting under everyone's feet. Ron finally rounded him up and ordered him to sit by the Anderson shelter and not move until given permission, and Harvey lay there as if he'd been shot, eyes mournful beneath the bushy eyebrows.

Ron grinned at the old chap who was making a fine job of repairing the flint wall even though he looked concerned about Harvey. 'Take no notice of him,' he said. 'Harvey is the Humphrey Bogart of the dog world and every performance deserves an Oscar, so it does.'

'Aye, I can see that,' he replied round the stem of his unlit pipe. 'He's a lurcher, isn't he?'

Ron nodded. 'A Bedlington cross greyhound, probably with a bit of Irish wolfhound thrown in. Fast as lightning and a good nose – but a bloody nuisance at times,' he said affectionately.

The older man grinned as Harvey rolled on his back, legs waving in the air as his tongue lolled. 'One of the family, eh? That's as it should be.'

Ron was about to offer him a pinch from his roll of tobacco when he heard a commotion going on in the kitchen. 'I'd better see what that's all about,' he muttered as he handed the tobacco over. 'With a house full of women there was always going to be fireworks. Help yourself to a pinch for your pipe.'

The men rebuilding the scullery wall and plumbing in the sink had paused in their work to listen to the argument going on upstairs, and they stepped aside as Ron pushed his way through with Harvey at his heels. '

'I'd take your boots off, mate,' warned the plumber. 'Sounds like they're on the warpath up there, and that's no place for a bloke at the best of times – especially if he drops muck on their nice clean floor.'

Ron realised this was good advice and toed off his wellingtons to reveal enormous holes in his socks. He yanked them off too and went, bare-footed, up the cold stone steps with Harvey padding closely behind him, to discover Rita and Fran in a heated argument with Doris, while the young Phyllis stood in mute anxiety in the hall doorway.

'You can't just come in here and start throwing your weight about,' snapped Fran.

Doris stood squarely in the middle of the kitchen, her expression implacable. 'They'll get very little done if they don't follow orders and do things properly,' she retorted.

'Every woman here has willingly given up their day to help clear up the mess because they love Peggy,' Rita fired back at her. 'It's not up to you to order them about as if they were your servants.'

'You've upset everyone,' said Fran crossly, 'and they've worked so hard today.'

'Then they should have the common sense to think before they waste time doing things in the wrong order,' retorted Doris.

Ron decided the situation needed cooling down, but diplomacy wasn't really his strength and he struggled to be pleasant to this woman whom he disliked intensely. He stepped into the room and between the warring women.

'It's nice to see you, Doris,' he fibbed. 'Have you come to help?'

The tact was clearly lost on her as she turned her beady eyes on him. 'Ah, Reilly. I wondered how long it would be before you deigned to put in an appearance.'

He swallowed a sharp retort. 'As you can see, Doris, we are rather busy at the moment.' He regarded her with a stiff little smile that he knew didn't reach his eyes. 'And my name is Ronan. I would appreciate it if you could remember that.' He rested his hand on Harvey's head to silence the low growl that came from the dog's throat as he sat at his feet. 'Now, Doris, what can we do for you on this fine afternoon?'

'I've come to bring organisation to this chaos,' she replied stiffly. 'It is patently clear that none of these women have the first idea of proper house management, for not only have they started here in the kitchen, they are now upstairs – which anyone with any sense knows is not the way to do things.'

Ron shot a glance at the silent Phyllis, who'd been joined in the doorway to the hall by several of the other women. 'To be sure, I'm not thinking any of these wonderful ladies need any advice at the moment, Doris,' he said carefully. 'They are doing a grand job, so they are.'

'Well, you would think that, wouldn't you?

Housework is hardly your forte.'

'I didn't realise it was yours either,' replied Ron mildly. 'I thought Phyllis did all the work in your place.'

'I employ Phyllis to do the rough work, certainly, but that does not mean I am ignorant of the proper management of a household.'

'To be sure, Doris, I realise your knowledge far outweighs mine – but in this instance, I think it would be wise to accept the good-heartedness of these lovely women, and be grateful for the sterling work that has been achieved here with love today.'

Perhaps realising there was little point in continuing the very public argument, Doris turned her attention to Ron and Harvey. Her cool gaze drifted from Ron's filthy bare feet and horny toenails to his grubby clothes and unshaven chin, then trawled over a bristling Harvey. She sniffed in disdain. 'I can see that things are going to have to change radically before my sister comes home.'

Ron felt the hairs prickle on the back of his neck. 'What do you mean by that?'

Doris pulled off her coat and hat and handed them to a flustered and anxious Phyllis as she continued to glare at Ron. 'You obviously cannot manage on your own once Daisy and Cordelia come home from the hospital. So I have decided to stay until Peggy is fully recovered.'

There was a gasp of horror from Fran and Rita and a murmur of dissent from the gathered audience as Ron's heart sank to his boots.

'But he's not alone,' protested Fran hotly. 'He has me and the other girls to muck in. We managed when Peggy was lying-in after Daisy, and we'll do it again now.'

'I don't see how,' she replied. 'You're all at work most of the time, with strange shifts that often mean you're out all night. Reil – Ronan, for reasons known only to himself, is heavily involved in running the Anchor – hardly the most salubrious of places to take my niece. He cannot be left in sole charge of a vulnerable baby and a half-witted old woman with a broken wrist.'

Diplomacy and pretence fled. 'Cordelia's not half-witted,' exploded Ron, 'and I'll thank you to mind your tongue and keep your nose out of this family's business.'

'You forget, Ronan, that this is my family too. And I'm staying, whether you like it or not.'

He certainly didn't want her here, but getting heated about it wouldn't help an already explosive situation. 'To be sure, Doris,' he said with a forced smile, ''tis grateful we are, but we can manage just fine, and I'm sure Ted would prefer to have you at home.'

'Edward fully understands the importance of my being here to make sure things are running smoothly while my sister is recuperating,' she said stiffly. She turned away to coldly regard Phyllis and the other women grouped in the doorway. 'Phyllis, hang my coat up and take my suitcase into Peggy's bedroom. I shall need clean bedlinen, and make sure you're careful when you unpack my silver dressing table set.' Phyllis scuttled off.

'Doris, I really don't think–'

'That's the point, Ronan – you never do,' she said flatly. 'I will be taking charge of this household from now on, and that is final.'

Ron realised that nothing short of a bomb would shift the bloody woman – and with no armoury to defend his home from this assault, he could do absolutely nothing about it.

Doris scented victory and was now in full flow. 'The rest of you, get upstairs and finish what you were doing. Once that's done, you will clean the hall floor again and scrub the sink properly.'

There was a general mutter of complaint from the other women as Rita rushed to their defence. 'The kitchen has already been done, and so has the hall,' she said, her arms tightly folded round her waist, her expression stormy.

Doris eyed Rita up and down. 'Not to my high standard,' she retorted, 'but then *I* was not born in a slum.'

Everyone gasped at this piece of nastiness, but Rita wasn't about to let her get away with it. She took a step towards Doris, her little fists tight at her side, her face pinched with dislike as they stood almost nose to nose. 'For all your posh clothes and fancy talk, you're the rudest, most ignorant woman, Doris Williams,' she said with quiet fury. 'If Peggy was here, she'd send you back home, bag and baggage, with a flea in your ear.'

'I hardly think you are in a position to decide what my sister might do,' said Doris as she looked coolly down her nose. 'After all, you're not even family.' Without waiting for a reply, she turned on her heel and headed for the hall and Peggy's bedroom.

The women parted like the Red Sea to let her through, and then swarmed into the kitchen, all

201

talking at once.

Ron could barely hear himself think in all the noise, but the message was clear. The women were united against Doris and not another stroke of work would be done today – not that there was much more to do, for they'd worked like Trojans since daybreak. He decided a cup of tea would soothe ruffled feathers, and set the large tin kettle back on the freshly blacked hob.

'To be sure, that woman will drive us all insane,' muttered Fran as she poured the tea into the thick mugs and handed them round.

'Aye, no doubt she will,' he replied, 'but she has no authority here, and if we go on as we've always done, she'll realise it soon enough and sling her hook.'

'I wouldn't hold your breath, Uncle Ron,' said Rita, who was still simmering with anger. 'Come hell or high water, that woman's here to stay until Auntie Peg comes home.' She followed the rest of the women who were now trooping down the cellar steps and out into the garden for a well-earned rest.

Ron poured himself a cup of tea and joined the women, who now seemed in a far more relaxed mood as they laughed and chatted with the men, lit cigarettes, drank their tea and enjoyed the sunshine. The camaraderie had always been strong, but he sensed it had been reinforced after that scene with Doris. He felt sick at the thought of having her here, but despite that, she'd had a valid point about caring for Cordelia and Daisy, which was even more galling.

Cordelia would be out of action with her arm in

plaster for at least six weeks, and although he knew how to bath, dress and feed a baby, it would take a great deal of planning to work round everyone's shifts, his duties with the ARP, the Home Guard and his responsibilities at the Anchor. He couldn't always rely on Pearl and Brenda – there were pipes to clean, heavy barrels to be changed, books to keep up to date, bills to be paid and orders to be sent to the brewery.

He lit his pipe and sat gloomily on the pile of discarded bricks and mortar as Harvey rested his muzzle on his knee and looked up at him in commiseration. Ron stroked his head and wished mightily that his darling Rosie was here. But even if by some miracle she did come home, he couldn't expect her to share the responsibilities of his household.

He gave a deep, weary sigh. He loathed Doris, but it looked as if he was stuck with her – and that could only bring trouble, for the battle lines had already been clearly drawn. The girls and Mrs Finch would form a united front against her and he would no doubt find himself stuck right in the middle of yet another war zone.

He gripped the pipe between his teeth. The next few weeks could prove to be the most difficult of his life, but he had to admit that he enjoyed a good tussle – it brought a zest to things as long as you didn't let it get under your skin.

Chapter Twelve

The canteen was a vast, echoing building at the heart of the factory complex, with long tables and benches and a serving counter that was managed by the men and women of the NAAFI. A wireless was playing some jolly music through a loudspeaker fixed to the rafters as the workers from the surrounding factories caught up with the latest gossip and exchanged funny anecdotes over their lunch. It was all very friendly, and Ruby and Lucy were greeted with smiles and asked how their first morning had gone as they stood in the long queue waiting to be served.

'It's all a bit like boarding school, isn't it?' said Lucy as they were served mashed potato, mince, cabbage and thick onion gravy, with jelly and custard for afters. 'Even the food's the same.'

'I wouldn't know,' said Ruby, who'd left school at thirteen to help her stepfather run his market stall of fake leather shoes and handbags. She waited for the girl behind the counter to fill her mug from the enormous tea urn and then looked round for somewhere to sit.

'There're two spaces over there,' said Lucy, pointing to the other side of the canteen. 'Come on, let's bag them before someone else does.'

Ruby couldn't help but smile at her youthful enthusiasm as she followed the girl across the room. She was still finding it hard to believe there was only a year between them, but could just imagine Lucy at her posh boarding school, with her plaits flying as she raced about the playing field with her hockey stick.

'What on earth's so funny?' asked Lucy with a frown as they sat down next to one another.

'When you was at boarding school, did you have pigtails and play hockey?'

'Of course.' She grinned. 'Captain of the first team in my last year,' she said proudly. 'But why do you ask?'

'I was just interested,' Ruby replied with a shrug. 'We only had a bit of yard at my school, so it was skipping and hopscotch while the boys kicked a ball about and had fights.'

The blue eyes widened. 'Really? How awful for you.' She blushed and bit her lip. 'I'm so sorry, Ruby. That sounded frightfully patronising.'

Ruby laughed. 'No offence taken, Lucy. Now eat up before this lot goes cold.'

Her stomach rumbled and her mouth watered as she picked up her knife and fork. She was looking forward to this, and no mistake. The first decent bit of food that she'd had in days, and probably the last until tomorrow if the previous night's offering was anything to go by.

'So,' said Lucy as she neatly placed her knife and fork on her empty plate, 'where are you billeted?'

'With Councillor and Mrs Fraser in Nelson Street.'

'Oh, that's nice. Mrs Fraser's lovely, isn't she? She and Mother are the stalwarts of the local Women's Guild, and they often hold their knitting circles in our drawing room.'

'I haven't really got to know them yet,' Ruby replied carefully. 'I only moved in there yesterday.'

'Well, you won't have any trouble there, not like some poor evacuees who have absolutely ghastly experiences.' She smiled at Ruby happily. 'I'm so glad you've fallen on your feet. It can't have been easy coming all this way on your own without a job to go to, or a place to stay. You are brave, Ruby.'

'Don't be daft,' she said lightly. 'I'm no braver than anyone else, and as you say, I've fallen on me feet with a good billet, a well-paid job and a new friend.'

'It's funny, isn't it?' mused Lucy. 'We obviously come from very different backgrounds and probably would never have met if it wasn't for this war – but I'm so glad we did, aren't you?'

''Course I am,' she muttered, a bit embarrassed by all this soppy talk. 'Now stop yer rabbiting and get on with yer jelly.'

Lucy giggled. 'You are funny,' she said as she picked up her spoon. 'Does everyone talk like you in the East End?'

'We got our own way of talking when we're all together,' Ruby murmured through a mouthful of rather lumpy custard. 'But you wouldn't understand the 'alf of it, 'cos we make it rhyme, see.'

'Really?' The blue eyes were wide, the expression expectant. 'Go on then, say something.'

Ruby thought for a moment. 'I were on me tod, so I come down the apples and took a butchers down the frog. I couldn't Adam and Eve me minces, so I stuck me titfer over me Barnet, cleaned me Hampsteads and went down to the dog to tell the strife.'

She grinned at Lucy's perplexed look. 'It means I were on me own (me Sweeney Todd), so I went downstairs (apples and pears) and had a look (a butcher's hook) at the road (frog and toad). I couldn't believe (Adam and Eve) me eyes (mince pies) so I put me tit-for-tat (hat) over me hair (Barnet Fair), cleaned me teeth (Hampstead Heath) and went down to the phone (dog and bone) to tell the wife (trouble and strife).'

Lucy giggled. 'You are a caution, Ruby,' she said happily before tucking into the jelly again. 'You'll have to teach me how to do that.'

'You speak ever so nice already,' said Ruby. 'You don't wanna learn my lingo.'

Ruby was still smiling as she listened to the gossip going on around her and enjoyed her pudding, but her smile faded as she picked out the unmistakable sound of East Enders further down the table. A surreptitious glance revealed three girls deep in heated discussion over the benefits and pitfalls of jacking in their jobs at the armaments factory for safer work and three square meals as Land Girls.

She didn't recognise them, and felt a modicum of relief. The last thing she wanted was word getting back to Bow – and ultimately to Ray and his family. But of course there were probably other women here from London and, even if she didn't know them by sight, any one of them could be related in some way to the Clark family. She would have to stay on her guard.

'You're looking very serious all of a sudden, Ruby,' said Lucy with a soft nudge of her elbow. 'If you don't want the rest of that jelly, I'll have it.'

Ruby grinned, forgot about the girls at the end of the table and dug in her spoon. 'Not likely,' she said. 'I love a bit of jelly and custard.'

They finished their pudding in companionable silence as the talk went on around them. Ruby noticed the peroxide blonde had surrounded herself with some of the plainest, dumpiest young women, who were wide-eyed and enthralled as she regaled them with some story, and flashed sultry looks at the men who were admiring her from the next table.

It was typical of her type, Ruby thought sourly. She didn't want the competition, so picked the dowdy ones who were easily impressed by having such a glamorous, sophisticated person taking an interest in them. But the glamour was brassy, the sophistication about as real as the fake handbags on her stepfather's stall.

The hooter went. Lunchtime was over, and they all began to traipse back to their various factories. Lucy tucked her hand into Ruby's arm and they were happily planning a trip to the film show at the big church hall at the weekend when they were joined by the blonde.

'Hello. My name's Flora,' she said as she flicked back a wisp of hair that had become caught in her heavy mascara. 'Are you two sisters?'

'No,' said Lucy with a welcoming smile. 'We only met this morning. I'm Lucy, and this is Ruby.'

Flora eyed the linked arms. 'How sweet,' she murmured, and sauntered away, hands in her pockets, slim hips swaying in the tight trousers as she passed two gawping youths.

'See,' said Lucy. 'She's not all that bad.'

'Give her time,' muttered Ruby. 'She'll show her true colours soon enough.'

By the time their shift had ended they both had aching feet and a throbbing head. Their hands were filthy from the oily machines and some of it had smeared over their faces, so they went to the washrooms and cleaned themselves up before they left for home.

Lucy took off the scarf and handed it back before brushing out her long fair hair. 'I'll bring my own tomorrow and some cotton wool to stuff in my ears. My head's ringing with all the noise.'

'So's mine,' Ruby admitted. 'And me plates are killing me far worse than they ever did after a session behind the bar in me high heels.'

'Plates?'

Ruby grinned. 'Yeah, plates of meat – feet.' They walked back into the late-afternoon sunshine. 'You got far to get home, Lucy?'

'Nowhere's too far away in Cliffehaven,' she replied. She pointed towards the west and the sea. 'I live down there near Havelock Gardens. It's very nice, with a lovely sea view from the back of the house.' Her eyes sparkled. 'Why don't you come with me? I'm sure Mother would love to meet you, and we could have tea in the garden.'

Ruby could think of nothing she'd like better, but there was an alarm clock to buy and Mrs Fraser would soon be cooking the evening meal, and she needed to be there to make sure she got a proper share of it. 'Sorry, Lucy, not tonight. I got things to do. But I'd love to come another day.'

'I'll hold you to that.' Lucy smiled shyly back at her. 'Thanks for being so nice today, Ruby. I don't know what I'd have done without you.'

'You'd've been fine. Now, I need to get to the shops, so I'll walk with you as far as the High Street.'

They set off, happily chatting about films and Hollywood stars, and soon came to the station, where there was still no sight of the elusive Stan. Lucy pointed out where the cinema had once been. 'There was talk of building a new one, but now that the Americans have provided us with a projector and turned part of the big hall into a cinema, there's no need. We can get all the latest films, and there's a cup of tea and a biscuit in the interval as well.'

They came to the small ironmonger's and Ruby drew to a halt. 'This is as far as I go, Lucy. I'll see you tomorrow.'

Lucy sketched a little wave goodbye, swung her gas-mask box from her hand and almost skipped down the road towards the sparkling blue of the sea.

Ruby watched until she was out of sight, and thought how nice it must be to have the freedom from any real worries or responsibilities. But with every word and gesture the yawning chasm of class and education widened between them, and Ruby wondered if this blossoming friendship would shrivel away once they acknowledged neither of them had a thing in common but work on a factory floor.

She rather hoped it would last and become something important to both of them despite their many differences, for each had something to give and it was lovely to feel like a young girl again, to forget momentarily about everything she'd left behind and talk about clothes and the pictures and giggle about nothing in particular.

With a warm smile she returned Lucy's wave as she reached her turning, and then went into the gloomy interior of the ironmonger's and found a cheap alarm clock. Tucking it, and the change, into her gas-mask box, she then headed back up the steep hill towards Nelson Street and the dubious delights of Mon Repos.

Mrs Fraser was boiling the ham bone with pearl barley, onions and chopped vegetables. Potatoes were simmering in a nearby pan and some pale fillets of fish were being poached in watery milk in a saucepan. The house stank of fish, but at least it looked as if there was to be a decent meal that night.

Ruby asked politely if she could help with anything, and Mrs Fraser told her that, no, she had it all under control. 'Then I'll just get changed out of me work clothes and come and help you dish up,' said Ruby.

She dashed upstairs, checked on her hidden stash of money and then changed into one of her worn cotton dresses and pulled on a cardigan. It was still warm, and she had no plans to go walking round the town once it got dark, so there was little point in wearing her good clothes. After tea she would sit down and write a long letter to her mother which she'd post to Fred at the Tanner's Arms first thing tomorrow. It could take a fair bit of effort, because she'd never found writing very easy, and by then it would be time for bed so she was fresh for the morning.

Back in the kitchen the soup was ladled into bowls and taken into the dining room, where Harold Fraser was already sitting at the table. He still wore his three-piece suit with the watch-chain across the straining buttons of his waistcoat.

He looked up from his evening paper and eyed Ruby through the thick lenses of his glasses as she put the soup in front of him. 'I see the worker has returned,' he said with an oily smile. 'And how was your first day, Ruby?'

'It were all right,' she said as she sat down. 'The work ain't hard, and I made a new friend, but me head and me feet was hurting something rotten by the end of the day.'

'That's nice, dear,' said Mrs Fraser, who clearly wasn't really listening.

'Simpson's is a reputable firm,' said Harold. 'I have known Arthur Simpson for years, and I'm sure that if I had a word with him, he could find you something less tiring to do.'

Ruby felt the swift, slight pressure of his knee and glared at him. 'Thanks all the same, but I'm not looking for favours, Councillor Fraser, and I ain't unhappy on the production line.'

He smirked before turning his attention to the thin soup. 'Well, if you change your mind, Ruby, you only have to say.'

Hell would freeze over before she went to him for anything, for there would be a price to pay with such a man. She glanced across at Marjory Fraser, but she was engrossed in a magazine and didn't seem to notice the tension in the room.

Ruby drank the soup and tried not to slurp it as she usually did. It didn't taste too bad, but could have done with a bit of salt and pepper to liven it up, and perhaps a bit of bread. But there was no bread on the table again tonight and she realised Mrs Fraser was not in the habit of serving it with tea.

The fish was pale and overcooked, the potatoes white and mushy with only a hint of butter, and the peas were like small green bullets. Pudding turned out to be a rice pudding that was as palatable as soft cardboard and just as thin. It seemed that Mrs Fraser's cooking abilities were non-existent – but it was a proper meal, with fair portions all round, so she couldn't really complain.

Ruby helped to clear the table, brushing non-existent crumbs from the cloth with a special little brush and pan. Then she dried the dishes and put them away while Mrs Fraser made a pot of tea.

'Mr Fraser is going to a council meeting this evening,' said Marjory once they'd drunk the tea. 'And I am attending our twice-weekly knitting circle. Neither of us is expected back before ten o'clock, so if you wish to take a bath, then do so.'

Ruby wasn't at all sure she did want to take a bath, but she listened dutifully to the long list of dos and don'ts and promised firmly that she would scrub out the tin tub when she'd finished and polish the kitchen linoleum of any spills.

They left the house half an hour later and Ruby watched them from her bedroom window as they went arm-in-arm down Nelson Street, As they reached the curve that would take them out of sight, Harold glanced over his shoulder at her window as if he was aware of her behind the curtains.

Ruby shifted back into the shadows and, after a moment's thought, returned to writing her letter. She didn't think it was wise to tell her mother or Fred Bowman exactly where she was, but she described the town, her billet and the job at the factory, and said she was well. It wasn't a long letter, but she had to concentrate hard on each word, and it took nearly an hour before she'd finished it.

Having addressed the envelope carefully to 'Mr Bowman Esq., The Tanner's Arms, Leather Lane, Bow, London', she licked the stamp, pressed it firmly in place and put the letter in her gas-mask box to be posted first thing tomorrow.

It was getting dark outside now, so she used the outside lavatory and ignored the tin tub hanging on the wall. Returning to the kitchen, she made a strong mug of tea, loaded it with sugar, and after checking on the time, went back to her room.

Once she'd jammed the chair under the doorknob and pulled the blackout curtains, she wound up the cheap clock, put the hands to the correct time and set the alarm. Then she drank her tea, stripped off her clothes and had a good wash in the basin before rinsing out her underwear and leaving it to dry on the towel rail. Tomorrow, she vowed, she would find out where the public baths were.

The house was very quiet, so when she heard the soft click of the front door closing she stilled instantly, the hairs rising on the back of her neck.

The door to the kitchen was being opened now, followed by muffled footsteps on the hall carpet and the creak of the bottom stair.

Ruby slipped on her clean pants and vest, turned off the light and sat on the edge of the bed and watched the door. The illuminated dial of her new clock showed it was eight-thirty, and that definitely wasn't the heavy-footed Marjory Fraser coming up the stairs.

She didn't have long to wait before she saw the doorknob turning. She held her breath, but the door didn't budge, and with a hiss of annoyance, the footsteps retreated back down the stairs.

Her mouth was dry and her heart was hammering against her ribs as she sank back into the pillows with relief. Her instincts had been proved right once again and she was very relieved that she'd followed them, for she'd known from the moment Harold Fraser had glanced back at her window that he'd return early in the hope of catching her in the bath.

The thought of those greedy little eyes trawling all over her made her shiver, and she vowed that she'd never use that tin tub. She opened the blackout curtains and lay on her bed watching the moon rise above the rooftops as her thoughts raced. Harold clearly couldn't be trusted, and although she could lock herself away in here at night, she couldn't avoid him completely. It was like living with Ray all over again – her nerves on a knife-edge, waiting for him to pounce.

The woman at the billeting office had said to go to her with any problem she might have, but would she be believed? She doubted it very

215

much, for the Frasers were hugely respected in this town and she was an outsider. They would think of her as a troublemaker – which would not only jeopardise her chances of getting another billet, but probably get her the sack from Harold's friend's factory as well.

Perhaps she could ask Lucy if her mother would be willing to take her in? But then how could she possibly explain why she needed to leave the Frasers, who were clearly great friends of Lucy's family? It was an impossible situation, she realised, and until something happened to change it, she was stuck here to fight her corner alone.

She closed her eyes on the tears that threatened, refusing to let them fall and weaken her resolve. She'd been through worse and would survive – but at this very moment, all she really wanted was the feel of her mother's loving arms around her, and the consolation of hearing her voice again.

Chapter Thirteen

As the day had waned the women had drifted back to their own homes and the men had finished their building work. Doris settled into Peggy's bedroom and began to write lists of all the things she wanted done over the next few days. Phyllis sulkily peeled the vegetables for the evening meal while Rita, Fran and Ron found an inordinate number of things to do that kept them out of the kitchen and as far from Doris as possible. Even Harvey was affected by the tension, for he never left Ron's side as he worked in the garden.

Ron had waylaid Sarah, Jane and Suzy as they had come home from work, and prepared them as best he could for Doris's presence in the house. Jane and Sarah had yet to meet Peggy's sister and therefore didn't really know what to expect, but Ron painted a picture that left them in little doubt that she was a very different kettle of fish to Peggy.

He'd warned them not to say a word to Peggy about the upset Doris had already caused, or about the damage that had been done to Beach View during the raid. None of them had looked very happy about keeping things from Peggy – and Suzy was horrified at the thought of having Doris at such close quarters – but as they didn't want to worry Peggy while she was so ill, they accepted his reasoning and promised to try and avoid any further confrontation.

Ron had done all he could to take the sting out of a nasty situation, and now he'd taken himself off with Harvey, his pipe and newspaper to his resurrected shed for a bit of peace and quiet before he went to the hospital with Rita to pick up Cordelia and Daisy. The warm, mild weather continued as the sun slowly sank beyond the rooftops, and it was very pleasant sitting here in a deckchair in the shed doorway looking out at the garden.

The pile of hard core would be collected by the council workers in the morning to be used to fill bomb craters in the roads, or as foundations for the emergency housing they were building up behind the station. The bonfire had long since gone out, leaving a pile of ash in the corner which, once cold, he would dig in round his surviving vegetables as a good fertiliser.

Sarah and Jane had taken in the washing now it was dry and were planning to iron it after tea, Fran and Phyllis were cooking the evening meal under the gimlet eye of Doris, and Suzy was checking on Cordelia's bedroom to make sure everything was ready for her return from hospital.

Ron's pleasant reverie was broken by Rita. 'I've borrowed one of the fire station vans,' she said. 'It's time we went to fetch Cordelia and Daisy.'

Ron eyed the three brown paper parcels in her arms. 'What are those for?'

'Clean clothes for Daisy and Grandma Finch, and nightclothes and wash bag for Peggy,' she replied. 'Suzy sorted them out because of course the clothes they'd been wearing would be filthy after all that rubbish fell on them, and Peggy will need a nightdress and hairbrush and things.'

The thought of clean clothing had never occurred to him – but then he had a house full of women who were adept at spotting such needs, and for once, he was grateful for it. He tipped some dog biscuit into a bowl and carried it into the scullery, where he ordered Harvey to stay until one of the girls let him out. Shutting the doors to the kitchen and garden firmly on his pitiful howls, he could only hope he didn't carry on like that for too long, otherwise he and Harvey would get it in the neck from Doris.

Rita drove the small van along Camden Road and into the hospital forecourt. Parking close to the steps so Cordelia wouldn't have far to walk, they hurried inside.

'I'll collect Daisy while you fetch Grandma Finch,' said Rita as they both reached the landing at the top of the long flight of stairs and she handed him one of the parcels. 'Then we'll drop in quickly on Peggy so we can give her the nightclothes and she can see that Daisy and Cordelia are all right before Cissy turns up.'

Ron had forgotten that Cissy was due to visit her mother this evening – but then he'd had so many things to worry about over the past few hours it was amazing he still remembered what day it was. 'Aye. I'll meet you there,' he said gruffly.

He strode off towards Women's Medical while Rita ran up yet another long flight of stairs to get to the nursery. This damned place was like a maze, and totally unsuited to the halt and the lame that had to negotiate the endless corridors and treacherous flights of marble stairs to get anywhere. There was a lift, but it rattled and shuddered so alarmingly that it was used only when absolutely necessary.

He arrived at the ward and peered through the circular windows in the double doors. Cordelia was sitting in a bedside chair in a hospital dressing gown, her arm in a casing of plaster and a sling. Her little face was bruised and he could see scratches on her cheeks and brow where she'd been hit by flying glass and concrete. It was a miracle that any of them had survived, and his heart swelled with deep affection and relief as he

219

pushed through the doors and headed straight for her.

'How are you, old girl?' he asked awkwardly.

Fierce blue eyes glared back at him despite the twitch of a smile at the corners of her mouth. 'I'm extremely well, thank you – old fellow. What kept you? It's almost six and I've been waiting for hours to get out of this place.'

'We've had a bit of a busy day, Cordelia, and as you were safely tucked in here, you were not at the top of my list of priorities.' He grinned and winked at her as he dumped the parcel of clothing on the bed. 'Suzy packed you some clean clothes,' he muttered. 'Will you need help getting dressed?'

Her eyes widened and she went scarlet. 'Not from you, you old rogue. Ask one of the nurses to come and help me.'

Ron backed away quickly, found a nurse and hovered by the doors as the curtains were drawn around the bed. He felt uneasy as he stood there under the curious gaze of eleven women in their nightclothes, and could only hope that Cordelia would hurry up.

The double doors swung back and almost pinned him to the wall as the doughty figure of Matron strode into the ward. Her gimlet gaze fell on him immediately. 'Mr Reilly,' she boomed. 'What are you doing lurking on my ward?'

He knew her of old, for he'd once been a patient here and had made his escape from her and the torture of this hospital on the back of Rita's motorbike. That escapade had become a bit of a legend in Cliffehaven, and rumour had it that she'd never quite forgiven him. 'I'm here to

220

take Mrs Finch home,' he replied.

'Then you can wait in the corridor.' She held a door open and he edged through it. 'Men are not allowed on this ward outside visiting time,' she said flatly.

Ron dared to glance at the clock on the wall. 'To be sure, Matron, there's but a minute to go, and Cordelia–'

'I've had quite enough nonsense from you, Mr Reilly. You'll do as you're told and stay here.' With that, she let the doors slam together again and marched off down the ward to Cordelia's bed.

Ron chewed on the stem of his pipe, not quite daring to light it in case Matron appeared again and did something unpleasant with it. 'Come on, Cordelia. What's taking you so long?' he muttered as he paced back and forth.

The minutes dragged by and eventually a little nurse held the doors open as another steered a regal Cordelia from the ward in a wheelchair. It seemed Matron was thankfully busy at the far end of the ward.

'Here we are, Mr Reilly,' the nurse said with a beaming smile. 'Mrs Finch is to rest and take it easy for a while, and here is an Outpatients' appointment for six weeks' time when the doctor will remove the plaster cast.'

Cordelia beamed and thanked both the girls before she looked up at Ron. 'I'd like to visit Peggy and make sure she's all right before we go home,' she said as the nurse settled the parcel of dirty clothes in her lap.

'Aye, we're meeting Rita and Daisy there before Cissy arrives.' He grasped the wheelchair handles.

'Are you ready, old girl? Hang on then, off we go.'

'Ron, stop it,' she protested with a giggle as they sped down the corridor. 'You're going far too fast and it's making me giddy.'

'Ach, to be sure, 'tis giddy you've always been, Cordelia, and it's nice to see you smiling again.' He slowed down and followed the signs to Women's Surgical, assured that he wouldn't get it in the neck from Matron now it was officially visiting time.

Peggy was feeling slightly more awake and able to take in things more clearly. She had shed some tears through the day for her lost baby and for the absence of her darling Jim who had yet to telephone home. How she longed to feel his strong arms about her, to know he was close and would help her to see this thing through. But of course he couldn't be here and she should be grateful for the caring skills of the lovely nurses, for the pain was being managed, and it only hurt now if she coughed or moved too quickly.

She was resting back on a mound of pillows, Daisy held tightly to her side in the crook of her arm. It was far too painful to lift her and of course she couldn't take any pressure on her poor stomach. 'She's so lovely,' she murmured as she softly fingered back the dark curls and blinked back her tears. 'Thank God she wasn't hurt, Rita. I don't know what I would have done if I'd lost her as well.'

'We're all thankful no one was seriously hurt last night,' Rita replied. 'It was a miracle, really, considering how much damage was done further

222

up the hill.'

Peggy immediately looked concerned. 'Was it very bad at Beach View, Rita? Is it still safe to live there?'

Rita patted her hand. 'As safe as it's ever been,' she soothed. 'There was a bit of damage to the scullery, but a couple of my friends at the fire station soon fixed that, and a whole army of women turned up to clean the place from top to bottom.'

'Oh, how kind,' Peggy sighed. 'How very thoughtful of them to do such a thing when they must have their own homes and families to look after.'

'They did it because they love you, Auntie Peg,' said Rita, 'and because you've always been a good friend and neighbour.'

Peggy hugged Daisy close, her little finger closely grasped by a tiny hand. 'People are so good, aren't they?' she murmured. 'I feel very blessed.'

She looked up and saw Ron struggling to wheel Cordelia through the double doors. 'Oh my goodness,' she breathed. 'Poor Cordelia.' Tears blinded her as she noted the bruises and cuts and the arm in the sling. She was a selfish, thoughtless woman, for she'd been so wrapped up in her own misery that she hadn't given darling Cordelia more than a passing thought.

As Ron parked the wheelchair by the bed Peggy held out her hand to Cordelia and the two women gently embraced. 'I'm so glad you're safe,' Peggy murmured as she dashed away the tears. 'Thank you for making the effort to come and see me.'

'Well, of course I had to see you before I went

home. I wanted to make sure you and little Daisy had come through all right.' Her blue eyes were bright with unshed tears. 'I was so sorry to hear about everything,' she said softly as she held Peggy's hand. 'But you'll come through this, Peggy, just like you do with everything else.'

'I'm sure I will,' she replied with a brave little smile, 'but at the moment I feel as if I've been flattened by a steamroller.'

'We're a couple of crocks, aren't we?' Cordelia joked as she fidgeted in the wheelchair. 'I feel positively ancient being carted about in this thing – and Ron's driving skills are questionable to say the least – but without my walking stick, I would never have made it down those endless corridors.'

Peggy regarded her closely. 'But apart from your arm, is everything else all right?'

Cordelia grinned. 'About as right as it ever was, if you discount age, decrepitude and general wear and tear.' She shrugged. 'Unfortunately I won't be of much use to anyone with my arm in this,' she said, pointing to the plaster cast. 'But I'm sure Ron and the girls will manage just fine until you get home, so you're not to worry about a thing.'

Peggy suddenly realised the seriousness of the situation and looked helplessly at Ron. 'But how can you possibly manage with all your other responsibilities?' she asked him. 'Daisy needs someone to watch over her all the time, and so will Cordelia, and the girls are so busy with their work...'

Ron cleared his throat. 'Well now, Peggy, you see there is a solution, and no doubt you'll find out soon enough, so I won't beat about the bush...' He shuffled his feet and stared at the floor.

Peggy was alarmed. 'What solution, Ron? For goodness' sake stop dithering and tell me.'

'Doris has moved in.'

Peggy closed her eyes and took a long, deep breath. 'Good grief,' she sighed. She opened her eyes again. 'Please tell me you're joking, Ron.'

'He's not,' said Rita. 'She moved in this afternoon, and when we left to come here, she had Phyllis and Fran cooking the tea.'

'Well,' said Cordelia with a humph of displeasure. 'That just about puts the tin lid on it, doesn't it? How long is she planning on staying?'

'Until Peggy is well enough to come home,' admitted Ron. He reached for Peggy's hand. 'You are not to fret about this, Peg, do you hear? The girls and me have agreed to carry on as usual and not let Doris get under our skins, no matter how difficult it might be. There will be peace and harmony, Peggy. I promise.'

'Not if my sister has anything to do with it,' said Peggy fretfully. 'But it's so unlike Doris to be charitable to me and mine like this – let alone to actually move into Beach View, which she's always loathed. There has to be a reason behind this, but I'm blowed if I can think what it might be.' She clutched his hand. 'Oh, Ron,' she sighed. 'I'm so sorry you've been left with all this to deal with.'

'I've dealt with worse,' he said with a wink. 'The Hun didn't get me in the trenches, and neither will Doris – so you rest easy and concentrate on getting better.'

Peggy reached up and tugged at his jacket collar until she could plant a kiss on his whiskery cheek.

225

'I'll be home before you know it,' she said softly. 'Thank you, Ron.'

Ron cleared his throat and actually went red. 'Yes, well, we'd better get these two home. Cissy will be here in a minute and this old woman probably needs a decent cup of tea after the dishwater they serve in this place.'

Peggy blew a kiss to Cordelia and then nuzzled and kissed Daisy before Rita plucked her from her arms. 'Promise me that one of you will bring her in every day.'

'I promise, Auntie Peg – and don't worry about Daisy, we all love her as if she was our own, and we'll take very special care of her.'

Peggy kissed her goodbye and watched as they left the ward with her precious little Daisy. She felt bereft all over again, and the ready tears fell as she thought of them being at home without her – and the difficulties they would all have to face over the next few weeks.

What made it worse was the prospect of Doris reigning over her home. What on earth had possessed her sister to take on such a challenge when she knew nothing of running a busy household or looking after a baby? She'd always had cleaners and cooks and gardeners before the war; still employed poor little Phyllis to do the rough work – and had had a nanny to look after Anthony from the moment she'd taken him home from the hospital.

She lay there imagining the sort of hurt her sister's spiteful tongue could cause, and the chaos she would bring to the easy-going routine of Beach View. She didn't doubt that she'd look

226

after Daisy, and that her home would probably be cleaner than ever before – but that wasn't the point. Beach View had its own heart and soul, and a woman like Doris could rip them out in an instant and destroy everything.

'There's only one thing for it,' she muttered. 'I'm going to have to get better very quickly – and the only way to do that is to get out of this bed and start moving about.'

She tugged at the blanket and sheet and sat up. A knife of pain shot through her, making her gasp, but she determinedly edged to the side of the bed and swung her legs down. As her feet touched the floor and she stood, she had to bend into the deep ache in her wound. But she would not be defeated, and she cradled her heavily bandaged scar with her hands as she began to shuffle down the ward. She must look like an old crone, she thought, but she didn't care, for there was a definite thrill of achievement gained with every step – the threat of Doris taking over at Beach View focussing her mind and bolstering her determination to get home as soon as possible.

'What *do* you think you're doing, Mrs Reilly?'

Peggy looked up to find herself staring into the granite features of the dreaded Matron. 'I need to go to the lav,' she replied.

'You will use a bedpan,' said Matron. She placed a very firm hand around Peggy's skinny arm and began to steer her slowly back to bed. 'I have had enough trouble already from your father-in-law, Mrs Reilly, and I will not stand any further nonsense from you.'

Peggy tried to free herself from her grip, but

simply didn't have the strength. 'I'm a mother and grandmother and I will not be spoken to as if I'm a naughty child,' she gasped as the pain surged through her and the room began to swim.

'If you behave as a child, you will be treated like one, Mrs Reilly. I seem to remember having the same conversation with that disreputable old father-in-law of yours.' Matron eased her down onto the bed. 'This is my hospital, Mrs Reilly, and all the time you are in it, you will do what I tell you without argument.' The grey eyes were steely as they looked down the long beaked nose. 'Is that understood?'

'Completely,' said Peggy, who had absolutely no intention of following her draconian orders.

'Good. You will soon be allowed to sit in the bedside chair, and then in about two weeks you will be permitted to walk to the end of the ward and back.'

Peggy stared up at her in horror. 'How long will I have to be in here?'

'At least a month,' Matron replied tartly as she drew the curtains round the bed and marched off in search of a nurse with a bedpan.

'I'll give it ten days – two weeks at the most,' Peggy muttered. 'You're not keeping me in here when my family needs me, you old dragon.'

Rita parked the van close to the front steps and Ron handed her Daisy before helping Cordelia onto the pavement. He glanced up at the front door, knowing that Doris was waiting somewhere behind it, and a long evening stretched ahead for all of them.

It was the first time in his life that he dreaded coming home and the realisation sickened him, but he put on a brave smile for the others, determined to make the best of things. 'Would you be after me carrying you up the steps, Cordelia?'

'I'm not a cripple or in my dotage just yet,' she retorted. 'I can manage perfectly well if you could just give me your arm.'

He let her grasp his arm as she made her slow way up the steps to the front door. Rita opened it and they were almost immediately swamped by the girls rushing to welcome them home. Daisy was plucked from Rita's arms by Fran, Suzy and Sarah took charge of Cordelia, and Jane gave Ron a hug and took the parcel of dirty clothing from him. 'She's in the kitchen,' she said in a hoarse whisper before hurrying off.

Everyone was talking at once and Ron left them to it. There was no sign of Harvey. From the sound of his frantic barking, it seemed he was still shut in the cellar. Ron stomped into the kitchen and found Doris sitting in Peggy's chair reading a magazine while Phyllis battled with the saucepans on the range.

Ron didn't bother to speak to either of them as he went to open the cellar door and was almost bowled over by an overjoyed Harvey. He ruffled his ears and patted his back as the dog licked his face and tried to climb up into his arms. 'Why did no one let the dog out?' Ron demanded as the girls trooped into the room with Daisy and Cordelia.

'It's not hygienic to allow a dog in the house,' said Doris. 'I gave strict orders to leave him there.'

'You do not – ever – shut my dog out of the house,' he said gruffly.

'But it was you who shut him in the cellar to begin with,' she said with maddening logic. She remained seated, the magazine on her lap. 'If you must insist upon that animal having free rein in here, then it should be kept under control. It's clearly undisciplined and far too big to be galloping about when there's a baby's welfare to consider.'

'Harvey is part of the family,' he replied, struggling to keep his temper, 'and he will have the freedom of this house as he has always done. Daisy will come to no harm from him.'

Doris balefully eyed the dog, who didn't seem to realise he was the subject of this tussle and rather spoiled everything by sniffing at Daisy and giving her face a resounding lick. 'That is precisely the sort of behaviour I will not allow,' she said coldly. 'Francis, you will wash Daisy immediately and prepare her for bed.'

Fran glanced at Ron, and at his nod, took Daisy to the sink and began to clear it of the dirty cooking pots and fill it with warm water.

'What on *earth* are you doing?' said Doris, aghast.

Fran tucked her wild auburn curls behind her ears and frowned. 'Well to be sure, Mrs Williams, I'm following your orders and washing Daisy.'

'Not in the sink!' she snapped. 'Good grief, girl, what sort of upbringing did you have?' The magazine fell to the floor as she stood and advanced on Fran.

'But Peggy always washes her in the kitchen,'

protested Fran, 'and I can see no harm in it.'

Doris snatched Daisy from Fran and dumped her in a rather startled Phyllis's arms. 'See to her, Phyllis – in the bathroom upstairs. Then bring her back for her bottle.'

Daisy didn't think much of being passed from pillar to post in such a rough manner, and started to yell, throwing herself back in Phyllis's arms so violently that it was only by a miracle that Phyllis didn't drop her.

Ron stepped in and took Daisy, holding her against his shoulder, his large, rough hand gentling her as she howled furiously in his ear. 'I will see to my granddaughter,' he said firmly. 'Someone give Cordelia a cup of tea, and the rest of you get on with laying the table, and dishing up tea. It's way past six and me stomach's so empty it's clinging to me backbone, so it is.'

Doris looked at him with undisguised disgust. '*Supper* will be eaten in the dining room from now on,' she said. 'And it will be served at eight.'

'I prefer to have my evening meal in the kitchen at six o'clock,' said Cordelia, who'd silently watched everything from her chair by the table. 'And it is a convenient time for the girls when they come in from work.' She regarded Doris with little affection. 'This is a busy household and the routine we already have suits all of us.'

Doris sniffed and eyed all of them disdainfully. 'In that case, I will have Phyllis bring supper on a tray to my bedroom.'

Cordelia smiled up at Phyllis. 'Are you moving in here as well, dear?' she asked.

'Of course she isn't,' snapped Doris. 'She has

231

her own home to go to.'

'As sweet and helpful as no doubt she is,' said Cordelia mildly, 'I do hope you're not expecting us to pay for her services.'

'Phyllis has a fixed wage and I will, of course, continue to pay that,' said Doris stiffly.

Cordelia reached for Phyllis's hand and gave her a warm, sweet smile. 'Are you happy about that, dear? Only you seem to work very long hours.'

'My arrangements with my staff are none of your business, Mrs Finch,' said Doris flatly. 'Phyllis, get on with the cooking, and mind you don't boil those potatoes to a watery mush.'

Phyllis swallowed and blushed, her gaze darting to Doris and back to Cordelia. 'I don't mind,' she stammered. 'Not really.' She ducked her chin so her hair veiled her face as she checked on the vegetables boiling away on the hob.

Cordelia watched her for a moment and then accepted the cup of tea from Suzy. Grasping it in her good hand, she blew on it to cool it down and took a tentative sip. 'Oh, that's better,' she sighed. 'A proper cup of tea at last. You wouldn't believe the dishwater they serve in that hospital.'

'There is a war on,' said Doris with a sniff. 'One can't expect luxuries now, you know.'

Cordelia's bright blue eyes regarded her over her half-moon glasses and slowly took in the angora sweater, the pearls, tweed skirt and expensive shoes. Her smile was enigmatic, her silence eloquent as her gaze drifted to the gold lighter and the rare packet of Sobranie cigarettes before returning to hold Doris's defiant glare.

Ron felt a warm glow of pride as he watched

this little show of strength from Cordelia. Doris had met her match, and it amused him to realise that gentleness and calm were powerful weapons. He hunted about for Daisy's clean nappies. They were usually stacked on the dresser, but for the life of him, he couldn't see them anywhere.

'I have put all of Daisy's clean clothes in the airing cupboard upstairs, and her toiletries are in the bathroom,' said Doris. 'It's unhygienic to change her in the kitchen.'

Ron followed Cordelia's lead and said nothing as he left the room with Daisy and clumped upstairs, Harvey shadowing his heels. 'To be sure, 'tis a fine thing to be ordered about in your own home,' he muttered as he gathered up a pile of nappies, a clean nightdress and the little tin of baby powder. 'We'll have you all warm and dry again, never you fear.'

He returned to the kitchen, dumped most of the nappies onto the dresser and carried Daisy down to his basement room to change her. It wasn't the most ideal place, but he was damned if he would let Daisy get chilled in that freezing bathroom. Once she was clean and dressed for bed, he wrapped the blanket round her again and went back up to the kitchen to find everyone but Doris sitting at the table.

'I've done her a little bowl of veg and gravy,' said Rita, 'and her bottle's ready.' She handed him a bib. 'You might need this,' she murmured. 'Daisy's a messy eater.'

Ron gave her a grateful smile and settled down to feed his granddaughter while Suzy put his plate of dinner in the slow oven to keep warm, and

Sarah cut Cordelia's food into tiny pieces so she could eat it with just a fork. There was no sign of Doris, and he could only guess that she'd taken herself off to her bedroom to await her supper tray.

'Are ye not sitting down to eat with us, Phyllis?' he asked the girl, who was still clattering pots at the sink.

'I've got to get home to feed me dad,' she replied shyly. 'But thanks fer asking.'

Ron finished feeding Daisy and as her eyelids drooped and her thumb found its way to her mouth, he gently carried her out into the hall and placed her in the pram. She usually slept in her cot in Peggy's room, but with Doris in there, he thought it wiser not to disturb her.

As he tucked into his rabbit stew, Harvey drooling at his feet under the table, Phyllis laid a tray and carefully carried it out and tapped on Doris's door. Ron had never known the kitchen to be so quiet, and he asked Suzy to turn on the wireless.

'I'm on duty tonight,' said Rita as she eventually pushed away from the table. The others followed in quick succession, as if relieved to escape the dour atmosphere. Fran and Suzy went straight upstairs to do the ironing in their bedroom, while Sarah and her sister Jane helped a weary Cordelia to her room and helped her change for bed.

Phyllis came back into the kitchen, her little face wan from a very long, tiring day. 'I'll just wash the pots,' she said, 'then I'll be off home.'

'Leave them be,' Ron replied as he filled his pipe and settled back in his chair. 'I'll do them after I've given Harvey a bit of a run.'

Phyllis wiped her hands down her apron and

reached for her thin coat which hung on the back of the kitchen door. She shot a wary glance towards the hall, bit her lip and slowly pulled on the coat, her gaze darting to him from beneath her untidy fringe of hair.

Ron didn't know much about Phyllis, only that she lived with her widowed father who suffered from lung trouble contracted in the trenches during the last war. She was only a slip of a thing, barely eighteen, and not the brightest button in the box, but he sensed that given the chance, she could do very much better than slave for Doris. As he watched her, he realised she was working up the courage to say something. 'How's your dad coming along, Phyllis?' he asked.

'He's not getting any better really,' she replied softly. 'The doctor's ever so kind, but there isn't much he can do.'

'It must be hard for you to work such long hours and then go back home to care for a sick man,' he said, gently probing to get to whatever it was Phyllis had on her mind.

'I don't mind, Mr Reilly, only... Only the hours are a bit more than I really...' She fell silent and fiddled with the buttons on her coat.

'If all this is too much, then you must say,' he said kindly.

Her eyes were bright with tears as she looked back at him. 'Oh, Mr Reilly, I want to help while Peggy's so poorly, really I do,' she blurted out. 'But I'm eighteen now and should be doing something proper for the war effort. I got a letter from the Labour Exchange yesterday and there's a job going at the tool factory.'

She seemed to run out of steam and her shoulders slumped. 'I'm supposed to start next week and the money's three times what Mrs Williams pays me,' she said quietly. 'It would help no end to have a decent wage coming in, 'cos Dad's medicines cost a lot, and I don't always have enough at the end of the week to get him the fresh veg and meat he needs to get him better.'

Ron got up from the table and put his arm round Phyllis. 'Ach, you poor wee wain, that's a lot of responsibility for such narrow shoulders. Of course you must take the job. Doris will understand.'

'I don't think she will,' replied a tearful Phyllis. 'She'll be ever so cross, and when she's like that I just get all tongue-tied and muddled up and cave in.'

'Don't you fret now,' he soothed. 'I'll square things with her.'

Her little face brightened as she looked up at him. 'Will you, Mr Reilly?' she breathed. 'Oh, thank you. Thank you so much.'

Ron cleared his throat, dug in his trouser pockets and pulled out a ten-bob note. 'Why don't you take yourself off for the rest of the week so you can prepare yourself for your job in the factory?' he said as he pressed the note into her hand. 'I'll see to it that Doris sends on any money you're owed, but that should see you through for now.'

'Oh, Mr Reilly,' she breathed, 'you are kind.' She blinked away her tears and pocketed the money. 'I don't like leaving you in the lurch like this when Peggy's so ill. Are you sure you don't want me to–?'

'Go home,' he said firmly. 'Peggy will understand, and no doubt feel all the better knowing you're settled in a proper job and doing your bit for the war.' As she opened her mouth to thank him again, he gave her a small nudge towards the cellar door. 'Best you go the back way, Phyllis. Now hurry before the dragon comes out of her lair.'

She giggled and then hurried down the steps and out onto the back path.

Ron watched her go and returned her wave before she disappeared into the twilight. 'Best of luck, Phyllis,' he murmured. 'I hope things turn out all right for you.'

He returned to the kitchen and eyed the dirty plates and pots waiting to be washed. Rolling up the sleeves of his ragged sweater and fraying shirt, he stacked everything to one side and turned on the taps. 'Your walk will have to wait, Harvey,' he said to the patient dog still sitting under the table.

'I'll do that,' said Sarah as she came into the kitchen. 'Jane's reading to Aunt Cordelia, and the others are finishing the ironing, so I'm at a bit of a loose end.' She patted Harvey who'd come out from beneath the table to greet her, and then reached for an apron.

'Would it be all right if I leave you to it, walked Harvey and nipped into the Anchor to check on Pearl and Brenda? Only they've been left to their own devices all day, and there are bound to be barrels that need changing and crates brought up from the cellar.'

'Of course,' she said cheerfully. 'I'll keep an ear out for Daisy, never you mind.'

'Ach, you're a good wee girl, so y'are.'

'Where's Phyllis?'

They both turned to see Doris entering the kitchen with her supper tray. 'I sent her home,' said Ron.

'You had no right to do that,' she said, dumping the tray on the table. 'There are still things I need her to do.'

Ron realised it would be better to get this over and done with as quickly as possible. 'That's as maybe,' he replied, 'but she'll not be back, Doris. She's handed in her notice.'

Doris waved this announcement away with a flick of her hand. 'She's always giving in her notice,' she said. 'She'll be back soon enough.'

'Not this time,' he said evenly. 'She's eighteen and has been allocated a job at the tool factory.'

Doris stared at him, the colour draining from beneath the carefully applied make-up. 'But she can't,' she breathed. 'I need her to help me here.'

'Her country needs her more,' said Ron. 'Don't worry, Doris. You'll soon get the hang of things around here, and with so many willing hands I'm sure you won't miss her one little bit.'

Doris stared at him, her mouth twitching as a tic pulsed in her neck. Ron watched, fascinated by the way her face muscles worked and a strange light came into her eyes. If he hadn't known her so well, he might have seen the light as tears, the expression one of profound loss tinged with fear. But before he could get his mind around such a strange phenomenon, she had turned on her heel and left the room.

'What a very odd reaction,' murmured Sarah.

'Aye,' muttered Ron. 'I've never liked the woman, but for a moment there she looked almost lost and vulnerable and I nearly forgot m'self and felt sorry for her.'

He pondered on this as he remembered what Peggy had said earlier. He grabbed his poacher's coat from the door hook. 'You know, Sarah, I'm wondering if there's not more to this than meets the eye.'

'How do you mean?'

'I'm not sure,' he admitted, 'but I have a suspicion that there's another motive behind this act of charity she's foisted upon us – for it's out of character, so it is – and the Doris I know never does anything that is not to her own advantage.'

Sarah eyed him quizzically as she dumped the cutlery into the hot soapy water. 'It's been a long, hard slog since dawn, and we're all exhausted,' she said. 'Are you sure you're not just imagining things, Uncle Ron?'

He shrugged into his coat as Harvey stood on the cellar steps waiting for him. 'Time will tell, Sarah,' he murmured as he pulled on his cap. 'But I'll lay odds on being right.'

Chapter Fourteen

Ruby had been living with the Frasers for two weeks, and in that time Harold had twice tried her door in the middle of the night, and his knee rubbed against her leg every time they sat at the dining room table. So far, she'd managed never to be alone with him, but she was getting tired of always being on her guard and had begun to think seriously about finding another billet.

Once again there was little food to be had for breakfast this morning, and although she'd been sorely tempted to cook one of Marjory Fraser's precious eggs, she hadn't quite got the nerve, so made do with toast and dripping and the heel of a bit of stale cheese. It didn't taste very nice, but it lined her stomach and the two big mugs of sweet tea filled her up nicely.

She had tiptoed back to her room and wedged the door shut while she retrieved her hidden stash of money and tucked it deep into the pockets of her dungarees. Her shift finished at four today, and this was the first chance she'd had to get to the post office and open an account before she went in search of Stan at the station. He was a difficult man to find, for he seemed to be absent from his post a great deal and she had no idea where he lived. The lovely red scarf was still tucked in with her gas mask, and she was determined to give it to him before yet another week passed. Having checked the room was neat and tidy, she put the chair back and opened the door.

'Well, good morning,' said Harold, who was again resplendent in his dressing gown and slippers as he stood squarely on the landing and barred her way. 'My goodness, you are an early bird, aren't you?'

'I'm on early shift and don't like to waste the day,' she replied. She eyed him coolly. 'Excuse me, Mr Fraser, but I have to get to work.'

240

'Please, Ruby, don't be so formal after all this time of living here,' he said as he came towards her. 'You must call me Harry.'

Ruby's back was almost pressed against her bedroom door, but she was also aware that Marjory was only in the next room and she doubted dear 'Harry' would risk anything much within her hearing. 'I were always taught to be formal with them what's a lot older than me,' she said flatly. 'Especially when they're in their nightclothes.' She took a small step away from the door. 'I gotta go to work, Mr Fraser, and you're in me way.'

'Harry, what's going on out there?' Marjory's voice drifted out to them from her bedroom.

'Nothing, dear,' he called back. 'Just passing the time of day with Ruby.'

Ruby took advantage of this distraction and tried to dodge past him.

But Harold was a fast mover for a fat man and in the blink of an eye he had her pinned against the wall, his soft belly pressing into her as his hands grasped her hips and his hot breath feathered her face.

Ruby stamped the heel of her heavy boot on his toes and ground it in as hard as she could. 'Do that again, and it'll be me knee in yer nuts,' she hissed.

'What on earth is going on out there? Harold? Harold?'

Harold's eyes were watering as he hopped about and tried to stifle the howl of pain and answer his wife.

Ruby fled down the stairs and slammed the front door behind her. She ran along Nelson Street, past the dairy and the allotments and finally reached the high fence that surrounded the factory estate.

She stopped for breath and began to chuckle at the memory of Harold's startled face and the way he'd hopped about in silent agony as his wife continued to question him from the other side of her bedroom door. He was a dirty old man and it served him right.

Ruby's laughter soon died and she sank onto a nearby garden wall, her thoughts very troubled. Harold would be furious about what she'd done this morning, and would probably be even more determined to have his wicked way with her. The situation wasn't at all funny; it was escalating too quickly. Sooner rather than later, Harold would make another move – and she might not be able to fight him off next time.

'You're looking terribly serious for such a lovely morning,' said Lucy as she came to sit beside her. 'Whatever's happened?'

Ruby thought about telling her and instantly dismissed the idea. Lucy was too young and innocent and would be horrified, tell her mother, and then all hell would break loose. 'I just didn't get a good night's sleep,' she replied instead.

'Poor old you,' said Lucy in sympathy as she knotted the square of bright blue cotton over her hair. 'With no raids on last night, I slept like a log.'

Ruby stood and hitched up her dungaree straps. 'It was probably the quiet that kept me awake,' she said lightly. 'I'm used to the noise going on all night every night back in London.'

They walked to the gate and showed their identity cards and then made their way towards the factory. 'You know, Ruby, even with the cotton wool in my ears, my head is still ringing for at least an hour after I get home.'

'So does mine,' said Flora as she joined them. 'And I've had to cut my lovely nails,' she said ruefully as she flashed them in front of Ruby. 'That Mabel's a right cow, isn't she? On my case all day, every day, just because I take care to look nice.'

'I suppose shorter nails would make it easier to work on the machine,' said Lucy, 'but it is a shame to have to cut them when they were so pretty.'

Flora preened and patted her hair. 'At least we're allowed to wear make-up,' she said, checking her appearance in a small compact mirror. 'I couldn't bear it if I wasn't allowed to put the slap on every morning.' She eyed Ruby and Lucy, who didn't have even a dab of lipstick on. 'Not all of us like to look dowdy.'

Ruby gritted her teeth and swallowed a sharp retort, but Lucy innocently replied to the jibe. 'Oh, I think make-up's all right in its place, but there doesn't seem much point in using it here, and of course with rationing and shortages it's expensive and hard to find.'

'A girl must always look her best,' said Flora as she glanced round to the men who were having a smoke by the gate. 'You never know when you might bump into someone interesting, and there are some definite possibilities here.'

'I'm not really interested in old men,' said Lucy as she wrinkled her nose.

'They're not *that* old,' laughed Flora, 'and don't knock it, Lucy, they've got money in their pockets and enjoy spending it on the pretty girls.' She turned to Ruby. 'What about you, Ruby?'

'I'm a married woman,' she replied, 'and I don't mess about with other men, old or otherwise.'

A carefully plucked eyebrow rose. 'Goodness, how self-righteous you sound. Anyone would think you were middle-aged.' She eyed Ruby thoughtfully. 'Mind you, with that scar on your forehead, and your sour expression, most men would run a mile.'

'In my experience, most blokes are nothing but flamin' trouble, and if my looks keep 'em at arm's-length, then that's all right by me,' she retorted flatly.

Flora looked rather disconcerted at this, but any further discussion was brought to a halt by the sound of the hooter.

Ruby immediately regretted her loss of temper and quickly steered Lucy into the factory before the girl could start questioning her. They clocked in, checked their scarves were securely fixed over their hair and went straight to their machines, the cotton wool divided between them so the noise was muffled. But Lucy still had questions in her eyes, and Ruby knew she would have to come up with some sort of explanation for her outburst by the time they had their break.

'I only said it to shut her up,' Ruby said as they were drinking tea a couple of hours later. 'The fact is, I ain't interested in being like 'er and flirting with anything in trousers.' She smiled at her friend. 'I like a quiet life, Lucy, and blokes aren't the answer to everything. Believe me.'

'She's a bit of a man-eater, isn't she?' murmured Lucy as she watched Flora accept a light for her cigarette from one of the men she was surrounded by.

'Yeah, and you wanna steer clear, gel. Going about with that one will get you a bad reputation.'

'Ah, there you both are.' Mabel came and sat next to them and lit a cigarette.

'We ain't done nothing wrong, have we?' asked Ruby in some alarm.

Mabel laughed. 'Goodness me, no. In fact it's the opposite. You're obviously quick to learn and your work over the past two weeks has been admirable, so I wondered if you'd like to go on to the more complicated machinery?'

'Do we get paid more?' asked Ruby.

Mabel grinned. 'An extra threepence an hour.' She regarded Ruby, her eyes still glinting with humour. 'I like your style, Ruby Clark. You're smart and quick off the mark, and not afraid to ask the important questions. So, what do you both say?'

'Yes please,' breathed Lucy as Ruby nodded.

'Right, come on then. I'll show you how we make the screws.'

They followed her back into the factory and stood close to her as she showed them the large machine where the thick stumps of metal were fixed securely so the threads could be ground into them. 'They must be evenly ground and cleanly finished off – and then you place them squarely into this aperture so you can grind out the notches where the screwdriver blade goes in to fix them in place.'

They made a bit of a hash with the first few, but

Mabel patiently made them repeat the process until they managed a dozen perfect ones. 'Right,' she said, shouting over the noise, 'when you've done your first hundred, put your hands up and I'll come and inspect them.'

Lucy and Ruby grinned at one another and set to their task. A hundred seemed an awful lot, but once they'd got the hang of the machine, they found a definite rhythm and the boxes at their feet were soon full.

'Well done,' said Mabel. 'Go off for lunch now, and finish your shift half an hour early this afternoon as you missed your morning break. Once you've really got the hang of it, you'll find the work will speed up, and then you can do as much overtime as you like.' She gave them both a thumbs-up and strode off.

'Golly,' breathed Lucy. 'She's not nearly as strict as I thought she'd be.'

Ruby grinned and grabbed her gas-mask box. 'Come on, let's have our lunch. I don't know about you, but I'm parched, and so hungry I could fall over.'

'But surely you had breakfast?' said Lucy as they hurried towards the canteen.

Ruby thought of the bread and dripping and the nub of cheese. ''Course I did,' she replied, 'but the thought of extra money and overtime's given me an appetite.'

There was no sign of Flora, for she was still working on the washers and her lunch break was slightly different – all the breaks were staggered so the machines were never still. Ruby and Lucy collected their meals, found a seat and were tucking in when the three London girls came to sit next to them.

'I hear you've just come down from the Smoke,' said the little dark-haired one. 'The name's Grace, and this 'ere's Gladys and Gertie.' She grinned. 'We're the three Gees from the Mile End Road.'

'I'm Ruby and this is Lucy,' she replied carefully.

'So what bit of old London you from then, Ruby?' asked Grace, who was obviously the spokeswoman.

'Bermondsey,' she said quickly. 'How long you been down 'ere then?'

'Almost a year,' Grace replied as she tucked into the stew and dumplings. 'But we're all a bit homesick, ain't we, girls?' She turned back to Ruby, her gaze dropping to the wedding ring. 'The old man gorn off soldiering, 'as he?'

'Yeah,' muttered Ruby as she chewd on a dumpling.

'Mine too,' Grace sighed. She perked up and smiled again. 'Still, we're having a good time and the work's not bad. Money's all right too, 'cos we're in the armaments factory making bullets all flamin' day.'

'That's dangerous work, isn't it?' asked Lucy.

'Yeah, if yer not careful you could blow yer 'and off, and the gunpowder makes yer skin go a funny colour an' all. Still,' she added cheerfully, 'we gotta beat old Hitler and win this war, and it's a livin', ain't it?'

Ruby liked her and wished things could have been different, for she missed her mates back in Bow and didn't like lying to the girl, who was

247

only being friendly. But Grace and her mates came from an area of London that was too close to home for Ruby's liking, and she knew she would have to watch what she said.

They finished their lunch and went their separate ways, and Ruby and Lucy continued to make their screws. The time sped past and they were both surprised when Mabel came to tell them it was time to go home.

Having washed the dirt and grease from their faces and hands and brushed out their hair, they set off down to the High Street, happily chatting about their day and the good fortune which had brought them a healthier wage.

Lucy waved goodbye and hurried home to help her mother host a tea party in aid of some charity, and Ruby went into the post office and opened an account.

She'd known that such a large amount of money would be questioned, so it was no surprise when she saw the girl's eyes widen as she pushed the roll towards her. 'It's me and the old man's savings,' she explained. 'What with him being called up, I thought I'd better put it somewhere safe in case we gets bombed out again.'

The girl took the money and slowly counted it out, then entered the sum into the passbook and stamped it. 'Keep the book safe, Mrs Clark. That's a lot of money.'

'Yeah, don't I know it,' she said. 'Could I rent a safety deposit box?'

The other girl nodded, filled in the necessary form and handed her the key. Ruby placed the passbook in the deposit box and locked it away with the food and clothing stamps with a sigh of relief. They had never really been hers, and she felt a great deal better now they were out of her possession.

She quickly left the post office and headed up the hill. She felt better now the money was out of her hands, for it made her feel grubby knowing where it had come from – but at least she had a bit of security if things went haywire.

She got to the station just as Stan was coming out of his Nissen hut. 'Hello, Stan. You're a difficult bloke to find.'

His expression brightened. 'Hello, Ruby. Nice to see you again. I hear you've got a billet and a nice job, so well done you.'

Ruby frowned. 'How did you know that?'

He grinned. 'This is a small town, lass, and I get to hear everyone's business sooner or later.' He regarded her thoughtfully. 'I'm glad you've settled in all right,' he said. 'I was worried about you – so worried, in fact, that I even asked my friend Peggy Reilly if she'd take you in. She owns a boarding house over in Beach View Terrace and takes in evacuees, and she said she had a spare room.'

Hope flared. 'That were very kind of you, Stan,' she said. 'I don't suppose she still has that spare room, has she?'

He frowned and shook his head. 'I'm sorry, lass, but she was involved in the air raid a couple of weeks ago and is in hospital. I shouldn't think she'll be taking in any more lodgers for a while yet.'

'Oh.'

He was silent for a moment. 'Is everything all

right up at Councillor Fraser's?' he asked, his expression concerned.

Ruby shrugged and was sorely tempted to confide in him. 'The house is lovely, but... Well, things ain't working out the way I'd hoped really,' she finished lamely.

Stan regarded her thoughtfully. 'Why don't you come in and I'll brew us a pot of tea while you tell me all about it?'

She wasn't sure she could say very much, for like everyone else in Cliffehaven, he probably thought highly of Councillor Fraser, and she didn't want him to think she was trying to cause trouble. 'I only come up to give you this.' She pulled the scarf from her gas-mask box and clumsily shoved it at him. 'It's just a bit of something to thank you for taking me in the night I arrived.'

'Oh, Ruby, you didn't have to spend your money on me, but it's lovely,' he said as he wrapped it round his neck. 'Just the thing for the cold nights when I have to wait for the late train – but a little too warm for today,' he added with a smile. He unwound it and carefully placed it in his pocket. 'That definitely deserves a cup of tea – unless you've got somewhere else to be?'

He looked so eager for her company that she couldn't refuse. 'I'd love a cuppa.'

He made the tea, found his sandwich tin and offered her a biscuit. 'They're a bit soft, but they're kind on my dentures,' he explained.

Ruby drank her tea and ate the biscuit as she perched on the canvas stool and happily listened to him talk about his late wife, the town and the people in it. It seemed he knew everyone and their business, so she was very careful not to say too much about herself and her life in London.

'It sounds to me as though you had it a bit tough up there,' said Stan after she'd mentioned the heavy bombing raids and the almost nightly shelter with her mother in the underground station. 'Staying in Cliffehaven with the Frasers must have come as a bit of an eye-opener.'

She saw the questioning look in his eyes but felt she didn't know him well enough to tell him what was really troubling her. 'It's not what I expected,' she conceded. 'The house is ever so nice, 'cos Mrs Fraser likes everything clean and shiny, and me room's like a little palace with a washbasin and everything. But she can't cook to save her life,' she added with an impish smile.

Stan chewed a biscuit and slurped his tea. 'I've heard she's inclined to boil everything to a pulp,' he replied, 'and that she's a bit mean with the rations.' He looked at her over the rim of his tin mug. 'How are you getting on with Councillor Fraser?'

Ruby gave a small shrug and couldn't meet his gaze. 'I can't take to him at all,' she replied.

Stan said nothing for a while, and Ruby glanced at him through her lashes to discover that he was regarding her with great solemnity.

'I heard that the Frasers have had trouble keeping their lodgers,' he said eventually. 'I know of at least three who left within a couple of weeks.'

Ruby held his gaze. 'I didn't realise they'd had other evacuees,' she said. 'All girls, were they?'

He regarded her steadily. 'So I understand.'

Ruby had the distinct feeling that Stan had an

inkling of what her problem was, but still she held back from blurting out the truth. 'I think I might start looking for another billet soon,' she said carefully. 'Somewhere with a woman on her own, or with a group of other girls.'

He nodded, his gaze still thoughtful, and then he looked away and reached for the tiny vase on the end of the counter that held a single, perfect rose-bud. He breathed in the fragrance and sighed. 'I get to hear and see a lot of things in this job, Ruby, and although snippets of gossip and little incidents don't always seem significant on their own – when brought together, they can sometimes be most illuminating.'

He examined the rose, his finger delicately touching the tightly curled petals. 'The human race can be ugly, with dirty little secrets hidden behind a smiling face or respected position, which is why I like to spend time in my allotment with my roses. Their smell is sweet and their honest beauty never lets me down.'

Ruby knew then that Stan understood, and the relief was so great it brought tears to her eyes. She hurriedly blinked them away as he handed her the vase. 'Yeah,' she murmured, 'things ain't always what they seem, are they? But this is very beautiful,' she murmured as she breathed in the delicious perfume. 'Do you grow lots of roses?'

'Yes, I do. They are delicate despite their thorns, and I enjoy nurturing and protecting them so that, like children, they can flourish and blossom as they should.'

'They're lucky you look after them so well,' she replied, 'and that you care about them.'

252

He nodded and smiled and replaced the vase on the end of the ticket counter. 'Would you like to see my allotment? Only there isn't another train for an hour and if you've nothing else to do...'

'I'd love to,' she replied. 'We never had a garden back 'ome, but it were lovely to go to the park and walk through the rose gardens. They're not the same now they've been turned into vegetable patches.'

Stan locked up behind them and they walked in companionable silence over the little humpback bridge and through the remains of what had once been row upon row of terraced houses. 'Blast bombs put paid to this lot,' said Stan, 'but they did the place a favour, for it was no better than a slum.'

They reached the allotment and as they walked down the narrow dirt paths between the rows of vegetables and flowers, Stan greeted the other old men who were digging and hoeing or sitting in their little sheds drinking tea or smoking their pipes.

His patch was right at the far end and backed onto the side wall of the dairy. Ruby stood and looked in awe at the way some of the roses had been trained to go along the wall, or to climb up bits of trellis. There were buds of bright pink, little blooms of yellow with red or orange on the tips of the leaves, and blowsy white and red roses that reminded her of the silk ones on her mother's favourite hat that came out on every special occasion.

'This is the best corner of the allotment because it's so sheltered and gets the sun all day. My roses

253

bloom earlier than most because of that. Those Harlequins,' he pointed to the red, yellow and orange blooms, 'shouldn't really be out until June, and here we are still in the middle of May.'

Ruby closed her eyes and let the heady scent drift all around her. 'This has to be the best place in the world,' she murmured, 'and I wish I could wrap it up and carry it with me.'

He chuckled. 'I think we can manage that,' he said mysteriously.

Ruby watched as he unlocked the narrow shed that sat in the middle of his vegetable patch, rooted about inside for a moment then emerged with some newspaper, string, a shallow wooden basket, and a pair of strange-looking scissors.

'These are secateurs, especially made for gardeners,' he explained, 'and this is what we call a trug. It's for carrying cut flowers or vegetables.'

He stood by the wall and regarded the blossoms thoughtfully before he cut through one of the thick stems and handed her a bud of the deepest red. 'Red for Ruby,' he said, and grinned. 'You can pin it on the strap of your dungarees with this, while I cut some more for Peggy Reilly.'

Ruby took the safety pin and fixed the perfect bud so she could smell the scent without even turning her head. 'It's lovely,' she breathed, 'and I promise to take great care of it.'

'That was my wife's favourite rose. The house was always full of them when she was alive. The scent of them reminds me of her, and it's as if she's come back to me when they bloom every summer.'

Ruby watched as he carefully chose which

254

blooms to cut and then placed them almost reverently in the trug. He must have adored his wife, she thought wistfully, and it was a lovely idea to grow her favourite roses and to feel that she was still with him as he worked in this peaceful place.

'There, that's enough I think.' Stan took the trug to the shed and spread out the newspaper on the wide shelf that jutted out from beneath the window. He trimmed each bloom, carefully snipping off the thorns and lower greenery, and then soaked a lump of moss in a nearby watering can before wrapping it round the stems.

'That will keep them fresh,' he explained as he neatly rolled the paper into a cone around the flowers, tied it with string and hunted out a stub of pencil and a scrap of paper. Swiftly writing a note, he tucked it in with the blooms, and then looked at his watch.

'It's not yet five and a bit early for visiting time, but I've got the incoming from Hastings due to arrive and then the outgoing from Dover to deal with.' He handed the bouquet to Ruby. 'Why don't you pop in and see Peggy for me?'

'But I don't know her,' said a startled Ruby.

'Well, she knows a bit about you, as I explained earlier, and I'm sure you'll both get along fine. Peggy Reilly's the salt of the earth and a lovely lady, but I simply don't have the time to go and visit her today. I very much want her to have the roses, because I know she loves them as much as I do, and they'll go some way to cheering her up.'

Ruby looked up at him and smiled. 'Then of course I'll take them to her. When is visiting time?'

'Six until seven, but I'm sure Matron won't

mind you slipping in a bit early so you don't miss your evening meal. If she says anything, just tell her I sent you.' He tapped the side of his nose with a grubby finger and winked. 'She and I belong to the local rose growers' society and I happen to know that her bark is far worse than her bite.'

Ruby grinned back at him. 'Thanks for everything, Stan. You're a diamond.'

His smile was almost shy as he tugged at his hairy earlobe. 'Get away with you and see Peggy before she gets swamped with visitors and you miss out on your tea.'

Peggy was sick of being in hospital, and although she'd managed each day to get out of bed and walk the length of the ward several times, she knew she wasn't ready yet to go home. She also knew that Fran and the other nurses weren't too happy about her breaking all the rules, but as her wound was clean and none of the stitches was coming loose, they turned a blind eye when they saw her shuffling past them.

The only panic had come when Matron was spotted in the corridor one afternoon, and Fran had swiftly got her into a wheelchair and back to bed before she marched through the doors. Fran had given Peggy a ticking-off once Matron had gone again, but it was done in good humour and they both knew she was wasting her breath.

Peggy lay against the mound of pillows and watched as Fran soothed the elderly woman in the far bed who'd woken from a nightmare. For all her wild hair and rapscallion ways, Fran was a good nurse, with endless patience and a cheering nature, and Peggy was feeling as proud as a mother hen of her little Irish chick. But she was also aware that she would have to be careful not to get the girls into trouble with Matron. It had been a close call that recent afternoon, and Peggy had come to the conclusion that her exercise must be tailored to Matron's busy – but fairly predictable – schedule so she was occupied elsewhere.

Today had gone remarkably quickly, all things considered. There had been the usual bed bath, the unappetising meals, the lovely visit this afternoon from Jane who'd brought in Daisy, and the surprise few minutes with Suzy as she'd dashed in during her break and told her what had been happening at Beach View.

It seemed that Doris was behaving herself, the household routine was uninterrupted despite her interference, and Ron and the girls were managing just fine. She'd been delighted to hear that little Phyllis had at last found the courage to leave Doris's employ, though how she was getting on in a noisy factory was anyone's guess. The girl was timid and shy, and not at all prepared for the loud and sometimes rough behaviour that went on in those factories.

Peggy closed her eyes and wondered who would visit her this evening. It had been lovely to see Cissy again last night, but she was on duty at the airfield, and probably wouldn't come again until the weekend. Her younger sister, Doreen, was in London, and didn't even know she was in hospital because Peggy had insisted she wasn't to be told. She certainly didn't want her to make the long journey down here when she was so busy, just as she didn't want Anne to come all this way. There was nothing any of them could do, and if her exercises went to plan, she'd be out of here – with or without permission – by the end of the week.

Her fighting spirit ebbed a little for there had still been no telephone call from Jim, and she suspected the telegram must have either gone astray, or simply not been passed on from the barracks mail room.

She gave a deep sigh, lit a cigarette and grimaced. It was not her usual Park Drive, but the horrid Pasha cigarettes that tasted foul and were always available because no one smoked them unless they were desperate. She stubbed it out in the tin ashtray and drank some water. This damned war had a lot to answer for, and she was sick of bad communications, lost letters, silent telephones, rationing, shortages, foul-tasting fags, and this blasted hospital bed.

A glance at the clock above the double doors showed there was still over an hour before visiting time. She would have liked to have stretched her legs a bit, but as Matron usually patrolled the wards before the visitors were let in, she realised it wouldn't be wise.

One of the doors opened and a young, very slight girl in dungarees peeked round it. Fran went over to her, and they exchanged a few words before the girl headed down the ward, her arms laden with the most glorious bunch of roses.

Peggy wondered who she was visiting, and was most surprised when she came right up to her bed. 'Mrs Reilly?' she asked.

Peggy nodded as she took note of the nasty scar

258

on her forehead and the waiflike figure that was almost swamped in the dungarees.

'I'm Ruby,' the girl said breathlessly, 'and Stan from the station asked me to bring you these.'

So this was Stan's little waif, and she could see immediately why he'd been so protective of her. Peggy's smile broadened in delight as the flowers were placed gently into her arms. 'Oh, how wonderful,' she murmured as she breathed in the heavenly perfume. She glanced down the ward. 'Pull the curtain a bit, Ruby, and sit down so you can't be seen,' she urged. 'It's so lovely to have a surprise visitor.'

'Stan said he were sorry he couldn't come himself, but he has trains to organise, and he thought we should get to know one another seeing how kind you was to offer me a billet.' She sat on the edge of the chair, her little face earnest. 'He's ever so nice, ain't he?'

'He's a dear, sweet man,' murmured Peggy, 'and a complete softie. Everyone in Cliffehaven is very fond of him, and his roses win all the prizes every year at the flower show.' She saw the piece of paper tucked in between the rose stems, pulled it out to read it, and then thoughtfully folded it into her dressing-gown pocket. 'I understand he looked after you the night you arrived?' she said softly.

Ruby nodded. 'I didn't have nowhere to go and it were bitter cold.' She went on to describe the sandwiches and very welcome tea, and the night she'd spent in the Nissen hut alongside the suitcases.

'I had the feeling he'd found you somewhere warm and safe to stay the night. He was very concerned about you when he telephoned me and asked if I could take you in.'

'Yeah, he told me about that, and I'm ever so grateful for the offer. I'm sorry things didn't work out and that you've been hurt, Mrs Reilly. Will you have to stay in 'ere for very long?'

'Not if I can help it.' She smiled. 'Home is the best place to get better, surrounded by family and loved ones.' She saw the sadness in Ruby's eyes and her heart went out to her, for despite the wedding ring, she looked so very young, and was probably terribly homesick. 'Tell me about your home and family, Ruby. You're from London, aren't you?'

Peggy listened as the girl described her home, her mother and her work at the pub. She noted that the husband, Ray, was mentioned only in passing and wondered at that. This little girl's life seemed so empty of hope and joy, that it made her want to reach out and give her a cuddle – but of course she didn't.

'So that's it really,' Ruby finished. 'I come down here, found a job and made a nice friend, and it's lovely to be so close to the sea. I ain't never been to the seaside before, and I like the way it smells, all clean and salty.'

Peggy noticed that she didn't include her billet with the Frasers in this catalogue of success. 'We're very lucky,' Peggy murmured. 'I've lived here all my life, and I couldn't imagine ever moving away.'

'Stan said you've got a boarding house,' said Ruby.

'I do indeed. It's three roads up from the promenade, and although you can only see the sea from one of the top windows, it's sort of comforting to know it's always there.'

Ruby grinned. 'A bit like St Paul's. As long as that's still standing, it gives us all hope we'll win this war, don't it?'

'It certainly does,' Peggy said warmly.

'I'd better go,' murmured Ruby. 'The nurses will get into trouble if Matron finds me here, and that little redhead said I weren't to be too long.'

'That's Fran,' said Peggy. 'She's one of my lodgers, and Suzy who's also a nurse lives with me too.' Peggy regarded Ruby kindly and resisted her natural instinct to offer her the spare room again. 'We have a happy household at Beach View. There's Sarah who works for the WTC, her sister Jane who delivers milk in the morning and does the accounts at the uniform factory in the afternoon – and then there's Rita who drives a fire engine, Cordelia who's everyone's grandma, and my father-in-law Ron.'

'It all sounds lovely,' Ruby said on a sigh. 'Do you have any children, Mrs Reilly?'

Peggy told her about her scattered brood. 'The only one at home now is my baby Daisy, and she's four months old and growing like a weed.'

'Oh, how sweet,' Ruby said wistfully.

Peggy picked up on that sadness immediately and wondered what was behind it, but she resisted asking. She hardly knew the girl, and some things were far too personal to share on a first meeting. 'Would you like to stay and meet whoever's coming in to visit me tonight? It's almost visiting time.'

Ruby pushed out of the chair. 'I'd love to, but I

261

gotta get back to Nelson Street for me tea. If I'm late Mrs Fraser gives me half-rations and don't bother to heat it up.'

'Good heavens,' gasped Peggy. 'How mean.'

Ruby tried to make light of it by giving a small shrug. 'I've eaten worse, and at least I get a decent meal at the factory canteen lunchtime.'

Peggy noticed the small, tight smile and the careful nonchalance and realised Ruby was reluctant to say more. 'Will you come and see me again, Ruby?'

'Yeah, I'd like that, and perhaps Stan could come with me next time.' She gave her a sweet, genuine smile. 'It's been nice to meet yer, Mrs Reilly. I 'ope you gets better soon.'

Peggy squeezed her little hand and then watched as she clumped down the ward in her heavy working boots. Once she was out of sight, Peggy plucked Stan's note from her pocket and read it again.

'Ruby needs your help, Peggy. Nelson Street is not at all suitable. I know it's a lot to ask – but you're the only one I could think of who could put things right for her. Stan.'

It was rather cryptic and she didn't really understand what Stan had been trying to convey. But it was clear he was deeply worried for the girl – to the point where he'd actually manipulated their meeting. Peggy folded the note and tucked it away in the bedside drawer.

In the normal run of things, she'd have gone straight to Nelson Street and taken Ruby home to Beach View – but she was tied to this blessed hospital bed and unable to do anything, which was

262

so frustrating, it made her want to scream. Having spoken to the girl and sensed that she was indeed unhappy with the Frasers, she'd been very tempted to offer her the spare room then and there, but no decisions could be made without consulting the others – and she doubted very much if Doris would agree to taking on another lodger.

She looked at the clock, impatient for visiting time. All she could do was hope that Ron came this evening. He could talk to Stan and get to the bottom of things, and if he thought the girl really was in trouble then she trusted him to make the right decision, regardless of any opposition from Doris.

Chapter Fifteen

Ruby had left the hospital and was just approaching the station when she saw the flash of a scarlet uniform jacket and the unmistakable figure of the Canadian officer she'd met on the train. He was talking to another officer as they emerged from the station, and she quickly darted into a shop doorway before he caught sight of her. She hadn't really expected to see him again, and the last thing she needed was for him to spot her, so she turned her back and watched their reflections in the shop window as they strolled down the High Street.

She felt faintly ridiculous as she peeked round the window to make sure they'd gone, for she was old enough to stand up to any nonsense from the likes of Michael Taylor – but her life was complicated enough, and the Canadian was far too handsome and charming to be trusted.

She waited until they'd reached the Town Hall, and then she ran past the station and all the way up the hill to Mon Repos. The Town Hall clock was striking six as she breathlessly stepped into the hall and closed the door behind her. She was panting hard and her heart was racing from that uphill run in her heavy working boots.

Mrs Fraser emerged from the kitchen with a tray of soup bowls and looked at her with disapproval. 'You're just in time,' she said. 'I could have done with a hand this evening, Ruby. My poor Harry is feeling most unwell.'

'Nothing serious, I hope,' she said with a distinct lack of sincerity.

'The poor man fell on the kitchen floor and has broken three toes. He's in the most awful pain.'

Ruby was delighted to hear it. She followed Mrs Fraser into the dining room and saw that Harold was enthroned in a wing-backed chair, with a tray across his lap, his left foot swathed in thick bandages and propped on a nearby stool. 'That looks painful,' she said as she sat down at the table.

His gaze was malevolent. 'It is. And I shall be laid up for at least a week.'

'Poor you,' she murmured before she tucked into her soup.

'It's all most inconvenient,' said Marjory as she fussed over him. 'The council has a great many things to plan and discuss over the next few weeks, and Harold really needs to chair the meetings.'

She finally sat down and started on her soup. 'I still don't understand how he could have taken such a tumble – unless you didn't dry the floor properly after your bath?' The pale eyes looked at her from across the table.

'I didn't have no bath last night,' said Ruby.

Mrs Fraser frowned. 'But I specifically told you to have one while we were out. This is the second week you've disobeyed me, Ruby, and I am not happy about it. I keep a clean house, and expect my lodgers to wash regularly to get rid of nits and fleas.'

Ruby dowsed the flare of temper at this insult. 'I don't have nits and fleas and I wash proper in the basin in me room. The public baths do for me twice a week, and they're cheaper than what you charge.'

'Well, really,' Marjory gasped. 'Do you hear that, Harold? The cheek of the girl – and to think I work my fingers to the bone to keep and feed her – and that's all the thanks I get.'

Ruby finished the watery, almost tasteless soup. 'I never said I weren't grateful,' she said calmly, 'but I gotta watch me pennies.'

Mrs Fraser sniffed and collected the bowls, but before she could say anything else, Ruby had picked up the tray and was carrying it into the kitchen. She didn't want to be left alone with Harold, for his angry, piggy eyes hadn't left her since she'd sat down.

'I must say, Ruby,' said Marjory as she dished out the corned beef hash, 'that I am disappointed in you. I thought that coming from the East End slums, you would appreciate a nice, clean, well-ordered home, and willingly comply with our routine.'

'Oh, but I do, Mrs Fraser. It's ever so nice – and that food smells lovely.' Ruby forced a bright smile. 'It's just that I'm used to public baths, with a cubicle and a bolt on the door for me money.'

Mrs Fraser made no further comment as she finished serving the soggy hash that was more potato than meat, and they returned to the dining room with the plates.

The rest of the meal was eaten almost in silence, with just the occasional fleeting exchange between Marjory and her husband, who continued to glare at Ruby.

Ruby had smothered the unappetising mess with tomato sauce. She scraped her plate clean then clattered her knife and fork together. 'That were lovely, thanks a lot,' she muttered mechanically.

'You can help me with the dishes, and then we'll listen to "Name that Tune" with Violet Carson before I have to leave for the WI meeting.'

Ruby felt a stab of alarm. 'I were planning on going out,' she said hurriedly.

'I'd prefer it if you stayed and kept poor Harold company until I get back. I should only be an hour or so, and I don't think it's too much to ask, do you?'

'I had other plans,' she muttered.

'What plans?'

Ruby thought fast. 'I were going to the public baths,' she said.

'They close at six,' replied Marjory as she carried the dirty dishes into the kitchen and dumped them on the wooden drainer. 'So that's settled

266

then. You and Harry can have a cosy evening in listening to the wireless, and I can go to my meeting and not worry about him taking any more tumbles.'

Ruby felt quite sick at the thought of being alone with Harold and wished with all her heart that she'd had the courage to tell the lovely Peggy Reilly straight out what it was really like here. But she hadn't, and now she would have to suffer the consequences.

By the time the washing-up was finished and the Frasers were ensconced in the sitting room by the wireless, Ruby's stomach was in knots. She left them trying to guess the names of the tunes Violet Carson was playing on her piano and ran up to her bedroom. She couldn't stay here alone with him, she simply couldn't – for even with broken toes he was a menace, and by the nasty looks he'd been shooting at her all through tea, he was eager to get his own back.

She changed out of her grease-stained dungarees and boots into her old cotton dress, cardigan and sandals, her thoughts working furiously as she put the sweet-smelling rosebud into a glass of water. Her only option was to leave the back way the minute Marjory closed the front door, and wander about until she saw her coming home again. The thought of sitting in her bedroom all night with Harold trying to get in – and perhaps succeeding – was just too awful.

Grabbing her coat, she carried it downstairs and quickly hung it up in the cupboard under the stairs alongside her gas-mask box. The show was all but over and Marjory would soon be leaving.

She went into the sitting room and froze. There was no sign of Harold.

'Has Councillor Fraser decided to go with you?' she asked Marjory, who had switched off the wireless and was slipping on her jacket.

'Of course not,' she said rather crossly. 'The Women's Institute does not allow men to their meetings.'

'Has he gone to bed then?'

'You seem very concerned as to the whereabouts of my husband,' said Marjory stiffly.

'I just thought,' stuttered Ruby, 'that if he's up and about, and don't need no help or nothing, I might go out anyway and visit me friend.'

'I need you to stay here and look after him in case he falls again,' Marjory retorted. 'Really, you are the most irritating girl, Ruby. I thought you understood how worried I'd be all evening if he was left alone.' With that, she picked up her gloves and handbag, adjusted her hat and walked into the hall to collect her gas-mask box from the newel post.

'But if he can't walk about on his own, where is he now?' Ruby persisted.

'If you really must know, he has gone to the lavatory,' Marjory snapped. 'I shall be back before ten, and if I find you've disobeyed me and left him alone, then you will be out on the street bag and baggage before morning.' Her steely gaze fixed on Ruby. 'Do I make myself clear?'

Ruby was tempted to tell her to stick Mon Repos up her jumper and that she was leaving anyway – right now, this minute. But she knew she was really in no position to argue, for where could she go? So she nodded, and Mrs Fraser left, the sound of the slamming door echoing through the silent house.

The bulb had been removed from the hall light in one of Mrs Fraser's economy drives, and there was only a feeble glimmer coming from the sitting room, which made the darkness of the rest of the house seem more profound. The escape route out the back was no longer an option. She would have to go out the front and risk Mrs Fraser seeing her leave.

Ruby felt the hairs on the back of her neck prickle as she walked past the partially open door to the dining room and reached into the cupboard under the stairs for her coat and gas-mask box. It was too quiet and there was no sign of Harold. Was he still outside in the back yard? Or had he come into the house and was lurking somewhere in the darkness?

She had one arm in the sleeve of her coat when she heard a noise behind her, but before she could react, a heavy shove caught her in the small of her back and sent her tumbling to the floor. Unable to catch her breath or cry out, she found she was pinned beneath him, his forceful hand mashing her face into the strip of carpet.

'You don't do that to me and get away with it,' he hissed in her ear as his free hand shot up her thigh and pawed at her knickers. 'If you want to play rough, little girl, then I'm happy to oblige.'

Ruby managed to free her head enough to yell, 'Get off me,' as she writhed and kicked, her hands reaching up to claw at his face. 'Leave me alone, you filthy old pervert,' she rasped as she struggled against the heavy weight on her back and the pressure of his hand grinding her face into the rough carpet.

'Not until I've finished,' he panted, his fingers tugging at her underwear and probing between her legs.

Ruby tried to scream, but her mouth and nose were smothered by the carpet, his weight squeezing the air from her lungs and threatening to crack her ribs. She tried to buck him off, to kick out and perhaps make contact with his broken toes as his breath rasped in her ear and his hand continued to explore beneath her dress. But she couldn't breathe and her struggles were weakening.

Ruby clenched her buttocks against his probing fingers and wriggled furiously, fighting for breath, determined not to be beaten. Then she went suddenly limp, felt the pressure lessen, and reared back with every ounce of strength she had until her head connected with a bone-crunching thud on his nose.

With a roar of fury and pain, he slumped over her, and she felt the warmth of blood dripping on her face. She was still pinned to the floor, but now she could breathe, and that gave her greater strength. She screamed as she kicked and wriggled, trying to roll from beneath him as she reached back to pull his hair and gouge his eyes. But he was too heavy, too aroused and angry – and her scream was smothered as he once again pressed her face into the carpet.

Ron had been deeply disturbed by Stan's note to Peggy, so he'd collected Harvey from Beach View and gone to the station to find him. They were old friends, and Ron knew he could rely on Stan to tell him everything man to man and not mince his words.

'Peggy sent me,' he said after they'd greeted one another and made themselves comfortable in the Nissen hut. 'What's all this about, Stan?'

Stan lit the small stove, boiled some water for tea, and gave Harvey a biscuit. 'There have been rumours over the years about Harold Fraser's liking for young girls,' he began.

'To be sure I've heard whisperings,' replied Ron around the stem of his pipe. 'He's not a man I've ever taken to, but 'tis dangerous to take such things as gospel when there's no proof to back them up.'

'I realise that, Ron, but you and me, well, we've lived long enough to know there's very rarely smoke without fire – and having spoken to Ruby this afternoon, I got the distinct feeling she's in some kind of trouble up there in Nelson Street.'

'Aye, that's what Peggy feels too. Did Ruby actually tell you that Fraser's been making a nuisance of himself?'

Stan shook his head as he poured the tea into tin mugs. 'Not in so many words, but she said enough for me to know she was feeling very uneasy about him.'

Ron blew on his tea and took a sip. 'I don't really know what you both expect me to do,' he said thoughtfully. 'I can hardly go up there and accuse him of something like that without being very certain of the facts. Fraser's an important man in the town, and if this all blows up in my

271

face, I could be facing charges of slander.'

'I wasn't suggesting you should do that, Ron – it would be foolhardy to say the least. But perhaps you could just go and have a quiet word with Ruby? Make it clear we both suspect what Fraser is up to and ask her straight out if he's threatening her in any way. I'm sure that once she realises you're there to help, she'll tell you everything.'

'But I haven't even met the girl,' he protested. 'To be sure, Stan, she'll not want to be confiding in me, and 'tis a terrible thing we're accusing that man of. What if we've got this all wrong?'

'Better to be wrong than to do nothing at all,' replied Stan flatly. 'There have been a succession of young women leaving that house over the past three years – and it's pushing coincidence too far when Ruby is already talking about finding another billet after only two weeks. She does her best to hide it, but she's frightened, Ron, and I can't rest easy until I know she's safe.'

Ron finished his tea and thought about it. Stan was astute and in a position to hear all sorts of things. He'd met and talked to Ruby and had sent her to Peggy with that note, in the sure knowledge that Peggy would know what to do for the best. Ron's first instinct, like Peggy's, had been to go up there and take the girl home to Beach View – but what if Stan had got the wrong end of the stick and Harold Fraser was innocent?

Ron had never been in this situation before and although he'd never liked the man, and had heard the rumours, he knew how dangerous it was to throw such accusations about.

'If you were so certain about all this, why didn't

you offer her a bed at your place?'

'Come on, Ron, think about it. I'm a man on my own in a tiny one-bed cottage. It wouldn't be right at all. She could sleep in here for another night, I suppose, but then what?'

'She could go to the billeting people and ask to be moved.'

'Only if she's prepared to answer a lot of very awkward questions,' he replied. 'Look, Ron, she's alone, and a stranger to the town. Fraser is an important man in Cliffehaven, and the odds are she won't be believed – and she's bright enough to know that.'

'Aye, you could be right,' Ron murmured.

'What if it was your Cissy in that situation, Ron? What would you do then?'

'Rumours or not, I'd have her out of there in an instant.' He held Stan's gaze and knew then what he must do. 'I'll go up and talk to her,' he said on a sigh, 'but God help the both of us if you're wrong, Stan.'

'God help the girl if I'm not,' he said flatly. He pulled the fob watch from his waistcoat pocket and checked the time. 'I'll come with you after I've dealt with the troop train. Should only take about an hour.'

'You see to the train and I'll deal with Fraser,' Ron rumbled as he set down the empty mug and rose from the canvas stool.

Stan shook his hand. 'Thanks, old friend. I knew the Reilly family would come up trumps.'

Ron pulled his cap over his ears and turned up the collar of his tweed jacket against the wind that tore up from the sea through the open door.

'We've yet to see the cards we're playing with, Stan,' he said grimly. 'But this will be dealt with tonight, you can be sure of that.'

With Harvey trotting along at his heels, he left the station and set off over the small humpback bridge and up the hill to Nelson Street. He was fully focussed on his mission now, determined to get to the bottom of this very worrying and distasteful situation with Fraser and to do what he could to put things right for Ruby.

It was very quiet up here under the hills, and his footfalls echoed as Harvey padded alongside him. Then he thought he heard a thin, high scream cut short, and looked at the dog. Harvey had heard it too and was standing stiff-legged, ears cocked.

Ron dismissed it as probably just some animal that had been caught by a fox, and was about to continue when he heard it again. The cry was definitely human, short and sharp and full of fear – but again cut brutally short.

Harvey was already standing outside Mon Repos, a growl deep in his throat as he pawed at the door.

Ron stilled and hushed him with a gentle hand, and listened keenly to the sounds of some sort of struggle coming from the other side of the door. He eased the letter box open and looked into a hallway dimly lit from a nearby room.

One glance was enough. He stood back and with one mighty kick the door flew open. Before Fraser had time to react, Ron had grasped his collar, hauled him off the girl and punched him hard on his already bloody nose.

Harold Fraser slid down the wall and slumped to the floor, his trousers around his ankles.

Harvey growled deep in his throat as he stood over him, his snarling muzzle inches from that bloodied face.

Ruby had scuttled away from Harold and was curled up in a corner, sobbing so hard she couldn't speak.

Ron sat on the floor beside her and tenderly gathered her into his arms. She clung to him in abject distress and relief, her small body trembling. 'There, there,' he soothed. 'It's all right, acushla. He'll not be hurting you any more.'

He continued to cradle her while Harvey kept Fraser pinned to the wall and Ruby's tears and terrors were slowly soothed.

He tried... He tried to...' she sobbed against his jacket lapel. 'But how did you know? Who are you?'

'I know what he was trying to do,' he said grimly, 'and I'm here because Stan and Peggy knew you needed help.' He gave a tremulous sigh. 'And thanks be to God that I listened to them,' he murmured. 'There there, you're safe now. He won't be touching you ever again.'

Her heartbreaking sobs stuttered to a halt eventually, but he could feel the tremors running through her little body as she continued to cling to him. She was like a frightened bird in his arms, and his rage at Fraser was a white-hot furnace building inside him.

Ruby slowly calmed enough to take his rather grubby handkerchief and blow her nose. She gently withdrew from his embrace and looked

275

back at him with large green eyes that were still haunted and swimming with tears. 'Thank you for saving me,' she breathed tremulously. 'But who are you?'

'I'm Ronan Reilly, Peggy's father-in-law, and I've come to take you home to Beach View where you'll be safe.' He saw her, tear-stained face brighten and the torment in her eyes replaced by hope, and his soft old heart melted. 'Why don't you go and clean yourself up and collect your things, Ruby?' he said gruffly. 'I'll wait down here for you.'

With his help, Ruby managed to get to her feet, and Ron watched with an ache in his heart as she straightened her torn dress and slowly dragged her way up the stairs. She was such a little thing, but she'd fought bravely. It was only by sheer chance that he'd been in time to save her.

He turned to look at Harold, who was weeping with pain and trying desperately to haul up his trousers and stem the flow of blood from his broken nose as Harvey continued to snarl in his face. It took all his years of specialist army training for Ron to hold in his rage and resist beating the bastard to a pulp. He watched him snivelling and cringing, and then clenched his fists and stepped closer. 'If you're not out of this town by the end of the week the authorities will know what kind of man you really are,' he said, his voice dark with menace.

'That's blackmail,' whined Harold. 'And no one would believe you anyway.'

'They will by the time I've finished,' he growled. 'The Mayor and I fought together on the Somme, and he knows me as a truthful man.' He saw Fraser's smirk of disbelief and kicked the bandaged foot.

Fraser howled in pain and curled up on the floor as Harvey continued to straddle him, his lips drawn back in a snarl to show wickedly sharp teeth.

'The rumours about you can easily be stoked again,' continued Ron. 'A few words in the right ears and the whole town will know what a fat, perverted little shite you really are.' He stepped closer, the toe of his boot hovering less than an inch from the bandaged foot. 'You're finished in this town, Fraser.'

'But I can't just leave,' he protested, his eyes wild with fear and pain. 'What about my wife and this house?'

'You should have thought about that before you started molesting young girls,' Ron said coldly. 'You've got until the end of the week – and that is not negotiable.'

Ruby emerged at the top of the stairs carrying a large pannier basket. She'd changed into a pair of trousers, a sweater and thick boots, and was clutching a red rosebud. Her little face was wan beneath the angry carpet burns, and she had to cling to the bannisters to steady her way down to the hall, but she seemed calmer.

Ron picked up the coat and gas-mask box which had been strewn across the floor in the struggle.

Ruby burst into tears again as she saw the blood on the sleeve and the tear in the silky lining. 'My lovely coat,' she sobbed. 'He's ruined it.'

'To be sure, we'll soon have that clean and

mended,' Ron soothed as he helped with the coat and gave her a swift, reassuring hug. 'As long as you're in one piece, that's all that matters.'

She looked back at him with her large, sad green eyes. 'He didn't... You know.'

Ron was glad to hear it, but he still felt a murderous rage over Fraser's attack, and knew that if they didn't leave immediately, he wouldn't be responsible for his actions.

'Come, Harvey,' he ordered. 'Our work's finished here.' He took the basket from Ruby and tucked her hand into the crook of his arm to steady her as Harvey gave one last growl and followed them out into the street.

Ruby was still in shock as she clung to Mr Reilly's arm. She forced one foot in front of the other as they slowly walked down Nelson Street, the lovely, brave dog padding along beside them. Every part of her was aching and she knew there were bruises and carpet burns on her legs and arms, and on her face, but what hurt most of all was the knowledge that yet again she'd been a victim.

Was there something about her that attracted violent men? She had to conclude that there must be, but she was tired of fighting, sick of always being on the end of an angry fist or preyed on by randy bastards like Fraser. Her life seemed to be one long catalogue of disasters, from her violent stepfather, to her vicious husband – and now this. So much for a new life and a new beginning, she thought with despair.

They reached the station, but a troop train

278

must have just arrived, for the ladies of the WVS had set up a mobile canteen and the whole area was swamped with young soldiers and sailors enjoying cigarettes and hot cups of tea. There was no sign of Stan, and for that she was grateful. She burned with shame at the thought of his seeing her like this – and of his knowing what Fraser had tried to do. And yet his kindness had saved her and tomorrow, when she felt more able to think coherently, she would come and thank him for bringing Mr Reilly to her rescue.

They didn't go straight down the High Street, which would have meant having to pass through the crowds that still spilled over the pavements, but through narrow, dark lanes she hadn't noticed before. She had to keep stopping to rest, for her legs felt like jelly and her head was swimming. Mr Reilly, bless him, had offered to carry her, but she was determined to make her own way. He'd done enough for one night.

As they eventually reached Camden Road and began to head east, the moon came from behind the clouds and drenched everything in a pale blue light. There had been little time to really look at her saviour before they'd left the house, and she'd simply had the impression of someone sturdy, square and strong, whose arms shielded her and whose voice soothed.

Now, as she examined him in the moonlight, she could see that her good Samaritan was far from the storybook knight in shining armour – but was, in fact, a rather scruffy, well-built man, probably in his sixties, with a grizzled chin, wayward eyebrows and the soft lilt of Ireland in his speech. It didn't

279

matter a jot that he wasn't young and handsome or riding a white horse, for he reminded her of her father, and it was the solid, reliable comfort of a father figure that she needed right now.

Ruby felt the dog's wet nose snuffle into the palm of her hand as they walked slowly down Camden Road, and for the first time in what felt like hours, she smiled. The man and his dog were well matched, for they were both rather scruffy, and yet she found that lovely and reassuring.

'That's the Anchor,' said Ron. 'I'm in charge there while my friend Rosie Braithwaite is away. These shops are where Peggy's registered her ration books. Fred the Fish and Alf the butcher are mates of mine, so they are, and there's often a wee treat for the tea table or a bone for Harvey.'

'My food stamps,' Ruby gasped. 'I left them in the kitchen.'

'To be sure, they'll have to stay there,' he said gruffly. 'Neither of us will be going back.'

Ruby shivered at the thought of ever going into that house again.

'Let's sit and catch our breath,' Ron said as they came to a bombed-out house where only a few walls and part of the garden wall were still standing. 'I can tell you're finding all this walking a struggle and there are things I need to warn you about before we get to Beach View.'

Ruby tensed as she perched on the rough stone. She'd known this was too good to be true.

He must have read her thoughts, for he smiled and patted her hand. 'To be sure, 'tis nothing too serious, but you see there hasn't been much time to warn everyone that you're coming, and I don't want you getting upset when Doris starts in on us.'

Ruby was still wary as he set about filling his pipe. 'Who's Doris?'

'She's Peggy's older sister and a bit of a dragon if the truth be told,' he said round the pipe stem. 'She moved in with us two weeks ago without invitation and is likely to cause a fuss about a new lodger moving in. Now, I don't want you to take heed of any of her nonsense. I know how to deal with Doris.'

Ruby didn't like the sound of this woman at all. 'I'm so sorry, Mr Reilly,' she said anxiously. 'If it's going to cause trouble, then perhaps it would be better if I found somewhere else to stay.'

'You'll not be going anywhere but Beach View,' he said firmly. 'Fran will be back from the hospital now, and I'm sure Peg's warned her that you might be coming, so she and the other girls will have got your room ready.'

Ruby's eyes filled with tears again. 'Everyone's being ever so kind,' she said unsteadily. 'And I ain't got the words to tell you how grateful I am – but thank you, Mr Reilly'

'Call me Ron; everyone else does,' he said gruffly. 'And there's no need for thanks – or for tears. I only did what any right-thinking man would do.'

Ruby shook her head and gave him a watery smile. 'Nah, you done more'n that, Ron, and I'll never forget it.'

'Come on then. Let's go home and face the Doris dragon.'

Ruby's hand was tucked back into the crook of

his arm and Harvey trotted happily alongside her, tongue lolling, ears flapping in the wind that was blowing the blossom from the trees and making it swirl like pink and white confetti. She and Ron had defeated one dragon already tonight, and she had little doubt that, together, they could slay another.

Beach View Boarding House was a tall, narrow terraced house, with the front steps shadowing a basement window. Most of the windows seemed to have been boarded over, but the front door and brass knocker were polished to a gleam and the steps had been recently whitewashed. There was a bit of damage to the walls, probably from flying shrapnel, but it clearly hadn't suffered like the houses at the end of the short street, which were no more than rubble.

'They went in a gas explosion right at the start of the war,' explained Ron. 'We had a bit of damage at the back the night Peggy was injured, but that's all been mended and now we're almost as good as new again.' He gave her an encouraging smile, turned the key in the lock and opened the door.

Ruby stepped into a square hall which led to three doorways and a wide, elegant staircase of dark, gleaming wood. The paint was faded, the wallpaper beneath the dado rail coming away in places, but there was a delicious smell of food and furniture polish and a lovely warm atmosphere that could only come from a real home.

Harvey licked her hand as if to reassure her and then stayed by her side as Ron led her into the kitchen. She got the impression of worn furniture, homeliness and clutter before the friendly chatter died down and everyone turned to welcome her.

She felt rather intimidated at being the centre of attention, but began to relax a little as she recognised Fran from the hospital, with her wild red hair and green eyes. As Suzy and Sarah introduced themselves, she marvelled at how sophisticated they looked with their blonde hair and elegant figures. She returned Jane's welcoming smile, admiring her creamy skin and artless manner, and then grinned at Rita, instantly recognising a kindred spirit.

'Welcome to Beach View,' said Rita. 'You don't have to be mad to live here, but it does help.'

'I'm sure it's all lovely,' she murmured, still feeling a little out of her depth.

'I'll get the first-aid kit out,' said Suzy as she eyed Ruby's battered face. 'Those grazes need cleaning and I've got some iodine for the bruises.'

Ruby dipped her chin as she felt the shame heat her face.

'It's all right,' murmured Rita as Suzy went to fetch the first-aid box and the others continued to fuss over Ron and Harvey. 'We don't need to know anything unless you want us to. We're just glad you're here.' She saw the blood on Ruby's coat. 'Give me your lovely coat, Ruby. Sarah's an absolute whizz at getting stains out, and it'll soon be as good as new.'

'I only bought it two weeks ago,' she replied as she slipped it off. 'D'you think she really can get it all out?'

Rita nodded and grinned, but their conversation was cut short by a querulous voice. 'I'm

283

not invisible, you know, and I don't appreciate being ignored.'

The girls parted to reveal an elderly woman sitting in a fireside chair with her arm in plaster. 'Ruby, this is Mrs Finch,' explained Rita. 'We all call her Grandma Finch and we love her to bits.' She leaned closer to Ruby. 'She's got her hearing aid in tonight, so you don't need to shout,' she said in a stage whisper.

Ruby thought the little woman looked ever so grand, with her white hair and nice floral frock – like the old ladies what lived up in Kensington and walked their lapdogs in the park – but there was a glint of naughty humour in her eyes which made her very approachable. 'Hello, Mrs Finch. Pleased to meet yer, I'm sure.'

'Hello, dear. I'm glad you decided to stay with us. You'll be all right here.' She eyed the others over her half-moon glasses and tried to be stern. 'They all talk at once and dash about like mad things on motorbikes and bicycles, wearing trousers and painting their legs with gravy browning. They're a lively lot, but they'll see to it that you settle in quickly.'

Harvey rushed between them all and tried to lick Mrs Finch's face before he was firmly pulled away and distracted by the sight of food in his bowl.

Ruby's legs could no longer hold her up and she sank gratefully onto a kitchen chair while Suzy cleaned her grazes and put iodine on the bruises. She was drained by the night's events and the boisterous welcome, and simply longed to crawl into bed.

'I expect you'd like something to eat,' murmured Ron. 'I know I would. What's left in the pot, girls?'

Fran checked in the large pot on top of the gleaming black range. 'The last of the rabbit stew, dumplings, carrots and onions. There's only a bit of apple and custard for afters, but I'm sure it'll be enough as you've already had one tea tonight, Ron.'

'Ach, to be sure, young Franny, I wouldn't say no to a second helping of that stew.'

'Then it's a good thing there's enough for two,' she said with a wink before ladling it out into bowls.

'This is a lovely coat,' said Sarah as she dabbed at the bloodstains on the sleeve and collar. 'I suppose you bought it in London?'

'Nah, I got it 'ere. Proper posh, ain't it? Never thought I'd 'ave summink like that, ever.'

'Good grief. Aye never imagined Aye would be assaulted by such ghastly gibberish. Is the gel actually attempting to speak English?'

An immediate silence greeted this remark and Ruby looked up at the woman who stood in the doorway. Not over-tall, but with a good figure for a woman of her age, she looked as if she'd just walked out of a department store window. But the eyes were cold, the lips curled in a snooty sneer. This could only be Doris.

'If you spoke the King's English then I could excuse that remark,' said Ron as he chewed on his stew. 'But as you don't, then I think you should apologise to Ruby for your lack of manners.'

'When it comes to manners, Ronan, you are hardly the one to make judgements.' The cold gaze swept over Ruby once more. 'Aye have no idea why you are here,' she said frostily, 'but Aye can only surmise that you were expelled from your billet as it is the middle of the night.'

'You can surmise all you like, Doris,' said Ron before Ruby could respond, 'but, unlike you, Ruby is here at Peggy's invitation and that's an end to it.'

'But she's no more than a guttersnipe,' she hissed. 'Really, Ronan, what was my sister thinking? I can't possibly run this house with yet another one of your waifs and strays cluttering up the place.' She shot Rita a meaningful glare, which was ignored.

Ruby thought she was a snooty cow and not worth the effort of another fight. She exchanged a knowing look with Rita and carried on eating the delicious stew as Ron continued the battle.

'She was, as usual, thinking of others, rather than herself,' retorted Ron. 'If you don't like the arrangement, then you're always free to go back to your own home.'

Doris ignored this broad hint. 'How long is she staying?'

'She's staying for as long as she wants, and you forget, Doris, you are not in charge here. I am.'

'If it wasn't for me there would be utter chaos,' she snapped. She slapped Harvey's inquisitive nose, which had gone up her skirt, and without another word stalked out of the kitchen in a huff.

Ron turned to Ruby and winked, his eyes sparkling with mischief. 'To be sure, she's riding a high horse tonight,' he said as he reached for his pipe. 'Don't mind her, Ruby, none of us take any notice of her either, and 'tis a wonder she's still here. We keep trying to get rid of her, but short of packing her bags and putting her out on the doorstep, she seems determined to stay.'

'We think she secretly likes it here,' said Suzy as she collected her nursing cape from the hook on the door. 'Anthony, her son, is away for a while and her husband seems to spend most of his time at the golf club, so she probably prefers even *our* suspect company to sitting on her own every night.' She chuckled. 'You'll find it's never dull around here, not with ferrets, Harvey and Ron to keep us on our toes.'

'Ferrets?' Ruby brightened a little. Her dad had kept ferrets.

'Flora and Dora,' said Ron proudly. 'I'll introduce them to you tomorrow.'

Suzy said goodnight to everyone and left for the hospital with a cheery wave.

'Suzy's courting Anthony,' said Rita, with a grimace, 'and Doris doesn't approve.'

Ruby wondered how on earth anyone could possibly not approve of the lovely Suzy. 'Is she snooty about everything?'

There was a general murmur of agreement and Rita giggled. 'Only if you don't live in the posh side of town or have a title, like that stuck-up Lady Chumley that she's always on about.'

Ruby sat at the kitchen table with its faded oilcloth and finished the deliciously rich and fragrant stew even though she was still trembling from her ordeal and her eyelids were drooping with weariness. Beach View Boarding House was a haven of warmth and welcome, and it didn't matter, that Doris had ideas above her station, for there was real friendship to be had here, and a chance to pick up the pieces and begin again.

Ruby finished the stew and drank a welcome cup of tea as the other girls settled down to their knitting and sewing. Ron disappeared with Harvey to check on the Anchor, and Mrs Finch twittered and giggled as she listened to ITMA on the wireless. Doris put in an appearance for a short while to wash out her sherry glass, but no one spoke to her and she went back to her room.

'Where's Mrs Reilly's baby?' Ruby asked.

'She's in with Doris,' said Rita, who was making a hash at knitting what might have been a scarf. 'Minding Daisy is about the only thing she's good at, and they seem to have become quite fond of one another, which is a complete mystery. Doris is hardly the maternal type.'

'No, she didn't look as if she was – more like one of them shop dummies, really – all clothes and no feeling.'

Rita giggled. 'You are a caution, Ruby. I'm glad you've moved in.'

'So, what brought you here, then? What's everyone's story?'

Rita told her how she'd been born in Cliffehaven, and had gone to school with Peggy's daughter, Cissy. Blast bombs had flattened her little home behind the station and she'd been billeted at the asylum. When that was blown to smithereens, Peggy had rescued her from the chaos of the Town Hall emergency accommodation and brought her here.

'Sarah and her sister Jane came all the way from

Singapore to be with their great-aunt Cordelia; and they still don't know what happened to their father, or to Sarah's fiancé, Philip,' she said quietly. 'But their mother's safe in Australia with her parents and her baby boy.'

'Blimey, that must be 'ard, not knowing – and to be on the other side of the world from yer mum and all.'

'Yeah, I think it is, but they don't go on about it.' Rita continued, 'Grandma Finch has been living here for years, and Fran and Suzy moved in before the war 'cos they didn't want to live at the nurses' home under Matron's nose.'

'I don't blame them. I've heard from my mate Lucy that she's a right tartar.'

Rita grinned. 'She can't be any worse than Doris. Poor Suzy,' she sighed. 'If she ever marries Anthony, she'll have the old bat for a mother-in-law, and it gives me shivers just thinking about it.'

Ruby grinned. 'Me too.' She regarded the happy scene of the girls and Mrs Finch gathered in peaceful harmony in the glow from the fire as they listened to the wireless. It was warm and cosy and a million miles away from Nelson Street.

'What about you, Ruby? Peggy didn't tell Fran very much, only that she thought you'd be moving in tonight, and that we had to make sure you were warmly welcomed.'

'It's a long story, Rita, and I'll tell you once I've 'ad a good night's sleep.' She gave a vast yawn and picked up the rosebud she'd carried with her from Nelson Street. 'I'm completely done in, and I have to be at the factory by eight in the morning.'

'Come on then. I'll show you upstairs and teach you how to use the water heater in the bathroom. It can have your eyebrows off if you're not careful.'

Ruby's eyes widened in disbelief. 'A bathroom? In the house?'

'Peggy and Jim worked long hours to save up enough to get it put in, but of course government regulations mean we can only have five measly inches of water in the bottom of the bath, and then we have to scoop it out in the big enamel jug and pour it into the water butt by the back door. Ron uses it to water his veg.' Rita grinned impishly. 'There's a proper lav upstairs as well. Which is a very good thing. The old outside lav got blown to bits a couple of weeks ago, and Ron hasn't got around to replacing it.'

Ruby said goodnight to everyone and thanked them again for making her first evening so lovely, and then followed Rita up the stairs with her basket. The bathroom was a revelation of white tiles, with a deep tub on clawed feet and polished brass taps. The boiler was a bit of a liability, but as long as she remembered to step back and count to three after putting the lighted match to it, she wouldn't lose her eyelashes.

Rita continued her guided tour, pointing out the airing cupboard where the towels and household linens were kept, the lavatory, Mrs Finch's bedroom and the three rooms on the floor above. 'Fran and Suzy still share, Peggy's daughter Cissy's room is at the end, and I'm in the middle up there. And this is yours, right next to Sarah and Jane's.'

Ruby stood in the doorway and looked in delight at the single iron bed, the neat little dressing table with a frilly skirt hiding the drawers, the comfortable armchair beside the gas fire and the pretty curtains that matched the eiderdown. 'It's lovely,' she breathed.

'It's all yours for as long as you want it,' said Rita with a broad grin. 'Now I need to get to bed too. I'm due to start my shift at the fire station at five-thirty, so I'll see you when you get back from work tomorrow.'

'What's the routine here in the mornings?' Ruby asked anxiously.

Rita rolled her eyes. 'I knew I'd forgotten something. Breakfast is usually porridge, and the first one up gets it warming on the stove along with the kettle. We drink a lot of tea in this house,' she added with a grin, 'so the kettle is always on the hob. Lunch is usually at twelve or thereabouts, and tea's at six, but again, it all depends on your shifts. If you write them down and leave them on the kitchen table, one of us will make sure your food's kept hot for when you get in.'

'Ta ever so, Rita.'

'Sleep well,' she replied, giving her a swift hug before she ran up the stairs to the top floor.

Ruby stepped into the room and closed the door. There was a key in the lock, but she didn't turn it. She would be safe here.

Chapter Sixteen

Ruby was having the running dream again, but this time it wasn't just Ray chasing her, but his uncles and brothers as well – and Harold. She knew that if they caught her, she would live long enough only to suffer great terror and pain before they snuffed out her very existence. So she ran, as fast as her bare feet could carry her over the rough ground. Her heart was thudding with fear, for she could hear their angry voices and their pounding footsteps gaining on her – and then she was flying, over the jagged edge of the white cliffs, and plunging with stomach-churning swiftness towards a black abyss.

In the instant before she hit the bottom she woke and reared up, eyes wide with terror, pulse racing as she fought to breathe. There was no abyss and no pursuers, just the pearly grey of a dawn sky shedding light between the open curtains. She slumped back into the soft pillows. It was only a nightmare, but the vestiges of it clung to her in cobweb tendrils, the sweat of fear still cold on her skin, and she knew she wouldn't be able to go back to sleep.

As Ruby waited for her heart to stop thudding, and the shadows of the nightmare to fade to nothing, she watched the sky lighten above the rooftops, and heard the first raucous screeching of the seagulls. She was in her lovely little bedroom at Beach View, safe and snug on this brand-new day, and she hugged that thought like a precious gift.

Her cheap alarm clock told her it was barely five in the morning when she heard a door click shut upstairs and soft footsteps on the landing. It had to be Rita, she surmised, but she wasn't alone, for as she reached Ruby's landing, Ruby heard another door open and a whispered conversation as they passed her door. She assumed this had to be Jane, who delivered milk from the enormous dray. She'd thought she'd recognised her last night as the girl who'd waved to her on that first morning at the factory – it was a strange coincidence that they should end up being billeted in the same house.

Ruby waited until the house was quiet again, and then padded out to use the lavatory and take advantage of the early hour to have a bath. The bathroom was icy, but there was a lock on the door and the five inches of hot water was wonderful, and she slid into it and revelled in the luxury of these private and pleasurable few minutes.

Once she'd wrapped herself in one of the soft towels and rubbed her hair dry she scooped the water out of the bath with the large enamel jug and placed it on the landing, ready to take downstairs once she was dressed. It didn't take long to pull on her shirt and dungarees and to tie the laces of her working boots – but a glance in the dressing-table mirror told her that although the bruises and carpet burns on her legs and arms were hidden, her face was a mess.

She sat on the little upholstered stool, feeling a bit like a film star, for she'd never possessed such a wondrous thing as a dressing table and stool, and carefully dabbed some Pond's cold cream on her face and then dusted it with powder. A bit of mascara on her lashes made her look less washed out, and once her hair was brushed to a gleam, she felt quite pleased with the effect.

Gathering up her gas-mask box and cardigan, she breathed in the scent of the rosebud that now stood in a glass by her bedside and then quietly left the bedroom. Having retrieved the enamel jug, she went downstairs to discover Ron and Harvey were already in the kitchen.

'Top of the morning to you,' Ron said with a beaming smile as he took the jug from her and Harvey left his saucer of tea to greet her enthusiastically.

Ruby managed to avoid getting her face licked by wrestling the dog's paws from her shoulders and pushing him away. 'Good morning,' she said, patting the animal's head as he nudged her with his nose.

'Harvey, ye eejit beast, leave the wee girl alone, and drink your tea,' Ron ordered. 'I'm sorry if he's a bit boisterous, but he means no harm,' he said to Ruby.

'He's lovely,' she said truthfully, 'not a bit like the savage strays we got round the tenement blocks. Most of them 'ave got the mange, and would bite you as soon as look at you.'

Ron poured her a cup of tea from the large brown pot and then ladled a good helping of porridge into a bowl and placed it on the table in front of her. 'You get on with that, and I'll empty the jug.'

Ruby tucked into the porridge and drank the sweetened tea as she took in her surroundings. She'd been so overwhelmed by everything last night that she hadn't taken anything in properly, but she could see now that her first impression had been right.

It was a shabby room, with faded walls and mismatched furniture, the upholstery on the armchairs worn away from years of use. But there was little doubt that it was the heart of this home, for the fire in the range glowed, the old furniture gleamed from industrious polishing, the linoleum looked quite new, and the gingham curtain beneath the sink added a dash of colour. There was a picture of the King and Queen above the cluttered mantelpiece where framed photographs had been lovingly placed, and she could only guess that the handsome man in army uniform must be Peggy's husband, Jim, and that the others were of their children.

The wail of a baby drifted through the house and Ruby felt a tug of longing which she quickly banished. There was no point in wishing things were different, and making a new start meant putting the past behind her – yet the memory of that poor, dead baby would always be with her, tucked away in the deepest recesses of her heart.

Ron returned to the kitchen and nodded with satisfaction as he saw her empty bowl. 'We'll soon put some meat on those bones,' he muttered as he reached into his trouser pocket and pulled out two perfect brown eggs. 'I'll boil one for you and do a bit of toast,' he said.

'There's no need,' she said hastily. 'The porridge was quite enough, and I know how precious them things are.'

'Ach, to be sure, these come free every morning from me hens. You'll be having the egg, and no argument.'

'I hope there are enough for everyone, in that case,' said Doris as she came into the kitchen with a grizzling Daisy in her arms. 'If the girl doesn't want it, there are plenty who will.'

Ron ignored her and placed the egg in a saucepan of boiling water.

Doris glared at him and then at Ruby. 'You might as well make yourself useful,' she said as she unceremoniously plonked Daisy into her lap. 'Take care of her while I prepare her breakfast.'

Ruby looked down into the baby's big brown eyes as she felt the solid, warm weight of her in her arms. Daisy smelled of baby powder, and her dark curls were still damp from her bath. Ruby's heart ached with loss as she caressed the chubby arms and legs and counted each of the tiny fingers and toes. Her own baby would have looked like this if it had been allowed to grow inside her, and the thought was almost unbearable. Her eyes filled with tears and she hastily blinked them away, determined to keep those treacherous emotions at bay.

Ron must have seen how Daisy was affecting her, for he gently took the baby from her arms and jiggled her against his shoulder. 'Eat your egg and soldiers,' he said gruffly, 'while I sort this one out. You don't want to be late for work.'

She shot him a grateful, rather watery smile and ate her egg and toast while Ron fed Daisy with some porridge, and Doris fussed over heating her bottle of milk. Ron was a sweet, thoughtful man who asked no questions, but seemed attuned to her needs and emotions, and she wished with all her heart that she could repay him in some way for all that he had done for her.

Ruby had just finished her delicious breakfast and was washing her crockery when Suzy came up the cellar steps into the kitchen. She folded her navy cloak over the back of a chair and sank into it to ease off her shoes. 'Thank goodness that shift is over,' she said on a sigh as Ruby poured her a cup of tea. 'Everyone was in a foul mood for some reason and I seemed to spend most of the time being bullied by either Matron or one of the surgeons.'

'In that case you must have been doing something wrong,' said Doris, who was now giving Daisy her bottle.

'One doesn't have to do anything wrong to be bullied by any of them,' said Suzy with admirable calm. 'It was a busy night, the theatres were running at full stretch and everyone was tense.'

'But there wasn't a raid last night,' said Ron.

'Not here, but there was a tip-and-run further along the coast. An ammunition dump took a direct hit and there were lots of civilian casualties. As we're the biggest hospital for miles around, they were sent to us.'

She finished the cup of tea and refused the offer of breakfast. 'I ate in the hospital canteen, and now all I want to do is go to bed and sleep. Anthony is picking me up at six, so I need–'

'Anthony's home?' asked Doris. 'He didn't tell me he was coming back today.'

'I expect he tried to ring you, and probably spoke to Mr Williams,' said Suzy as she gathered up her things. 'Never mind, you can have a chat with him this evening before we go out.'

Doris's expression was grim, her lips forming a thin line beneath her patrician nose, her eyes narrowed and steely. 'If you spoke to my Anthony, you could at least have told him where Aye am. He must be worried sick about me.'

Suzy bit her lip. 'It was a very short conversation, and we were cut off before we–'

'That is not the point,' snapped Doris. 'May Anthony has a very important job to do with the MOD, and he must not be allowed to fret over his mother's whereabouts.' She eased Daisy over her shoulder and rubbed her back rather forcefully to bring up the wind. 'Really, you girls are so selfish. Not a thought for anyone.'

Suzy's wan face flushed scarlet but, with admirable control, she didn't respond to this insult, and simply walked out of the room.

Ruby decided it was time to leave for the factory before Doris started in on her and Ron.

Ron had put Daisy into her pram so he could wheel her to the Anchor. Doris, of course, had kicked up a fuss, but Daisy was his granddaughter and Doris was getting far too possessive of her – which could cause ructions with an already jealous Peggy.

He gave a deep sigh as he walked down Camden Road with Harvey trotting along beside the pram. With a house full of women he was feeling beleaguered and looked forward to a bit of peace and quiet before the lunchtime session began.

He went through the side door and wheeled the pram into the bar. Opening the diamond-paned windows to let out the fug of cigarettes and spilled beer, he parked the pram beneath one of them so Daisy could watch the dappled shadows of the nearby tree dance across the ceiling.

As Harvey settled, nose on paws, beside the pram, Ron stood in the silence as dust motes danced in the rays of sunlight that gilded the room, and felt the peace enfold him. It was a lovely old pub, built over two centuries ago when fishing and smuggling had been thriving industries in Cliffehaven, and the parson, the fisherman and the innkeeper formed an alliance which was the backbone of this illicit and very profitable trade.

The cellar had a secret hidey-hole where the smugglers used to store their goods – and where the odd black-market crate of bottles, illicit cigarettes, or barrel of rum could still be hidden. This hiding place led into a warren of tunnels that spread beneath the houses and pavements of Cliffehaven to the other pubs, and ultimately to the crypt of the large church that had been recently flattened by the Luftwaffe.

Ron looked up at the ceiling, which was low and beamed with scarred and blackened ancient oak, then his gaze drifted to the fireplace, which was wide enough to accommodate a bench on either side where the old men would sit for hours with their pipes and pints of beer. The brick floor rippled and dipped, and the heavy oak door was studded with iron. Light barely penetrated the small diamond-paned windows, but when it did at this time of the morning, it brought a rich glow to the solid mahogany of the bar and a gleam to the many pewter pots that hung above it.

He heard the latch turn in the side door, and the creak as it was opened. He didn't take much notice, for he was expecting his doughty middle-aged barmaids, Pearl and Brenda, to arrive soon, and Harvey hadn't bothered to get up, but was simply thumping his tail on the floor.

But as he shrugged off his jacket and rolled up his sleeves to get stuck into cleaning the place up, he saw Harvey leap to his feet, then heard the unmistakable click-clack of high heels and his heart leaped with hopeful joy. He whirled round, and there she was – his Rosie.

'Hello, Ron,' she said with a soft smile.

'To be sure and you're a sight for these poor auld eyes,' he said through the lump in his throat as he took in the hourglass figure, the lovely face with the blue eyes and sensuous mouth, framed by the halo of platinum hair. Rosie might be in her fifties, but she was one fine-looking woman – in her prime, and utterly glorious.

She put down her suitcase and eased the handbag and gas-mask box straps from her shoulder and made a fuss of the welcoming Harvey. 'I wasn't sure if you'd be here,' she said, 'but I'm glad you are. This place wouldn't be the same without you and this old rogue.'

Ron longed to sweep her into his arms and kiss

the breath out of her, but he was suddenly uncertain about how she might react to such ardour after they'd been apart so long. He took a tentative step towards her. 'Welcome home, Rosie, me darlin' girl.'

Her blue eyes glistened, and without another word she abandoned Harvey and stepped into his arms and clung to him. 'Oh, Ron, I've missed you so very much,' she murmured against his cheek.

His arms willingly encircled her and he felt the rounded softness of her breasts press against his chest as her sweet perfume engulfed him and roused his senses. 'I've missed you more than words can say,' he whispered. 'Oh, Rosie, I've waited so long to have you in my arms again.'

She took his face in her hands and brought her lips to his in a lingering, sweet kiss and then stepped out of his embrace. 'We'd better stop now before things get out of hand,' she said, her voice choked with emotion.

'But, Rosie...'

She put a soft finger on his lips. 'I'm still not free,' she said, her eyes bright with unshed tears. 'My husband is extremely sick, but he's alive, and as long as he is, then you and I must respect that.'

'But you still love me, don't you?' he dared to ask.

'Oh, yes, Ron. I love you – nothing has changed that.'

He felt helpless, for he loved the bones of her and would have married her in an instant if it had only been possible. But her husband was locked away in an asylum and divorce was out of the question according to the law – and Rosie was not the sort of woman to break her marriage vows and give herself to another man while he was alive.

He cupped her lovely face in his rough old hand and resisted the temptation to kiss her again. ''Tis proud I am to be your closest, dearest friend, my sweet Rose,' he said gruffly, 'but if you keep looking at me like that, I shall not be answerable for my actions.'

She giggled and stepped away from him. 'You haven't changed, you old rapscallion,' she teased as she gathered up her handbag and suitcase and headed for the door that led to the upstairs rooms. 'I'll sort myself out and make us a pot of tea while you change the barrels and tidy up down here.'

She turned in the doorway and gave the bar an appreciative glance. 'Though I must say, the old place looks very well looked after, even though it seems to have been turned into a nursery.' There was a teasing light in her eye as she raised a brow. 'Not yours, I hope, Ron?'

He chuckled and winked at her. 'Go and make that tea and I'll explain everything when you come back down,' he said.

She shot him a naughty grin and went upstairs, and Ron wasted a bit of time just listening to her walk back and forth, imagining her in her little private domain above the bar. Then he got to work and quickly changed barrels, brought up crates of bottles from the cellar and made sure everything was polished to a gleam by the time she returned, looking very businesslike in her black skirt and frilly white blouse.

He took the tea tray from her and placed it on one of the low tables. 'That's my granddaughter,

Daisy,' he said proudly as Rosie leaned over the pram to inspect the sleeping baby. 'Peggy had her on the same day the Japs bombed Pearl Harbor, but I'm sure I wrote and told you that.'

'Yes, of course you did. I was only teasing.' She softly touched the dark curls. 'She's absolutely lovely,' she breathed. 'I hope Peggy knows how very lucky she is.'

Ron saw the wistful expression and the sadness in her eyes before she quickly masked them with a smile, left the pram and busied herself by pouring the tea. 'Aye, she does that, but things have changed at Beach View these past two weeks, and at the moment she doesn't feel particularly lucky at all.'

Rosie listened as she drank the tea and fed biscuits to Harvey, her large blue eyes widening as Ron told her about the bombing raid, the emergency operation and Doris's arrival. 'Poor Ron, what a nightmare – and on top of all that, you've had to keep this place going and carry on with your Home Guard duties too. You must be worn to a frazzle.'

'I might be past me best, but there's plenty of life in this auld carcass yet,' he said with a chuckle.

She laughed. 'I don't doubt it. But what I really want to know is what happened to my nefarious brother. You never did explain, and my sister-in-law hasn't answered my letters.'

'Tommy was caught with black-market booze and cigarettes hidden in the cellar,' he explained, carefully avoiding the fact that he'd been the one to inform the police so he could be certain that the slippery Tommy Findlay got his just deserts and was put out of action – and distanced from Cliffehaven for a very long time.

'He'd been running this pub like a bawdy house and there had been numerous complaints to the police,' he continued. 'When he was arrested, I took over with Brenda and Pearl, and you'll find the books are up to date and the profits have grown.'

Rosie gave a deep sigh. 'I might have known Tommy would let me down, but at the time I had little choice but to ask him to take over.' She placed her hand over Ron's as it rested on the tabletop. 'Thank you, Ron. I don't know what I'd've done if this place had fallen to rack and ruin.'

He knew she'd invested all her savings into the Anchor, which was why he'd stepped in so quickly to rescue it and get rid of Tommy. 'It was the least I could do,' he said modestly.

Rosie's gaze turned to the pram as Daisy began to burble and wave her arms and legs about. After a questioning look at Ron, she gently lifted the baby out and sat her on her lap. Resting her cheek on the dark curls, she held her close and played with the tiny fingers. And then she looked up at Ron, her expression earnest. 'If I ask you something, will you answer me truthfully?'

It was a startling question and Ron was cut to the quick that she should think he'd ever be dishonest with her. 'Of course,' he said rather stiffly.

'Did Tommy let Eileen Harris in here?'

'He had lots of women in here, but I don't think Eileen was one of them.' He regarded her steadily. 'Peggy saw them together once outside. According to her, Eileen was giving him a piece of her mind and he was arguing back. It was quite a heated exchange by all accounts, but Peggy was too far away and, much to her fury, couldn't catch what they were saying.'

Rosie grinned. 'As long as they weren't a cosy twosome, then that's fine.' She returned to playing with Daisy's fingers. 'The thought of that woman in my home makes me go cold.'

Ron was concerned about this change in her mood and the turn in the conversation. Eileen Harris worked for the council, and there had been rumours many years before that she and Tommy Findlay had had an affair. Tommy was married, and when he wasn't roving, lived with his wife and children a bit further down the coast, but he was a regular visitor to Cliffehaven, and was usually involved in some shady deal. If there had been an affair, it was long over, and yet, in some inexplicable way, Rosie seemed to have been tangled up in it – and whatever had happened, it had left deep scars.

He'd broached the subject once, but Rosie had simply told him that Eileen Harris had betrayed her in the worst possible way, but refused to elaborate. Puzzled by her vehemence and her determination to keep this past betrayal secret, he'd asked Peggy if she knew anything. Peggy, the fount of all knowledge when it came to the truth behind rumours, had remained tight-lipped and told him to mind his own business.

'You never did explain what happened between you and Eileen all those years ago,' he probed.

She regarded him evenly. 'No, I didn't, did I? And I'm not about to now. It's almost opening time and this baby needs changing and feeding.' She got up with Daisy still in her arms. 'Do you have clean nappies and a bottle I can give her?'

Ron dug about in the basket beneath the pram and found everything Daisy would need to make her comfortable. 'I'll see to Daisy while you sort out Brenda and Pearl – they're due any minute.'

'I'd prefer to deal with Daisy,' she said with a soft smile for the gurgling baby. 'You carry on, and I'll see you when this sweet little flower is all fresh and fed.'

Ron was so amazed by Rosie's unexpected maternal streak that he couldn't think of a thing to say. He watched her carry Daisy out of the bar and then shook his head. 'T'be sure, Harvey, I'll never understand women – God love 'em. They're a different species, so they are.'

As Ruby walked past the station she caught a glimpse of Stan, who was watering his pot plants at the far end of the platform and chatting to an old man sitting on a bench nearby. He was engrossed and didn't see her, so she carried on up the hill towards the factory.

Lucy was already waiting for her outside the gates. 'You must have been up very early to manage a walk down to the seafront and back before eight – and what's happened to your face?'

Ruby had realised this moment could be awkward, but she knew Lucy deserved at least part of the truth. 'I tripped on the stairs and bashed me face on the carpet in all the excitement of moving into Beach View Boarding House with the Reilly family,' she said.

The blue eyes widened. 'But you never said anything about moving yesterday.'

'I'm sorry, Lucy, I would have told you, but it was all a bit last minute,' she replied.

Lucy frowned. 'But why? I thought you were happy with the Frasers?'

'Ron and Peggy Reilly invited me to move in with them, and with all the other girls living there, it's much more lively,' she said carefully. She linked arms with the other girl and grinned. 'I know it's a longer walk to the factory every morning, but it takes me less than two minutes to get to the promenade – and I can't get enough of the sea.'

Lucy still didn't look overly convinced. 'But how do you know the Reilly family?'

'Remember I told you about how Stan looked after me on my first night here? Well, he introduced me to Peggy and things just went on from there,' she replied. Unwilling to continue this awkward exchange, she changed the subject. 'Do you fancy going to the pictures tonight? Only they're showing *Lady be Good*, with Eleanor Powell, Robert Young and Red Skelton.'

Lucy shrugged off her curiosity and smiled. 'I've heard it's really good, and some of the tap dancing is supposed to be amazing – Eleanor apparently does a whole dance routine with her dog.'

'That's settled then,' said Ruby. 'But we'll have to go to the late showing, 'cos I need to pop in and visit Peggy first.'

Lucy regarded her with unveiled curiosity. 'You look different today,' she said.

Ruby laughed. 'I put on a bit of make-up for a change.'

'Yes, I noticed that, but it's not the make-up – there's a sort of glow about you this morning.'

'That's because I'm happy,' she replied. She caught a glimpse of Flora bearing down on them, and tugged Lucy's arm. 'Come on, Flora's gaining on us and we're in danger of being late to our workbenches.'

They were both giggling as they scampered through the milling women to avoid the other girl, and Ruby felt a lightness of spirit that she hadn't experienced in a long while as she and Lucy clocked on and headed into the heart of the gloomy factory to begin another long shift. She was young and free and safe for the first time in years. Life was definitely on the up.

Chapter Seventeen

Peggy had been fretting over Ruby, for she hadn't seen Suzy at all, and Fran had only just come on duty and had been occupied with one of the other patients. Restless and worried, she'd done her four circuits of the ward and was feeling a bit tired and out of sorts as she waited for her visitors to arrive that Wednesday afternoon. She was definitely getting stronger by the day, and now the stitches had been taken out, she was determined to be out of here by Friday evening at the latest. All she had to do now was convince Alf the butcher to help her, and then run the gauntlet of Matron. This last hurdle would be the toughest, but Peggy's mind was made up and nothing would change it.

She plucked the latest of Jim's letters from her dressing-gown pocket and tried once again to make sense of it through the judicious pruning by the censor. It seemed he still had no idea that she was in hospital, which was puzzling – but he'd been sent to yet another barracks, which could explain why the telegram hadn't got through.

Folding the letter back into the envelope, she held it to her lips and tried very hard not to give in to the yearning to cry. She missed him so very much, and she hated the thought of him being so far away and out of reach. If only he could get some leave, just a few days, or even an hour or two. It would make all the difference.

Fran bustled over, saw her woebegone face and squeezed her hand. 'To be sure, Uncle Jim will come home on leave when he can,' she soothed. 'Don't upset yourself, Peggy. Just concentrate on getting better so that when he does come home, you'll be able to enjoy the time you have together.'

'I know it's silly to worry about him,' said Peggy, 'but we've been together almost every day since we married, and it feels so strange not having him around.'

''Tis the same for thousands of others,' Fran murmured, 'so you're not alone. I expect it's just the effects of the operation that are making you feel low. Once you're home again, you'll be amazed at how much more cheerful you'll be.'

Peggy blinked back the tears and didn't dare catch Fran's eye, for her planned escape must be kept secret, and Fran was very astute at picking up things. 'Yes,' she murmured. 'I expect I will.'

Fran smoothed the sheet, tucking it in as tight as a tourniquet over her hips. 'I'm sorry about this, Peggy, but Matron insists everyone has to be trussed up like mummies before visiting time.'

Peggy grimaced. 'How are things at home? Did Ron bring Ruby back with him last night?'

Fran smiled as she plumped the pillows with rather unnecessary vigour. 'To be sure, Peggy, 'tis life as usual at Beach View. Ruby has settled in just fine, and she and Rita have hit it off straight away, so you've no need to worry about her.'

Peggy sighed with relief. 'How was she when she arrived? Did Ron say anything about what had happened up at the Frasers'?'

Fran shook her head. 'We didn't know that was where she'd been staying,' she said. 'But she looked as if she'd been through the mill a bit and was clearly upset about something, but as she didn't say anything, we didn't like to ask.'

Peggy didn't like the sound of that at all, but she'd have to wait until she got Ron on his own before she could discover what had happened. At least the girl was safe now, and that was all that really mattered. Her thoughts turned to her second worry. 'What about Doris?'

'Doris is in a bate over the fact Anthony telephoned Suzy and not her – and that he didn't tell his doting mother that he was actually coming back to Cliffehaven tonight to see Suzy.'

Peggy rolled her eyes. 'When will Doris realise that Anthony has his own life? He's a grown man, for heaven's sake.'

Fran lingered for a spot of unnecessary tidying of the top of the bedside cupboard. 'It's all a wee bit odd, though,' she murmured. 'From what Doris said this morning, it sounds as if Anthony doesn't know she's living with us – but surely, if he'd telephoned home, her husband would have told him.'

Peggy shrugged. 'No doubt Ted's making the most of being left to his own devices. I suspect he's all but living at the golf club while Doris is out of his hair.'

Fran nodded and smiled, then went off to make sure the other nurses had the ward neat and tidy before the visitors arrived.

Peggy surreptitiously loosened the sheet and blanket so she could get into a more comfortable position, and then settled down to watch the doors in eager anticipation. She'd written a note to her friend Alf, the butcher, and Suzy had dropped it into his letter box on the way home this morning. She just hoped he'd managed to find someone to watch the shop so she could talk her plan of escape over with him.

There was a general rush on the dot of two and she was beginning to think no one was coming to see her today when a beaming Ron appeared with Daisy in his arms, followed by Alf, who was trundling Cordelia along in an ancient wheel-chair.

Her smile touched them all as she reached out for her tiny daughter and held her close, breathing in her lovely familiar scent and revelling in the feel of her sweet little hands touching her face. She caught Ron's eye over Daisy's curls, and her questioning look was answered by a wink, so she knew for sure that whatever had happened last night, Ron had sorted it and Ruby was safe.

She smiled at Cordelia Finch. 'My goodness, Cordelia, that was quite a regal entrance.'

'I hate the blessed thing,' she said after she'd kissed Peggy, 'but Alf borrowed it from his grandmother and it's a means to an end if I'm to get anywhere in this vast place.'

Alf's large ruddy face was glowing with pleasure as he pecked Peggy's cheek and handed her a small paper bag. 'My Lil made the fudge especially,' he said, 'and you're not to give most of it away, there's another lot in Cordelia's handbag to share out when she gets home.'

'Oh, Alf, how kind of Lil to use her sugar ration so generously.' Peggy took a small square of creamy fudge, fed a tiny piece to Daisy and popped the rest in her mouth. It was soft and very sweet and absolutely heavenly after so many months of going without sugary things. 'Hmm,' she managed. 'Hmm, hmm.'

They sat and chatted while she finished the treat and then carefully tucked the paper bag away in the bedside cupboard. Holding Daisy close, she kissed her little face and laughed back at her as she gurgled. 'She's looking wonderfully bonny,' she said wistfully. 'You all seem to be coping very well without me.'

'We muddle through,' said Ron. 'But the auld place isn't the same without you, Peg.'

'Me and Lil miss you and all,' said Alf gruffly, his Cockney accent still strong even after the many years he'd lived in Cliffehaven. 'That Mrs Williams is a tricky customer, forever poking me meat about and complaining about me sausages.'

'Are you coming home soon?' asked Cordelia fretfully. 'Only I don't know if I can stand living with Doris much longer.'

'I'm surprised she's lasted this long,' said Peggy as she eased the baby's weight off her bandaged stomach and kept hold of her as she tried to crawl across the bed. 'Perhaps now Anthony's back, she'll go home.'

'Aye, it would be a blessing. And now Rosie's home again and eager to help out, I can't see we need Doris at all.'

Peggy giggled. 'I noticed there was a glow about you today, Ron. I might have known it had something to do with Rosie.' She squeezed his fingers. 'I'm so glad she's home. Was she pleased with everything you've done at the Anchor?'

Ron's cheeks were suspiciously red as he nodded. 'Aye, she approves of the way I've converted the cellar into an air-raid shelter bar, and she's very pleased with the accounts and her freshly painted rooms. All in all, I think I've earned me stripes while she's been away.'

Peggy saw the happiness in his face and the sparkle in his eyes that had been missing for too long. Ron was back to his old self again, and Peggy's heart swelled. He was such a good man, he deserved all the joy he could get in the autumn of his life, and Rosie Braithwaite was the perfect mate for him. 'I suppose I'll have to dust off my wedding hat,' she teased.

He shook his head. 'Afraid not, Peg. She's still tied to that husband of hers – but we'll certainly throw a welcome home party.'

Daisy was growing restless, wanting to crawl and explore the bed, threatening to topple off the sides or get entangled in the blankets. As Peggy retrieved her yet again from the very edge, she felt the painful pull on her scar. 'Could you take her, Ron? She's too heavy to lift, and far too adventurous to keep still.'

Ron took the squirming baby, who immediately began to howl in fury at being thwarted. 'I'll take her for a wee walk before she has Matron marching in here complaining about the noise.'

Peggy watched as he carried the wailing Daisy out of the ward, and then turned to Cordelia. 'Do you have your hearing aid switched on?'

'Of course,' she replied. 'I can hear you perfectly well if you don't mutter.'

'Good, because there's something I want to discuss with you and Alf, and I don't want the rest of the ward listening in. In fact,' she added, 'I don't want this conversation going any further than this bed.'

'Goodness, that sounds intriguing,' breathed Cordelia as she edged the wheelchair closer, her eyes bright with excitement. 'Are we plotting something?'

Alf sat down in the chair by the bed, his expression anxious. 'This ain't gunna get me into trouble with the wife, is it?' he asked.

Peggy grinned. Alf adored his wife, but for a tiny woman, Lil had a fierce temper and a sharp

314

eye which missed very little – and despite his size, Alf was terrified of upsetting her. 'It will probably get all of us into hot water one way or another, but needs must when the devil drives,' she said purposefully. She beckoned them even closer. 'I'm coming home on Friday afternoon,' she said quietly.

'Oh, but that's wonderful news,' squeaked Cordelia.

Alf wasn't so easily taken in, and he eyed her suspiciously. 'Have you actually got the doctor's permission to come 'ome, Peg?' he rumbled.

'They said I was making excellent progress,' she said airily, 'and I feel so much better that I've decided it's time for me to leave and make way for someone who needs this bed more than I do. The wards are full at the moment after that tip-and-run and I–'

'Peggy Reilly, you can't just up and leave,' hissed Alf, going very red in the face. 'Jim would never forgive me if anything 'appened to you, and I'll not be a party to any daredevil escape.'

'Oh, Alf, and I thought you enjoyed a bit of an adventure,' she retorted with a teasing smile. 'You see, I'm going to need you to drive me home in your van.'

Alf shook his large head, his brawny shoulders hunched mulishly. 'I ain't doing it, Peg – and there ain't nothing you can say what will change me mind.'

She shot him a sweet smile: 'Are you sure, Alf?' she murmured.

He looked decidedly uneasy and Peggy could almost see the cogs churning in his mind as he tried to figure out exactly which of his many guilty secrets she knew. 'Positive,' he said without much conviction.

'Remind me,' she said softly, 'how did you *really* pay off the loan for that van?'

His eyes widened and he went quite pale. 'How did you know about that? I didn't even tell Jim.'

'I have my ways,' she said enigmatically. 'Does Lil know the truth, Alf?'

At the mention of his little wife, Alf's face went from ashen to puce and his Cockney accent thickened. 'Lil don't know nothing, 'cos if she did she'd 'ave me guts fer garters.' He looked quite terror-stricken. 'You ain't gunna tell 'er, are yer?'

'No, but I could drop enough hints for her to put two and two together,' she replied, struggling to keep a straight face.

'Bloody hell, Peggy, that ain't playin' the game. I thought you was my friend?'

'I am,' she said evenly, 'which is why I'm asking you to drive me home on Friday.'

'That's blackmail, Peggy Reilly.'

'Putting ten quid on a horse is gambling,' she retorted, 'and you were lucky it came up trumps, otherwise Lil would have had something to say.'

'Lil would have done more than 'ave a word,' he muttered, his expression grim. 'She made me promise to stay away from the gee-gees.' He looked at her in appeal. 'But it were a sure-fire thing. Got it from the 'orse's mouth, so ter speak. I couldn't let an opportunity like that pass me by, could I?' He wrung his great beefy hands.

She managed to keep her expression stern, but it was very difficult. 'So, Alf, do we have a deal?'

316

'Yeah, all right,' he muttered. 'But I ain't 'appy about this, Peg.'

'But you promise you'll drive me home on Friday?' He nodded and looked so woebegone that she relented. 'Thank you, Alf,' she sighed with relief. 'And don't worry, your secret's safe with me because I never had any intention of telling Lil anything.'

His face split into a grin and he roared with laughter. 'Peggy Reilly, you're a devious woman, and I should have known you'd never drop me in it with Lil. I've a good mind to call yer bluff and keep the van at 'ome on Friday.'

'But you won't,' she said, 'because you're a good friend and I trust you to keep this particular promise.' She smiled at him and wondered how long it would be before he confessed to Lil and discovered she already knew about his lucky win at the races.

'I'll be 'ere,' he said, 'though Gawd knows how we'll get past Matron.'

Cordelia had been silent during this exchange, her gaze following the banter back and forth like a spectator at a tennis match. 'You're both no better than naughty children,' she twittered, her eyes bright with laughter. 'But I too like a challenge, and I know exactly how I can help.'

They both looked at her in puzzlement, and she tapped a finger against her nose and grinned impishly. 'You get on and plan the escape. I will deal with Matron,' she said mysteriously.

Ron could understand Peggy's need to be at home, but he wasn't at all sure it was wise for her

317

to leave hospital after such a big operation until the doctor gave his permission. And yet, he'd been incarcerated in the damned place himself a couple of years back and had made his escape, so he supposed he had to go along with this mad idea and just hope it didn't have any long-lasting or disastrous repercussions.

He'd returned from the hospital with Cordelia and Daisy in Alf's van. Alf was still very nervous at the idea of helping Peggy escape, but Ron had assured him that Lil would never find out what they were up to, and he'd gone back to his shop feeling slightly better about things.

Having settled Cordelia in her chair with a cup of tea and a biscuit, he'd gone back down to the basement to check on his ferrets. What with all the responsibilities on his shoulders at the moment, he hadn't had the time to take them out or walk Harvey properly, and after the stifling atmosphere in the hospital, he felt the need to stretch his legs and get back up into the hills.

The scullery was better than new with its freshly plastered wall, replacement door and shiny stone sink, but his bedroom was in its usual state of chaos. He decided he'd clean it up before Peggy got back, but as there were a couple of days to go it seemed silly to waste a lovely day by doing it now.

He cleared away the discarded socks and pants, pulled the wooden cage from under his bed and knelt down to greet his young ferrets as Harvey whined and tried to sniff them through the wire mesh. Flora and Dora were looking sleek and quite plump, and their eyes were bright. They

318

seemed delighted to be taken out of their cage and carefully tucked into one of the deep pockets of his poacher's coat.

Harvey thumped his tail on the cellar floor, ears pricked in anticipation of an outing as Ron tied the laces on his sturdy boots, found his woolly hat and dug the specially adapted army-issue canvas bag out from beneath the pile of boots and wellingtons he'd left in the corner.

He'd carried this bag across his chest throughout his time in the trenches, and it had once carried maps, identification papers, first-aid kit and compass, as well as his tobacco and pipe – but after he'd come home he'd adapted it for a far more pleasant task, and with the long shoulder strap, it had proved ideal. Once he had gathered up everything he would need, he carried it all upstairs to the kitchen.

The house was quiet and, thankfully, there was no sign of Doris, so after feeding Daisy, he dressed her warmly and wrapped her like a cocoon in one of her small blankets before fitting her snugly into the canvas bag.

'What on earth are you doing?' asked Cordelia in alarm.

'I'm taking my granddaughter onto the hills,' he explained. 'She'll be quite safe. I used to do the same with Frank's boys when they were this size – and with Peggy's brood as well.'

'Doris won't like it,' she muttered.

'I don't care if she likes it or not,' he retorted as he hung the bag from his neck and secured it around his waist with the long tapes he'd sewn into its seams. 'It's time Daisy got to know what lies beyond this town of ours.'

Daisy gurgled and he looked down into the smiling little face and grinned back, remembering all the times he'd carried Frank's sons against his heart. The memories were warm and happy, but the reality of knowing that only one of the three had survived this awful war, and that his own sons were now back in the army, was quite sobering.

'You realise, of course, that you look quite ridiculous,' Cordelia said with a twinkle in her eyes.

'Aye, and you don't look much better,' he replied with a wink. 'Can I get you anything before I go?'

She shook her head. 'I have my book to read, and there's always the wireless to keep me company.' She gave a great sigh. 'It's such a nuisance being helpless like this,' she muttered as she eyed the plaster on her arm.

'You enjoy being lazy while you can,' he said. 'To be sure, there'll be work for you enough when that's taken off.' He pulled on his long, heavy coat and yanked the knitted cap over his ears. 'I'll be back in time to help cook tea,' he said before he turned and clumped down the cellar steps.

Harvey was already waiting impatiently by the back door, and as Ron waved him on ahead, he dashed off, jumping over the gate and disappearing along the alleyway that ran between the backs of the houses.

Ron felt the weight of his granddaughter tug round his neck, and heard her babbling happily as he plodded after the dog. It had been years since he'd done this, but with Rosie home and the whole glorious afternoon ahead of him, he felt as if he'd been given a new lease of life.

'Ronan Reilly, what *do* you think you're doing?'

'Uh oh,' he murmured to Daisy. 'Looks like we've been rumbled.' He kept his head down and lengthened his stride as Doris shouted from the bedroom window.

'Come back *immediately*. I know you can hear me, Reilly. Don't you *dare* pretend you can't.'

Ron heard the slam of the sash window which had only just been repaired and hoped to goodness she hadn't cracked the new glass in her temper. He quickened his pace again and was at the far end of the alleyway and starting the steep climb onto the hills by the time she could shout at him from the garden gate.

He ignored her furious demands and continued up the hill as Harvey raced ahead of him. Freedom was in the tough, windblown grass and gorse – in the sweep of the clear blue sky – and the sough of the breeze in the trees. This was a part of Daisy's heritage, and although she was far too young to take much notice of it, he knew it was important to show it to her.

He reached the top and stood for a moment to catch his breath. The colours were bright on this early summer's day, the air sweet with the smell of wild garlic and thyme and the salty sea which glittered in dazzling beauty beyond the white cliffs. The delicate blossom of apple and wild cherry drifted like confetti along with the feathery dandelion seeds, and the white heads of the cow parsley bobbed beside the Michaelmas daisies underneath the elderflower trees, which were almost in full bloom now.

From his vantage point above the valley, Ron could see fields of rippling green shoots of wheat, and a swathe of magnificent scarlet where the early poppies had taken over the fallow land. He turned away from this glorious sight, for it was a sharp reminder of his fallen comrades who hadn't come home from the last war.

He looked down at his small granddaughter, and discovered that she'd fallen asleep against his chest, a tiny thumb plugged into her rosebud mouth. His smile was soft as he headed down into the valley towards the line of dark trees and the high wire fence that marked the boundaries of the Cliffe estate. Daisy might not realise it, but the air she breathed and the scents she could smell would be instilled in her, and maybe, one day, she would bring her own children up here.

'It's disgraceful the way he conducts himself,' snapped Doris as she came back into the kitchen. 'I know he heard me.'

'I should think half of Cliffehaven could hear you,' said Cordelia mildly as she looked up from her book. 'As for being disgraceful, I think that's going a bit far.'

'Surely you don't approve of him taking a baby up there in such a dangerous manner?'

'Why not? He evidently did it with all his other grandchildren, and she'll be safe with him, I assure you.'

'But he's taken the ferrets and that blessed dog with him,' she said, her fists tight at her sides. 'Goodness only knows what he's planning to do up there.'

'He'll be hunting for rabbits, I expect,' said Cordelia, who was getting a bit tired of this and wanted to get on with her very exciting book. She reached up to turn off her hearing aid.

'Don't you *dare* turn that thing off when I'm talking to you,' snapped Doris. 'I'm sick and tired of having everyone ignore me – and I will *not* stand for it any more.'

Cordelia didn't appreciate being talked to in such a way, and she gave up on the book with a sigh. 'If you had something interesting to say, then I'm sure we'd all listen quite happily,' she said. 'But no one appreciates being bullied and bossed about, and there are times, Doris, when you can be most unpleasant.'

Doris went pale beneath the carefully applied make-up. 'You have no right to say such things when you aren't even part of this family.'

'I have as much right as you to express my feelings,' said Cordelia calmly, 'and this family has embraced me as one of their own for many years, so I feel quite justified.'

Doris glared at her and then lit a cigarette. 'One would have thought that after all I've done for this household, I'd be shown at least a modicum of courtesy and gratitude – even from you.'

'I'm sure we all appreciate your good intentions,' said Cordelia, 'but what exactly is it that you've done for us that must earn this gratitude?' She held Doris's gaze unflinchingly. 'Suzy and Fran take it in turns to help me wash and dress, Ron and the girls organise the shopping, the cooking, cleaning and Daisy's care throughout the day.'

'I bathe and feed Daisy and tend her through

323

the night,' she said stiffly. 'At least she isn't bathed in the kitchen sink any more, and I take great care to see that the dog does not slobber all over her, and that her food is wholesome.'

'Her food is the same as ours, and the milk comes out of a tin,' said Cordelia. 'As for bathing her in the sink, it's practical and much warmer than that icebox of a bathroom.' She relented a little, knowing that Doris really did have Daisy's welfare at heart. 'I agree, Harvey can be a bit of a nuisance at times, but that's all part of the rough and tumble of life in this house. A peck of dirt never hurt anyone, Doris.'

Doris seemed to run out of steam, for she plumped down onto a kitchen chair and silently smoked her cigarette, her gaze fixed on the flickering flames in the range.

Cordelia regarded her over the top of her half-moon glasses and realised that the other woman was having some sort of inner battle. It had to be galling to be ignored all the time, and to realise that she really wasn't wanted here, and although Cordelia didn't like her, she felt a twinge of conscience. Perhaps she'd been a little harsh – but then Doris's manner was aggressive and unkind at times, and she was old enough to know that was not the way to treat people if she wanted them to like and appreciate her.

'It will be nice to see Anthony again,' Cordelia murmured in an attempt to placate her. 'Where has he been these past couple of weeks?'

Doris stubbed out her cigarette in the ashtray. 'Anthony has a very important job with the MOD, and his whereabouts are top secret.' She squared her shoulders. 'Aye shall, of course, not question him when he comes here tonight – but Aye am disappointed that he didn't see fit to telephone me instead of that silly, thoughtless girl.'

'Suzy is neither silly nor thoughtless,' said Cordelia, rushing to her defence. 'You know, Doris, it is a mother's burden to watch our children grow and become independent. It's a bit different with daughters, who seem to stay closer to home, especially when they start a family of their own. But they all leave in the end to make their own way. And that is how it should be. Anthony is no longer a boy and dependent upon you or his father. He has his own life, and I believe that, whether you like it or not, Suzy is an important part of it.'

Doris's expression was stony as she picked up her gold cigarette case and lighter and pushed back the chair. 'I hardly think you're in a position to offer homespun advice on raising children,' she said coldly. 'From what I understand, your sons couldn't wait to get as far away from you as possible, and now you're all but forgotten – just a lonely old woman living out her last years feeding off the kindness of strangers. I hardly think that is a template for a lecture on motherhood.'

Cordelia felt the barbed words strike her heart; but determinedly kept her expression blank. 'I don't know why you feel you have to lash out at everyone like that,' she said flatly, 'but it strikes me you're a very bitter, angry woman – and it makes me wonder why that is, when you seem to have everything you could possibly want.'

Doris didn't reply as she strode out of the kitchen and slammed the bedroom door.

Cordelia dipped her chin and looked down at the plaster cast on her arm and the hands gnarled with arthritis that lay on the open pages of the book. Doris's cruel words still rang in her head, and although she rarely heard from her sons and their families, it had been she who'd encouraged them to find new lives in Canada. She who'd tearfully stood on the quayside and waved them off as they'd sailed away, knowing she would probably never see them again.

They had written regularly at first, long, interesting letters full of their trials and triumphs of settling in, but as the years had passed and they'd married and had families of their own, the letters had become fewer. She knew she hadn't been forgotten, but hoped that the birthday cards and letters at Christmas were sent with love and not out of a sense of duty.

Cordelia blinked away tears and sat for a moment in the peaceful silence of the house that had become her home. She knew she was loved here, knew she was an intrinsic part of this family and didn't feel sad. Life was a challenge, especially when you were a mother, and she'd learned to accept the way of things. But she sensed that Doris, for all her money and pretentions, was a deeply unhappy woman, and Cordelia wondered why that was.

Chapter Eighteen

Ruby didn't have any flowers to take to Peggy today, but she had managed to buy some sherbet lemons from her stash of illicit food stamps. It was still a few minutes to visiting time, but seeing Fran on duty, she pushed through the doors.

'I know I'm early, but I just wanted to speak to Peggy before the others arrive,' she said before the other girl could order her back outside.

'Well, seeing as it's you, I'll let you in, just don't let Matron catch you,' whispered Fran.

Ruby saw Peggy's welcoming smile as she hurried down the ward. 'You look ever so much brighter today,' she said as she handed over the little bag of sweets. 'I just come to say thank you for what you and Ron and Stan done fer me yesterday.'

'Bless you,' said Peggy warmly as she took her hand. 'You didn't have to bring me anything, or even thank me. I'm just glad you're safely home at Beach View.'

Ruby sat on the edge of the chair by the bed and tweaked the curtains a bit so she couldn't be seen from the door. 'But I do, Peggy, 'cos without your help, I'd've been in real trouble last night and no mistake.' She saw the alarm on Peggy's face, felt the warm, encouraging pressure of her hand round her fingers and slowly, hesitantly, told Peggy what had happened at Mon Repos.

There were tears in Peggy's eyes. 'Oh, my dear, I didn't realise...'

'Men like Fraser are clever at 'iding what they're really like,' said Ruby flatly. She grinned back at Peggy. 'Ron give him a bloody nose and told 'im he had a week to get out of town. Harvey were snarling and growling like he was about to rip his face off, and Fraser was sobbing like a baby.'

'I would have loved to have been a fly on the wall when Marjory arrived home. I wonder how he explained everything to her.' Peggy looked sharply at Ruby. 'You don't think she had some idea of what kind of man he was?'

Ruby shrugged. 'Gawd knows, but if she's got any sense she'll leave him, 'cos he'll do it again, you can bet on that.'

'Do you think so? Oh dear, perhaps it would be better if Ron reports him to the police. At least then he'd be locked away and other girls would be safe.'

'I already told Ron I don't want the police involved,' she said hurriedly. 'He's been found out and has to face his wife with a broken nose, which he'll find very hard to explain – and then have to come up with some reason for leaving the town in an 'urry. I reckon that's enough.'

Peggy's expression sharpened. 'But the police will...'

Ruby felt a stab of alarm. 'Nah, Peggy, I don't want to have nothing to do with them. Best we leave them out of it.'

'Is there another reason you don't want the police involved, Ruby?' she asked softly. 'Did something happen before you came down here?

Is that why you were covered in bruises and had that cut on your head?'

She stared at Peggy in confusion. 'Who told you about them?'

'Stan told Ron and he told me,' said Peggy. She held tightly onto Ruby's hand, her expression concerned. 'You can tell me, Ruby, and it will go no further, I promise. Whatever it is you've done – or witnessed – or had done to you, will stay between us. This is a new start for you, and it's always better to clear the air before you begin again.'

Ruby saw the honesty in her eyes and was drawn to her gentle, motherly concern. She wanted so very much to confide in her, but was terrified that if she did, Peggy would not want her living in her home. 'We don't trust the police where I come from,' she muttered instead. 'And we got our own way of dealing with things what need sorting out.'

Peggy patted her hand, her warm smile understanding. 'It's all right, Ruby, you don't have to say anything more. But if you ever do want to confide in me, then I'll be happy to listen.'

Ruby nodded, unable to speak through the lump in her throat.

Peggy reached out and cupped her chin. 'I take people as I find them, Ruby, and don't judge – and if you think I'll turf you out of my home because of anything you might tell me, then be assured I would never do that.'

'Thanks, Peggy, you're a real diamond.' Ruby could hardly see her for the tears as she nestled her cheek in the warm, soft hand and was reminded of her mother. She sniffed back the tears and gripped Peggy's hand. 'If there's anything I can do for you, then you only gotta ask. I owe you and Ron so much.'

Peggy smiled and handed her a clean handkerchief. 'As it happens, there is something you could do for me, Ruby, but you must promise not to tell anyone.'

Ruby dried her eyes and leaned closer, her curiosity piqued. 'That sounds mysterious,' she murmured with a tentative smile. 'What are you up to?'

Peggy told her about her planned escape. 'But I need you to get me some outdoor clothes. I can't possibly leave here in a nightdress.'

Ruby frowned. 'Are you sure you're well enough to come 'ome?'

'Ruby, don't be tiresome, love,' she said on a sigh. 'I've only had a hysterectomy. Just get me some clean underwear, a skirt, jumper, shoes and a coat. It wouldn't occur to Ron and I doubt Cordelia will think of it either, she's too busy plotting how to distract Matron.'

'Just how many people are involved in this?' asked Ruby with a grin.

'Alf, Ron and Cordelia – now you. And not a word to Fran, she's already suspicious about the amount of walking I do every day.'

Ruby thought about this task for a moment and realised it could be quite tricky. 'I'll have to wait until Doris is out of the way. She's moved into your bedroom, and if she catches me going through your things there'll be hell to pay. She's already made it clear she don't like me.'

Peggy grimaced. 'My sister doesn't like anyone very much. I wouldn't let it bother you, Ruby.

330

Just do what you can to get her out of the way long enough to put together some clothes before visiting time tomorrow night. Can you manage that, do you think?'

Ruby chuckled. 'I'll do me best, I promise.' She peeked round the curtain as the doors opened and the visitors came pouring in. 'There's Sarah, Jane and Rita. I'd better be off. I'm supposed to be going to the pictures with my mate Lucy, and if I don't hurry up, I won't have time to change out of this lot before the last show starts.'

Peggy kept hold of her hand. 'Remember, Ruby, I'm on your side, and if you need someone to talk to, then don't be afraid to come to me.'

Ruby kissed the soft cheek. 'I know, thanks for everything, Peggy,' she murmured.

Ron was already at the Anchor with Harvey, Ruby had dashed in to get changed before she'd charged out again, and Suzy was getting ready for her evening with Anthony while Doris remained in Peggy's bedroom with Daisy. Cordelia had been left in charge of keeping the evening meal hot for when the other girls came back from visiting Peggy.

Cordelia found she could stir the soup with one hand, and lay the table, but what she couldn't do was keep secrets, and that really bothered her. She'd never managed to keep her thoughts from showing on her face and would have been a terrible poker player, which was why she was finding it so hard not to blurt everything out to Suzy as she came downstairs, refreshed from her sleep.

'You look a bit on edge, Grandma Finch,' Suzy

said with a frown. 'Is your arm hurting? Would you like an aspirin?'

'No, dear, my arm's fine,' she said hurriedly. 'It itches a bit, but my knitting needle soon sorts that out.'

Suzy didn't look terribly convinced, but before she could continue this minor inquisition there was a knock on the front door. 'Anthony,' she breathed, her face lighting up as she dashed into the hall.

Cordelia could hear the murmuring of sweet nothings, and not wanting to eavesdrop, she went across the kitchen to turn up the wireless. But her fingers never reached the knob, for Doris had come out of Peggy's bedroom and all but pushed Suzy out of the way to fervently embrace her son.

'Anthony, my dearest boy,' she said as she hugged him fiercely and smoothed back his hair. 'I'm so thankful you're back in one piece.'

Anthony didn't look at all delighted as he disentangled himself and pushed his glasses back up his nose. 'I haven't actually been involved in anything at all dangerous,' he said, 'so I don't really see why you have to make such a fuss.' He frowned as he looked down at her. 'What on earth are you doing here, anyway, Mother?'

'I've come to help out while Peggy is in hospital,' she said stiffly. 'I left a note on the kitchen table. Haven't you been home yet?'

'No. I came straight here to see Suzy.'

'I see.' Her expression was stony. 'So you aren't in the least concerned about your mother's welfare now you've had your head turned by this ... this girl.'

He kept his hand firmly clasped in Suzy's. 'Why should I be concerned about you?' he asked, genuinely puzzled. 'You seem to be healthy and robust as usual, and I'm sure that Father is quite capable of dealing with any other problems.' He put his arm round Suzy's shoulders. 'Suzy's my girl, and of course I want to be with her as much as possible. I thought you understood that.'

Doris made a strange noise in her throat. 'Oh, I understand well enough,' she rasped as she reached for the front door and swung it open. 'Don't let me stop you,' she said coldly. 'I'd hate for you to miss a second alone with your precious Suzy.'

'Mother, don't be like that,' he sighed in exasperation, his glasses once more slipping down his nose. 'It's really unbecoming and rather embarrassing, if the truth be told.'

Doris turned on her heel and went back to Peggy's bedroom, the door clicking shut behind her.

In the heavy silence she left behind, Anthony gave Suzy a hug. 'I can't seem to do anything right, just lately,' he muttered. 'Do you think I should try and talk to her? Would it do any good?'

Suzy kissed his cheek before reaching for her coat. 'I don't really think anything would appease her at the moment,' she said softly. 'She's jealous, Anthony, and nothing you can say will change that.'

'But that's ridiculous,' he hissed. 'She's my mother, for heaven's sake.'

'Mothers can be horribly possessive,' she murmured as he helped her on with her coat. 'Especially when they have only one, very clever, handsome son to cherish, and some girl happens along to whisk him away.'

Anthony pulled Suzy into his arms and held her tightly, his chin softly resting on her fair head. 'I'm not handsome, or particularly clever, but I am a lucky man – and that's because of you, Suzy.' He cupped her face in his hands and kissed her lips. 'You can whisk me away to anywhere you like. Come on, let's get out of here.'

Cordelia returned to stirring the soup as the front door closed behind them. What a fool Doris was, she thought, for if she carried on like that, she would lose the son she adored, and become even more bitter in the process.

She let her thoughts wander as she pottered about collecting plates and bowls and checking that she'd remembered to put the bread and salt on the table. The girls would be back just after seven, probably starving hungry after a long day at work, and she didn't want anything to spoil their enjoyment of this rather late evening meal. But her mind kept returning to the problem of Doris.

Cordelia had only met her husband Edward on one occasion, and he'd seemed a quiet sort of man – a real gentleman – but Doris had almost been dismissive of him. Suzy had said much the same thing after the dinner party the other week, so things clearly hadn't changed. What was the matter with the woman? Couldn't she see the damage she was doing?

The vast assembly hall behind St Saviour's Church now served as the local cinema, thanks to the generosity of the Americans billeted at Cliffe estate. They had provided a projector and one of their corporals to run it until a couple of the local men learned enough to take over, and they were also the source of many of the latest Hollywood films and cartoons which they'd had flown in from America. It seemed the Americans could perform miracles even in these troubled times, and the residents of Cliffehaven were extremely grateful, for going to the pictures was an escape – a chance to forget the war and become lost for just a few hours in the fantasy of another world.

The large white screen had been set up on the stage and chairs of varying shapes and sizes had been scavenged from every corner of Cliffehaven, and the distributors who'd once serviced the Odeon now provided this makeshift cinema with a seemingly endless supply of newsreels and old films as well as the latest releases from the British studios. An enthusiastic army of women swept the hall clean every day, and beat the dust from the heavy velvet curtains that hung on either side of the stage, and then served the tea and biscuits that were sold during the interval in support of the local Spitfire Fund.

Ruby had dressed quickly in her lovely new skirt and jumper, and although she didn't possess any stockings, the soft leather shoes didn't rub her bare feet. She'd applied powder, lipstick and mascara and had brushed her hair so it fell to her shoulders in a rich brown sheen. With her freshly cleaned coat over her arm, she'd run all the way to St Saviour's and was out of breath by the time she reached the queue that stretched all the way down the street.

Lucy waved and called to her from near the front, and she hurried towards her. 'I thought I were going to be late,' she panted, 'and I've missed me tea. Luckily, Grandma Finch made me a couple of sandwiches to keep me going.'

'We'll treat ourselves to a fish supper after the show,' said Lucy, who was looking very pretty in a pink sweater and grey skirt. Her face lit up with a smile. 'You look very smart, Ruby, and I love those shoes.'

Ruby felt a glow of happiness as they stood and chatted while the queue grew even longer. And then the double doors were flung open and they slowly shuffled up the steps, bought their tickets and found two spaces to sit. Ruby fidgeted a bit on the rather rickety kitchen chair while Lucy folded her coat on the seat of another so she could see over the heads of the people in front. Ruby pulled the packet of sandwiches out of her gas-mask box. 'Do you want one?'

Lucy shook her head. 'I'll wait for the fish supper, but thanks, anyway.'

Ruby sank her teeth into the meat paste sandwich and munched happily as the hall began to fill up and the noise level rose along with the cigarette smoke. She loved going to the pictures, and as it had been a treat denied her by Ray, who thought it was a waste of money, she'd made sure she went at least twice a week now she was free to do what she wanted.

'Hi there, Ruby. Is it okay if we sit here?'

The soft burr of the Canadian voice startled her and she almost choked on her sandwich as she looked round to find Michael Taylor standing beside her. She hurriedly finished the mouthful and dabbed her finger along her lips to make sure there were no crumbs or smears of paste left behind. 'Hello, Michael,' she said awkwardly. 'What are you doing here?'

'Waiting for the film to start,' he said with a twinkle in his very blue eyes as he settled onto the chair beside her. 'I love the movies, don't you?'

She nodded, unable to think of a thing to say as his bright gaze and wide smile held her enthralled. And then she felt a soft nudge in her ribs and realised Lucy was feeling a bit left out of things. 'This is my friend, Lucy,' she told him. 'We work together at the tool factory.'

Michael was all smiles as he introduced himself and then turned back to the equally handsome young officer sitting beside him. 'This is my buddy, Steve Cameron.'

Ruby saw Lucy blush as her hand was enveloped in the large Canadian's paw, and couldn't blame her, for both men were quite something to look at and their manners were impeccable. And yet she felt awkward sitting beside Michael, whose broad shoulders and long legs seemed to take up too much space – whose wide smile and blue eyes were far too close for comfort. She felt a subtle change in the light-hearted mood she'd been in, for her senses had sharpened and her heart beat a little faster as his arm brushed against hers.

'I guess these chairs weren't built for us big guys,' he said as he and his friend tried to get comfortable.

Despite all her misgivings, Ruby giggled. 'It strikes me all you Canadians are twice the size of

337

normal blokes. What do they feed you on over there?'

He chuckled. 'I guess we eat the same as you, but Canada's a big, empty country, and I suppose we have to grow tall and broad to fill it.'

Ruby was saved from replying to this, for the room was plunged into darkness and the beam of the projector's light flashed onto the screen as the familiar cockerel crowed to announce the Pathé News. She tried to concentrate on the battles being fought in the Coral Sea, and on the North African front, but she was all too aware of the man sitting beside her and couldn't resist taking surreptitious peeks at him.

He was dressed in the scarlet tunic and black trousers that were so reminiscent of the guards who protected Buckingham Palace. His boots were highly polished, and the brass buttons and gold braid on his jacket gleamed in the flickering light which enhanced the sculptured planes of his face. Now he'd removed the peaked hat, she could see that his fair hair was cut brutally short, and, that his brows were several shades darker above the blue eyes, long, straight nose and chiselled chin. He could certainly have passed as a Hollywood star with those looks, she mused, but if he thought she was an easy sort of girl who could be flattered by his attention, then he had another think coming.

He seemed to realise she was watching him and turned his head with a questioning smile.

Ruby blushed and quickly turned back to the screen. She'd have to watch herself with this one and no mistake, for he unsettled her, and that wasn't at all what she wanted or needed right now. She'd had enough of men to last her a lifetime, and if Michael Taylor thought he could change her mind, then he was sorely mistaken.

When the lights went up half an hour later she realised with a jolt that she hadn't taken in a single thing, and she silently cursed Michael for ruining what should have been a relaxing, pleasant evening. Yet she couldn't be cross with him, for he and his fellow officer showed no sign of getting fresh as they bought tea and biscuits and asked about their work at the factory and life in Cliffehaven.

Steve Cameron and Lucy seemed to be hitting it off rather well, and they all shuffled around so they could sit beside one another and continue their discussion about winter skiing – which was a passion that Lucy had never revealed to Ruby.

Michael kept his questions almost impersonal, never probing too deeply into her marriage or her life in London, and seemed happy to tell Ruby about his growing up on a ranch in Saskatchewan, and his interrupted career in the Canadian Mounted Police before he enlisted into the Royal Regiment of Canada.

'Is it true that a Canadian Mountie always gets his man?' Ruby teased.

'Yes, ma'am,' he replied and grinned. 'And the uniform helps to get the girl sometimes, too.'

Ruby laughed and resisted asking him if he had a girl at home. 'I just bet it does. Is that why you chose to join a regiment with such a glamorous uniform?'

He looked a little bashful. 'I always admired the Grenadier Guards, and the uniform is very similar. We even wear busbies when on regimental parade.'

Ruby giggled, feeling much easier with him now he wasn't flirting with her. 'I used to go and watch them changing the guard at Buckingham Palace with me mum and dad when I were little – and I never did work out 'ow they could see where they was going under all that fur.'

'Bearskin,' he gently corrected her. 'And we lift our chins and look down our noses to see where we're going, and I don't mind telling you, it can get mighty hot under there at times.'

'I thought it were freezing cold in Canada?'

He smiled at her. 'It is in winter, with snow piled higher than the rooftops, but the summers are warm.'

The lights went out and they settled down to watch the main feature film. Ruby was still on her guard, but he'd shown no signs of trying to hold her hand or get fresh, and she'd enjoyed listening to his stories about Canada He seemed to be a genuinely nice man – but then they all were until they got what they were after, she thought cynically. Better to keep him at a distance and her guard up than to fall foul of yet another sweet-talking predator.

The film slowly drew her away from the church hall and the people surrounding her and she found she was laughing at the jokes, her feet tapping along in time to the music as the dance routines swirled across the screen. It was a happy, lively film and she felt quite sad when it was over and the lights went back on.

'Can we walk you girls home?' asked Michael.

'Or we could go to the pub and have a drink, if you'd prefer. We don't have to be back on base until midnight and Steve has borrowed a car.'

'We were planning on having fish and chips,' said Lucy before Ruby could think of a polite way of refusing their offer.

'Hey, that sounds a great idea. I've heard a lot about your English fish and chips, but never had a chance to try them out.'

Ruby realised she would be seen as a bit of a spoilsport if she demurred, so she linked arms with Lucy and they led the way back to the High Street and the chippy. There must have been a fresh delivery of fish, for there was plenty on offer, and Ruby ordered four cod with chips and plenty of salt and vinegar, and insisted each of them paid for their share – it might only be fish and chips, but they didn't know these men well enough for them to buy their dinner.

The heat seeped through the newspaper as they carried their supper down to a low brick wall which stood in front of a bomb site. Despite the blackout, there was enough light from the moon to see that Cliffehaven High Street was bustling with life. The drinkers spilled out of the pubs onto the pavements to escape the noise of badly played pianos and the fog of cigarette smoke. Girls were dressed up to the nines and walked arm-in-arm in giggling gaggles down the street as the servicemen strolled about in hunting packs, and the Yanks roared up and down in their jeeps, wolf-whistling and catcalling every girl they passed.

'It's a lively little town, isn't it?' said Michael as he finished the last of his supper and lobbed the

341

newspaper into a nearby rubbish bin. 'How about we go for that drink now? The pubs are open for another half hour, so we've time.'

'Me and Lucy have to be at work early tomorrow,' Ruby said quickly before Lucy could answer. 'And I gotta finish me letter to me 'usband so I can post it in the morning.' It would do no harm to remind Mike Taylor that she was a married woman. 'Ta ever so for your company.'

'Do you have far to go?' he asked. 'Only Steve and I would gladly see you both home safely.'

Ruby could see that Lucy was beginning to waver and so quickly tucked her hand into the crook of her arm. 'Nah, it ain't far, but thanks for the offer. Goodnight.' She turned away and set off at a brisk walk down the High Street.

'Why didn't you let them see us home, Ruby? We haven't got to be at work tomorrow and they were ever so nice.'

'Because walking us home might give 'em ideas if they should pass a dark alley or a shop doorway,' Ruby replied. 'Nice they might be, but give 'em an inch and they'll take a mile. Trust me, Lucy. I know what I'm talking about.'

'But Steve's not like that. I'm sure he isn't – and neither is Mike.'

'You know what they're sayin' about the Yanks, Lucy. Over-paid, over-sexed and over 'ere. Who's to say the Canadians ain't just the same?'

Lucy tugged on her arm, forcing her to stop walking. 'You've been sharp all evening. What's got into you, Ruby?'

She drew a deep breath. 'I'm sorry, Lucy. I didn't mean to be so cross. But you're only seventeen, and you don't really know nothing about either of them to judge what they're like. They could be married for all we know – or engaged – and I bet that at the very least, they've got girlfriends at home who are trusting them not to stray.'

Lucy looked thoughtful as she dug her hands into her coat pockets. 'You kept very quiet about Mike,' she said finally. 'How come you know him?'

'We met on the train coming down here,' she replied with studied nonchalance. 'I never expected to see him again, so it was a bit of a shock him turning up like that out of the blue.'

Lucy giggled. 'You've gone all red, Ruby. But I can't say I blame you. He obviously likes you, and is quite the thing, isn't he?'

Ruby did her best to appear unfazed. 'I'm a married woman, Lucy,' she reminded her – and herself, 'and blokes that 'andsome are dangerous.'

Lucy gave a shiver of delight. 'I know,' she sighed. 'Lovely, isn't it?'

Ruby giggled as she once again linked arms. 'Come on, Lucy. The sooner you gets home, the sooner you can dream about 'im.'

Chapter Nineteen

Ruby lay in the comfortable bed and watched the sky turn pearly grey as she thought about the previous evening. She'd probably been a little hard on Mike and Steve, darkening their intentions with her cynicism, but Lucy was far too naïve for her own good, and she'd felt responsible for her. And yet she regretted being so bossy, for she'd enjoyed the evening, and against her better judgement would have liked to see Mike again, for she'd found him interesting to talk to. Hopefully he would take her none-too-subtle hint that she wasn't interested, and stay away from now on, for he was an added complication to her life that she simply didn't need.

Ruby's thoughts turned inevitably to her mother and Ray. It was frustrating and very worrying not to know what was happening up in London, and because she couldn't give anyone her address, there was no way of discovering if Ray was still alive – or, more importantly, if her mother was safe. Perhaps, once Peggy came home, she'd ask if she could use the telephone to call the Tanner's Arms.

Deciding this would be a good idea, she then turned her mind to the difficult task of getting into Peggy's bedroom. She had no idea of Doris's daily routine, and if she was discovered poking about in the cupboards, there would be hell to pay. Ron and Cordelia were part of this secret plan of escape, and it seemed logical to ask one of them to get the clothes, or at least distract Doris while she went in there.

Ruby finally climbed out of bed. It was still very early, but the habits of years were deeply ingrained, and she knew she wouldn't be able to get back to sleep again. Having washed, she dressed in trousers, blouse and sweater, in preparation for the promised ride on Rita's motorbike, and then spent a few minutes applying make-up to hide the grazes on her face, and the still-angry red scar on her forehead.

When she eventually went into the kitchen, it was to find Ron washing out Harvey's food bowls and boiling up a mess of bread, egg and milk for his ferrets while Doris tutted her disapproval and warmed Daisy's bottle.

Cordelia was eating porridge and scanning the newspapers. She looked up and smiled at Ruby. 'Good morning, my dear,' she said brightly. 'Lovely day, isn't it?'

Ruby glanced out of the heavily taped kitchen window. 'It looks as if it might be quite sunny,' she replied before ladling some of the porridge into a bowl and pouring a cup of tea.

'If you like your eggs runny, then you should only put them in for a minute or two,' said Cordelia. 'I'd eat that porridge first, if I were you. Eggs need watching.'

Ruby frowned at this and then saw Ron twirling his fingers by his ear and realised Cordelia's hearing aid wasn't working.

Cordelia seemed oblivious to this. 'Have you got any plans for your day off? Only the WI has arranged a charabanc outing for the Cliffehaven pensioners, and I'm sure they wouldn't mind if you came along with me.'

Ruby grinned at the thought of an outing with a busload of pensioners. 'Ta ever so, but me and Rita are going out on her bike today,' she said loudly and clearly.

Cordelia wrinkled her little nose. 'Nasty smelly thing,' she muttered. 'I really don't see the attrac-

345

tion, but Rita seems to like nothing better than to charge about on it. I suppose she's told you about the races she organises?'

Ruby nodded. 'Yeah, and I think it's a brilliant way to raise money for a Spitfire. She told me there's almost three hundred quid in the kitty, so with only another couple of hundred to go, she's almost on target.'

'Rita is not the only one who helps to raise funds,' said Doris as she fed Daisy her bottle. 'Aye sit on several highly respected charitable committees in the town and it has always been our aim to provide Cliffehaven with its very own Spitfire.' She sniffed. 'Motorcycle racing is hardly the most appropriate way to fundraise.'

Cordelia fiddled with her hearing aid, clearly confused by the conversation she couldn't hear properly.

'It doesn't matter how it's raised,' said Ron, 'and I wouldn't mind betting that Rita pulls in more money with her races than you do with your snooty tea parties.'

Doris looked down her nose at him and made no comment as she finished feeding Daisy. Having wiped her face clean with a damp flannel, she carried her into the hall and strapped her into the pram with some of her toys.

'I would appreciate it if you could lift the pram down into the back garden, Ronan,' she said on her return. 'Daisy needs some fresh air.'

'Aye, I'll do that when I've fed Flora and Dora.'

He stumped down the cellar steps and Doris gave an exasperated sigh. 'It comes to something when ferrets take precedence over a granddaughter,' she muttered. She eyed the sink full of dirty dishes with distaste and turned back to Ruby. 'When you've finished eating you can do the washing-up,' she said in her commanding voice. 'There is also a pile of dirty nappies that need seeing to, and as it's your day off, you might as well do something useful to earn your keep.'

'Ruby and I will see to the washing-up,' said Cordelia firmly. 'But the nappies are down to you, Doris. I did warn you they needed doing every day, and as you've taken it upon yourself to organise Daisy, then you must also see to the less pleasant tasks.' Cordelia regarded her without affection. 'After all, Doris, you're the only one in this house with time on your hands, and so far, you've managed to avoid doing both the dishes and the laundry.'

'I had plans for today,' she said stiffly.

'It's still early enough to do the washing and get it on the line before you have to be anywhere.'

There was a hint of panic in Doris's expression. 'But I don't know how to light the boiler, and my manicure will be ruined.'

'Ron will show you how to light the boiler,' said Cordelia, 'and there are rubber gloves under the sink.' She smiled at Ruby. 'I can't do much with this arm in plaster, but if you see to the dirty crocks, I'll put everything away and tidy up.'

Doris wrinkled her nose as she reached under the sink for the bucket of nappies and rubber gloves, and carried them at arm's-length down to the scullery. 'Ronan,' she ordered, 'hurry up and bring Daisy into the garden, and then you must show me how this infernal boiler works.'

Cordelia rolled her eyes. 'Do you think that woman regards all of us as her servants?' she asked in exasperation.

Ruby grinned. 'Yeah, I think she does,' she agreed. Now that Cordelia's hearing aid was working properly, Ruby saw her chance to have a quiet word with her. She turned on the taps and began to fill the sink with hot water. 'Peggy asked me to do something for her today,' she said quietly, 'and I'm going to need your help'

'What's that, dear? Peggy's going away?'

Ruby realised she couldn't hear her properly over the sound of the running water, and Doris was still too close to talk any louder, so she shook her head. 'It doesn't matter,' she replied.

'She's not going away, dear,' said Cordelia with a chuckle. 'Or rather, she is leaving, but I'm not allowed to say because it's secret.'

Ruby put her finger to her lips. 'I know,' she mouthed.

Cordelia was looking a bit flushed as she giggled and nudged Ruby. 'I do love secrets, don't you?'

Ruby nodded and again put her finger to her lips to warn Cordelia to keep quiet. Her only option now was to get Ron on his own. As she began the washing-up, she could hear him telling Doris how to light the boiler, and her loud complaints about being forced to do such menial work when there were others in the house far more suited to such tasks. It seemed Doris really did think they were all her servants. It was a puzzle to Ruby that two sisters could be so very different, for Peggy wasn't in the least bit grand or snobbish.

The dishes were clean and most of them were

dried by the time Ron stumped up the stairs into the kitchen. She could see by his expression that he was not in the best of moods after dealing with Doris, but this might be the only opportunity she had to get him alone.

She left Cordelia to put away the clean crockery, caught Ron's eye and beckoned him into the hall. Ron frowned. 'What is it, Ruby, girl?'

'It's something I need you to do,' she said urgently. As his frown deepened she quickly explained about Peggy's clothes. 'Can you keep Doris down in the cellar for ten minutes while I go into her room to get them?'

'Aye, I'll do that.' He looked over his shoulder. 'Better get in there now, and I'll talk loudly if she decides to leave the scullery.'

'And warn Cordelia I'll be gone for a bit. I don't want her calling out or coming to find me.'

'Oh, what a tangled web we weave when Peggy Reilly practises to deceive,' he said on a sigh. Then, with a conspiratorial wink, he strode back into the kitchen.

Ruby didn't waste time, and quickly went into the bedroom, leaving the door ajar so she could hear if Ron raised his voice. The room smelled of Doris's expensive perfume and was as neat as a pin, with a highly polished chest of drawers, a dressing table adorned with silver hairbrushes and little crystal jars, and a large wardrobe which took up an entire wall. Daisy's cot was jammed in close to the bed beneath the window which overlooked the back garden, and a froth of lace and silk nightwear had been draped over the pillows.

Her heart was thudding as she stood on the

dressing stool and took a canvas holdall from the top of the wardrobe. Shoving the stool back in place, she opened the cupboard doors. She could see immediately what belonged to Doris, for the quality of the clothing that hung from the padded hangers was a world away from Peggy's rather shabby and well-worn skirts, dresses and costumes that dangled from wire hangers – the shoes an entirely different breed to the others, with their soft leather and fancy bows and buckles, each one with a shoe tree inside it so they kept their shape.

Ruby selected a loose cotton dress, a linen jacket and a flat pair of sandals, which she carefully placed in the bag, and then turned her attention to the chest of drawers. Again it was easy to pick out Peggy's hand-knitted cardigan from the cashmere sweaters. Underwear was in the dressing table, and she quickly pulled out knickers, vest, bra and petticoat, dithered over the corset, stockings and suspender belt and decided they wouldn't be at all comfortable on her scar, so left them in the drawer.

With everything neatly packed into the holdall, she glanced round the room to make sure she hadn't left any sign of her being there, and then listened keenly at the door before easing through it and closing it with a click. She was about to heave a sigh of relief when she heard Ron's loud voice coming from the kitchen.

'To be sure, Doris, I'm sure those gloves are perfectly adequate.'

'There is no need to shout in such a vulgar fashion,' retorted Doris, her footsteps loud on the kitchen lino. 'Not all of us are deaf.'

Panic spurred Ruby into flight and she took the stairs two at a time, dashed into her bedroom and closed the door. Her heart was pounding and her mouth was dry as she leaned against the door, the holdall clasped to her chest, listening for the sound of following footsteps.

But all was quiet, and it seemed she'd got away with it. With a sigh of relief, she tucked the holdall under her bed, making sure the bedspread draped over the end to hide it so it couldn't be seen from the doorway. Satisfied that she'd fulfilled part of her promise to Peggy, she waited until her pulse was steady before returning to the kitchen.

There was no sign of Doris, but Ron was helping Cordelia put away the last of the crockery. 'I've done it,' she murmured. 'Thanks for that.'

''Tis my pleasure,' he whispered back.

'What are you two whispering about?' Doris had emerged from the scullery, her arms encased to the elbows in yellow rubber gloves, her expression and tone aggressive.

'Nothing that concerns you, Doris,' said Ron airily. 'What's the matter? Has the boiler gone out?'

'I cannot possibly wash nappies while that filthy dog of yours keeps sticking his nose up my skirt,' she snapped. 'Remove it immediately.'

'To be sure, Doris, that's an offer I'm having to refuse,' said Ron woefully. 'I wouldn't dream of removing your skirt.'

Neither Ruby nor Cordelia could quite smother their giggles as Doris grew red and snorted. 'Don't be disgusting. Remove the dog, Ronan, or I shall be forced to tie it up to the garden gate.'

His look said that it was she who should be tethered in the garden and he stomped back through the kitchen.

'What are you sniggering at, girl?' Doris's eyes were steely as they settled on Ruby. 'Get on with your work.'

Ruby's laughter died. 'You don't order me about, lady,' she said coldly. 'I ain't yer maid.'

'You will not speak to me in that rude manner,' snapped Doris.

'It ain't your business how I speak,' retorted Ruby, her hands on her hips, 'and you should mind yer own manners before you start on at me.'

Doris was bug-eyed, her mouth working like a fish out of water as she tried to respond. 'Well, really,' she gasped finally, and then turned on her heel and went back into the scullery.

Ruby closed the door behind her and grinned at Cordelia. 'I ain't usually that rude, but she really winds me up.'

'She winds everybody up,' said Cordelia, who was still chuckling.

Once the kitchen was tidy, Ruby swept and mopped the floor, and then took the mop and bucket into the hall to give the lovely red and blue tiles a good clean. She opened the front door to let the fresh air dry the floor while she scrubbed the steps, just as her mother had done every morning when her father was alive and they'd been living in the little back-to-back terraced house in Bow. The physical labour, fresh air and the warmth of the sun on her back restored her spirits, and she was humming to herself as she finished the last step and gathered up her bucket and brush.

Cordelia came out of the kitchen clucking with amusement. 'The silly woman's moaning and groaning and making a complete drama out of having to do the washing and use the mangle and scrubbing-board,' she said in a stage whisper. 'Goodness only knows when she last did the laundry – but it'll do her good to experience real life for a change.'

'I suppose she always had a char to do the rough work,' murmured Ruby. 'My mum used to do it for a lady in South Ken, and she told me the woman had never been down into the kitchen in all the years she'd lived there.' She grinned back at Cordelia. 'It's another life for some, ain't it?'

'Indeed it is, but some forget who they are and put on airs and graces.' Cordelia glanced over her shoulder towards the kitchen and sniffed with disapproval. 'Money might buy nice clothes and expensive manicures, but it does *not* buy class.' She jabbed her walking stick onto the damp tiles and carefully began to make her way across the hall floor.

Ruby abandoned the mop and bucket and rushed to her side. 'Mind how you go,' she warned. 'The floor's still a bit slippery in places. Do you want me to help you upstairs?'

'I'm quite capable, dear,' she said, 'but a steadying hand is always welcome. I need to get ready for my outing.'

Ruby stayed at her side as she slowly climbed the stairs to her bedroom. She could see the excitement in the lovely old face, and her heart went out to her. She was clearly very happy here and everyone loved her, but the promise of a rare outing with all the other old dears had brought an added sparkle to her eyes.

Ruby saw her safely into her room then went back downstairs to empty the bucket into the water butt, and put away the mop and broom. Doris was pegging out the rows of dazzling white nappies, but they didn't acknowledge one another as Ruby said hello to Daisy and earned a beaming, almost toothless smile. She was a sweet, chubby baby, and Ruby found it hard to resist picking her up and giving her a cuddle – but she satisfied her longing by caressing the sweet cheek before hurrying back into the house.

She went back up to the kitchen, found some cleaning cloths under the sink and began to polish the brass stair-rods and the heavy oak bannisters, taking pride in how she made them shine. As Fran and Rita were still asleep, she didn't like to start on the hoovering, so she began cleaning the bathroom. It was a joy to be doing something useful for those who'd given her such a happy refuge, and a delight to have such a big house to clean and polish and make ready for Peggy's homecoming.

She had finished the bathroom and was about to start on the lav when Cordelia emerged from her bedroom. 'I'm sorry to be a nuisance, dear,' she said fretfully, 'but do you think you could help me finish dressing?'

'Yeah, of course,' she replied happily. She stepped into the cosy bedroom, glancing at the family photographs sitting on the narrow shelf above the gas fire and little treasures dotted about. It was a lovely room, smelling faintly of lavender and mothballs. There was a comfortable chair by the gas fire, a beautiful patchwork cover on the bed and little lacy cloths draped over the small tables where pretty ornaments were displayed.

Ruby fastened the row of buttons down the front of Cordelia's sprigged cotton frock, buckled the narrow white belt, and then, tied her shoe-laces. Taking the triple string of beautiful pearls Cordelia handed her, she carefully secured them around the slender neck and then helped her on with her pale yellow linen jacket and adjusted the sling.

'I thought that as I don't get the chance to go out much these days, I'd wear my hat,' said Cordelia. 'Could you fetch it, dear? It's on the top shelf of the wardrobe.'

Ruby opened the wardrobe and was enveloped in the smell of mothballs. She reached for the hat, which had silky roses fixed to a yellow ribbon around the crown, and blew off the accumulated dust.

Settling it on the thick white hair, she stood back and admired the effect. 'You look proper lovely,' she breathed. 'And them roses in yer 'at match the jacket just right.'

'I don't scrub up too badly, do I?' Cordelia regarded her reflection in the pier glass and nodded with satisfaction. 'Though I suspect Mr Wilkins will only grumble as usual about mutton dressed as lamb.' She realised Ruby had no idea what she was talking about. 'He's the Chairman of the Pensioners' Club, and is inclined to look down his nose if he doesn't approve.'

'I'm sure he'll be delighted to have the company of such an elegant lady,' Ruby said stoutly.

'I don't know about that,' muttered Cordelia. 'He was once considered quite a catch, you know, and some of the old ladies have been trying to snare him now he's widowed and rattling round that big house of his. He used to be quite handsome, but he's gone to seed a bit now he's turned eighty and is grumpy about everything.'

Ruby didn't dare laugh, for Cordelia was looking very serious, and she didn't want to hurt her feelings.

Cordelia's expressive eyes became curious. 'Is your husband a handsome man?'

'He's good-looking, I suppose, but looks ain't worth a light if you ain't got the manners to go with 'em.' She regretted the words the minute they were spoken, for Cordelia was suddenly as alert as a whippet.

'Oh dear,' she said. 'That sounds as if things aren't very happy between you.'

'It's one of the reasons I left London,' she replied dismissively. 'D'you want an 'and to get down the stairs?'

'Not yet,' said Cordelia. She sat down in the chair, her expression determined. 'Tell me about your husband, Ruby.'

She realised Cordelia wouldn't budge until she'd told her something, so she perched on the edge of the bed and tried to calculate how little she could get away with. 'There ain't much to tell,' she said quietly. 'He's a wrong'un through and through, and I were daft to fall for his charms.'

Cordelia's gaze was steady. 'Was he violent? Is

that why you left him?'

Ruby just nodded. She couldn't tell this lovely, genteel lady what life with Ray had been like – or even touch on the terrible violence that had sent her fleeing from London in fear of her life.

'Why don't you get a divorce?'

Ruby blinked at her in astonishment. 'I didn't think people like you approved of such things?'

Cordelia clucked her tongue. 'I might be from a generation who believed divorce was a terrible scandal to be avoided at all cost, but I'm fully aware that some marriages should be brought to a swift end – especially if there is violence. I don't know much about how to arrange such things, but I could telephone my solicitor and make an appointment for you to go and see him, if you'd like.'

Hope flared and died within an instant. 'Ray would never agree to a divorce and all the stuff it involves,' she said with a sigh. And then she smiled. 'But thanks for the offer.'

'Does he know where you are?'

Ruby shook her head. 'And I never want him to find out, neither.'

Cordelia regarded her for a long, silent moment and then nodded and struggled out of her chair. 'We'd better go downstairs,' she said. 'The chara-banc will be here soon.'

Ruby was about to open the door when Cordelia's soft hand rested on her arm. 'Thank you for your help this morning, Ruby,' she said. 'I know I can't do much about your situation, but if you ever need to talk, you know where I am.'

Ruby nodded as the tears formed a lump in her

throat. They had been strangers until two days ago; now she felt blessed to have this family's loving support and understanding and felt the stronger for it. 'Thanks, Grandma Finch. I'll remember that.'

She took the walking stick and handbag as Cordelia clung to the bannister with her uninjured hand and slowly negotiated the stairs. Ruby's hand hovered beneath her elbow, ready to steady her if she lost her footing on the damp floor, until they finally reached the kitchen.

Cordelia settled onto one of the chairs by the table. 'It looks as if Doris has taken Daisy for her morning constitutional,' she said. 'I expect she'll head straight for her home in Havelock Gardens to interrogate poor Anthony over his evening out with Suzy.'

'At least we'll be left in peace for a bit,' said Ruby. 'Do you want a cuppa before you set off?'

'I'd better not,' replied Cordelia as she checked in her handbag for her door key, handkerchief and purse. 'It's not wise at my age to drink anything if one is about to spend several hours on a charabanc.'

Ruby glanced at the clock, shocked at how early it still was. 'Is there any shopping to get? I could do it while Rita's still asleep.'

'That's very kind of you, dear. We're forever out of something, and I see that Doris has left the list behind as usual.' Cordelia plucked the scrap of notepaper from beneath the empty fruit bowl that sat on the table. 'The ration book is up there on the mantel. Peggy gets extra because of the number of people living here – and of course because of Daisy. We're registered at the shops in Camden Road.'

Ruby took the list and ration book, found the shopping basket and housekeeping purse, and gave Cordelia a peck on the cheek. 'Have a lovely day out and I'll see you later,' she said, before hurrying out through the back door and down the garden path.

It was almost nine-thirty and the queues stretched right along the pavement outside nearly every shop. She looked at the list, realised most of it could be found in the grocer's, and joined the queue.

Standing there in the warm sunshine of this late May morning, she listened to all the gossip as the time ticked away. She was quite amazed by the goings-on in this posh little town, what with girls going out with a different Yank every night, and the French Canadians causing trouble in one of the pubs, and someone's daughter getting pregnant while her husband was away in North Africa. But as interesting as it all was, she knew she couldn't afford to stand about for too long. Rita would soon be up and about and they'd planned to be at the race circuit before lunchtime.

As the queue slowly shuffled forwards along the pavement, a large saloon car pulled up. Everyone turned to look at it, for there weren't that many civilian cars about these days because of petrol rationing.

Ruby's pulse shot up as Michael climbed out of the car and walked towards her. He'd caught her out in the lie about going to work this morning, and now she was trapped and could do absolutely nothing about it.

She became aware of the envious looks and the muttered comments and oohs and aahs of the women around her, and tried to appear non-chalant, despite the panic fluttering in her midriff. 'Hello, Mike,' she said with what she considered to be admirable calm. 'How on earth did you know where to find me?'

'I didn't,' he admitted with a smile. 'Not after I went to the tool factory, anyway. Since then, I've been driving round the town hoping to spot you.'

'Oh.' She could feel her face getting redder by the minute.

'I wanted to ask if you'd like to come for a run out into the countryside. I'm off duty today, and my buddy lent me his car.'

He towered over everyone and was so much the focus of attention that Ruby could almost hear the ears tweaking and the eyes coming out on stalks. 'Thanks ever so,' she stammered, 'but I got things to do today.' She dared to glance up at him. 'I'm sorry,' she finished lamely.

The queue shuffled forward and Ruby followed it, only to discover that he was still at her side. 'Have you made plans for the end of next week?' he asked, as aware as she that every word was being listened to. 'Only there's a dance in the mess on the Saturday night, and I wondered if you and your friend Lucy would like to come? You can ask any other girlfriends as well if you like,' he added hastily.

Ruby felt the colour deepen to a blazing heat in her face as she inadvertently caught the inquisitive eye of the woman standing behind her in the queue. 'I'm not sure,' she hedged, not daring to look at him, 'but I'll ask the girls when they get back from work.'

'Okay, that's great,' he said cheerfully. He dug into the pocket of his scarlet tunic and handed her a slip of paper. 'You can reach me at the barracks on that number to let me know how many are coming and where you want to be picked up. I hope you can make it, Ruby,' he added, his blue eyes glinting with humour, 'because I happen to know you're not on shift that particular weekend.'

Ruby stood like a stunned mullet on the pavement as he climbed back into the car and drove away.

'Blimey, love, if you don't want him, I'm free that weekend.'

'Yeah, you lucky thing. Who is he?'

Ruby looked at the curious faces all around her and wished the pavement would open and swallow her up. 'He's just someone I met a couple of weeks ago,' she muttered.

An elbow nudged her arm. 'He'll not be on his own for long,' said the middle-aged housewife with a wink. 'I'd grab him quick, if I were you.'

'I've already got an 'usband,' said Ruby as she flashed her wedding ring.

There was a snigger of laughter from one of the younger women. 'Don't you know there's a war on, love? What the eye don't see, and all that.'

'Yeah, you have a bit of fun, love. You're only young once.'

Ruby giggled, despite her uneasiness at the whole thing. 'Sounds like you're all trying to lead me astray,' she said.

'I wouldn't mind being led astray by that one and no mistake,' said one of the younger women with a deep sigh. She grinned at Ruby. 'Don't mind us, love, we're just having a bit of fun. Life can get too serious these days, and we were only teasing.'

The queue seemed to move faster and the time went quickly now everyone was chattering to her, and before she knew it, she had a basket full of groceries and was heading further along Camden Road to buy bread and any kind of meat the butcher might have. Within the following hour she was on her way back to Beach View.

'Blimey, you must have got up with the lark,' said Rita cheerfully as she tucked into egg and toast. 'Are you ready for our ride out to the racing circuit?'

Ruby put the basket on the table. 'I could do with a cuppa first,' she said. 'Queuing and listening to gossip is thirsty work.' She put away the groceries and then poured the tea and sat down. 'It's very quiet. Where is everyone?'

Rita scraped the last mouthful of egg out of the shell and ate it with a bit of toast. 'Grandma Finch left about an hour ago. Suzy's upstairs asleep, having gone straight on to her night shift after seeing Anthony; Fran's meeting a friend at the Lilac Tearooms before she goes on duty this afternoon and Doris is still out with Daisy. Sarah and Jane are at work and Ron's disappeared to woo the wondrous. Rosie at the Anchor,' she finished with a naughty grin.

Ruby drank her tea while Rita explained about Ron's ongoing pursuit of the Anchor's landlady as she washed up her breakfast things and tidied everything away.

'I met this Canadian bloke a couple of weeks ago, and me and Lucy bumped into him last night at the pictures,' Ruby said in a rush once Rita had finished talking. 'I saw 'im again this morning, and he's invited us all to a dance in the officers' mess at Wayfaring Down Saturday week.'

Rita turned from the sink, her eyes sparkling with delight. 'Well, you're a dark horse, Ruby, I must say – and you being a married woman and all.' She grinned and sat down at the table. 'Come on, Ruby, spill the beans and tell me everything about him.'

'He's tall, good-looking and far too sure of his flamin' self,' she said abruptly. 'He even had the cheek to go to the factory and find out what me shifts were. There ain't nothing going on between us, Rita, and I don't want you getting any funny ideas about it.'

'He sounds very keen on you, though,' she murmured, 'and it could be fun if it's anything like the parties the Yanks put on up at Cliffe estate. I'm not sure what Fran and Suzy's shifts will be, but Sarah and Jane are sure to want to go, and I'm up for it as long as there isn't a raid or anything – what about you?'

Ruby shrugged. 'I dunno,' she admitted. 'I'd like to go, but I don't think it'd be a good idea. It would only encourage him, and I don't want him to think I'm keen on him or anything.'

Rita folded her arms and huffed with im-patience. 'It's just a dance, Ruby, not a marriage proposal – and you should be flattered that some nice Canadian is taking an interest in you.'

'It's all right for you,' she muttered. 'You ain't married.'

Rita took her hand. 'Look, why don't we drop in and see your friend Lucy, and ask her if she'd like to go too?' She grinned. 'Peggy always insists that there's safety in numbers, and why turn down such an offer when it could be fun for all of us?'

Ruby was torn. If she refused to go then the others wouldn't feel right about going without an invitation – but if she did go, then she'd have to be very careful not to let Mike Taylor think she was in any way interested in him. 'All right,' she said with a sigh. 'But I ain't got nothing to wear to such a posh do.'

'With so many girls in the house there's always something to wear,' said Rita firmly as she rammed her feet into her sturdy boots and tied the laces.

Ruby felt a flutter of excitement at the thought of going to a proper party, but she determinedly ignored it and turned to more practical matters. 'I didn't have time to get everything on the shopping list this morning,' she said, 'but perhaps we can get them on the way to the racing circuit?'

Rita grinned back at her. 'Fine by me. But are you sure you want to go on the back of my bike, Ruby?'

'I'm game if you are,' she replied, despite the tingle of apprehension.

Rita picked up her fleece-lined flying jacket – a relic of the First World War – and gathered up her goggles, leather helmet and gas-mask box. 'Right, come on then, before you change your mind and

Doris gets back and finds other things for us to do. The bike's at the fire station.'

They set off down Camden Road and managed to get the washing powder, toothpaste and formula milk without too much hanging about, and Rita stowed it all in her locker at the fire station. Having introduced Ruby to her boss, John Hicks, and the rest of her colleagues, Rita gave her a guided tour and proudly showed off the gleaming red fire engine which she drove during her shifts.

'And this,' she said triumphantly as she flung back the tarpaulin, 'is my bike. She's a Norton ES2, and me and my dad rebuilt her.'

Ruby was impressed. 'You built it?' she asked in awe.

'Yeah. Dad found it abandoned amongst the rubbish and weeds at the back of an empty house. We had to strip it right back and start from the beginning, but we managed to get it finished before he was called up. He taught me everything I know about mechanics, and I passed all me exams with flying colours,' she said wistfully.

Ruby noticed the light dim in her friend's eyes as she lovingly stroked the rather ugly piece of machinery, and knew she was missing her dad, just as much as she was missing her mum. She swallowed the tearful lump in her throat and broke the awkward silence. 'Are we going for a ride on it then? Or do we just stand about admiring it?'

Rita shook off the solemn moment with a wavering smile, and unhooked a fleece-lined jacket from a nearby peg. 'This is for you,' she said. 'It belongs to one of the other firemen, but you'll need it 'cos it gets cold on the bike even when the sun's shining.'

The jacket swamped her, but she fastened it to her chin and pushed back the sleeves while Rita wheeled the bike out through the side door and then kick-started it into a thunderous roar. At Rita's beckon, she hooked her leg over the seat and settled behind her friend, determined not to let her nerves get the better of her.

'Put your arms round my waist and hang on,' shouted Rita above the noise. 'I don't want you falling off.'

Ruby hung on, gripping even tighter as the motorbike shot off the forecourt, leaned dangerously into a left-hand bend and then a sharp right until they were roaring up the High Street and towards the humpback bridge.

As the bike left the ground altogether and sailed into the air before thumping back down again on the other side of the bridge, Ruby felt no fear, but a great surge of excitement. This was like flying, and she'd never experienced such a thrill.

She leaned against Rita's back and watched over her shoulder as the wind whipped the hair from her face and made her eyes water. They were going very fast now, weaving their way through the back streets of Cliffehaven and further up the steep hill until they reached the top and Rita drew the bike to, a skidding, stomach-churning, exhilarating stop.

Ruby's pulse was racing, her heart thudding with excitement. She could see the whole of Cliffehaven spread beneath her on one side of the hill and a broad valley on the other. The sea sparkled with sun diamonds, fields of green rippled like a great ocean in the warm wind and the air was fresh and clean.

'Hold on,' shouted Rita.

Ruby hung on and the motorbike leaped forward and soon they were hurtling down the hill, past a huge forest and into a country lane. Rita leaned the bike into the long bends, still going at some speed, the hedgerows and cottage gardens flashing past as chickens and cats scattered out of the way.

Ruby was grinning broadly as they passed a five-bar gate and turned off the lane to head down a narrow dirt track and then through a narrow opening in a tall hedge. She felt a wave, of disappointment as Rita drew the bike to a halt and switched off the engine. Their journey was at an end, but she could have happily spent all day racing through the countryside.

'See, I told you it was fun,' said Rita as she took off her helmet and goggles and grinned back at her. 'Do you fancy giving it a try?'

Ruby was very tempted. 'Let me get me breath back first,' she replied. 'That were the best thing ever.'

Rita giggled and helped her climb off the bike. 'Come on, I'll show you round. Then if you want, I'll give you a driving lesson.'

Ruby saw that the centre of the field had been cleared to accommodate a cinder track. This track didn't just form a loop, but dipped into hollows, arced left and right into long bends and then into a sharp hairpin halfway round. Heaps of worn old tyres had been placed beside the bends to protect the riders should they fall off, and there were wooden stands erected by the finishing post.

'I got a couple of the men from the fire station to help me get the stands and the track back into good order, and when we have the races there's always a refreshment tent, a spare parts tent, which is always popular, and of course a beer tent. It's two bob to get in and ten bob to enter a race. The boys love it, and there's a lot of rivalry between the services – especially now the Yanks are here. The girls come too, and families bring picnics and deck-chairs and enjoy a good afternoon out. All the profits go straight to the Cliffehaven Spitfire Fund, and when we have enough, the name of the town will be painted on the side of our very own plane.'

'Blimey, you've thought of everything,' breathed Ruby. 'It's a smashing idea, Rita. You are clever.'

Rita shrugged, but her expression told Ruby that she was pleased with the compliment. 'The circuit's been here for years, but since the war started it fell out of use. I've just tidied it up a bit and got the council to agree to me using it again.' She squinted into the sun as she looked back at Ruby. 'You could help out if you're not working. We can always do with a hand behind the bar, or selling raffle tickets.'

'I can do the bar with me eyes shut,' said Ruby. 'Count me in for the next meeting when I'm off work.'

'In that case, you'd better learn how to ride a motorbike. Come on, hop on and I'll show you how to get her started.' Rita grinned as she handed over the goggles and helmet. 'I'm ever so glad you came to live with us, Ruby. You're what the Aussies call a "bonzer Sheila, too right", and I reckon you and me are, going to be good mates.'

Ruby gave her a swift hug and then climbed onto the bike and pulled on the helmet and goggles. The other girl's open-hearted friendship meant more than words could express, and she was a bit embarrassed to discover there were tears in her eyes.

Chapter Twenty

Ruby had learned to ride her dad's old bone-shaker bicycle when she was small, but she hadn't realised how difficult it was to keep a heavy motor-bike upright and steady while she controlled the speed. There had been one or two near tumbles and heart-stopping moments before she'd got the hang of it and managed to hiccup her way round the cinder track without falling off or stalling the engine. Her confidence had grown after that, and by the time they had to head for home, she'd dared to go a bit faster, even into the bends.

Now she was happy to perch on the seat behind Rita as they roared down Camden Road to the fire station. Rita parked the motorbike in the rear of the vast garage and covered it with a tarpaulin while Ruby returned the borrowed jacket and collected the shopping, and then, arm in arm, they strolled out to the sunlit forecourt. Their faces were dirty, their clothes blackened by the dust from the cinders and Ruby's trousers had a tear in one of the knees, but they were happy, and looking forward to a nice bath and some tea before they went down to the Anchor for a drink and a sing-song.

As they reached the hospital, Ruby thought about the holdall hidden beneath her bed. 'If Ron's not planning to see Peggy this evening, then I'll have to pop in there for a few minutes before I come with you to the Anchor.'

'There's still just time to see her now,' said Rita as she drew to a halt. 'Visiting time doesn't finish until four.'

'Good idea, but I need to go and fetch something first.'

Rita eyed her keenly. 'You're being very mysterious all of a sudden. What's Peggy asked you to do?'

'Just to fetch her something from Beach View,' said Ruby vaguely.

Rita chuckled. 'Okay, I get the hint. It's a secret.' She quickened her pace as they walked down Camden Road, and they both broke into a run, racing to reach Beach View Terrace and the front door first.

Rita won and they were both laughing and out of breath as she slotted in the key. 'I'll have my bath while you're out,' she panted as they stepped into the hall.

'You're not going anywhere, Ruby Clark.' Doris stood there, arms folded, her expression thunderous.

Both girls stared at her in amazement, and the

370

joy in Ruby drained away, leaving her cold and empty. 'I can go wherever I like,' she stammered.

'Not if you're in prison,' snapped Doris.

Ruby felt the colour drain from her face as her legs threatened to buckle. How did Doris find out about Ray? Did this mean he was dead and the police were waiting for her somewhere in the house? 'What do you mean?' she asked, her voice barely above a whisper.

'You are a thief, Ruby Clark. And there's no use in denying it, because I have the proof.'

'That's a bit strong, even for you, Mrs Williams,' protested a stunned Rita. 'You can't go about accusing people like that.'

Ruby was staring at Doris, her thoughts confused. This wasn't about Ray – it was something entirely different. 'I ain't a thief,' she rasped, 'and you got no right to say such things.'

'Really?' Doris's eyes were like flint as she turned to the chair behind her and picked something up. 'How do you explain this then?'

Ruby couldn't take her eyes off the tartan holdall. 'I can explain,' she stammered. 'It ain't what you think.'

'Ruby?' Rita put her arm about her waist.

'This is my holdall,' said Doris flatly, 'and it was on the top of my wardrobe this morning. I'd be most interested to know how it came to be hidden beneath your bed.'

'I didn't realise it were your bag,' said Ruby, swallowing the lump in her throat.

'So you admit stealing it?'

Ruby, was aware of Rita's frown and the way her comforting arm had tightened about her waist. 'I only borrowed it,' she said, 'and if you ask Peggy, then she'll tell you why.'

'I fail to see how my sister can have anything to do with this – this act of *treachery*,' Doris hissed. 'My family took you in, trusted you – and you repay us by creeping round in other people's rooms and stealing their possessions.'

'I didn't steal nothing,' shouted Ruby. 'And if you bothered to open the bag you'll see there are only Peggy's clothes in there.' Ruby snatched the bag from her, opened it, and tipped everything out onto the floor. 'There – see? There ain't nothing there that's yours.'

'What the divil is going on out here?' Ron stomped into the hall with Harvey at his heels as Cordelia, Suzy, Fran and Jane crowded into the kitchen doorway. He looked from Doris to Ruby and Rita and then down to the pile of clothes scattered at Ruby's feet.

'She's a thief,' barked Doris.

'I'm not,' stormed Ruby. 'Peggy asked me to get her some clothes, and I thought that were her bag.'

'I hardly think my sister needs outdoor clothing when she's stuck in a hospital bed,' snapped Doris.

'She needs them because she's coming home tomorrow,' said Ron. He put his arm round Ruby's shoulder.

'No one told me she was coming home,' retorted Doris.

'It was supposed to be a secret,' he replied flatly, 'but because of you, the whole surprise has been spoiled.' He glared at Doris, his eyebrows lowered in a deep frown. 'I knew what Peggy asked Ruby to do, and gave her my full support. You owe her an apology, Doris.'

Doris stared at him. 'You knew she'd been in my room?' she gasped. 'Knew she'd been poking about in the cupboards amongst my most intimate things?'

'It's Peggy's room,' he said firmly, 'and you still owe Ruby an apology, Doris.'

'Why the secrecy? Why wasn't I told that Peggy was coming home tomorrow?'

'Because it was none of your business,' said Ron. 'Apologise to Ruby, Doris, or pack your bags and get out.'

Ruby's face was burning with embarrassment. She hated being the centre of attention and certainly didn't want any more trouble. 'Look,' she stammered, 'everything's been explained and I'm willing to forget this if Mrs Williams agrees. It were just a misunderstanding, that's all.'

'I apologise,' said Doris stiffly, 'but I still don't like the thought of you creeping about and rifling through my things. See it doesn't happen again.'

'It won't,' said Ruby.

'You'll have to move to Cissy's room if you're planning on staying, Doris,' said Ron. 'Peggy will need her own bedroom back.' He regarded her with clear dislike. 'Or you could go home to your husband where you belong and leave us to get on with things the way we've always done.'

Doris glared at him, then turned on her heel and slammed the bedroom door behind her so hard it shook the walls and startled the sleeping baby into a storm of high-pitched bawling.

Ron gave Ruby's shoulders a reassuring squeeze as Suzy rushed to pluck Daisy from the pram and console her. 'To be sure, I'm sorry it came to this, Ruby. You were only trying to help.'

'I'm sorry too,' said Rita, her face scarlet with humiliation. 'I should never have doubted you, not even for an instant.'

'It's all right,' she assured them all as they rallied round her in support and Harvey licked her hand. 'Doris made a pretty good case out of it, and I don't blame you for believing her.' She gave a shaky smile as she knelt to gather Peggy's things from the floor, but hot tears were threatening and she had to dip her chin so her hair veiled her face while she tried to rein in her emotions. 'Do you have something else we can put these into, Ron?'

'Aye, I do that. And I'll see Peggy gets her clothes tonight.' He gave her a reassuring smile, took the bundle and carried it into the kitchen.

Ruby shot Rita a watery smile as she placed the empty holdall outside Doris's bedroom door. 'I don't know that I feel much like going out tonight after all that,' she said.

Rita took her hand and gave it a squeeze, her little face full of contrition. 'It strikes me that a drink and a sing-song amongst good company is exactly what you need.'

'Rita's right, Ruby,' said Suzy, 'and if I wasn't on duty tonight, I'd join you. Come on into the kitchen and let me pour you both a cup of tea. The kettle's just boiled.'

Ruby was feeling decidedly fragile and not at all sure she wanted to do anything much but climb into bed and hide from the world beneath the blankets. The unfair accusation had hit her hard, but not as hard as the realisation that she was still on a knife-edge over what she'd done to Ray, and the fate of her mother.

'Never mind, dear,' said Cordelia as she patted her hand. 'A good cup of tea and a long hot soak in the bath will soon have you to rights again.' She grimaced as she shot a glance at the bedroom door. 'Doris always was a cat – and it's about time someone clipped her claws.'

Ruby smiled despite herself and followed them all into the kitchen, where Ron was packing Peggy's clothes into a large cotton shopping bag. She took the cup of tea and, after the first soothing sip, turned to him. 'Ron, can I ask a favour?'

'Fire away,' he replied, his blue eyes twinkling.

'Could I use the telephone to call someone in London? I'll pay for the call,' she said hurriedly. 'Only I need to know if my mum's all right.'

'If you can get through, then of course you can,' he said. 'The lines aren't good at the moment, but it's worth a try to set your mind at ease.'

Ruby finished the tea and then went back into the hall and lifted the receiver, all too aware that Doris was only feet away behind the closed bedroom door. She would have to be careful what she said, for she wouldn't put it past her to eavesdrop.

She hadn't used a telephone very often, and was used to the one in the box on the corner of Bow High Street. There was no slot for pennies in this one, so she waited for the operator to answer. 'I want to make a call to London,' she

375

told the woman at the exchange.

'What's the number, dear?'

'Bow Lane three-one-nine,' she replied, 'and is it possible to let me know how much the call costs, 'cos I'll need to pay Mrs Reilly back.'

'Of course, dear. How is Peggy? I meant to visit, but–'

'She's doing all right,' replied Ruby, impatient now to get on with her call.

'Putting you through,' said the other woman, rather too briskly.

Ruby heard the buzzing tone and then the click of an open line. 'Tanner's Arms.' Fred Bowman's voice was unmistakable.

'Fred? This is Ruby. Can you talk?'

'Blimey, girl, didn't expect to 'ear from you after I got that note for yer mum. Ain't nothing wrong, is there?'

'I'm fine. More to the point, how's Mum?'

'She's doin' all right, gel. She and me 'ad a bit of bother from Ray's family, but we managed to convince them we don't know where you are, and they've left us alone since.'

Ruby gripped the phone in her anguish. 'They didn't hurt no one, did they?'

'Nah, nothing like that. Just a bit of strutting about and making their presence felt, but I don't reckon they're that bothered now Ray's causing them so much grief.'

Overwhelmed with relief that she hadn't killed him, Ruby couldn't have cared less about the trouble Ray was causing his family. 'What's he done?' she asked tentatively.

Fred cleared his throat, and his tone became

376

conspiratorial. 'He beat up Micky Flannigan so bad it were a miracle he survived, and now the plods are after him for attempted murder as well as a long list of crimes connected to his black-marketeering. They've rounded up most of the Clark family as well as the thugs what worked for 'em, and now Ray's gone to ground. He's a loose cannon, Ruby, and you'd be wise to stay well away and keep schtum.'

Ruby discovered she was trembling so badly she almost dropped the receiver. 'I ain't planning on leaving here for a long while,' she managed to assure him. 'But will you keep an eye on Mum for me, Fred, and tell 'er I'm all right?'

'Yeah, I'll do that for you, Ruby, gel. You take care now, y'hear?'

'And you, Fred.' The line went dead, the woman at the exchange came on to tell her how much the call had cost, and Ruby replaced the receiver.

She sank into the nearby chair, her thoughts in a whirl. Ray's vicious temper had finally led him into real trouble, and she just prayed the police would run him to earth quickly before someone else got hurt. Isolated and in hiding, Ray would now be more dangerous than ever. The only comfort she could take from her conversation with Fred was that Ray had absolutely no idea where she was, and certainly wouldn't risk being seen anywhere near his old haunts – therefore Fred, his family, and her mum were safe.

Peggy had heard about the fracas between Doris and Ruby from Ron – and then from Suzy, who'd taken a few minutes off her night shift to come and see her. Peggy had been most distressed by it all, and although her secret was out, she knew she'd made the right decision. She had to get home to Beach View before Doris did any further damage.

She hadn't slept at all well, for her thoughts and emotions were jumbled. Excited about going home, and a little nervous about her planned escape, she was nonetheless concerned about how to deal with her sister. Doris hadn't visited at all during the past two and a half weeks, and that in itself was a mystery – but according to the others she'd taken great care of Daisy, and had proved she did indeed possess some sort of maternal feelings.

Peggy dozed on and off through the night, wondering why Doris steadfastly refused to leave Beach View when it must be clear to her that she wasn't welcome. She knew that her eldest sister could be stubborn to the point of pig-headedness, but she'd thought she had more pride than to stay where she wasn't wanted. It would be tricky facing her, Peggy realised – and it would require every ounce of tact she possessed to make her see it was time for her to leave. If that didn't work, then she'd pack her bags herself and dump them and her damned sister on the doorstep.

Feeling slightly mollified by this flare of temper, she'd fallen into a fitful doze and had been woken up by the rattle of the tea trolley. The morning progressed as it always did with lumpy porridge for breakfast, followed by temperatures being taken, bed baths, pills and cups of bland tea. Peggy could feel her pulse begin to pick up speed as lunch was cleared away and the time drew nearer for her escape.

It was ten minutes to visiting time when Matron came through the swing doors to do her inspection. She marched from bed to bed, checking the charts and the hospital corners on the sheets and blankets, and harrying the nurses over a wrinkled pillowcase or a forgotten teacup.

She arrived at Peggy's bed and glared at her. 'You look flushed, Mrs Reilly,' she said as she reached for the chart. 'It seems you have a temperature. Bed rest for another two days,' she ordered the nurse hovering behind her before she marched to the next patient and told her off for leaving her knitting on top of the bedside cupboard.

Peggy caught Fran's eye and resisted winking at her. They both knew there would be no bed rest – not in this hospital, anyway.

Once Matron had left the ward, Fran hurried over. 'I'm off duty now,' she whispered, 'and Suzy is already at home, but would you like me to stay and help you escape?'

'No,' said Peggy firmly. 'I want you and Suzy well away from here so you don't get the blame.'

Fran's expression was troubled. 'Are you sure about this, Peggy? Only it was a big operation, and you're not really...'

'I'm as ready as I'll ever be,' she said firmly. 'Stop fretting, Fran, dear, and take the last of my things out of the bedside cupboard, go home and put the kettle on. I could do with a really good, strong cup of tea after two weeks of dishwater.'

Fran still didn't look convinced, but Peggy's

determined expression brooked no argument and she quickly emptied the bedside cabinet before hurrying off the ward.

Peggy lay back against the pillows, her gaze flitting between the clock and the swing doors. She could have done with a cigarette and no mistake, but they were in the handbag Fran had taken home.

The doors were opened on the dot of two, and amongst the visitors she could see Ron and Jane. 'Where's Cordelia?' Peggy asked as they reached her bed.

'Ach, to be sure, she has her own plan to distract the enemy, so Jane offered to come and help.' He grinned back at her, his eyebrows wriggling like two hairy caterpillars. 'Are ye ready for this, Peg?'

'You bet I am,' she breathed. She pulled back the sheet and blankets and swung her legs over the side of the bed. 'I need to use the bathroom,' she said, loudly enough to be heard by one of the nearby nurses. 'Jane, dear, would you help me?'

Jane played her part beautifully, helping her on with her dressing gown and slippers and fetching the spare wheelchair that always stood at the end of the ward. 'Where are your clothes, Auntie Peg?' she whispered.

'Fran put everything in her locker,' she whispered back. 'I've got the key in my pocket.' She looked up at Ron. 'Stay here for five minutes and then wander out as if you're going for a cup of tea. We'll meet you by the lift.'

It was all very cloak and dagger, and Peggy was feeling quite excited as Jane wheeled her down the ward and informed the nurse on duty that she was taking Peggy to the bathroom before they went to the dayroom for a cup of tea. Then they were out of the doors and heading for the deserted nurses' cloakroom. 'Hurry up, Jane, before someone comes,' Peggy urged as she gave her the locker key.

Within minutes they were on their way again, the bag of clothes firmly held on Peggy's lap. Jane wheeled her into the bathroom. 'Do you want me to help you get dressed?'

Peggy shook her head. 'I can manage, dear. Go outside and keep watch. If you see Matron, tap on the door twice and I'll know to stay in here until she's gone.'

'I say,' said Jane with a grin. 'It's all frightfully good fun, isn't it?'

'Not if we get caught,' muttered Peggy as she dragged off the dressing gown.

Jane took the hint and left the bathroom, and Peggy locked the door. It was a bit of a struggle to get into her clothes and they felt strange after being in her nightdress for so long. She was quite hot and sweaty by the time she'd pulled on her coat and headscarf. With her nightclothes tucked into the shopping bag along with her slippers, she unlocked the door.

'All clear,' whispered Jane, who seemed to be thoroughly enjoying the subterfuge. 'Ron's waiting by the lift.'

'Has Alf parked the van close to the front door?' asked Peggy anxiously as Jane wheeled her down the long corridor. 'Only I don't think I'll be able to walk too far.'

'He's parked it off to one side and has the

engine running so that the minute he sees us, he can pull up at the steps,' replied Jane in a hoarse whisper.

Ron had wedged himself in the lift doorway so it couldn't go anywhere until he was ready. 'Hurry up,' he muttered. 'I've just seen one of the senior nurses off your ward, and she was asking where you'd got to. I told her you were in the dayroom, but that won't keep her away for much longer.'

Jane quickly pushed the wheelchair into the lift and Ron removed his foot, closed the door and drew the metal gate shut before stabbing the button for the ground floor.

Peggy's pulse was racing and she could feel the sweat running down her back as the ancient lift rattled and jolted its way down. The next bit would be the hardest, for they would have to pass right by Matron's office door and then through the busy reception hall. 'I hope to goodness Cordelia has a proper plan,' she muttered. 'If Matron catches us, we'll all be for the high jump.'

The lift shuddered to a halt and Ron glanced down the hall to where Cordelia was standing outside Matron's door.

At his signal, she rapped on the door with her walking stick. 'I wish to make a complaint,' she said stridently. 'Open this door at once.'

Ron, Peggy and Jane peeked round the lift doors as Ron kept them jammed open, and watched wide-eyed as Cordelia continued to beat on Matron's door. It opened, and Cordelia took full advantage of a surprise attack. 'About time,' she snapped, prodding her walking stick at the startled matron as she marched into her room and

382

slammed the door shut.

With Matron firmly imprisoned in her room, Jane quickly wheeled Peggy along the corridor and into the echoing reception hall where the milling crowds shielded their hurried departure.

Ron went on ahead and signalled to Alf, who screeched the van to a halt at the bottom of the steps. Jane grabbed the bag from Peggy's lap and Ron lifted her out of the wheelchair and dumped her unceremoniously into the passenger seat before clambering into the back of the van with Jane and slamming the doors shut. Alf put his foot down on the accelerator and they shot out of the hospital forecourt as if the demons of hell were snapping at their heels.

Peggy began to laugh as they reached the end of Camden Road. 'I never realised Cordelia could shout that loudly, or look quite so fierce,' she gasped. 'Poor Matron. I almost feel sorry for her.'

Ron chuckled from the back of the van. 'To be sure, the wee woman is a fine actress at heart. She's missed her calling, so she has.'

'What complaint was she making?' Peggy asked. 'After all, she isn't even a patient at the hospital.'

'She decided a touch of dottiness was called for. Having mistaken the hospital for the Grand Hotel, she was incensed that no one seemed to have prepared her room, or could show her where it was. As far as she was concerned, Matron was the manager, and she was determined to read her the riot act.'

By now Peggy had got the giggles, and when she saw the grim look on Alf's face as he parked outside Beach View, she was almost in tears with it and had to hold her stomach. 'Do cheer up, Alf,' she managed to splutter. 'You've done your good deed for the day and should be pleased it went so well.'

'This is the last time I help you, Peggy Reilly,' he grumbled. 'Lil's bound to badger me with questions for the rest of the day. I were supposed to take her to her mother's this afternoon.'

Peggy dried her eyes and tried to control the giggles which still bubbled away inside her. 'Just tell her the truth for once, Alf. She'll understand. Really she will.'

Any further conversation was halted by the sight of the front door opening. Harvey galloped down the steps, swiftly followed by Fran, Suzy and Rita. He planted his big paws on the van door, stuck his head through the open window and barked his welcome before trying to scrabble inside to lick Peggy's face.

'Get that flamin' dog outta there before 'e damages me paintwork,' shouted Alf.

Peggy tried pushing Harvey away, but the more she pushed the harder he scrambled to get to her. 'Ron!' she called frantically. 'Come and help me.'

Ron grabbed Harvey's collar just as Alf stormed round the van to inspect the damage to his door. 'Come on, you eejit dog,' Ron rumbled. 'Let Peggy alone.'

Fran and Suzy rushed to help Peggy out of the van and up the steps while Jane carried her things and Rita took charge of Harvey so Ron could try and appease an enraged Alf about the scratches on his door before they had to set off to rescue Cordelia.

Peggy felt very guilty about the damage to Alf's van and sincerely hoped that one of Ron's many friends could repair it, for the poor man didn't deserve such ill-treatment after he'd been so kind.

She was feeling decidedly wobbly on her feet as she reached the hall and had to lean quite heavily on Fran's arm as she made her way into the kitchen. With barely a glance at the po-faced Doris, she sank into her chair by the range, closed her eyes and gave a deep sigh of relief. 'Home at last,' she breathed. 'You have no idea how good that feels.'

'I suppose you think you've been very clever,' said Doris coldly. 'But I regard the whole nefarious escapade as irresponsible and selfish.'

'You're welcome to your opinion,' said Peggy as she took a well-earned cup of tea from a smiling Suzy. 'I'm just thankful to be home.' She spotted the empty playpen in the corner. 'Where's Daisy?'

'She's having an airing in the back garden,' said Doris.

'Good grief,' Peggy sighed, 'you make her sound as if she's a piece of laundry. Go and get her, Rita. It's been too long since I had a cuddle.'

'She's asleep and isn't due to wake for another fifty-eight minutes,' said Doris as she blocked Rita's exit. 'We have got into a strict routine, and–'

'I'm very grateful, Doris, but she's my baby, and if I want to cuddle her, then I'm sure she won't mind.'

'Selfish, that's what you are,' snapped Doris. 'You have no thought for the poor nurses who will get it in the neck because of your cavalier behaviour, and neither do you give a thought to how a disturbed afternoon sleep will affect your daughter.'

Peggy looked at her, her expression stony. 'I have written a letter to Matron so no one gets into trouble, and Ron will deliver it to the receptionist when he collects Cordelia.' She glanced across at Rita. 'Go and fetch Daisy, love,' she said quietly.

Doris lit a cigarette and snorted smoke from her nose like an angry dragon. 'After everything I've done for you, I would have expected at least a modicum of gratitude and respect.'

Peggy held her arms out for Daisy, who was warm and sleepy. 'My precious girl,' she murmured as she softly caressed the rounded, sweet cheeks and marvelled at the long, dark eyelashes that fanned across them as her baby slept. 'Mummy's home now and she promises never to leave you again – not ever.'

Doris made a rude noise in her throat and Peggy glared at her before turning to the others. 'Thanks for all your help and support, girls,' she said. 'Now, I'm sure you have lots of interesting things to do with the rest of your day, so run along – and I'll see you at teatime.'

Silence fell once their footsteps had faded away and Peggy looked from her sleeping baby to the woman who sat so stiffly opposite her. 'I am neither selfish, nor ungrateful,' she said calmly, 'and I truly appreciate how well you've looked after Daisy for me these past two weeks.'

Doris dipped her chin in a rather grand gesture

of acceptance.

'I also appreciate what a sacrifice it must have been to move in here when I know how you've always hated Beach View and everything it stands for. I'm sure you've missed your lovely home in Havelock Gardens, and that Ted and Anthony will be only too pleased to have you home again. Please don't think I'll be offended if you want to leave straight away. I'll quite understand.'

'I have no intention of leaving until I am sure you are well enough to cope on your own,' said Doris stiffly. 'I have moved my things into Cissy's room.'

'But I'm not on my own,' Peggy replied firmly, 'and you have done far more than I could ever have expected. It's time for you to leave, Doris.'

She watched her sister's face, becoming alarmed at the way the muscles were working beneath the perfect make-up as she chewed her lip and rapidly blinked away the tears. 'Doris? Whatever's the matter?'

'Nothing,' she said hoarsely as she stubbed out her cigarette and battled to keep her dignity.

'Then why are you crying?'

'I'm not,' she protested, dabbing her eyes with a lace-edged handkerchief. 'It's just a touch of hay fever making my eyes sting.'

Peggy struggled out of her chair and carefully carried Daisy over to the playpen and placed her on the thin mattress. She felt a twinge of pain, but ignored it as Harvey settled by the playpen. She closed the kitchen door, then turned back to her clearly distressed sister. 'You've never suffered from hay fever in your life,' she said softly.

'What is it, Doris?'

'If you must know, it's everything,' she rasped. She balled the handkerchief in her hand and waved her fist distractedly. 'It's this house, these people – the lack of respect and the sheer vulgarity of it all. Rita and Ruby are little more than guttersnipes, Suzy's a conniving little witch, and that Irish tart has no manners. Sarah and Jane aren't too bad, I suppose – at least they speak the King's English – but Cordelia Finch has a vicious tongue, and it's time she was put into a home. As for Ronan and that dog of his ... they are disgusting.'

Peggy stared in amazement as the vitriol poured from her sister. But as each cruel word struck her heart she hardened it, and the last shred of her patience disintegrated. 'If you hate it so much, why insist upon staying?' she asked coldly.

Doris fiddled with the handkerchief and didn't reply.

'You might think we're beneath you,' said Peggy, determined not to lose her temper. 'But my girls are all good girls, and I will not have you talk about them like that. Cordelia will remain here until her last breath as this is her home and we love her. As for Ron and Harvey, they are the mainstays of this household now Jim is away, and Cordelia and I owe Ron our lives after that raid. If you find them so abhorrent, then you should have left long ago when it became clear that nobody wanted you here.'

Doris's black mascara made tracks on her powdered cheeks as the tears rolled down and dripped from her chin. Her lips formed a thin line and her eyes hardened. 'How comfortable you must be up there on that smug, sanctimonious mountain of yours. You clearly have no idea what it's like to be derided, ignored and sniggered at – to be cast aside like an old shoe that is no longer of any use.'

Peggy shivered at the coldness in her sister's voice. 'Doris, that wasn't what–'

'I know when I'm not wanted,' Doris interrupted. 'I'm not stupid, but I stayed for you – and for Daisy – and this is the thanks I get. A nod and a wink and then it's pack your bags and get out.'

Peggy realised the posh voice had disappeared and that a real passion was boiling inside her sister that had far deeper roots than this current spat. Her anger dissolved and she reached for her sister's hand. 'What's happened to make you so bitter, Doris?' she asked softly.

Doris snatched her hand away. 'What do you care? You've got your precious family to look after you now. What happens to me doesn't matter.'

'That's not true and you know it,' retorted Peggy. 'Talk to me, Doris. Tell me why you suddenly decided to change the habit of a lifetime and come to my aid. Tell me what happened to make you stay here when it was obvious you hated it and weren't needed – and why you've been avoiding me these past two weeks.'

'Why should I?' she sniffed. 'You'll only gloat – and there's absolutely nothing you can do to change things.'

Peggy gave an exasperated sigh. 'Oh, for goodness' sake, Doris, stop making a drama out of everything and tell me what the heck is going on

389

with you.'

'I've been abandoned,' she said as fresh tears washed the black mascara from her face. 'Phyllis has gone off to work in a factory. Edward is never home, and Anthony rarely visits any more since he's become involved with that silly girl. He hasn't even bothered to ring me since he's come back from his conference.'

Peggy gave a sigh of relief. 'Is that all? Honestly, Doris, you do make a mountain out of a molehill at times. Anthony is a man now and entitled to come and go as he pleases. You can't expect him to be tied to your apron strings for the rest of your life.'

Doris blew her nose and made a visible effort to pull herself together as she lit another cigarette. 'I was made very aware of that fact the other night.'

'Well, there you are then,' Peggy soothed.

'But where am I – tell me that?' Her voice broke. 'I can't stay here, but I can't go home either, and Lady Charlemondley has asked me to resign from her charity committees, and…'

Peggy felt a pang of alarm as she grasped her hand. 'What do you mean, you can't go home, Doris? Has the house been bombed?'

'It might as well have been,' she sobbed in deep distress.

Peggy hadn't seen Doris cry like this since they were children, and an overwhelming sense of pity made her reach out and take her in her arms. 'Tell me all about it, Doris,' she murmured. 'Come on, don't keep torturing yourself by bottling things up and trying to put on a brave face.'

Doris allowed Peggy to hold her for a moment,

then she drew back, her shoulders squared, her chin lifted in defiance of the tears she couldn't seem to stem. 'Edward has not been playing golf,' she rasped. 'He's been having an affair. And it's been going on for three years. Now he's packed his bags and left, and wants a divorce.'

Peggy froze, stunned that the quiet, mild-mannered and rather boring Ted Williams had it in him to conduct an illicit affair for three whole years – let alone have the gumption to ask Doris for a divorce. 'Good grief,' she breathed. 'Oh, Doris, my dear, how awful for you. No wonder you've been so reluctant to go home.'

'I feel so betrayed,' she sobbed. 'And as if that isn't bad enough, the woman is one of his shop assistants and lives on the council estate.' She lifted her tear-streaked face to plead for Peggy's understanding. 'How could he do that to me, Peggy? How could he lie and cheat like that for all those years with some fat, plain, common woman who drops her aitches and has a laugh like a hyena?'

If it hadn't been so tragic it might have made Peggy smile, for despite everything, it seemed Doris's pain and humiliation had more to do with the class of woman Ted was having the affair with – rather than the affair itself. 'I'm sure he'll soon see the error of his ways,' she soothed, 'and once he realises how unhappy he's made you after all the years you've been together, he's sure to come back home.'

'I don't want him now I know he's been with *her*,' she snarled.

'But I thought...'

'It's the shame of the thing,' she hissed through a cloud of cigarette smoke. 'How can I hold my head up in this town once this becomes common knowledge? My good name and reputation will be besmirched and Lady Charlemondley – who I thought I could count on as a confidante and friend – has made it very clear that this sort of scandal will not be tolerated. She asked me to resign my seat on the charity boards.'

'Oh, Doris,' Peggy sighed. 'I'm so sorry.'

Doris puffed furiously on the cigarette and then mashed it in the ashtray as if it was Edward's head she was mangling. 'It's Anthony I'm really worried about,' she confessed. 'I've yet to tell him, and he'll be devastated to know how badly his father has treated me. If this endangers his important work for the MOD, I will never forgive Edward. *Never.*'

Peggy realised that the suppurating bitterness and shame that had been eating away at her sister was finally finding some release – but there was very little she could do but offer tea and sympathy and Cissy's bedroom until things could be brought to some sort of conclusion. 'You can stay with me for as long as you need, Doris,' she said quietly.

Doris gripped her arm as the front door opened and they heard Ron talking to Cordelia in the hallway. 'Promise you'll say nothing to anyone,' she said fiercely as Harvey scrabbled to greet them. 'I couldn't bear it if they were all sniggering behind my back.'

'No one will know, I promise you,' Peggy soothed. 'Now, dry your eyes and I'll put the kettle on while you telephone Anthony and ask him to come and see you after Suzy has left for her night shift this evening.'

For once in her life Doris looked bewildered and unsure of herself. 'I don't know how to tell him, Peggy,' she whispered.

'We'll do it together,' soothed Peggy.

Fresh tears threatened as she looked up at Peggy. 'You're being very kind,' she murmured, 'and I know I don't deserve it.'

'You're my sister, Doris, and although we don't always see eye to eye, I'll always be here for you,' she replied softly.

Chapter Twenty-One

Ruby glanced repeatedly at the big clock on the factory wall, wondering if Peggy's planned escape had gone smoothly. It would be lovely to have her home and get to know her properly, and if it meant that snooty cow Doris was finally booted out, so much the better.

She had managed to catch Lucy before they started work and tell her about the invitation to the Canadians' dance. Lucy's eyes had sparkled with delight and she'd said immediately that of course they should go. They had started a later shift today, so their lunch break was at three, and coincided with that of the girls working on the washers and in the armaments factory. Having collected their food from the serving counter, they looked around the crowded canteen and discovered the only two spaces were next to the girls from the Mile End Road, and across from Flora.

'Hello, girls,' said Ruby cheerfully as she ignored Flora and sat down. 'The weather's turning out nice, ain't it?'

'Yeah,' replied Gertie through a mouthful of stew. 'Better than the smog we gets back 'ome, that's for sure. We thought we'd take a picnic up in the 'ills this Sunday if the weather holds. Do you two fancy coming along?'

'We'd love to,' said Lucy and Ruby in unison, and then giggled.

'Well, well,' murmured Flora. 'It's little Miss Goody Two-shoes and her soppy friend. Are you two joined at the hip?'

'Put yer claws in, Flora,' drawled Ruby. 'You ain't impressing no one.'

'We are in a sour mood today,' she purred. 'Get out of the wrong side of bed this morning, did we? Or was it the wrong bed you were kicked out of?'

Ruby chewed on the rather gristly meat stew and tried to ignore her as Grace, Gladys and Gertie pretended they hadn't heard this exchange.

But Flora seemed determined to provoke some sort of reaction from Ruby. 'It's no good you trying to pretend to be prim and proper, Ruby Clark,' she said as she lit a cigarette and blew smoke across the table. 'I saw you both last night, all cosy in a huddle with those Canadians.'

'They were just being friendly,' protested Lucy, flapping ineffectually at the smoke, 'so don't try and make something out of it, Flora.'

A finely plucked brow arched and the eyes narrowed. 'Oh dear,' she sighed. 'How naïve you must think I am. You were both positively drooling. Don't tell me you didn't let them have a bit of a kiss and a cuddle after they'd treated you to the pictures and a fish supper.'

'Actually we paid for ourselves,' said Lucy in her snootiest voice, 'and I don't appreciate your innuendo.'

'Get you!' Flora sniggered. 'All posh and bristling with self-righteousness – if that isn't proof you've got something to hide, I don't know what is.'

'Wind yer neck in, Flora,' snapped Ruby. 'We ain't all like you.'

'And what do you mean by that?' she bristled.

'Anything in trousers might be fair game to you,' she shot back, 'but me and Lucy ain't like that. So don't tar us with the same brush.'

'Goodness me,' Flora said with a dramatic sigh. 'How fiercely you defend your dubious honour. I'm sure your husband will be eternally grateful to know that his little wifey has kept herself pure for him while he's being a hero on some battlefield.' She shot Ruby a sneer as she pushed back from the table. 'It's a good thing he's not here to witness you flirting with Canadians, isn't it? But then, when the cat's away...' She turned away and was gone before either girl could reply.

'Bitch,' muttered Ruby.

'You wanna watch that one,' said Grace as she tucked her short dark hair back under her headscarf. 'She's got the morals of an alley cat and a vicious tongue, and if you ain't careful, Ruby, she'll cause you trouble.'

'She can try,' said Ruby darkly, 'but it won't get 'er far.'

'You were right about her not being very nice, Ruby,' said Lucy as she put her knife and fork neatly together on her empty plate. 'She certainly showed her true colours today.'

Ruby took no pleasure in being right, but at least Lucy had learned a lesson in how to see beneath the brassy gloss and glamour. She finished what she could of the stew and pushed her plate away. 'You can have my jelly and blancmange, Lucy,' she said, eyeing the gelatinous pink mess in the bowl.

'But I thought you liked jelly.'

'I did until I were given it every flamin' day,' she said, pushing the bowl towards her. 'Besides, I get a decent breakfast at Beach View, and I ain't that hungry.'

'Oh,' said Lucy, her blue eyes sparkling, 'I meant to tell you. It's the most extraordinary thing.'

Ruby smiled indulgently at her friend. 'What you done? Bought a new frock without yer mum knowing?'

Lucy giggled and wiped a smear of jelly from her bottom lip. 'I have, actually. It's a gorgeous blue and just right for the dance next weekend. But that's not what I meant to tell you.' She leaned closer. 'Councillor Fraser has resigned his position on the Town Council and left his wife,' she said breathlessly.

Ruby's attention sharpened. 'When was this?'

'Yesterday afternoon. Marjory came round to

see Mother, and she was in a terrible state, poor woman.' She fiddled with the spoon. 'Mother bustled her quickly into Daddy's study and shut the door – no doubt thinking I was far too young and innocent to be a witness to such hysteria. But I was so curious, I'm afraid I did eavesdrop a bit,' she confessed with a blush.

'What did you hear?' prompted Ruby.

'Well, it seems he's run off with some woman, and has told Marjory he will provide her with the evidence she'll need for a divorce. It all came as a terrible shock, because she'd had absolutely no idea what Harold had been up to.'

The truth would have been an even greater shock, thought Ruby sourly.

'You don't seem terribly surprised, Ruby,' said Lucy with a frown. 'Did you suspect something when you were living there?'

'Nah,' she replied quickly. 'I weren't in the house much, so I didn't get to know either of them that well.' She realised she was expected to say something sympathetic, and after a momentary hesitation, she said, 'Poor Mrs Fraser. She's a proud woman and will find it hard to deal with the gossip.'

Lucy scraped the last of her jelly from the bowl. 'She's planning to rent out the house and go and stay with her sister in Surrey until the scandal dies down,' she said. 'Mother will miss her. They were close friends.'

Good riddance to the pair of them, thought Ruby.

Lucy finished both helpings of pudding as Gladys and Gertie left to sit outside in the sun and smoke their cigarettes. 'I'll get our tea,' she said brightly, and went off enthusiastically to join the long queue by the urn.

'She's a caution, that one, ain't she?' said Grace.

'She's lovely,' said Ruby with a soft smile, 'but far too naïve for her own good at times. I'm surprised she's lasted this long, what with Flora and the sort of high jinks some of the other girls get up to here.'

Grace shrugged. 'Working 'ere will teach her far more than that posh school she went to, you mark my words.' She puffed on her cigarette, her expression thoughtful. 'I reckon she's tougher than you give 'er credit for, Ruby – but then we all gotta have a bit of steel to get through this flamin' war, ain't we?'

Ruby nodded and watched idly as Lucy chattered to the other girls in the queue and firmly slapped away the wandering hand of one of the male technicians. Her perceived naïvety was her charm and, with her sunny disposition, she'd become popular amongst the other women – but she was certainly no fool and had swiftly learned to ignore the often crude jokes, and to fend off the unwanted advances of some of the men. Grace was right, she realised with a sense of surprise. Lucy was far more capable than she'd thought.

Grace tapped cigarette ash into her saucer. 'I didn't realise yer name was Clark,' she said casually. 'Are you related to the Clarks in Bow?'

Ruby's blood ran cold, and all thoughts of Lucy disappeared as she fought to keep her expression bland. 'I wouldn't know,' she replied. 'Clark's a common name. Especially in Bermondsey where

398

I comes from.'

Grace eyed her steadily. 'I don't doubt it,' she murmured, 'but the Clarks I'm talkin' about have got a bad reputation all over the East End – especially that toerag, Raymond.'

Ruby's heart was hammering and she could barely breathe as her gaze was fixed by Grace. 'Just 'cos we got the same name don't mean nothing,' she managed.

Grace continued as if she hadn't spoken. 'I got a letter from me cousin what lives over that way, and the gossip is that Ray got a taste of his own medicine from 'is wife, and is as mad as 'ell 'cos she done a runner and he can't track 'er down.' The brown eyes remained steadily focused on Ruby through the cigarette smoke. 'It strikes me,' she said quietly, 'that she done 'erself a favour by scarpering – he's a nasty piece of work.'

A trickle of cold sweat ran down Ruby's back but she found she couldn't tear her gaze from those knowing eyes.

'If I was her,' continued Grace, 'I'd lie low until the coppers catch up with him for what he done to Micky Flannigan.'

Ruby stared at her, unable to think or speak.

Grace gripped her hand and leaned closer, her voice barely above a whisper. 'You got nothing to fear from me, gel. I ain't about to blab to no one, and the other gels don't know nothing.'

Ruby clasped her hand, the tears of relief and gratitude blinding her as all pretence was swept away. 'You're a diamond, Grace,' she breathed. 'A real diamond.'

Grace shot her a warning look as Lucy approached the table. 'We gels gotta stick together,' she muttered as she flicked ash into the saucer, 'and I just wish I'd 'ad your courage to hit back when my old man belted me one.'

'It weren't courage, Grace – it were sheer, blind, bloody terror.'

Grace grinned as she mashed out the cigarette and gathered up her things. 'You'll do right enough, Ruby – now I gotta get to work. See ya later.'

Doris had hurriedly dried her tears and composed herself before she followed a joyful Harvey into the hall, curtly acknowledged Ron and Cordelia, and lifted the telephone receiver to call Anthony's office.

Peggy sighed. Her homecoming hadn't turned out at all as she'd planned, and now she was feeling decidedly dispirited by her sister's revelations, and more than a little guilty at how cold-heartedly she'd planned to get her out of the house. She wanted nothing more than to climb into bed and go to sleep, but she had responsibilities and a promise to keep, so she plastered on a smile for Cordelia and Ron as if nothing had happened.

'Is she telephoning Anthony to come and collect her?' asked Ron hopefully as he pointed the over-excited Harvey in the direction of the hearthrug and settled Cordelia in her usual chair.

'No,' replied Peggy. 'I've asked her to stay on for a bit.'

Ron's eyebrows lowered as he glared at her. 'Ach, 'tis soft you are, Peggy Reilly. To be sure we can cope without her now you're home safely.'

'I'm not as strong as I thought I was,' she confessed, 'and Doris has been so good with Daisy, I've asked her to help out for a while longer.'

'Oh dear,' twittered Cordelia. 'I do hope you haven't made yourself ill by coming out of hospital too soon.'

'Not at all,' she hurried to assure her. 'But I will need time to fully recover, and Doris will be a godsend with everyone else being so busy.' She smiled and patted Cordelia's hand. 'I know it's all been very difficult, but I think you'll find things will settle down now I'm in charge again.'

Ron snorted as he freshened the teapot with boiling water. 'The woman's a menace, and I'm amazed you're letting her stay after the way she's treated everyone.' He handed out the cups and sat down with a thump on a kitchen chair.

Peggy understood their reluctance and fully shared their misgivings, but she'd promised her sister refuge, and was not about to renege on it. 'I'd like both of you to give her a second chance,' she replied. 'After all, she is my sister, and Daisy has become very fond of her.'

Cordelia didn't look convinced, and Ron eyed her suspiciously. 'You've changed your tune, Peggy,' he grumbled. 'What's going on that you don't want to tell us?'

She smiled back at him, her eyes wide and innocent. 'It's a woman's prerogative to change her mind, Ron. Surely, after all the years you've lived here, you've realised that?'

'Hmph. I know you too well to let you pull the wool over me eyes,' he retorted. 'I'll get to the

401

bottom of this, never you fear.'

Peggy grinned and reached for the new packet of Park Drive cigarettes. 'You know, Ron, you're too sharp for your own good – and one of these days you're going to cut yourself.'

He tried to continue looking stern but couldn't quite manage it, and returned her grin. 'You and me both, Peggy Reilly,' he said.

She decided it was time to change the subject. 'How's the lovely Rosie?' she asked.

'Blooming as always,' he replied proudly. 'She's promised to cook me a spot of supper tonight, and then I'm taking her to the pictures.'

'I'm glad things are back to normal between you,' she said warmly. 'Let's just hope nothing else happens to take her away again.'

Ron concentrated on filling his pipe. 'She's got no plans to leave Cliffehaven. Rosie's contented with the life she's made here – even if it is only half a life because of that mad husband of hers. As far as I can make out, the only fly in Rosie's ointment is something I can't do anything about until she trusts me enough to talk about it,' he said gruffly.

Peggy eyed him sharply. 'She's not still troubled by what happened with Tommy, is she?'

Ron shook his head. 'She's accepted that her brother deserved to be arrested and locked up. It's his links with Eileen Harris that are still niggling her.'

'But their affair was over years ago,' she replied. 'Surely she isn't still harbouring the hurt Eileen caused her?'

'It seems so,' he muttered around the stem of

402

his pipe. 'And if I knew how and why that hurt had been inflicted, then I could maybe do something about it.' He looked at her expectantly.

'We've had this conversation before, Ron,' she said firmly, 'and I will not discuss Rosie's private business. It's clear she has no wish to drag it all up again, even with you. She's got enough on her plate.'

Ron scowled and was about to protest when he saw the glint of steel in Peggy's eyes and realised it wouldn't be wise to push his luck. He finished his cup of tea and went down to his basement bedroom with Harvey at his heels.

'The poor man is only trying to help,' murmured Cordelia.

'There's nothing he could do even if he knew all the facts,' Peggy replied. 'It all happened such a long time ago, Cordelia, and now it's far too late to do anything about it. Rosie's wise to keep the past where it belongs, and I just hope that Ron has the sense to understand that.'

'I suppose so,' murmured Cordelia, 'but secrets have a habit of casting long shadows, and that isn't good for any relationship.'

Peggy felt weighed down by her knowledge, and the awful gloom that had overshadowed her homecoming, and decided to lighten the mood. She determinedly dredged up a smile. 'I can see you've thoroughly enjoyed your afternoon of dramatics,' she said to Cordelia. 'Why don't you tell me all about it?'

Cordelia went rather pink and giggled before she enthusiastically described every bang on the door and the shocked expression on the woman's face as she was prodded in the middle by the walking stick.

'She recognised me, of course, because I'd only recently been a patient. I thought for a moment she might have me carted off in a straitjacket,' Cordelia confessed with another giggle, 'because I did rather over-egg the pudding. I'm sure she thought I was completely potty.'

'Oh dear,' sighed Peggy. 'You put yourself in a very tricky situation, Cordelia – and all because I wanted to come home. Doris was right, I've been horribly selfish.'

Cordelia frowned. 'Nonsense,' she retorted. 'I was having the time of my life, and wouldn't have missed it for anything.'

Peggy chuckled how did you manage to avoid being locked in a padded cell?'

'I pretended to suddenly realise what a terrible mistake I'd made, blamed it on the pills I was taking for the pain in my arm, and apologised profusely as I was backing out of the door.' She adjusted her half-moon glasses and blew her nose. 'She was gracious about the whole thing and even offered me a ride home in an ambulance – which of course I refused. I ended up feeling rather sorry for her, actually.'

'Never mind, Cordelia. All's well that ends well. We'll just have to hope none of us needs the services of that hospital for a long while – or we could find ourselves transferred to some place fifty miles away.'

Daisy was squirming and stretching as she woke from her afternoon sleep, and as she managed to roll over and sit up, she caught sight

404

of her mother and, with a beaming smile, lifted her arms towards her.

Peggy gathered her up and smothered her little face in kisses as she held her close. Despite all the dramas and tears, and all the subterfuge involved, it was good to be home again.

Ruby had spent the rest of her shift worrying about the fact that Grace knew exactly who she was, and why she'd fled London for Cliffehaven. She had no choice but to trust her to keep her mouth shut – and her promise to do so had seemed genuine enough. By the time the hooter went Ruby had decided to accept Grace's promise at face value, for she liked her and enjoyed her company. But the niggle of doubt meant she couldn't trust her completely, and Ruby realised she would have to keep their friendship on a casual level, and mind what she said in future.

She and Lucy left the factory compound on the dot of seven o'clock. Grace and her friends caught up with them at the gates and they stood about chatting and making plans for the weekend picnic before they went their separate ways.

The three London girls set off for their billet, which was a large Victorian house that had been turned into a hostel for young single females. It lay to the north-east of the factory estate and was one of several such houses which nestled high above the town within the sheltering arc of a leafy copse of trees. According to Grace, these houses were really posh and, before the war, were considered to be the most exclusive in Cliffehaven, so she and the others agreed that they'd fallen on

405

their feet by being billeted there.

Waving goodbye to them, Ruby strolled arm in arm down the hill with Lucy. They were both tired after a long day, so their talk was desultory. They reached the station and when Ruby saw that Stan was sweeping the platform, she drew to a halt. 'I just want to pop in and say hello to Stan,' she said. 'I ain't seen him for a while, and he's a nice old fella.'

'I'll see you tomorrow then,' said Lucy through a vast yawn. She hitched up her gas-mask strap and continued down the hill, her heavy boots clumping on the paving slabs.

Ruby hurried through the remains of the station building and onto the platform. 'Hello, Stan. You're keeping busy, I see.'

He turned and beamed at her. 'Ruby, what a lovely surprise. Have you got time for a cup of tea before you go home to Beach View?'

She shook her head. 'I can't, I'm sorry, Stan. Peggy's come home today and I need to get back.' She grinned up at him, squinting a bit as the sinking sun almost blinded her. 'I just come to say thank you for what you and Ron done the other night. You saved me bacon and no mistake.'

He regarded her a bit bashfully. 'No need to thank me,' he murmured. 'I'm just glad Ron got there in time.' He smiled at her. 'You'll be all right with Peggy,' he said as he awkwardly patted her arm. 'Now you run along and tell her I'll be over with some more roses on Sunday.'

Ruby stood on tiptoe and swiftly kissed the prickly cheek before she turned away and ran down the High Street.

There was a lump in Stan's throat as he touched the spot she'd kissed. He slowly walked to the station entrance to watch her race down the hill and, through his tears, he saw her wave as she reached Camden Road. And then she was gone. He was glad she couldn't see how deeply that sweet gesture had affected him, for she would think him a sentimental old fool. But Ruby had touched his heart – had become the child he and his darling wife had never been blessed with – and he was eternally thankful that he'd played a part in keeping her from real harm.

Ruby was out of breath by the time she reached Beach View, and she had to lean against the door for a moment to steady herself before she went into the kitchen. She could hear laughter and Daisy's gurgling, could smell the delicious aroma of fried onions, and feel the lighter atmosphere in the house now that Peggy was back in the heart of her family.

She walked into the kitchen and did her best to mask her shock and disappointment at seeing Doris firmly ensconced at the kitchen table. She avoided looking at her and went straight to Peggy. 'Welcome home,' she murmured as she took her hand. 'I see you managed to escape all right. How's it feel to be home again?'

'It feels just right,' replied Peggy with a soft smile. 'Now, you must be starving after being at work all day. I've put your plate to keep warm in the slow oven, so you sit down and tuck in before it spoils.' She chuckled. 'Alf's wife, Lil, popped round earlier with a treat for us all to celebrate my homecoming – even though poor Fred got it in the neck for getting his van scratched by Harvey.'

Ruby fetched a tea towel and gingerly lifted out her supper, removed the plate on top of it and gasped with delight. There were two lovely fat sausages and a pile of mashed potato all covered in thick onion gravy. 'Cor,' she breathed. 'It's a right feast and no mistake.'

There was a tut of disapproval from Doris. She was also glaring furiously at Jane, who was bathing Daisy in the kitchen sink. Ruby shot Rita and Sarah a conspiratorial grin and tucked into her food. Doris could tut all she liked, but it was clear that with Peggy at home, she was no longer in charge.

Jane wrapped Daisy in a large towel and carefully handed her over to Peggy to be dried, while Sarah took the water down to the garden butt and Rita disposed of the soiled nappy and baby clothes. Cordelia was wittering on about how she'd sidetracked Matron so Peggy could escape, and Fran was making appropriate noises as she tried to read the evening paper.

Ruby ate her meal and, to Doris's disgust, mopped up the last of the gravy with bread and then licked her fingers clean. 'That were the best bangers and mash I've had in an age,' she sighed as she sat back and patted her full stomach. 'Now I'm fit to bust.'

Rita set a cup of tea in front of her and reached for her jacket and goggles. 'I'm off on fire-watch,' she said. 'See you in the morning.' She softly tickled Daisy under her chin and made her giggle before giving Peggy a kiss on the cheek. 'It's lovely to have you back again, Auntie Peg,' she murmured before she stomped past Doris, down the cellar steps and slammed the back door behind her.

Peggy continued to struggle to put a wriggling, gurgling Daisy into her nightdress, and had to pass her to Doris when it became clear that she couldn't cope. 'She's too strong for me at the moment,' she murmured, 'and far too heavy to lift. Be a dear and tuck her into her cot, will you? And then leave my door open so I can hear her if she gets fractious.'

Doris planted Daisy on her hip and looked down in disapproval at Peggy. 'I told you it was too soon to come home,' she said flatly.

Peggy smiled up at her. 'Then it's a very good thing I still have you to help me, isn't it?'

Doris took Daisy into the bedroom and Peggy lit a cigarette. 'Have you girls got any plans for the rest of the evening?' she asked casually.

'Jane and I have both got early starts,' said Sarah, 'so we thought we'd keep Fran company and listen to the concert and the late news on the wireless.'

'No doubt Lord Haw-Haw will be throwing in his tuppence-worth on "Germany Calling", said Peggy with a grimace. 'Detestable little man.'

'Detestable, yes,' said Fran as she folded the newspaper, 'but he tells us more about what's happening in Europe than our government do.'

There was a short moment of silence following this statement, for although everyone found the man loathsome, he did indeed reveal much more about the war in Europe than their own newspapers.

'Well,' said Ruby to break the awkward moment, 'I don't have to be in until eleven tomorrow, but it's been a long day, so I got no plans to go out.' She glanced across at Peggy, who was slumped in her chair. 'Why don't you go to bed, Peggy? You look all in.'

'I'm enjoying sitting by my own fire in my own kitchen,' she said firmly as she sat straighter and glanced up at the clock. 'I'll sit up for a bit longer, I think.'

Doris came back into the kitchen and sat down at the far end of the table as Sarah twiddled the knobs on the wireless. She lit a cigarette and opened her book, but Ruby noticed that she wasn't really reading it, and that her gaze frequently went to the clock. She and Peggy were waiting for something – or someone, and although they were both trying hard not to show it, they were both tense.

Ruby shot a glance at Jane, who gave a small shrug to acknowledge that she had felt it too.

The concert had just started when there was a knock on the front door. 'I'll go,' said Doris, and hurried out of the room, closing the kitchen door firmly behind her.

'That's the quickest I've seen that woman move since she arrived here,' muttered Cordelia with a grimace. 'I hope to goodness it isn't that ghastly Lady whatnot. I can't stand *her* either.'

Peggy slowly got out of her chair and eased her back. 'I think I'll just pop in and check on Daisy.

Enjoy the concert, girls,' she added just before she too closed the kitchen door firmly behind her.

'It's not like Peggy to shut the door,' said Cordelia as she peered over her half-moon glasses. 'In all the years I've lived here, I don't ever remember her doing that. Something's going on.'

'You're right, Aunt Cordelia,' whispered Jane. 'But I'm blowed if I can figure out what it might be – and I could have sworn I heard Anthony's voice when Peggy opened that door.'

Cordelia fiddled with her hearing aid. 'Blowing a wig in the hall out of choice? Oh, I don't think Anthony wears a wig, dear.'

Fran giggled and leaned closer to Cordelia to carefully repeat what had been said.

'I thought I heard his voice too,' murmured Sarah. 'But Suzy would have said if he was coming over tonight, and it's not like him to call in if she's on night shift.' She shook her head and sighed. 'No doubt we'll find out what's going on sooner or later, but I agree, it is all a bit mysterious.'

'It's probably something to do with Doris still being here after Peggy swore she was leaving,' whispered Jane. 'If that is Anthony out there, perhaps Peggy's wheeled him in to help get rid of her.'

'But why *is* she still here?' asked Ruby.

'That's what we'd all like to know,' said Cordelia rather sourly.

'They went into a huddle just after Peggy got back from the hospital,' said Fran. 'Peggy shooed us all out of the kitchen and shut the door, so none of us knew what they were talking about.'

411

She leaned across the table towards the other girls. 'But they were in here for ages, so it must have been something serious.'

They sat, each with their own thoughts, until Sarah finally broke the silence. 'Let's listen to the concert and leave them to it,' she said. 'It's really none of our business, and I feel a bit uncomfortable talking about Peggy behind her back.'

Ruby and Jane eyed one another shamefacedly, as Fran picked up her knitting and Cordelia settled more comfortably in her chair and closed her eyes. They all tried very hard to concentrate on the beautiful music and not on whatever might be going on in the room across the hall – but it was almost impossible.

Peggy felt rather awkward sitting there in her dining room while Doris poured out her sorrows and hurt and fell sobbing into Anthony's arms. She could tell that her nephew was deeply shaken by his mother's revelation, and she silently blessed him for being so patient with her, but Peggy knew she wasn't really needed by either of them and wondered if she could just quietly slip out and leave them to it.

Anthony caught her eye over his mother's head, and he looked so woebegone that Peggy realised she couldn't desert him, so she hunted out an old bottle of sherry from the back of one of the cupboards. 'Come along, Doris,' she soothed. 'Dry your eyes and have a little drink. You"ll make yourself ill with all this crying.'

Doris bravely tried to gather her wits as she blew her nose, settled into a chair, and finally reached for the sherry. She took a sip and grimaced. 'Don't you have any decent drinks in the house, Margaret? This is no better than vinegar.'

Peggy took umbrage at being called Margaret after the tentative closeness they'd shared earlier that day, for Doris knew how much it wound her up. 'There's a war on, Doris,' she said wearily. 'And I don't have the money to buy gin and whisky, even if they were available.'

Anthony pushed his glasses over the bridge of his nose and gamely sipped the revolting sherry as his mother abandoned her glass and lit another cigarette. 'I really don't know what to do for the best,' he said into the heavy silence. 'If Father is determined to make a fool of himself, then I think it would be wise if Mother went back home.'

'I can't go back there,' sniffed Doris. 'The house is so empty and I shall feel very alone.'

Anthony reached for her hand as he leaned towards her. 'But you won't be alone, Mother. I shall be there. It's your home – our home – and possession is nine tenths of the law. If Father is that besotted, and the house stands empty for too long, what's to stop this woman from persuading him to move back in and take her with him?'

Doris stared at him in horror. 'He wouldn't,' she gasped. 'He's not that sort of man.'

The hurt was clear in Anthony's expression. 'We might have been certain of that three years ago, Mother. But who's to say what sort of influence that woman has had on him?'

Doris sat bolt upright, her gaze steely as she absorbed this unpalatable truth. 'I'd rather die than let either of them over the threshold ever again,' she breathed.

He squeezed her fingers and gave her a loving smile. 'You're in shock, Mother, but I'm sure that once you've settled back at home and had time to think about things more clearly, you'll see that all is not lost.' He hurried on as she was about to interrupt. 'You and Father have been married for over thirty years, and although it appears to be the end, there is still a chance you could both sit down and talk things through – and see if there's a way to repair things between you and even, perhaps, start again.'

A flash of something akin to hope lit in her, eyes and then her shoulders slumped and she dipped her chin. 'I could never take him back,' she murmured. 'Not after this.'

'Give it time, Doris,' pleaded Peggy. 'It's all still too raw to make hasty decisions, and I'm sure Ted regrets the hurt he's caused you.'

'Hurt?' Doris's tear-swollen eyes widened and her lips thinned. 'There isn't a word strong enough to describe what that man has done to me – and if he thinks I'll just–'

'Mother, you're getting upset again,' said Anthony as he clasped her hands. His voice softened. 'You've been a marvellous wife and supportive mother, and now it's my turn to look after you. But I can't do that here. As lovely and homely as it is, it isn't *our* home. Why don't you let me take you back to Havelock Gardens, and we'll see this through together?'

Doris regarded him in silence and then reached up to touch his face. 'My darling boy,' she mur-

414

mured. 'I knew I could count on you to know what to do for the best. I'll go and pack.' She rose from the armchair and moved in stately fashion across the room and into the hall.

'I hope you realise what you've taken on, Anthony,' said Peggy.

His smile was of weary acceptance. 'I'm fully aware of how demanding she can be, Aunt Peg, but I love her, and wouldn't be any sort of honourable chap if I deserted her when she needs me the most.' He reached into his jacket pocket and pulled out a battered cigarette case, which he stared at for a long moment. 'Whether things can be fixed between them is debatable, but after all the years they've been together, I think it's worth trying, don't you?'

'She's been horribly betrayed,' said Peggy, 'and for a woman like Doris, the shame may prove too much.' She gave a deep sigh. 'It's all terribly sad, but if there's no love or respect any more, then perhaps divorce is better than living a lie.'

He opened the silver, cigarette case and offered one to Peggy. Having lit them both, he rested back in his chair and watched the smoke curl towards the ceiling. 'Only time will tell, Aunt Peg, but in hindsight, I can see now that the marriage has been in trouble for many years. In a way, I can almost understand why Father had to leave – it's just the manner of it I'm finding hard to forgive.'

Peggy said nothing, for she could see how deeply this was wounding Anthony. It couldn't be easy for any son to see his parents in such a glaring, unflattering light.

415

Anthony smoked his cigarette and then stubbed it out in the ashtray. 'Suzy didn't say it in so many words, but I know how insufferable Mother has been while living here.' His smile was weary. 'It's time she came home, for her own sake, as well as yours.'

'But what about your work at Cliffe Fortress?'

'I can cycle back and forth. It isn't that far.'

'And you and Suzy? It won't be easy to carry on courting if you're living at home again.'

His slow, sweet smile lit up his face. 'We'll manage somehow – and once things have settled down, I shall ask her to marry me.'

'Oh, Anthony,' she breathed. 'I'm delighted for you both – but you do realise that Suzy and Doris will never be able to live under the same roof?'

He chuckled as he brushed ash from the lapel of his tweed jacket. 'I'm not as daft as egg-looking,' he said. 'There's a lovely little house for sale near Badger's Wood, and the owners have accepted my offer. I shall rent it out until things are resolved with Mother and Father, then, if Suzy will still have me, we'll start our lives together there.'

Peggy grinned at him in delight. 'You're a dark horse, Anthony Williams, and I can't wait to see the house.'

He grinned back at her. 'Suzy doesn't know anything about it yet. It's to be a surprise on our engagement, so don't say anything, please.'

'So when's the engagement?' she asked breathlessly.

'I was going to ask her on her birthday in June, but with everything that's happened, I don't think it would be very tactful.' He frowned and fiddled with his shirt-cuffs. 'What about Christmas Day? Does that sound better?'

Peggy thought that another seven months was a bit too long, but she smiled and patted his hand. 'It sounds perfect,' she said.

Doris returned, having recuperated enough to make up her face and tidy her hair, and there was a sense of energy in her that had been missing throughout the day. 'I can't carry that heavy case downstairs,' she said as she patted the string of pearls round her neck and adjusted her neat little hat.

Anthony left the room and they heard his feet thudding up the stairs as they stood facing each other in awkward silence.

'I'm trusting you not to breathe a word of this to anyone,' said Doris as she checked the contents of her handbag and pulled on her gloves.

'I made a promise and I won't break it.' Peggy held her arms out to her sister and pulled her stiff body into a tight embrace. 'I'll call in regularly once I can get about more easily,' she said. 'And if you need me for anything, just pick up the telephone.'

Doris drew back from the embrace and gathered up her overcoat. 'Thank you for being so understanding,' she murmured. 'I know I'm not the easiest person to live with, and I haven't always been fair to you – but I do appreciate your support.'

Peggy smiled inwardly as Anthony returned with the case and they trooped out into the hall. Her sister would never really change, even though

417

Ted's betrayal had shocked her rigid. But perhaps, when the storm had died down, she would look back on her marriage and realise that she had played a major part in its failure, for if a man was unfulfilled at home – if he was treated with little respect and barely acknowledged – he would seek comfort elsewhere.

She stood on the doorstep and waved until Anthony's borrowed car disappeared around the corner. Closing the door, she leaned on it for a moment to bolster the last of her depleted energy, and then went into the warmth and comfort of her kitchen to tell everyone that Anthony had persuaded Doris to leave Beach View and return home.

Chapter Twenty-Two

There had been rumours coming out of Europe and the Far East during the past few months that were so horrific, no one wanted to believe them. And yet there had been reliable witness accounts of appalling conditions in the Japanese POW camps in the jungles of Malaya, Burma and Siam, where captured servicemen were being forced into hard labour despite the Geneva Convention that forbade such things.

In Europe, the SS leader, Heydrich, had called a conference in January to co-ordinate what he termed the 'Final Solution of the Jewish Question', and now there were dark whispers of cattle

418

trucks transporting hundreds of thousands of dispossessed European Jews, dissenters and gypsies to vast concentration camps where they simply disappeared.

Peggy could hardly bear to listen to the news any more, for she didn't understand the inhumanity of it all, and knew that every rumour, every snippet of information, coming out of the Far East was another knife-thrust to poor Sarah and Jane, who still didn't know the fate of their father or Sarah's fiancé. She would have cancelled the newspapers and banned everyone from listening to the wireless if she could, but of course it was impractical and unwise, for the mood of this war was changing daily, and it was important to keep abreast of things.

Peggy and Cordelia were sitting in deckchairs in the back garden to make the most of a lovely warm late May afternoon as they read the letters that had come in the second post. Ron and Rosie had taken Daisy in her pram for a stroll along the seafront, and the girls had yet to get home from work, so, despite the inordinate number of planes landing and taking off from Cliffe airfield, it was the calm before the usual evening rush.

Peggy had been home for almost a week. Cissy had paid a flying visit, and Peggy had also managed to get through to Somerset and reassure Anne and her younger sons that she was rapidly on the mend. It was a half-truth to allay their fears, for although her scar had healed nicely and she was able to get about more easily, she was always tired and found it hard to dredge up the energy needed to look after Daisy and get back into the swing of things.

The nub of it was, she was missing Jim, and although his many letters were a small comfort, she longed to talk to him, to see Kim and to hold him. The telegram had clearly never reached him, for he made no mention of her operation, and there had been no further telephone calls. Yet in a way it was a blessing, for it would have caused him unnecessary worry and he might have been tempted to do something silly.

'The censor has had a field day with this,' she said in tearful frustration as she tried to piece together Jim's latest letter. 'There are so many cuttings-out, it barely makes any sense. I have no idea where he is or what he's doing, and there's not even a hint of any leave. Don't the army realise how unfair it is on us wives not to tell us anything?'

'I can understand how hard it must be for you,' soothed Cordelia, 'and I wish I knew what to say that might stop you fretting.' She patted Peggy's hand. 'He's bound to get leave soon, you'll see.'

Peggy sniffed back the tears and stuffed the tattered, useless letter back into the envelope. Cordelia was just being kind, and she knew she should be thankful that Jim was still in England and not fighting Rommel's troops in Africa – but that didn't make her miss him less, or stop her from worrying about him.

Peggy lit a cigarette and shielded her eyes with an old pair of sunglasses, rather ashamed of her tears of self-pity when the rest of the world was going to hell in a handcart. It was time to pull herself together, she decided, to find that old fighting spirit and snub her nose at Hitler and all the inconveniences and frustrations this war brought to her door. There would be an end to it, a rightful victory that would see Jim and the other brave boys coming home having vanquished a brutal enemy. She just had to keep believing that, to live each day with hope and look towards a brighter, peaceful future – for if she didn't, then she would be lost.

'Oh dear,' breathed Cordelia as she finished reading her own letter.

Peggy was jolted from her thoughts by the sad expression on Cordelia's face. 'What's happened?'

'This letter is from my sister's solicitor,' she explained. 'As you know, poor Amelia passed away a few months ago. This is her will, and it appears that apart from a few charitable bequests, I am the sole beneficiary.'

'As her only next of kin, it's hardly surprising,' said Peggy carefully, for she knew that the sisters had been estranged for years. When Amelia had become deluded and muddled, she had had to be admitted to a special hospital and had died a few weeks later.

'Well it surprises me,' said Cordelia. 'I thought she'd leave everything to some church school she'd terrorised as headmistress.' She gave a deep sigh. 'I'm far too old to have to deal with such things,' she muttered, 'and I feel a bit of a hypocrite seeing as how I didn't speak to her for years or even attend her funeral.'

'Amelia was a difficult woman, and the funeral was two counties away,' said Peggy firmly, 'and it was she who decided not to have anything to do with you and the rest of your family, so don't start blaming yourself.'

Cordelia folded the thick, creamy paper, and slipped it back into the matching envelope. 'You're right, of course,' she replied softly, 'but her passing has made me realise that perhaps I could have done more to heal the breach. We are the last of our generation and she must have been lonely, with no husband or children to care for her.'

'She chose her own way of life, Cordelia; you can't be blamed for that.'

'I've been a very lucky woman,' she murmured with a wan smile. 'Not everyone has a Peggy Reilly to love and look after them when they get old and feeble.'

'Now you're talking nonsense and making me tearful,' chided Peggy softly. 'Come on, Cordelia, it's far too nice a day to get gloomy. What have you inherited?'

'The bungalow and everything in it, some stocks and bonds, and the residue of her savings once probate has been granted and all the bequests and bills have been paid.' Cordelia tipped the brim of her sunhat so her eyes were shaded. 'The investment income and the savings will last me out and perhaps provide a few treats to make life a bit easier once this war is over. But I don't need the bungalow.'

'It's not a good time to sell property,' said Peggy as she remembered how little Anthony had paid for his cottage. 'Why don't you rent it out for the duration?'

Cordelia took off her half-moon glasses and squinted into the glare of the sunlit garden as yet more planes droned in the distance. 'I could, I suppose, but tenants can be difficult, always complaining and damaging things because they don't own the place, and I simply don't have the energy any more to have to deal with all that.'

'Ron and I could manage it for you,' Peggy offered. 'It would be a shame to leave it empty when so many people are desperate for somewhere to live, and the rent will give you some added income as well.'

'I have more than enough,' said Cordelia. 'But I wonder. Would Sarah and Jane like to move in there, do you think? It would give them a bit of independence. I wouldn't charge them rent, of course, and then, when I'm gone, it will be theirs.'

Peggy didn't want to think of Cordelia's demise, and quickly turned to more pleasant matters. 'You'll have to ask them,' she said, 'but I think it's an excellent idea. Sarah's an adult and Jane is maturing very quickly, and although they don't seem to mind sharing a room, it's time for them to have their own privacy and space. The bungalow would provide that, and of course we'll always be on hand to help if there are any problems.'

Cordelia nodded and smiled. 'Then I'll ask them this evening,' she said. 'Now, I think it's about time we had a cup of tea and a biscuit. I don't know about you, but all this sunshine and decision-making has given me a terrible thirst.'

'There's something going on at the airfield,' said Ron as he tucked into his breakfast the following morning. 'I was up there at dawn with Harvey,

423

and the number of planes coming in and flying out again was quite staggering.'

'They've been making a terrible racket for the last four days,' said Ruby. 'Me and Rita went up on the motorbike to have a look after I finished me shift yesterday – but of course we weren't allowed nowhere near the place.'

Ron continued to eat his porridge, his expression thoughtful. 'Something's up, that's for certain. I'm thinking it would be wise to batten down the hatches and sleep in the Anderson shelter tonight, just to be on the safe side.'

'But we're supposed to be going to the party at Wayfaring Down,' protested Fran, 'and I've made a new frock especially.'

'There will be other parties,' said Suzy as she gathered up their nursing cloaks and gas-mask boxes, 'and you'll still get to wear your new frock. But Ron's right, better to stay home tonight rather than get caught out in a heavy raid.'

Fran stuck out her bottom lip as she swung her cape over her shoulders. 'To be sure, I'm sick of this war,' she muttered.

'Aren't we all?' retorted Suzy, who was still edgy about Anthony moving back in with his mother. 'Now, come on Fran, or we'll be late on duty.'

Ruby's disappointment was tinged with relief. Despite her initial misgivings about how it might be interpreted by Michael if she went, she'd begun to look forward to the dance, but now the decision was out of her hands, she no longer had to worry. She cleared the table and started on the washing-up as Peggy tried to stop Daisy from smearing porridge all over her high chair.

After Suzy and Fran had left for the hospital, Ron went down to the Anderson shelter to do his weekly clean-up and restock the drinking water, candles, matches, kerosene and box of provisions. Jane was out on her milk round, Sarah was sleeping in on a rare day off, and Rita was due back from her night shift at the fire station.

'I don't know why everyone hates sleeping in the Anderson shelter,' said Cordelia as she closed the newspaper and set it aside. 'I find I can sleep just as well there as anywhere.'

'That's because you take your hearing aid out and can't hear anything,' said Peggy fondly.

'Old age certainly has its advantages,' she agreed, 'and at least I don't have to put up with Ron's dreadful snoring.'

'You'll not have to put up with me at all tonight,' Ron said as he carried the empty water container into the kitchen. 'I'll be on fire-watch duty.'

'You mean you'll be drinking tea with your cronies and talking rubbish as usual,' Cordelia retorted with a sniff.

'Ach,' he countered with a twinkle in his eye, 'it's better than listening to you twittering away like a demented bird, so it is.'

Cordelia swiped at him with a tea towel and Ruby smiled as she finished the washing-up and began to dry the dishes. She'd come to love this warm, welcoming home and the people who lived here, and she enjoyed listening to the gentle banter that spoke so clearly of a deep and abiding affection. It reminded her of how it had once been when her father was alive, and they'd lived in the two-up, two-down just off Bow High Street. The kitchen had been the heart of their home then, and although the memories were faded and fractured, the essence of that sense of being loved and secure remained with her.

The sharp summons of the telephone snapped her out of her thoughts.

'Would you get that, Ruby, dear?' asked Peggy as she tried to mop up the porridge.

Ruby carefully put down the pile of plates and hurried into the hall to find Rita had come home and already had the receiver against her ear.

'Yes, I'm not surprised,' said Rita. 'Of course I will. Yes, she's here, do you want to speak to her?' She listened and then replied, 'Thanks for letting us know. TTFN,' and replaced the receiver.

'Who was that?' Ruby asked.

Rita shrugged off her thick waterproof coat. 'It was your Canadian friend Mike. All leave has been cancelled and the party is off. There's something of a flap on up there, so he didn't have long to speak. He sends his apologies and said he'd telephone once things have calmed down.'

Ruby felt a shiver of apprehension as the deep drone of another squadron of bombers passed over the hills behind the house. 'It's going to be big, whatever it is, isn't it?'

'Looks like it,' said Rita cheerfully, 'but the RAF can deal with anything the Luftwaffe can throw at them, so I wouldn't let it worry you too much.' She toed off her thick boots and padded into the kitchen to get a cup of tea.

'John Hicks obviously knows more than he's letting on,' she told Peggy and Cordelia. 'He's called us all in for an extra shift today, and I have to go back on duty at six, so I'll have this cuppa and get some shut-eye.'

The atmosphere had become charged as they went about their usual daily chores, for the skies above Cliffehaven were suddenly too quiet and they were all tense, waiting for something to happen. Ruby took the shopping list and joined the long queues, but the tension was tangible, the speculation rife, for no one really knew anything, and that only made it worse.

Having quickly gone to tell Lucy that the party was cancelled, Ruby returned to Beach View with the shopping and eyed the Anderson shelter with some misgivings. She had lived through the rivers of fire that had been the London Blitz and couldn't imagine how anything could be more terrifying. But if Gerry was planning a big raid, she'd have preferred to shelter in the London Underground than under that flimsy bit of rusting corrugated iron.

The day dragged on and they ate their tea almost in silence as they listened to the early news in the hope that there might be a clue as to what was about to happen – but, as usual, they were disappointed.

Suzy telephoned at eight o'clock to say she and Fran had been ordered to be on standby at the hospital, and this only served to increase the tension. Having decided it would be wise to take Ron's advice and spend the night in the shelter, they reluctantly began to get organised.

The range fire was dampened down, buckets of water were filled in case they were needed and the blackout curtains were pulled. Ruby helped Peggy by running about collecting Daisy's clean nappies and making up bottles of formula milk, while Jane and Sarah got Cordelia into her overcoat and gathered up her precious bits of silver and important documents and stuffed them in her capacious knitting bag.

Laden with blankets, overcoats, gas-mask boxes and pillows, Jane and Ruby followed the others down the cellar steps and into the garden. It was twilight now and all was still – too still – as if the town was holding its breath, poised for whatever might come with the night.

As Sarah and Jane settled Cordelia into the deck-chair that was jammed in one corner of the Anderson shelter and surrounded her with pillows, Ruby tucked the provisions box under the bench and placed the candles and matches on the back shelf, so they could be easily reached when needed.

Peggy tucked Daisy into her special gas-mask cradle and then set about lighting the primus stove and making tea. 'As the sirens haven't gone yet, we can leave the door open,' she said. 'It's quite a warm night, and this place gets claustrophobic.'

'I've got an even better idea,' said Jane. 'Why don't I fetch the other deckchairs so we can sit outside until the sirens go?'

At Peggy's nod, Ruby went with Jane to the shed and brought back the chairs, setting them out close to the shelter so they could still carry on chatting to Cordelia, who'd opted to stay inside. With rugs over their knees and a freshly made mug of tea in their hands, it was almost like being on holiday.

'We must look proper daft,' giggled Ruby, 'but anything's better than sitting in there all night.'

Peggy smiled at her. 'It's not so bad,' she replied. 'You get used to it.'

Ruby hoped she'd never have to, but at least the smell of damp and mouse droppings was slightly more pleasant than that of human waste, prevalent in the Underground stations.

They spoke in murmurs as the time ticked away, awed by the night sky and the silence that settled around them.

Ruby eased back into her deckchair and marvelled at how coldly bright the stars were, and how close they appeared to be. The full moon had a halo around it as it slowly rose above the rooftops, and she watched the great golden globe in awe. The London skies before the war were never like this, for the stars were dimmed by the thousands of lights pouring from every street and window, and were veiled by the smoking chimney pots and thick smog.

'Has Cordelia talked to you about the bungalow she's inherited?' Peggy asked Sarah some time later when it was clear Cordelia was fast asleep.

Sarah nodded. 'It was very sweet of her to offer it, but we'd rather stay here if it's not too much trouble.'

'Of course it's no bother,' said Peggy. 'You can stay as long as you want, you know that. I just thought you and Jane might like to set up on your own, rather than be cooped up here with all of us.'

'We love it here,' said Jane, 'and we're used to sharing.'

'We were a bit worried that Aunt Cordelia might be upset by us turning her down, but she didn't seem to mind too much. In fact she seemed quite open to the idea of renting it out for the duration if she can find someone she can trust to look after it.'

'I'm sure we'll sort something out between us – but what about after the war, Sarah? Will you stay in England?'

'We'll probably go to Australia to be with our mother and grandparents, and get to know our new little brother while we wait for news of Pops and Philip.'

'So you still haven't heard anything?'

'Nothing tangible, and if one started believing all the horror stories, then all hope would be gone.' Sarah shot Peggy a brave little smile. 'If Mother can stay positive like she does in her letters, then so must we.'

Ruby felt a great deal of admiration for Sarah and her sister, for they were always cheerful and optimistic. It was bad enough being separated from her own mother, but at least she wasn't on the other side of the world – and to have the added worry over their father and Sarah's fiancé must be torture.

Peggy was the first to go back into the shelter. After checking on Daisy and tucking the blankets more firmly around the sleeping Cordelia, she curled up on the bench and was asleep within minutes.

'I think I'd rather sleep out here,' said Ruby

through a vast yawn. 'It's got to be more comfortable than that hard bench.'

'We'll get awfully cold if there's a heavy dew,' said Jane, 'but I agree, this is much more fun.'

The three girls settled down, snug beneath their blankets as their eyelids drooped and sleep beckoned. It was eleven o'clock now, and it looked as if nothing much was going to happen after all, for the sirens remained silent and tranquillity lay softly across the sleeping town.

Ruby was on the cusp of sleep when she thought she heard a distant roll of thunder. She reluctantly forced her eyes open and wondered at first why she seemed to be in the garden and not in her lovely comfortable bed. Then she became aware of the deep growl of menace that seemed to be coming from beyond the hills, and was instantly awake.

'What was that?' asked a drowsy Jane.

'I think we're in for a nasty thunderstorm,' replied Sarah as she gathered up her blanket. 'We'd better get into the shelter before the rain comes.'

'Wait,' said Ruby, her head turned towards the sound, which seemed to be growing stronger and was now all too familiar. 'That's not thunder.'

Peggy had heard it too and she gathered up a squalling Daisy and held her close, the shadows of unspoken fear clouding her eyes as she came outside to join them. 'Is it a raid? I didn't hear the sirens.'

'It's coming from the north,' murmured Sarah, 'and if I'm not very much mistaken, it sounds like a huge squadron of bombers.'

'Enemy bombers?' gasped Peggy. 'But why haven't the sirens gone?'

They had no answer for her, and despite the threat, they seemed unable to move as they looked to the skies. The thunder was louder now, rolling across the hills and creeping over roofs and down the narrow streets and alleyways. The sound grew and swelled, drawing a confused Cordelia from her sleep.

'What's happening? Why are you all out here if there's a raid on?' she quavered as she fiddled with her hearing aid and then leaned on her walking stick.

'It can't be a raid,' shouted Peggy above the noise. 'The sirens haven't gone.'

They stood in the garden, as if in a trance, as ominous dark shapes appeared over the hills to the north and spread across the peaks, blocking out the moon and the twinkling stars. Ever nearer they came, the deep-bellied roar of the bombers' engines shattering the silence.

Now Ruby could see the individual planes – could identify the Wellingtons from the new Lancasters, and the Halifaxes, Manchesters, Hampdens and Whiteleys. The deep rumble vibrated in the ground beneath her feet and throbbed in the walls and roofs of the surrounding houses. They came in wave after wave, filling her head with their heavy drone, too numerous to count as they headed towards the Channel.

It was an awesome sight – a magnificent, heart-swelling display that brought tears to her eyes and great pride to her soul – and before she knew it, she had joined in with the others and was shouting encouragement and waving furiously.

And still they came, escorted now by the Blenheims and Havocs of Fighter Command who would attack the enemy night-fighter airfields along the bombers' route.

Ruby's ears were ringing with the sound, her heart thudding with excitement and a deep sense of national fervour as she ran out of the garden, down the alley and into the main road. From here she could see yet another phalanx of bombers coming from the west, their lights mere pinpricks in the darkness as they too headed across the Channel.

Transfixed, she watched until they had become a dark shadow on the horizon. The silence they had left behind was deafening, and it hummed in her head as she tried to absorb all she'd just witnessed and come to terms with her overwhelming emotions.

Her trance was broken by the sound of cheering and applause, and she suddenly realised she was not alone, for the others had joined her and now the streets were crammed with the townsfolk of Cliffehaven, who had come out to celebrate the mighty show of strength from England's Bomber Command that would surely bring this war to an end.

'That'll teach Gerry to bomb our cathedral cities,' said Cordelia, who was quite pink with excitement. 'Perhaps now they'll realise we won't be beaten, and give up on this beastly war.'

Ruby wondered if that hadn't been Churchill's plan all along, for the show of strength in the skies above Germany, and the number of bombs that would be dropped that night, would surely have the enemy cowering and on the run.

They all finally went back to the house, still awed by what they'd seen and heard, and far too awake to go upstairs to bed. More tea was made, the biscuit tin raided and Daisy settled once more in her pram. Then they sat and talked, and at just after three in the morning, they heard the bombers returning from their mission, their vast numbers rumbling over the houses and making the windows rattle. The raid was over, and their brave boys had come home.

Chapter Twenty-Three

Sundays didn't count when there was a war on, for the factories never closed and the machines were never silent. Ruby dragged herself out of bed at five-thirty, still bleary after only two hours' sleep. Her shift began at six, and after a cup of tea and a piece of toast, she left Beach View and tramped slowly but determinedly up the steep hill to the factory complex.

'You look as bad as I feel,' said Lucy through a vast yawn. 'But my goodness, what a show the RAF put on last night.'

Ruby almost dislocated her jaw by yawning too, but the fresh air and the long hike up the hill had gone some way to waking her up. 'We'll have to work carefully today,' she warned as they headed for the factory. 'Those lathes are deadly and our concentration won't be good this morning.'

'But we need to reach our daily quota,' protested Lucy as they clocked in.

'We'll catch up on it tomorrow. I don't fancy losing a finger like that girl the other day.'

She and Lucy worked side-by-side, the pounding and whining of the machines and the stench of hot oil and metal doing nothing to improve their muzzy heads. When the klaxon went at lunchtime, they gratefully stepped outside into the clean, cool air and then headed for the canteen, where all the talk was still about the massive RAF raid.

'It's a shame we couldn't go to the party,' said Lucy, 'but actually, I think we had a much better time watching those planes. I wonder what their mission was, and who got bombed.'

Ruby rubbed her eyes. 'I expect we'll hear all about it on the news tonight, but I doubt I'll be able to stay awake long enough to listen to it. I'm dead on me feet after only two hours' kip.'

They wandered back outside after they'd finished eating and tried to sharpen their wits before they had to go back to their lathes. For the rest of their shift, they continued to work slowly and carefully, fully aware that there had been several accidents this morning, and any carelessness could cost them dearly.

It was now three in the afternoon and their shift was finally over. Ruby slung the strap of her gas-mask box over her shoulder and took a deep breath of the clean, salty air. 'How's about we go for a bit of a walk by the sea, Lucy? I still need to clear me 'ead.'

'Yes, let's, and then we could go home and have a cuppa in the garden. It's such a lovely day, and Mother will be out playing bridge, and our two evacuees will be working at the clothing factory, so we'll have the place to ourselves.'

They linked arms and strolled down the hill. Just as they reached the humpback bridge, a tram pulled in and they were shrouded in a great cloud of smoke. Laughing and spluttering, they began to run, their heavy boots pounding on the High Street pavement as they raced each other to the seafront.

Stan had seen the girls on the bridge, and had watched them with an indulgent smile as they'd raced down the hill. It was good to know that little Ruby had made such a nice friend – she wouldn't go wrong with Lucy, who was well brought up and as straight as a die.

Which was more than he could say for some, he thought sourly, as the peroxide blonde in the tight slacks sauntered past. That one had the glad eye for anything in trousers, and she'd even had the nerve to wink at him once.

He reached for his cap and shut the door to the makeshift ticket office, then went to see if there were any passengers getting off at Cliffehaven. A flashily dressed youngish man he didn't recognise got off the train before it had come to an absolute stop, thrust the ticket at him and, after quickly glancing over his shoulder, strode off.

Stan was a bit startled by this, but he didn't have time to think about it, for young Linda Grey needed help unloading her bicycle from the guard's van, and there were four other passengers to deal with. He looked down the length of the train and was about to signal to the driver that all was clear when the door to the rearmost carriage opened and two men alighted.

Stan noted from their tickets that all three strangers had come from London, but they didn't seem to be travelling together and none of them had any luggage. As it was unusual to see men of that age out of uniform these days, he blew his whistle so the train could leave, and then went outside to the forecourt.

The younger man was halfway down the High Street now, and lighting a cigarette for the simpering blonde floozy. 'That was quick work, even for you,' Stan muttered in disgust before he trawled the busy street for sight of the other two. They were standing outside the tobacconist and engrossed in the daily newspaper.

Stan watched them for a moment, for he was suspicious of strangers now there was a war on, and there were posters everywhere warning of Fifth Columnists – Nazi sympathisers and spies. Then he shrugged and turned away. They didn't look like spies, and it was no business of his why they'd come to Cliffehaven – and besides, there was another train due in less than five minutes.

Ruby was feeling very much better after the walk along the promenade and the leisurely cup of tea and slice of home-made cake they'd eaten on Lucy's lawn. It was lovely sitting here looking out to sea, and she could have stayed there quite happily for several more hours, but the sun was beginning to drop behind the hills and it was getting chilly.

'I'd better go,' she said regretfully as she looked at the cheap wristwatch she'd recently bought. 'It's nearly five and I promised Peggy I'd finish off the ironing before tea, and if I don't get back she'll do it herself.'

'She's got a son-in-law in the RAF, hasn't she?' asked Lucy as they headed for the front door. 'I wonder if he took part in that raid last night?'

'She thinks he probably did, and is hoping she'll get news that he got back safely. It must be a terrible worry for her – and for her daughter down in Somerset.'

'We worry about Daddy being out in the Atlantic, but it must be far worse having a loved one in Bomber Command – the odds on their making it through are narrowing with every day.' Lucy gave a wan smile. 'I'll see you tomorrow. Get a good night's sleep, Ruby, because we've got another early start.'

'Don't I know it,' she said on a sigh. 'I'll be glad when this rota changes, and no mistake.' She tramped across the weed-infested gravel driveway and turned to wave goodbye before going through the gate and along the tree-lined pavement.

Despite the gloomy talk of war and death, she was in a happy frame of mind as she crossed the bottom of the High Street and headed down Camden Road. Life in Cliffehaven might have been challenging at the start, but now she was living at Beach View, she felt she could finally embrace this little town and settle down here. The factory work paid well and she'd made new friends, and with

Peggy and Ron to guide her, she knew she would blossom. If only she could divorce Ray and persuade her mother to come and live here, her life would be perfect.

The thought of Ray dimmed her happiness, for he'd never agree to a divorce, and as long as she was stuck with him, she could never really move on with her life.

The sudden roar of a motorbike engine made her jump and she realised she was outside the fire station and Rita was grinning at her. 'You done that on purpose,' she said with a giggle.

'You were miles away and I thought you needed waking up,' replied Rita. 'Want a lift home?'

Ruby clambered onto the back of the motorbike and held on as Rita swerved off the fire station forecourt and raced down Camden Road.

Neither of them noticed the man in the fedora and tailored overcoat watching from the shadows of the nearby bomb site as they parked the motorbike outside Beach View Boarding House and then closed the front door behind them.

Peggy's daughter, Cissy, had telephoned that morning from the airfield to reassure her mother that Martin Black had made it safely back from the raid. She'd refused to say anything more because it was against the rules, and so Peggy had to wait like everyone else for the late news on the wireless.

When the time came, they all gathered in the kitchen and listened intently as the newsreader informed them about the raid. The target had been Cologne. The force dispatched to fire-bomb the city – a thousand bombers – was more than two and a half times greater than any previous single night's effort by Arthur Harris's Bomber Command. In addition to the bombers there had been over forty Blenheims of 2 Group, reinforced by thirty-nine aircraft of Fighter Command and fifteen from the Army Co-operation Command, who had carried out intruder raids on the German night-fighter airfields near the route of the bomber stream. The raid had apparently been a great success, despite the loss of over forty aircraft.

Ruby woke at five the following morning, feeling much better after a long, deep sleep, and was looking forward to the day. She washed and dressed and hurried downstairs to find that Jane had finished preparing her flask and sandwiches and was already halfway out of the door on her way to the dairy.

'Don't you mind having to get up at this time every day?' asked Ruby as she poured a cup of tea.

'I love it,' said Jane with a happy smile. 'I get to talk to the horses while I muck them out, and it's peaceful without lots of people about.'

'You'll probably change yer mind once winter comes, and it's blowing a gale and tipping it down with rain.'

Jane's smile remained sunny. 'I don't mind wind and rain,' she said. 'It's lovely after the sticky heat of the tropics.' She waved goodbye and was gone, trundling the old bicycle along the garden path and then freewheeling down the alleyway.

Ruby had just poured a second cup of tea to go with her porridge when Rita came clumping into the kitchen in her heavy boots. 'I can give you a lift to work, if you like,' she said as she helped herself to tea and porridge.

'Won't that be out of your way?'

'Nah, I'm going out to the track this morning to put her through her paces. She's misfiring a bit, and I want to make sure she's tuned properly for the races next weekend.'

They finished their breakfast and were on their way out just as Peggy came into the kitchen with a grizzling Daisy. 'She's teething, bless her,' she murmured. 'Have a good day, girls, and I'll see you both later.'

They left the house and Rita wiped the heavy dew from the motorbike seat. Within minutes they were roaring up the High Street, over the hump-back bridge, then screeching to a halt outside the factory gates. Ruby clambered off and tried to bring some order to her hair as Rita turned the bike around and shot off back down the hill.

'She'll come a cropper on that thing one day,' said Lucy as she approached. 'Why does she have to go so fast?'

Ruby laughed. 'Because she can – and because she knows what she's doing.'

They clocked in and set to work neatly and swiftly, for they had quite a lot of catching up to do if they were to reach their daily target and make up for their lack of concentration the day before.

As the hooter went and they handed the machines over to the next shift, Ruby stepped out into the sunlight and breathed a sigh of relief. 'I need a bath and hair-wash, and then I'm going to spend the rest of the afternoon helping Peggy with the mending. You wouldn't believe how 'ard we all are on our clothes, and these overalls are coming apart at the seams.'

'I don't think you'll be doing any such thing, actually,' said Lucy and grinned. 'Look who's waiting at the gate.'

Ruby turned and her emotions went haywire as she saw Mike Taylor waving to her. 'Oh, Gawd,' she breathed. 'I must look a right fright. What on earth is he doing turnin' up 'ere without giving a girl any warning?'

'I thought you weren't interested?' giggled Lucy.

'I'm not,' she retorted, 'but it's a matter of pride, gel. It ain't no fun to have a bloke like that see me looking like this.' She hitched up the strap of her filthy overalls and decided against taking off the scarf to reveal her tangled, sweaty hair.

'Hi there, Ruby, Lucy,' he greeted them with a broad smile. 'Steve and I were wondering if we could buy you both a drink tonight?'

'I ain't going nowhere looking like this,' replied Ruby, her face reddening with embarrassment.

'Well, the pubs don't open until six, so you've plenty of time to get changed,' he said, his bright blue eyes twinkling with humour. 'Come on, Ruby. We just want to apologise for letting you all down over the dance.'

Ruby glanced at Lucy, who was starry-eyed and obviously eager to meet Steve again. She gave a nonchalant shrug, not daring to look Mike in the eye. 'All right. But our shift starts again at six tomorrow, so we can't be too late.'

'Where do you live? We could come and pick you up.'

'We'll meet you in the Anchor. That's in Camden Road,' she said quickly.

'Six o'clock?' He was smiling at her still, and there was a teasing light in his eyes.

'Make it half-past,' she replied, for no real reason.

'That's a date,' he said.

'It's not a date. It's meeting for a friendly drink.' She bit her lip, afraid she would giggle and let him see how much he was affecting her.

'Can I offer you both a lift home?' He pointed at the car parked on the other side of the road. 'Or is that off limits too?' he teased.

Ruby relented, for he was being nice and she was close to the point of being far too starchy with him. 'As long as you don't mind getting grease and muck on the up'olstery, a lift 'ome would be nice.' She peeked up at him through her lashes. 'Thanks.'

He opened the car's back door with a flourish and they climbed in. Slamming it shut, he got behind the steering wheel and started the engine. 'Where to?' he asked, his gaze finding her in the rear-view mirror.

'You can drop us both off at the end of Camden Road,' said Ruby. 'Me and Lucy don't live in the same place.'

'Okay,' he drawled. 'But I don't know why you're being so cagey. It's not as if I plan to climb the drainpipe in the middle of the night and break into your bedroom.'

Ruby went scarlet and Lucy giggled. 'All right,'

Ruby conceded. 'Lucy lives in Havelock Road and I'm at Beach View Terrace.'

He drove down the hill and over the humpback bridge, along the High Street and into Havelock Road. Parking outside Lucy's house, he leaped out, opened the door, and waited until she'd waved goodbye to Ruby and gone inside before he climbed back behind the wheel. 'I often wondered what it must be like to drive a taxi,' he said cheerfully. 'Are you okay in the back there?'

'It's ever so comfortable,' she admitted, 'and the leather smells lovely.'

His eyes smiled at her from the rear-view mirror, and all too soon they had reached Beach View Terrace.

Ruby rather liked the way he opened the door for her, and she clambered out feeling quite the lady despite her filthy working clothes and the muck smeared on her face. 'Ta ever so,' she said breathlessly as she backed away from him towards the front steps. 'I'll see you in the Anchor at half-six.'

He closed the car door and leaned against the bonnet, his expression serious. 'Is that a promise, Ruby, or are you just saying it to get rid of me?'

She shot him a nervous smile. 'Nah, I'll be there. I promise.' She turned away, unlocked the door and swiftly closed it behind her. 'Blimey,' she breathed, 'I'm gunna 'ave to watch meself there.'

'I saw the car – and the very handsome young man driving it,' said Peggy as she came out of the dining room carrying a large glass vase. She grinned. 'It looks as if you've made quite a conquest.'

444

'Oh, Gawd, Peggy, I dunno what to do,' she groaned. 'He's ever so nice, and I really like 'im, but I got an 'usband – and he ... he...' Ruby folded her arms tightly about her waist in an effort to keep her seething emotions under control. 'He's a wrong'un and I wish I never married 'im – now he's on the run from the law, I'm hiding from him, and I can't see no way out.'

'There's always a way out if you really want one,' said Peggy quietly as she set the vase on the nearby chair.

'Not for me there ain't,' said Ruby, hot tears running down her face. 'He'll kill me if he finds me – and there's no way he'll give me a divorce.'

'Oh, Ruby, my dear,' crooned Peggy as she drew her into a warm embrace.

Ruby clung to her, fighting the tears and the confusion – and the longing for her mother. She hadn't meant to blurt it all out like that, but Peggy's arms were so comforting, the tears a balm to all the hurt she'd been harbouring for too long.

'Come, Ruby, let's go into the dining room where we can talk in private. It seems to me you've been carrying a heavy burden on those narrow shoulders, and it will help you no end to share it.'

Ruby sniffed as she nodded. 'Yeah, I need to talk to someone, and you're the nearest person I got to me mum.' She looked at Peggy, her green eyes awash with tears. 'You don't mind, do yer?'

'That's what I'm here for,' murmured Peggy as she steered her towards the dining room and closed the door behind them.

Raymond Clark quietly settled back into the shadows of the bombed-out house at the corner of Camden Road, and pulled his camel-hair coat more tightly about him. He was cold and hungry after the long hours he'd spent watching the house, but his fury was white-hot, stoked by frustration at not being able to grab her earlier, and what he'd just witnessed.

He'd managed to give the law the slip but still, he'd taken a huge risk by coming here. And yet, once the little tart on the exchange had told him about the telephone call from Cliffehaven to the Tanner's Arms, he knew he had to come. Ruby had his money – and he wasn't about to let her get away with putting him in hospital and doing a bleedin' runner like his feckless mother. He'd make her pay for that.

He bunched his fists as he leaned against the remains of the kitchen wall and thought about how good it would feel to smash her face in. 'I'll get you, Ruby,' he whispered. 'And when I do, I'm gunna teach you a lesson you ain't never gunna forget.'

Chapter Twenty-Four

Ruby felt much calmer after the storm of tears and the quiet, loving way Peggy had listened to her story without judging and comforted her. She hadn't realised how much she'd bottled things up, or what a heavy burden she'd been carrying ever since her baby had died and she'd been forced to run for her life. Now the burden seemed lighter, and although things remained the same regarding her marriage to Ray, and her exile from London, the love and support she'd found here in Cliffehaven would make it easier for her to cope.

She finished dressing after her bath, and took extra care with her make-up before brushing out her freshly washed hair. There were russet lights in it again, she noticed, and her green eyes, although a little swollen after the tears, were sparkling. She could start to see the old Ruby emerging again, clear-skinned and bright-eyed – no longer the dreary, wan drudge, but the young girl she was meant to be.

Dressed in her new sweater and skirt, the lovely two-tone shoes cushioning her feet, she gathered up her warm overcoat and ran downstairs and into the kitchen to find Peggy arranging an enormous bunch of beautiful roses into a vase while Rita finished the washing-up. 'I see Stan's been visiting,' she said.

'Yes, he called in at lunchtime. Beautiful, aren't they?' Peggy smiled. 'And you look beautiful too,' she said softly.

'Yeah,' laughed Rita, 'you scrub up all right for someone who isn't at all bothered about meeting the handsome Mike for a drink.'

Ruby blushed. 'A girl's gotta have some pride, Rita. I looked a right mess this afternoon.'

Peggy looked at the clock and became business-like. 'What time are you meeting the others?'

'Oh, Gawd, I'm late,' groaned Ruby. 'He'll think

447

I ain't coming, even though I promised.'

'He'll wait,' said Peggy implacably as she put the plate of food on the table. 'You can't go out without something in your stomach.'

Ruby sat down at the kitchen table, aware that it was almost seven o'clock – but that her stomach was rumbling. She tucked into the corned beef hash with a will and soon cleared the plate. 'That were lovely, Peggy, but I ain't one to break me promises, so I gotta go.' She looked across at Rita. 'Why don't you come too?'

Rita shook her head and picked up the hessian bag of tools she'd dumped on a nearby chair. 'I've still got a bit of work to do on the motor-bike. And as there's just enough light to finish up, I want to get it done before I go to bed.'

'Have a lovely evening, dear,' said Peggy warmly, 'and if you see the other girls, tell them there's hot cocoa when they get in. Ron somehow managed to get a big tin of it this afternoon.'

Ruby kissed her cheek, grabbed her coat and hurried down the steps to the back door. It was just after seven and the sky was darkening, threatening rain. Rita would have to get a move on if she wanted to finish tinkering with that bike.

She carefully picked her way along the rough alleyway until she reached the main road, and then pulled her coat over her shoulders as the chill wind came up from the sea. Crossing the road, she hurried down the hill towards the turning for Camden Road where the large corner house had been almost flattened in an air raid. She was very late and she wouldn't be at all surprised if Mike had given up on her.

The arm grabbed her round the waist, lifting her off her feet and holding her so tightly she could barely breathe. The hand clamped over her mouth, stifling her scream as she was carried into the black shadows of the burnt-out house. 'Hello, Ruby. Remember me?'

Ray! She kicked at his legs, squirming and flailing her arms, fingers clawed to scratch his face and eyes as she desperately fought to wriggle free. She tried to bite his hand, but it was pressed too firmly over her jaw, threatening to crush the delicate bones. Her heart was pounding with terror, and although the fear engendered greater strength, he was stronger – and she could do nothing to stop him from pulling her across the rubble, deeper and deeper into the shadows and down steps into what smelled like a coal cellar.

The resounding thud of a trapdoor stole the final glimmer of light and sealed them off from the rest of the world.

'It's no good you fighting me, Ruby,' he hissed in her ear. 'I got you now, and there ain't nothing you can do about it.' His arm tightened around her waist as he held her against him. 'Where's me money?'

She made a high-pitched keening sound in her throat as she tried to wrest away from his smothering hand.

'I know you got it,' he continued. 'And I ain't going nowhere till you give it back.'

She felt his hand ease from her mouth, but the grip of his fingers was now a vice around her jaw as he thrust her head back against his shoulder. 'I … I…'

'Where is it, Ruby?'

'In ... post office,' she managed. 'The passbook's ... safe ... deposit box.'

'Where's the key?'

'In me bag.' The tears were hot and rolling down her face; her terror was a living, breathing thing that crawled through her and electrified every nerve and sinew.

His grip remained as firm as ever on her jaw. 'Give it to me.'

She scrabbled for her shoulder bag, her fingers slick with sweat, and fumbled to undo the catch and feel inside. She knew the key was in her purse, but she was so terrified, she couldn't seem to make her fingers work properly. She dropped the bag.

'Bitch! You done that on purpose,' he hissed. 'Pick it up.'

She felt his arm relax round her waist, his hand move from her jaw to grasp a handful of hair, yanking her head back until her neck was stretched to its limits. She gasped with the pain and then felt his knee jab into the backs of her legs so she fell to the cellar floor. Scrabbling in the dense darkness, her breath coming in ragged gasps as his fingers threatened to pull her hair out at the roots, she felt the handbag strap and grasped it.

'Hand it up to me,' he ordered.

Terrified he'd break her neck, she did as she was told. 'Please, Ray,' she begged. 'Just take the money and go. I won't tell no one.'

He was still kneeling behind her, his fingers still cruelly entwined in her hair as he fumbled in her bag, clicked open her purse and then tossed them away. 'It's not just about the money, though, is it?' he said softly in her ear, his breath warm and foul as he slowly traced the sharp edges of the cold key over her cheek. 'You left me to die, Ruby. And for that you gotta pay.'

Daisy was asleep in her cot in the bedroom, and Rita had been forced to abandon her work on her motorbike as the rain came down in wind-blown sheets. The other girls were out at a fundraising event, so Peggy and Rita were keeping Cordelia company as they waited for their favourite show, 'It's That Man Again', to come on the wireless.

It had just begun when someone rapped on the front door, and with a cluck of annoyance, Peggy went to answer it. As she opened the door and saw the Canadian officer standing on her doorstep she frowned. 'I thought you were meeting Ruby at the Anchor?'

'She's not here?'

Peggy felt a stab of alarm. 'She left over fifteen minutes ago.'

The handsome young Canadian ran his fingers through his hair. 'But there's no sign of her. Are you sure?'

'Positive.' Peggy quickly reached for her coat. 'We'd better go and look for her.'

'But where can she be? The pub's only minutes away. She can't have just disappeared.'

Peggy shivered as she thought of Ruby's brutal husband and the revenge she feared he would take on her if he found her. 'I'm telephoning the police,' she said briskly.

'Surely that's a bit–'

'It might be – but I'm not prepared to risk it.'

The first punch came without warning. It landed hard against the side of her head. The second caught her jaw. The third sent her sprawling to the concrete floor.

Ruby's head was ringing, the pain like a knife in her jaw, and a sickening ache in her side. But she knew that if she didn't move quickly he would kill her. The darkness was profound, but her only protection, and she scrabbled away from him through the remnants of the coal, her hands desperately searching for something to use as a weapon.

'You can't get away from me this time,' he snarled. 'It's just you and me, Ruby – and there's nowhere to hide.'

She had lost a shoe and was pressed against a wall, the strong smell of coal rising all around her, the crunch of it beneath her feet as she blindly peered through the darkness. She couldn't see him, to move silently was impossible, and there was very little room in here to manoeuvre. But she could hear him getting nearer, could smell his rancid breath and almost feel the rage emanating from him.

He stumbled into her, pinned her to the wall and caught her another glancing blow under the chin. She was spun across the coal cellar, stumbling and then crashing against the concrete steps. She slid to the floor and felt something hard beneath her leg. Hardly daring to breathe and almost passing out with the pain, she examined it with her fingers. It was long and round, like a thick wooden pole, the splinters slicing into her exploring fingers. She found the metal plate at the end of it and felt a spark of hope. It was a heavy shovel.

Grasping it firmly, she stayed on the floor, her back pressed against the side of the steps. She could hear him moving about, trying to find her in the pitch-black, his breath harsh in the silence. Her heart was hammering so loudly she was certain he could hear it, but she held her nerve, waited until she gauged he was standing very close, and then swung the shovel with every ounce of her strength.

He cried out and she heard his feet lose their purchase on the floor. She advanced on the sound of his heavy breathing and swung the shovel again, felt the strike resonate through her arm, and heard his grunt of pain. Keeping the shovel firmly gripped in front of her, she edged back until she found the steps.

'I'll kill you for that,' he groaned as he crunched coal beneath his feet.

He was getting too close. Ruby stealthily climbed the cellar steps until her head came into contact with the wooden trapdoor. She reached up and pushed hard, feeling the trapdoor lift and then clatter to the floor above her. One step. Two. And then freedom.

His fingers grasped her ankle, bringing her to her knees and making her drop the shovel. She kicked out wildly, felt his hold loosen and scrabbled free. Slipping, sliding and stumbling over the wreckage and bomb debris, she started to scream for help. The rain soaked her to the skin as she ran up the road towards Beach View, still screaming.

Ray was behind her, hobbling from his injuries, but moving fast enough to catch her. She swerved and darted across the street, her screams echoing through the twilight.

Suddenly there was an ear-piercing blast of police whistles and two men came running from the darkness of a nearby alley, leading a group of uniformed policemen.

She saw Ray hesitate. Saw him turn this way and that like a hunted animal before he raced into Beach View Terrace. The men gave chase and Ruby could only stand and watch as they pounded past her.

The roar of a motorcycle engine drowned the shouts and whistles, and the policemen scattered as Ray shot out of Beach View Terrace on Rita's bike and roared down Camden Road. The policemen quickly gave chase in their cars, their clanging bells bringing the startled citizens of Cliffehaven to their doors and windows.

Ruby's legs felt as if they'd been turned to jelly, her head seemed stuffed with cotton wool and the pain from Ray's blows was throbbing in every part of her. She staggered to lean against a wall, the shock and terror rushing in to overwhelm her as her eyelids fluttered and she began to sink into oblivion.

'It's okay. I've got you.'

The reassuring Canadian voice soothed her and she felt his strong arms about her. She sank into his embrace as he lifted her up and carried her through the cold, wet darkness to the light and warmth and love that was Peggy Reilly and Beach View Boarding House. She was safe.

Ruby opened her eyes to discover she was lying on a bed in the hospital emergency ward, and a careworn Peggy was sitting beside her, holding her hand.

'It's all right, Ruby,' she said softly. 'You were out cold so we brought you in. But the doctor says there's no lasting damage and you can come home with us once he's organised the medication to help with the pain.'

She tried to sit up, but her head swam and the pain in her jaw shot through her head. 'Ray? What happened to Ray? Did they catch him?'

Peggy took a firmer hold on Ruby's hand, her expression suddenly very serious. 'They chased him through the town and caught up with him by the humpback bridge. He was going too fast and lost control of the motorbike on the wet road. The bike crashed into the bridge wall and he was flung over it and landed on the railway lines. He's dead, Ruby. It's over.'

Ruby closed her eyes, wanting to mourn the man she'd thought she'd loved so deeply – but feeling nothing. He'd killed her love and her unborn child and now he was gone and she was free.

'How did the police get to me so quickly?' she asked softly.

'They got information from London two days ago that he might try to get to you once he knew where you were hiding. There was a girl on the telephone exchange in Raymond's pay that they'd been watching since he'd gone to ground, and it didn't take much to persuade her to talk.'

Ruby nodded her understanding. There was always someone ready to take a bribe, especially when Ray was involved. 'So why didn't they arrest him earlier? Why wait until he'd half killed me?'

Peggy licked her lips, clearly unhappy about having to continue. 'Two detectives from London followed him down on the train. They needed to know where he'd hidden his money and account book, you see, because it was evidence against him. They thought you might be acting as his accomplice.'

'Gawd,' Ruby breathed, 'coppers can be thick at times. Didn't they realise I was the last person to help him?'

'But you had his money, Ruby. They found your passbook, and all those food and clothing stamps in your safety deposit box.'

Ruby closed her eyes. 'I needed it to get away – to see me through until I could go home again.'

'I do understand, Ruby, and I don't blame you one bit. Unfortunately the police will want to ask you lots of questions, and they've taken the money and stamps as evidence.'

Ruby sighed. 'It were never really mine to begin with, I know that – and I did feel guilty about spending some of it. But I can tell them where he hid that little black account book and the gun. That should 'elp me case.' She looked at Peggy and saw only understanding and sympathy in her expression. 'But I still don't know why they didn't nab 'im sooner. Surely they was keeping an eye on 'im?'

'He gave them the slip shortly after he arrived, so they set up surveillance of Beach View in the hope they could catch him.'

'But he was already in the bombed-out house right under their noses,' she muttered.

Peggy nodded and then gently smoothed back the hair from Ruby's forehead. 'We're all just so thankful you weren't seriously hurt,' she murmured.

'Poor Rita. I bet she's heartbroken about her precious motorbike.'

Peggy smiled. 'She's learned never to leave the key in it again, that's for sure. It's a bit bent and buckled, but she says she'd rather have a damaged bike than an injured friend.' She glanced towards the drawn curtains that surrounded the bed. 'They're all waiting for you out there,' she said. 'Do you feel ready to come home?'

Ruby smiled through her tears. 'I can't think of nowhere I'd rather be,' she replied.

Chapter Twenty-Five

There had been no sign of Mike when Ruby returned to Beach View, for he'd had to return to his barracks. But he'd left her a long letter explaining that he was being sent away the next day on a training course for some mysterious mission and hoped to see her on his return. He expressed his relief that she was safe, warned her that a Canadian Mountie always got his girl, and signed it with a flourish.

Ruby kept that letter under her pillow and took it out frequently to read it as she rested and recuperated over the next few days. Perhaps, when he returned, they could get to know one another properly – but for now, she was content to know she was safe and no longer had to live in fear.

The police came to question her and she told them about Ray's hiding place in the skirting board. To her great relief they didn't press charges over the stolen money and stamps – and she suspected that was down to Peggy and the respect in which she was held in this town.

She'd finally got bored with lying in bed and went back to work, where she became the reluctant focus of attention, for the rumours of what had happened that night had spread all round Cliffehaven. The girls from Mile End were hugely supportive, treating her almost like a heroine, which was embarrassing, and even Lucy looked at her with admiration. Flora had had the grace to admit she'd told Ray where Ruby was living, and actually apologised for causing her so much trouble. Ruby kept her head down and concentrated on her work, knowing she'd soon be yesterday's news and it would all blow over.

Two weeks had passed since Ray's attack, the bruises had healed and she was no longer in any pain, but her thoughts had inevitably turned to her mother, and after managing to speak to her on the telephone at the Tanner's Arms, a plan began to form. It was a plan that she would need to discuss with Peggy if it had a chance of becoming reality.

She pushed through the back gate of Beach View that June afternoon to find Peggy and Cordelia sitting in the garden, with Daisy safely busy with her toys in the playpen.

'Hello, dear,' twittered Cordelia from her deckchair. 'We're just enjoying the sunshine. There's tea in the pot, and Anthony brought round some lovely cake from the Cliffe Fortress canteen.'

Ruby went to fetch a cup and another deckchair. The sun was warm, so she pulled the straps of her filthy dungarees off her shoulders, unfastened her blouse buttons and took off the headscarf. 'How's Anthony doing?' she asked.

'Very well, considering how demanding Doris can be,' said Peggy. 'But he's managed to persuade her to meet Ted on neutral ground to see if they can come to some sort of armistice. Suzy has been a real brick – it's clear she absolutely adores Anthony, and has been a terrific support to him.' She gave a wry smile. 'I think Doris now realises she's lost that battle.'

Ruby sipped her tea and nibbled on the lovely sponge cake before feeding a small piece to the bewitching Daisy, who immediately smeared it all over her face and laughed uproariously. 'She's a right little smasher, ain't she?' she said wistfully.

'You'll have one of your own some day,' Peggy replied softly.

'I hope so,' she sighed. 'But London ain't the place to bring up kids – not if you're poor. My mum's had a hard life since Dad died, and although she done her best, the East End slums grind you down until you lose all hope of anything better.'

459

'You don't have to go back there,' said Peggy. 'You have work and a home here for as long as you want it; you know that, Ruby.'

Ruby took her hand and smiled. 'I do know, and I can never express how much that means to me, Peggy. But I miss my mum, and I want her to share what I've found here in Cliffehaven.'

'Then write to her and ask her to move in here,' said Peggy immediately. 'You'd have to share, because I don't have any spare rooms, but–'

'That's really kind of you, Peggy, but I have a much better idea,' she broke in before turning to Cordelia. 'Is that bungalow still empty, Grandma Finch?'

'Well, yes,' she replied. 'I keep meaning to find a tenant, but somehow I haven't found the time.'

'Would you rent it to me and Mum? We'd pay the going rate and look after it for you,' she added swiftly.

The little face brightened and the blue eyes twinkled. 'What a splendid idea, but I won't charge you rent as long as you pay all the other bills.'

Ruby gently hugged her. 'We'll pay a proper rent and the bills,' she said firmly. 'I get good wages at the tool factory and me mum will soon find work there or in one of the other factories on the estate.'

Cordelia smiled. 'I think that as you're family you should get a discount. Would you agree to that at least?'

Ruby laughed. 'I've got to persuade Mum to leave London first and that may take some doing – but yes, I'll agree to a discount.'

'That's all settled then,' said Peggy as she poured them all another cup of tea. 'When are you planning to go up to London?'

Ruby felt a flutter of excitement at the thought of seeing her mother again. 'I've asked for two days off next weekend.'

Peggy took her hand and squeezed her fingers. 'We'll miss you, Ruby, but I think you're doing the right thing. You and your mother can settle into the bungalow and make a brand-new start – but you've got to promise me you'll come and visit at least once a week. I don't want to lose sight of you.'

Ruby's heart was full as she kissed Peggy's cheek. 'You won't get rid of me that quick,' she said through the tearful lump in her throat, 'and once Mum settles in and sees how lovely it is here, I wouldn't mind betting you and her will get on like a house on fire.'

Ruby had said her goodbyes to everyone at Beach View, knowing it wouldn't be long before she saw them all again. She reached the station to find Stan waiting for her with a bunch of beautiful roses.

'I thought your mum might like these,' he said bashfully.

'Oh, Stan, she'll be over the moon.'

He reached into his ticket office and drew out a small parcel and a thermos flask. 'I made you some cheese and pickle sandwiches and a flask of tea to take with you. There could be some long delays going into London, and I don't like the thought of you going hungry.'

Ruby blinked away her tears and softly kissed his bristly cheek. 'You're a diamond, Stan. Did I ever tell you that?'

He cleared his throat and picked up her case, his own eyes suspiciously bright. Having deposited the case on the overhead rack, he dusted the seat with his large white handkerchief. 'Now you have a good journey, and be careful up there. And I'll see you in a couple of days.'

'Thanks, Stan – for everything.'

He stepped down from the carriage and slammed the door. Quickly blowing his nose, he shouted, 'All aboard,' to the empty platform, then blew his whistle and waved his flag. The train began to chuff slowly away from Cliffehaven.

Ruby leaned out of the window and waved until he was a mere speck at the end of the platform. Then she settled into her seat, the scent of the roses drifting up to her, promising a new beginning and a brighter tomorrow – her tomorrow.

This Large Print Book for the partially sighted, who cannot read normal print, is published under the auspices of

THE ULVERSCROFT FOUNDATION